THE
BONE
SEASON

THE
BONE
SEASON

Tenth Anniversary Edition

Fully Revised with New Material

SAMANTHA SHANNON

BLOOMSBURY PUBLISHING

NEW YORK • LONDON • OXFORD • NEW DELHI • SYDNEY

BLOOMSBURY PUBLISHING
Bloomsbury Publishing Inc.
1385 Broadway, New York, NY 10018, USA

BLOOMSBURY, BLOOMSBURY PUBLISHING, and the Diana logo
are trademarks of Bloomsbury Publishing Plc

First published in 2013 in Great Britain
First published in the United States 2013
This edition published 2023

ISBN: ANNIVERSARY EDITION HB: 978-1-63973-223-4; EBOOK: 978-1-63973-405-4

Library of Congress Cataloging-in-Publication Data is available.

2 4 6 8 10 9 7 5 3 1

Typeset by Integra Software Services Pvt. Ltd.
Printed and bound in the U.S.A.

To find out more about our authors and books visit www.bloomsbury.com
and sign up for our newsletters

Bloomsbury books may be purchased for business or promotional use.
For information on bulk purchases please contact Macmillan Corporate
and Premium Sales Department at specialmarkets@macmillan.com.

For the dreamers

Author's Note on this Edition

The Bone Season was originally published in 2013, when I was 21.

The Tenth Anniversary Edition you're about to read has been significantly revised. It follows roughly the same course of events, rewritten with a bit more experience under my belt.

If you jump straight from this edition to the sequels, you may come across some minor inconsistencies. These will be corrected in the revised sequels, which will be published together in 2024.

I hope you enjoy this series as much as I've loved working on it for the last decade.

Samantha Shannon, 17 April 2023

Besides this earth, and besides the race of men, there is an invisible world and a kingdom of spirits: that world is round us, for it is everywhere...

CHARLOTTE BRONTË

Contents

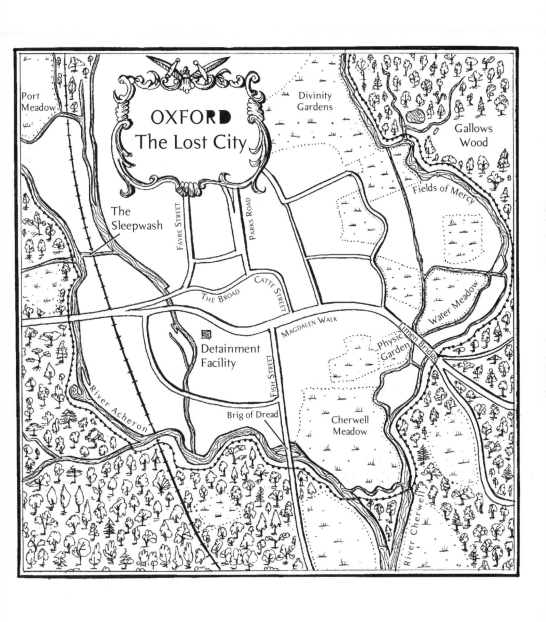

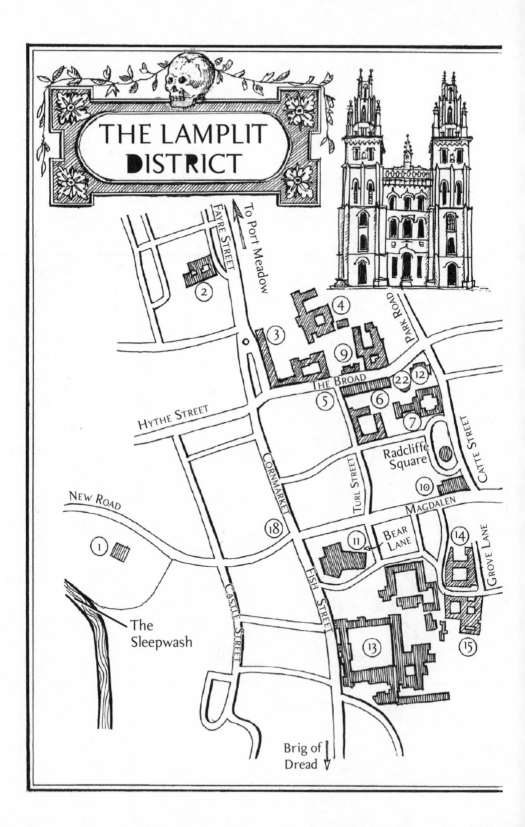

THE LAMPLIT DISTRICT

To Port Meadow

FAYRE STREET

PARK ROAD

HYTHE STREET

THE BROAD

CORNMARKET

NEW ROAD

The Sleepwash

CASTLE STREET

Radcliffe Square

TURL STREET

CATTE STREET

MAGDALEN

GROVE LANE

BEAR LANE

FISH STREET

Brig of Dread

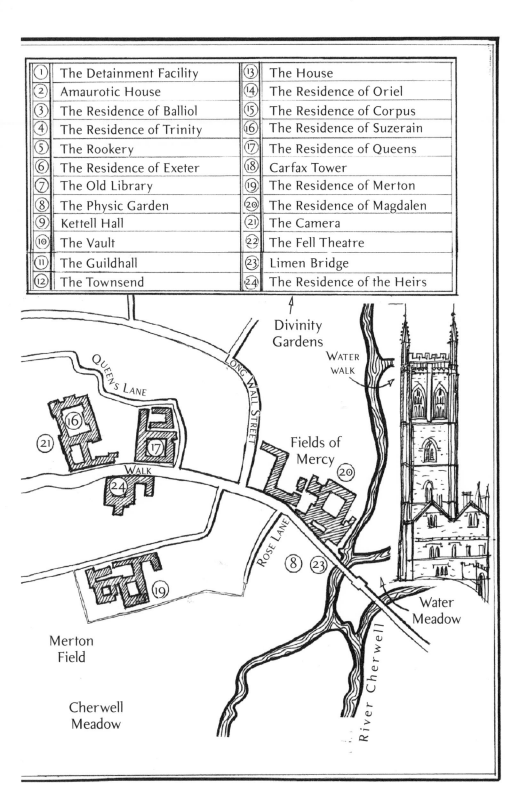

①	The Detainment Facility	⑬	The House
②	Amaurotic House	⑭	The Residence of Oriel
③	The Residence of Balliol	⑮	The Residence of Corpus
④	The Residence of Trinity	⑯	The Residence of Suzerain
⑤	The Rookery	⑰	The Residence of Queens
⑥	The Residence of Exeter	⑱	Carfax Tower
⑦	The Old Library	⑲	The Residence of Merton
⑧	The Physic Garden	⑳	The Residence of Magdalen
⑨	Kettell Hall	㉑	The Camera
⑩	The Vault	㉒	The Fell Theatre
⑪	The Guildhall	㉓	Limen Bridge
⑫	The Townsend	㉔	The Residence of the Heirs

Divinity
Gardens

WATER
WALK

QUEEN'S LANE

LONG WALL STREET

WALK

Fields of
Mercy

ROSE LANE

Merton
Field

Cherwell
Meadow

Water
Meadow

River Cherwell

PART ONE

SPRING

I

THE CURSE

I like to imagine there were more of us in the beginning. Not many, I suppose. But more than there are now.

We look like everyone else. Sometimes we act like everyone else. In many ways, we *are* like everyone else. We are everywhere, on every street. We live in a way you might consider normal, provided you don't look too hard.

Not all of us know what we are. Some of us die without ever knowing. Some of us know, and we never get caught. Either way, we're out there.

Trust me.

I had lived in London – Islington, officially – since I was eight years old. I attended a private school for girls, leaving at sixteen to work. That was in the year 2056. My father thought I would lead a simple life; that I was bright but unambitious, complacent with whatever work life threw at me.

My father, as usual, was wrong.

From the age of sixteen, I had worked in the criminal under-world of the Scion Citadel of London. I worked among ruthless gangs of clairvoyants, all fighting to live and thrive in a syndicate headed by the Underlord. Pushed to the edge of society, we were forced into crime to prosper.

And so we became more hated. We made their worst fears true.

I had my place in the chaos. I was a mollisher, no less – second in command to Jaxon Hall, better known as the White Binder, the mime-lord who ruled the district of I-4. There were six of us in his direct employ. We called ourselves the Seven Seals.

My father believed I was an assistant at an oxygen bar – an uninspired choice of occupation, but a legal one. The truth would probably have killed him.

I was nineteen years old the day my life changed. By that time, my syndicate name was notorious – the Pale Dreamer, heir of the White Binder, renowned for being the only known dreamwalker.

After a trying week among my fellow criminals, I had planned to spend a few days with my father. Jaxon could never understand why I bothered – for him, there was nothing worth our time outside the syndicate – but he didn't have a living family, to my knowledge. London could have crafted him from candle wax and hair, for all I knew.

It was raining that day. The day my life changed – not for the first time, but for ever.

In the gloom of the den, I lay on a couch, wired up to life support. Physically, I was in Seven Dials. My perception was some way north, in Marylebone.

I said I was a dreamwalker. Let me clarify. Among the many strains of clairvoyance, mine was especially intricate. In its simplest form, it allowed me to reach farther into the æther than other voyants. I wasn't a mind *reader* – more a mind radar, hypersensitive to the spirit world. My gift attuned me to it for about a mile outside myself.

When strangers arrived on our streets, I knew first. Nobody could hide from me. Consequently, Jaxon used me as a surveillance tool.

All clairvoyance was prohibited, but the kind that made money was downright depravity. For those caught dabbling in mime-crime (as we called it among ourselves), the official method of execution was nitrogen asphyxiation. There were still public hangings, naturally, and torture for certain sorts of high treason.

I committed high treason just by breathing.

But I digress.

Back to that day. I was tracking an elusive visitor to the area – a strange and remarkable dreamscape, which had appeared twice before. Jaxon had been stumped by my description of it. From the layering of defences, I would have said it was centuries old, but that couldn't be right. This had to be a voyant of unprecedented strength.

Jaxon was suspicious. By rights, a newcomer to his section of the citadel should have announced themself by now, but there had been nothing.

I had sensed it again while I drifted that day. Jaxon would be furious if I lost it.

Find the one who treads so brazenly on our turf, darling. I will have this insult answered.

Thousands of dreamscapes thronged the nearby districts. I strained to keep tabs on the one that stood out. It drew my attention through the æther like a lantern – quickly, as if the stranger could sense me, as I sensed them.

It was slipping out of range. I should have pulled back a while ago, but this stranger had Jaxon unusually perturbed. If any of us mentioned it, he would sink into a sullen mood, often for days.

I forced my perception to its very limit, pulling against the constraints of my physical location, but it was too late. One moment the dreamscape was there; the next the æther seemed to swallow it, and it was gone.

Someone was shaking me. I let out a faint sound of protest, and they stopped.

My silver cord – the link between the body and the spirit – was unusually flexible, letting me sense dreamscapes at a distance. Now it snapped my awareness back into place. As soon as I opened my eyes, Danica shone a torch into them.

Danica Panić, our resident genius – an engineer and unclassified fury, second only to Jaxon in intellect. She was three years older than me and had all the charm and sensitivity of a punch to the nose.

'Rise and shine,' she said. 'What day is it?'

'Friday,' I rasped.

'Very good.'

Danica switched off the life machine. I unfastened my oxygen mask.

The garret of our den came into focus. The building was a secret cave of contraband – penny dreadfuls, stacks of forbidden pamphlets, all manner of trinkets from the black market. This was the only place in the world where I could read and watch and do whatever I liked.

'I don't feel great.' I rubbed my brow. 'How long was I drifting?'

When Danica was ominously silent, I checked the timer on the machine. It stabilised me when I sensed the æther at long range, providing a safety net in case I ever went too far. Jaxon wanted me to learn to force my spirit from my body, but to date, I had failed. I was content with that.

'Dani,' I said, seeing the digits, 'are you trying to kill me?'

'Yes, actually.'

'I'm serious.'

'Jax told me to leave you for an hour,' she said. 'What did you find?'

'That dreamscape is back.' I sat up, a familiar headache swelling. 'I still can't get a clear read on it. I think it was heading towards Park Square.'

'I'll send Zeke.' Danica reached for her phone. 'I hear Jaxon gave you the weekend off. How did you swing that?'

'Psychological reasons.'

'What does that mean?'

'It means you and your contraptions are driving me mad.'

She dealt me a dark look. 'My contraptions are what keep you alive, ingrate. I could always let your sad excuse for an encephalon dry up.'

'I have no idea what you just said.'

'I know.'

Danica handed me my beaten leather boots. I pulled them on, then retrieved my peaked hat. She offered my revolver, but I declined.

'I take it you'll update Jax,' I said. She grunted. 'Where is everyone?'

'Zeke is now looking for your stranger. Nadine is at a séance in Cheapside,' she said, distracted by her phone. 'Eliza had an episode.'

An unsolicited possession. 'Was it Pieter?'

'No. Her new muse.'

'Has Nick checked on her?'

Danica shook her head. 'Jaxon took him out for dinner.'

'He said he would drive me to Islington.'

'They're at Chat's, I think. You should go over there.'

'It's fine.' I tucked my hair into my hat. 'I'd hate to interrupt their huddle.'

'You can't go by train now. It's too late,' Danica said. 'Don't you have to go through Inquisitors Cross?'

'Yes, but I'll be past the turnstiles. I've never seen an Underguard at Leicester Square.' I stood. 'Breakfast on Monday?'

'Unless something more interesting than you crops up.' Danica glanced at the clock. 'Don't die.'

'I won't. See you on Monday.'

I swung on my jacket and made for the door, greeting the spirit in the corner. Pieter gave a dull hum in reply. Being dead sometimes got to him.

Pieter was a muse, the spirit of the Dutch artist Pieter Claesz, found by a binder in Haarlem and traded along the ley line into Scion. Eliza – our medium – would let him possess her now and again, allowing her to paint a masterpiece. When she was done, I would flog it to unwary collectors at the black market.

Spirits could be temperamental, of course. Sometimes we could go for months without a painting. Even when we did get one, it left Eliza drained for days.

I locked the door behind me, glad to see the rain had stopped. The streetlamps were luminous blue, the moon a smirk of white.

Seven Dials was always lively on a Friday night. Airlift, the local oxygen bar, overflowed with laughing amaurotics. To my right, one of our couriers sat by the sundial pillar, the heart and namesake of the district. The rain had washed its six blue faces.

The courier gave me a nod. I returned it. As I walked down Monmouth Street, I subtly called a spool of ghosts to my side.

London had so much death in its history, it was hard to find a spot without spirits. They could be hostile, or willing to help. I liked to keep a few to hand when I went out at night, in case of Vigiles.

The amaurotics in that bar were none the wiser. They were the normal ones, the naturals – the people Scion was built to protect from unnaturals like me, who conversed with the dead. I strode away from them.

'Fortune for a bob,' came a whisper. I stopped. 'Best oracle in London, I promise you. A bob or two for a poor busker?'

The voice belonged to a thin man, huddled in an equally thin jacket. I read his aura. Not an oracle, but a soothsayer. I shot a glance over my shoulder before I yanked him into the nearest doorway.

'You're not an oracle, but you are loud,' I said, my voice low and dark. 'We're surrounded by amaurotics, you fool. Are you off the cot?'

His eyes flared wide. 'Pale Dreamer,' he said, his voice rough. 'Please, don't tell the White Binder I lied. I just wanted—'

'You need to go before he sees you.' I dug into my pocket and crushed a few notes into his hand. 'Get out of here. Use this for a doss.'

'Thank you.'

He slipped the notes into his jacket. I watched him leave, wondering if he had meant to beg for a place in the syndicate.

If so, he had chosen the wrong district. Any voyant who wanted to ply their trade here would first have to seek permission from Jaxon, and he rarely gave it. I was among the lucky ones, to work in Seven Dials.

Leicester Square was mercifully quiet. I had missed rush hour. As usual, most of the commuters were amaurotic. They had no auras to put them in danger.

Underguards came on duty at six to monitor the transport network. Like the rest of the Night Vigilance Division, they were uniformed voyants, bound to serve Scion for thirty years before submitting to execution. For some, that was easier than fighting to survive longer.

Their main duty was to hunt their own. Unlike amaurotics, they could see auras. That made them essential to Scion.

I had never considered joining. There was cruelty among voyants, but I could never condemn anyone to a miserable death on the Lychgate.

Still, occasionally, when I had worked hard for days and Jaxon forgot to pay me, I was tempted.

There were no Underguards to be seen. I scanned my travel permit, releasing my spool. Ghosts resented being taken too far from their haunts, and spot checks on the trains were rare – once you were past the turnstiles, the risk of detection plummeted.

As I descended, my headache grew worse. I was in no mood for the busy interchange at Inquisitors Cross, but I couldn't face Jaxon. He would only try to wheedle me out of visiting my father.

I reached the platform with a few minutes to spare. The pre-recorded voice of Scarlett Burnish came through the speakers: '*The next train is northbound to Inquisitors Cross. Please have your identity cards and travel permits ready for inspection. Thank you, and have a pleasant evening.*'

What I wanted was a *quiet* evening. Jaxon had run me ragged all week. He only gave me a lunch break if he was feeling generous, an event as rare as blue apples these days. Seeing my father was always an agony of evasions and small talk, but he let me sleep in for as long as I wanted. I would have a hot bath and call it a night.

A message appeared on the screens that lined the platform, black text on a white background. The other commuters barely looked up, even as it lit their faces.

RDT: RADIESTHESIC DETECTION TECHNOLOGY

'*In a citadel as populous as London,*' the voice of Scarlett Burnish said, '*there is a high probability that you may be travelling with unnatural individuals.*'

A dumbshow of silhouettes appeared on the screen, each representing a denizen. One turned red, and the others backed away.

'*RDT Senshield is now being trialled in Paddington Terminal and the Westminster Archon. By 2061, we aim to have Senshield installed in all Underground stations in I Cohort, allowing us to reduce the number of unnatural guards in the capital. Visit Paddington or ask an SVD officer for more information.'*

The notice disappeared, replaced by adverts, but it played on my mind.

Scion only brought out its unnatural officers at night. From sunrise until dusk, it was relatively safe for voyants to walk the streets of London. That was when the Sunlight Vigilance Division patrolled the citadel. They were amaurotic, unable to sense us.

Senshield would change that. According to Scion, it could detect aura – the connection between a voyant and the æther. If there wasn't a major delay to their plans, even amaurotic officers would soon be armed with the ability to see us. The entire NVD would be retired, depriving voyants of any chance to live within the law.

So far, the Unnatural Assembly had ignored the matter. The mime-lords and mime-queens of the citadel apparently had greater concerns.

A moist hand gripped my wrist. I tensed.

'Commuting, are we?'

Another voyant had come up behind me, dark hair falling to his shoulders from beneath a bowler hat. I had missed his dreamscape among all the others, but I could have recognised him just from his stink.

'Underlord,' I said stiffly.

'Pale Dreamer.' His grip tightened. 'Your mime-lord has crossed me for the last time.'

'What, by winning a game?'

'Nobody cheats me in my own den.'

'Good thing nobody has.' I waited for an amaurotic woman to pass. 'I'm honoured you'd come all this way to badger me, but surely the head of the syndicate has better things to do. Cleaning your teeth would be a good start.'

Look, I never claimed to be sensible.

'Oh, no. I wanted to see you in person.' Hector kept his voice low. 'Jaxon has been feathering a nest of troublemakers. I know what he plans. All seven of you have grown far too bold – and you the downiest of all, Pale Dreamer. It's past time he paid for his insolence.'

'Excuse me.' The woman had clocked us. 'Is everything all right?'

I nodded, forcing a smile. Hector mimicked. Even the Underlord wasn't fool enough to conduct underworld business in front of amaurotics.

'London belongs to me. Learn your place,' he whispered. 'Have a safe journey.'

With that, the Underlord was gone. I drew my cuff over my reddened wrist.

I had to watch my step – and my tongue – around Hector. As Underlord, he ruled over the entire syndicate. Most of my gang stayed out of his followers' way, but Jaxon treated him with open contempt. I also liked to win at cards, and certain lackeys did not enjoy losing.

If he ever cornered me without an audience of amaurotics, I was dead.

I boarded the train and held on to a handrail. It soon arrived at Inquisitors Cross, where a web of lines took denizens all over the citadel. It was a cold and sterile maze, full of security cameras. On any other night, I would have walked, but I was already late for dinner.

The next platform was almost deserted. When my eastbound train arrived, I sank into a vacant seat. There was just one other person in the carriage – a seer, reading the *Daily Descendant*. I took out my data pad and opened an approved novel.

Without a spool, my only real protection was to look as normal as possible. Jaxon was not without enemies, and plenty of voyants knew me as his mollisher.

As I flicked through the pages, I kept one eye on the seer. I could tell I was on his radar, too – but since he had neither beaten me senseless nor shown any sign of respect, he probably had no idea who I was.

I switched to a digital copy of the *Descendant*, the only sanctioned newspaper in Scion. The typical news glowered back at me. Two young men hanged (on trumped-up charges); a penny gaff shut down in I-3. A feature about the spike in free-world tourism to London and Paris. A letter from a reader, praising the cohesion and stability of the nine countries in the Republic of Scion.

Almost two centuries it had been growing. Scion had been established to end the scourge of clairvoyance. It had taken its first steps in 1901, when five murders had been pinned on Edward VII, son of Queen Victoria. According to the official story, he had drawn on a source of indeterminate evil, bringing clairvoyance – unnaturalness – upon the world. Soon it had spread across the continents, infecting and warping those it touched.

That year, the monarchy had been overthrown. An ostensible republic had been established in its place, built to hunt unnaturals. According to a new generation of officials, all crime and vice was our doing. Within a few years, this system of government was called Scion. It remained a republic only in name – no opposition, no elections.

Over decades, a voyant underworld had developed, forming a cutthroat syndicate. To protect ourselves, we had grown hard and cruel. Since then, Scion had worked even harder to root us out.

Once Senshield was installed across the citadel, the syndicate would collapse. We had two years to act, but with Hector as Underlord, I doubted we could save ourselves. His reign had brought nothing but corruption.

It had been fun while it lasted.

The train went past three stops without incident. I had just closed the *Descendant* when the lights went out, and the train came to a sudden halt. The other passenger straightened in his seat.

'They're going to search the train.'

I tried to reply, but suddenly my tongue was a thick piece of folded cloth.

'To maintain a regular service, this train will be held here for a short time,' the voice of Scarlett Burnish said. *'Thank you for your cooperation.'*

We both looked out of the window, seeing only the tunnel wall and our own reflections. Just ahead, I sensed two dreamscapes. A door must have opened somewhere in the darkness.

'We have to do something.' The seer got up. 'What are you?'

I still couldn't speak.

'I know you're voyant,' he pressed. 'Don't just sit there. We can fight.' He wiped his brow with his sleeve. 'Of all the days for a spot check—'

Just then, two beams of light shone into the carriage. The other voyant retreated at once.

This could not be happening.

I could not be this unlucky.

They stepped inside. A summoner and his backup, a medium, both in black uniforms with scarlet accents, helmets with visors that covered their eyes. The doors hissed shut in their wake.

The Underguards went to the seer first. The train resumed its journey, inching on with the lights dimmed.

'Name,' one of them said.

'Linwood,' the seer whispered. 'Please. I can pay you.'

'I don't think so.' The helmet distorted his voice. 'We had a report of an unnatural travelling on this line, but it seems we'll be hanging two with one rope.'

'Tell us where you were going,' the backup said. 'A séance?'

'I was visiting my daughter in hospital. She has cystic fibrosis,' Linwood said. 'I have the necessary permit from—'

'Get up,' the first Underguard barked at me. I stood. 'Where's your identity card?'

I slowly reached into my coat for it. He pointed his scanner, reading my notes from the database: Paige Eva Mahoney, born in 2040. A resident of I-5, employed in I-4. Five foot nine. No distinctive features but dark lips, probably caused by excessive smoking.

I had never smoked in my life.

'Mahoney.' His voice held a familiar disdain. 'Show me your travel permit.'

Once I had found it, I handed it over. He was going through the motions, forcing me to do the same, but this was a mockery of justice. It didn't matter who I was or where I was going.

I was still a dead woman.

'An attendant at an oxygen bar. Not with that aura,' he said. 'Who issued this permit?'

It took me a moment to find my voice: 'Bill Bunbury, my supervisor.'

He angled his torch into my eyes. All I could do was let him.

'No spirit sight,' he stated. 'An oracle, I'd say.'

'I haven't seen an oracle in years,' said the backup. 'We'll make a killing from this.'

Most voyants mistook me for an oracle. The auras were the same colour.

All at once, Linwood made a break for the door. He threw a spirit at the Underguards – not just any spirit, but a guardian angel. The backup shouted as the angel crunched into him, sending him to the floor in a heap.

The summoner was fast. Before anyone could move, he had mustered a spool of poltergeists. I backed away, my heart pounding.

'Don't move,' the summoner warned us.

Linwood stared him down. He was in his forties, small and wiry, brown hair greying at the temples.

'Tell me,' he said, 'why did a summoner of your talent turn on his own kind?'

The Underguard said nothing. I wished I could ask the same question, but my voice was still caught in my throat, my nerves unravelling.

Eleven years of hiding in plain sight, and it could end right here.

'That helmet can't hide what you are,' Linwood said. 'Those poltergeists certainly know.'

Their presence raised goosebumps all over me. I had rarely seen anyone control *one* poltergeist, let alone a trio. Linwood was right – the syndicate would have snatched this man up.

Which meant he was an Underguard because he *liked* eating his own.

As the angel rallied for a second attack, the poltergeists circled their Underguard. I could hardly breathe, with so much pressure in the æther.

'Come with us quietly,' the Underguard said, 'and they might not torture you.'

'Let them try.' Linwood raised a hand. 'I fear no man with angels at my side.'

He flung his angel back down the carriage. The poltergeists flew to meet it, the collision scalding my sixth sense. I broke out in a cold sweat.

Linwood had some mettle, for a seer in a crumpled suit. The other Underguard, recovered from the shock, was now reciting the threnody – a series of words that compelled spirits to leave. The angel turned. They would need to know its name to banish it, but so long as that chant went on, it would be distracted.

Spirit, be gone into the æther. All is settled. All debts are paid …

If Linwood lost this battle, I would be detained as well. I saw myself in the Tower, on the waterboard, ascending the gallows …

As the poltergeists converged on Linwood, my vision trembled at the edges. I homed in on the Underguards – on their dreamscapes, close to mine; on the spirits within those dreamscapes, two flames inside a pair of lanterns.

A black tide overwhelmed me. I heard my body hit the ground.

That was the last thing I heard.

The summoner never saw it coming. Before I knew what I was doing, I was in his dreamscape, and my spirit was charging straight into his, and then I was hurling it into the æther. I followed it into the dark. Before his crony could draw breath, I had slammed into him as well.

I snapped back into my own skin.

A moment passed. I drew one slow breath, realising I was on the floor. My ears rang, and I tasted metal. Swallowing, I tried to sit up.

Pain erupted in my head. I had never felt anything like it in my life; it was hot knives through both eye sockets, fire in the very nerves of my brain, leaving me heaving in panic. Even my vision crackled, laced with shivering white light. I clamped my fists on both sides of my skull.

Whatever I had just done, I was never doing it again.

The train must be getting near the next station. Little by little, I managed to get on to my hands and knees. Every finger and limb felt loose.

'Linwood—'

I crawled to his side. Shining my phone on his face, I saw his broken neck, scarred with silver. The poltergeists had killed him and gone. I had to speak the threnody, or he would haunt this carriage. Fumbling in the pockets of his coat, I found his identity card.

'William Linwood,' I said, my voice quaking, 'be gone into the æther. All is settled. All debts are paid. You need not dwell among the living now.'

His spirit was nearby. The æther quietened as both he and his angel faded.

I used a handrail to get to my feet. My clammy palm could hardly grip it. A few feet away, the summoner lay dead.

The other Underguard was on his back. I stepped closer and brushed his dreamscape. When I understood, I made a strangled sound.

I hadn't pushed his spirit all the way from his body. It was trapped in the outermost ring of his mind – the fifth circle, the darkest, the very brink of death. His silver cord might not have broken, but I had stretched it far enough that all his sanity was gone.

I sank to my knees beside him and found the switch on the side of his helmet, lifting the visor. He looked vacantly at the ceiling, a ribbon of saliva slithering down his chin.

As I stared at him, he focused on my face. With his last flicker of lucidity, he rasped out two faint words:

'Kill me.'

Tears spilled down my cheeks. I placed my cold hands on his shoulders and steeled myself for a mercy kill.

When the next station came into view, I was farther along the train, waiting. As soon as the doors opened, I stepped out and got straight into the nearest lift. By the time a group of passengers discovered the scene, one man in that carriage was still breathing.

I was gone.

2

NO SAFER PLACE

7 March 2059

I slipped almost unnoticed into the Barbican. Since it housed so many key employees of Scion, this residential wing had a security guard, who had been mercifully distracted when I arrived. He hadn't seen my ashen face, the drying blood under my nose.

Somehow, I had managed to leave the Underground before anyone raised the alarm. I must have escaped with seconds to spare. I should have gone straight to ground, but some buried instinct had driven me here, to my father.

He was in the kitchen, watching ScionEye, the flagship broadcast network of the Republic of Scion. I paused to listen to Burnish. Due to an incident on the Underground, one branch was suspended until further notice.

Scarlett Burnish, the Grand Raconteur – the voice of Scion, responsible for public announcements and reading the approved news. She had clear skin, smoothed by cosmetic enamelling, and lips painted to match her red hair, which she wore in an elegant tuck. The high collars she favoured put me in mind of the gallows.

Soon she might be telling the whole citadel my name.

'In news from elsewhere, the Grand Inquisitor of the Scion Republic of France, Benoît Ménard, will visit Inquisitor Weaver for Novembertide this year,' Burnish said, with her usual fixed smile.

'With eight months to go, the Westminster Archon is already preparing for the arrival of our closest friend on the Continent.'

'Paige?'

I hung up my jacket. 'It's me.'

'Come and sit down.'

'I just need a shower.'

I headed for the bathroom, sweating not so much bullets as shotgun shells. As soon as I had locked the door, I vomited my guts into the toilet.

Jaxon had always said I was capable of killing with my spirit, but I had never really believed it. Now I was a murderer, and worse, I had left evidence in the carriage: my data pad, smothered in my prints.

There was blood on my fingers. With a shudder, I shucked my clothes and stumbled into the shower. Hot water pounded on my skin.

The scene replayed, over and over.

I hadn't meant to kill them. I had only meant to send pressure at them through the æther, a tactic I had used for years. It might have caused them enough pain and panic to let me get away with Linwood.

What I had done was unprecedented. It had been instinctual, beyond my control.

My knees suddenly buckled. Huddled in the corner of the shower, I drew them to my chest, shivering.

I wouldn't be able to hide for long. Scion would match the fingerprints soon. A torch in my eyes, a needle in my neck, and I would disappear.

My head throbbed as I tried to think. I needed to get back to Seven Dials, but I couldn't lead Scion to Jaxon. Vigiles would be swarming this cohort, making it hard to escape on foot. With the nearest stations closed, there was no way I could get to the den unless I found a bob cab, and they rarely came to this part of London.

Shit.

My father moved to the kitchen. By coming here, I had already implicated him.

He had worked for Scion for over a decade. I had to hope that would protect him when they came.

Until then, I would pretend. I couldn't bear to tell him to his face what I had done.

Once I had changed, I went mechanically to the kitchen and put a pan of milk on the stove, following my old routine. My father had left my favourite mug out, the big one that said GRAB LIFE BY THE COFFEE.

Scion was still deciding whether caffeine was a cause of unnaturalness. The same doubts had doomed alcohol. Most denizens played it safe and stuck to Floxy, the only Scion-approved high. (Then again, GRAB LIFE BY THE FLAVOURED OXYGEN just wouldn't have the same ring to it.) As I poured the milk, I looked out of the window.

London sparkled before me. The complex was lit by a transmission screen, mounted on the highest tower of the Barbican Estate. It often ran live broadcasts of the latest public hangings.

At present, it showed a stylised anchor – the symbol of Scion – against a clinical white background. And that chilling motto:

NO SAFER PLACE

When I was young, my father had tried to protect me from that screen, to no avail. If I didn't get myself out of this, my death would be next to appear.

Clasping the mug, I left the kitchen. Jaxon would tell me what to do. Before I could reach my bedroom, my father intercepted me in the hall.

'Paige.'

My father worked in the scientific research sector of Scion, and had the frown lines to prove it. He wore the expression he usually did around me, composed mostly of caution.

'Hi,' I said, mustering a smile. 'Sorry I'm late. I did some overtime.'

'It's all right. I'm always grateful for a visit,' he said. 'Let me get you something to eat.'

I followed him back into the kitchen. When he turned the lights up, my eyes watered with the pain in my skull.

'You look a bit peaky.' He opened a cupboard. 'Are you well, Paige?'

His accent was pure Dublin. Working there for so long had rubbed off on him, and eleven years here had failed to erode it.

Not only did we sound like we came from different ends of Ireland, but we also looked nothing alike. He was a redhead, while my curls were icy blonde, kept in a bob. Where his pale face was freckled, mine was not. Apparently I looked more like my mother.

'Just tired.' I leaned against the counter. 'It's been a long week.'

'I was reading about the oxygen circuit earlier. Horrible case in IV-2. Underpaid waitrons, pneumonia, seizures—'

'The central bars are fine. The clients expect quality.' I watched him lay the table. 'How's work?'

'The usual.' He set down two glasses. 'Paige, your job at the bar—'

'What about it?'

A daughter scrubbing counters for her keep. Nothing could be more embarrassing for a man in his position. How his colleagues must have sneered when they realised I worked at *a* bar, not *the* bar.

Soon he would learn what I really did, and wish I had been telling him the truth.

'I know it isn't my place – you've told me so – but I think you should consider the University,' he said, after a moment. 'That job is a dead end. If you got your head down, qualified in French—'

'I'm happy where I am.' My voice came out harder than I had intended. 'Besides, you think they'd let me graduate, with our last name?'

He hadn't been there when the Schoolmistress gave me my final report. For a suffocating moment, I was back in that room, facing her.

I'm sorry you chose not to apply for the University, Paige, but it might be for the best, given your … temperament. A folder bearing the school crest. *Your employment recommendation. We note your aptitude for Physical Enrichment, French, and Scion History.*

She had been rigidly polite, for the sake of the other teacher in the room. But just as I left, she had gripped my shoulder and whispered her parting words in my ear: *I've waited years to be rid of you. The only way you could have brought more disrepute on this school is if you were unnatural, too.*

'I could arrange something,' my father said. 'I'd say I've earned their trust by now.'

'Do you really believe that?'

'Yes, and I'll use it to do right by you, for all the good it does me.' The corners of his mouth tightened. 'I had no choice, Paige.'

'I know,' I said softly. 'And so do your colleagues. They'll always know exactly how we got here, and they'll always know we're a pair of kerns, whether or not I attend your University.'

He gave me a weary look.

'Well,' he said, 'thank you for that.'

I clenched my jaw. Last time I was here, I had managed not to argue with him.

Fortunately, my father preferred a quiet life. He brought out some cutlery and said, 'Still living with your boyfriend, are you?'

The boyfriend lie had always been a mistake. Ever since I had invented Steve the Invisible, my father had been asking to meet him.

'We broke up,' I said.

'Sorry to hear that. No harm to the lad, but I did wonder where you were hiding him,' he said. 'Where are you staying now, then?'

'Suzette has a spare room in Holborn.'

'Suzy from school?'

'Yes.'

Jaxon must have got back to the den by now. I needed to cut this short.

'Actually, I might not eat. I've had a headache all day,' I said. 'Do you mind if I turn in early?'

'You have so many of these headaches.'

To my surprise, he came up to me and touched my cheek. More often than not, he avoided my gaze, but now he looked me in the face.

'You rest,' he said. 'I'll make us breakfast tomorrow. I want to hear all your news, seileán.'

I stared at him. He hadn't made breakfast since I was about twelve, nor called me by that nickname since we had lived in Ireland.

Eleven years and a lifetime ago.

'I'd like that,' I said.

'All right, then. Goodnight, love.'

'Goodnight.'

I headed for my room. He left the parlour door ajar, as he always did when I was home.

He had never known how to show he cared. To see him trying now was like a knife beween my ribs.

My old bedroom was always warm. I had moved to Seven Dials as soon as I left school, but officially, I still lived here. Scion would surround the estate when they realised.

By now, they would be analysing my data pad. All denizens provided their fingerprints to Scion. I had surrendered mine when I was eight.

Beneath my blouse, my skin had gone from cold to feverish. All I could see were the bodies on the train. All that damage in one breath.

Jaxon had been waiting for this – the day my spirit became a weapon. Hands shaking, I switched on my second phone and dialled the number for a call box in Mayfair.

There was always a contact near that box, paid to keep an ear out for it. I let the phone ring four times – my personal signal – then hung up.

For several minutes, I waited for the underworld to do its work. At last, my phone vibrated. I had barely accepted the call before Jaxon was off:

'There you are, light of my life. Have you reconsidered the holiday?'

'Jaxon—'

'Of course you have. My mollisher would never squander an entire weekend with an amaurotic, not when London is aquiver with fresh opportunities. Now, Jane Rochford is finally being auctioned tomorrow, and I need you to—'

'I killed someone.'

A long silence. I heard a faint crackle before Jaxon spoke again. 'Who?'

'Underguards,' I said. 'It was a spot check. They tried to detain us, me and a seer.'

'So you killed them.'

'No. Just one.'

'And the other?'

'He's … in his hadal zone.'

'Wait.' His voice softened. 'You did it with your spirit?'

When I didn't reply, he began to laugh. I could hear him clapping his hand on his desk.

'Paige, you little thaumaturge,' he erupted, 'you did it. Didn't I always say you could?'

'Jax, I fucking *killed* someone—'

'You certainly did. Magnificent work,' Jaxon said, with relish. 'You've bloomed like the rare flower you are, my wilful wunderkind.' I pictured him in the gloom of the den, taking a celebratory puff of his cigar. 'The second Underguard. He's still alive?'

'Yes.' I sleeved the sweat from my brow. 'I couldn't do it.'

'Well, never mind. He'll only babble, in that state, if he can speak at all.' He said it without a care in the world. 'So my dreamwalker has finally entered – and emptied – a dreamscape. Did they have any idea what hit them?'

'No.' I paced the room. 'They thought I was an oracle.'

'Amateurs.'

Just then, a new message appeared on the screen, accompanied by the cool tones of Scarlett Burnish.

DUE TO PASSENGER ACTION, ALL PUBLIC TRANSPORT IN I-4 AND I-5 HAS BEEN SUSPENDED. UNDERGROUND STATIONS ARE NOW CLOSED. PLEASE STAND BY FOR FURTHER ANNOUNCEMENTS.

'Jaxon,' I whispered. 'Did you hear that?'

'Try not to panic, Paige. It's unbecoming. Are you with your father?'

'Yes.' I blotted my face again. 'You'd better have a plan.'

'Don't worry about that. Just sit tight, before you run headfirst into a dragnet.'

'I can't just wait to be detained.'

'Darling, I have fired you into firmer stuff than this. The last thing they'll expect is for you to have fled to your registered address. Why *did* you do that, by the way?'

'I couldn't think of anywhere else. I'm not on your turf, Jax.'

'Don't remind me. Ognena Maria *might* have aided you,' Jaxon mused, 'but then, I would hate to be in her debt, and I doubt she would want to involve her own voyants. She is rather precious about their wellbeing.' His tone grew serious. 'Now you're there, stay out of sight, and dispose of that phone. If they come, you know what to do.'

There was a warning in those words. None of us could be captured.

'Hold your nerve for the next hour. Scion will take at least that long to match your fingerprints,' Jaxon said. 'When you see an opportunity, make for the river. Eliza will find you in the morning.'

'I'll be a fugitive. For good.'

'That only makes you more interesting. See you soon, Pale Dreamer.'

I hung up.

Jaxon Hall didn't know how to worry. He had danced on the edge of a knife all his life, and I doubted his blood could run any colder.

I removed the battery from the phone. Jaxon could be a colossal bastard, but three years ago, I had chosen to trust him. He could help me disappear.

There was a pocket pistol in one of the drawers, concealed under a stack of clothes. I loaded it, checked the knife in my boot.

Next, I needed my first edition of *On the Merits of Unnaturalness*, the most notorious pamphlet in the citadel. Written by Jaxon, it detailed every known type of clairvoyance and sorted them into seven orders.

My copy was covered in annotations: new ideas, explanatory notes, contact details for promising cases. Last time I stayed here, I had dropped it between my bed and the wall. It was still there, covered in dust. I fished it out, then retrieved my emergency back-pack from the wardrobe.

I fastened *On the Merits of Unnaturalness* into a pocket. If they found it here, they would never believe my father hadn't known what I was. That was his only chance now, to deny it. Even if I warned him, he had nowhere to go. Better he pleaded ignorance.

Finally, I sat on my bed, the pistol in my hand. Somewhere in the distance, in the darkness, there was thunder.

Whatever my spirit had done, it had drained me to the quick. Before I could stop it, I had passed out, still with the taste of blood in my throat.

When I woke, I knew something was wrong. The æther warned of unfamiliar dreamscapes in the building. I could hear an echoing clamour in the stairwell, closer by the moment.

That wasn't old Alice Heron next door, who used a frame and always took the lift. Those were the boots and radios of a detainment squad.

They had come for me.

They had finally come.

I was on my feet at once, throwing a jacket over my shirt, pulling on boots and gloves, pulse racing. Nick had prepared me for this day, but the escape would test my stamina to the limit – and no matter what happened, I could not lead Scion to the others.

They were on this floor now, slowing to mask their approach. I slung on my backpack, tucked the pistol into my waistband, and opened the door to the balcony.

I could do this.

Rain battered my clothes. I stood on the balustrade, finding my balance, then jumped for an eave and climbed on to the roof. By the time the Vigiles reached the apartment, I had started to run.

In London, Scion usually avoided killing amaurotics. My father would be tranquillised, to shut him up while they detained me.

I hoped that was all they would do to him.

The complex was quiet. I glanced over the parapet. No sign of the security guards. It didn't take me long to spot the paddy wagon in the car park, the van with tinted windows and gleaming white headlights. If anyone had taken the time to look, they would have seen the anchor on its back doors.

My boots had decent grip, but these conditions could be lethal. Nevertheless, I kept moving.

I didn't know the rooftops of the Barbican. They were a concrete labyrinth. Fighting to see through the downpour, I edged around dormer windows and planters, slid across the arched glass ceilings of the corridors.

So far, I had no pursuers. I swung my boot up to a wet ledge and scaled a ladder, the rain plastering my hair to my face. At the first opportunity, I hurdled on to a balcony, where I found a door unlocked. Breathing hard, I tore through the deserted apartment, seizing the opportunity to get rid of my phone, then ran down several flights of stairs, towards the front door of the building. I needed to get to the street, to vanish into a dark alley ...

Red lights stopped me in my tracks. I doubled back and slammed the door. Turning wildly, I pulled a fire axe from its case, smashed a window, and scrambled into a small courtyard, cutting my forearms on the glass. Then I was back in the rain, shinning up a drainpipe.

My heart stopped when I saw them. The rooftops were infested with masked figures in red jackets. Several torch beams moved towards me, glaring into my eyes.

These weren't Vigiles. I had never seen a uniform like this in London.

'Stay where you are.'

The nearest stepped towards me, a gun in one gloved hand. I backed away, feeling the aura of a powerful medium. The torch-light revealed a gaunt face, sharp chips of eyes, a thin mouth.

'Don't run, Paige. It's too late,' he called. 'Why don't you come out of the rain?'

I did a quick sweep of my surroundings. A helicopter came to hover overhead.

The next building was an office block. The gap was wide – at least twenty feet, farther than I had ever dared to jump. Unless I wanted to attack the medium and abandon my body, I would have to try.

I had nothing to lose.

'I'll pass,' I called back, and took off again.

Muffled shouts broke out in my wake. I dropped to a lower stretch of roof, escaping the searchlight that beamed from the chopper, and drew my pistol.

The medium sprinted after me. I could hear his boots pounding on the roof, seconds behind mine. He was trained for these pursuits. I was nimble and slim, narrow enough to slip between rails and under fences, but so was my pursuer. When I squeezed off two shots from the pistol, he eluded them without stopping.

I aimed blindly over my shoulder again. My lungs were already at bursting point. A flare in my ankle alerted me to an injury.

The medium was returning fire. I leapt over flexipipes and ventilation ducts, trying to turn my sixth sense on him, but I couldn't keep my focus on his dreamscape. There was nothing I could do to deter him.

Cold rain thrashed at my eyes. As I gathered speed, adrenalin snuffed the fire in my ankle.

A fifteen-storey drop yawned in front of me. I told myself that if I could only clear this gap, I could disappear into the shadows for good. I could leave Paige behind and embrace the Pale Dreamer.

Knees towards your chest, Nick had taught me. *Eyes on your landing spot.*

The edge rushed closer. Too late to stop or turn back now. My boot hit the very end of the roof, and I launched myself over the precipice.

For a strange moment, I was in flight, nothing to hold me up or down.

I collided with solid brick. As I fell, I grabbed a ledge, clinging on by my fingertips. Kicking for purchase, boots scraping the wall, I started to haul my body upward. A coin fell out of my jacket, into the darkness below.

My victory was short-lived. As I struggled on to the other roof, a bolt of agonising pain tore up my spine. I slipped down the wall, one hand still clinging on, and craned my neck to look over my shoulder. A dart was buried in my back.

Flux.

They had flux.

The drug surged into me. Behind me, I heard shouting above the chopper, the rain. Soaked and numb, I formed two last thoughts. First, that Jaxon was going to kill me – and second, that he wouldn't have the chance. I was already dead.

My fingers lost their strength.

I let go.

3

DELIRIANT

I t lasted a lifetime. I didn't know when it had started, didn't see
when it would end.

I remembered movement, a throaty roar, and being strapped
to a hard surface. Then a needle was pushed into my arm, and pain
took over.

Reality unravelled at the seams. A candle burned nearby, and its
flame kept erupting into an inferno. Sweat dripped from my pores
like wax – and then I was freezing, desperate for warmth, feeling
as if I would die from the cold. There was no middle ground. Just
limitless pain.

Fluxion 14 was a deliriant. Made with purple aster, it attacked
both the body and the dreamscape, causing phantasmagoria – a vivid
series of hallucinations, worsened by fever and chills. I fought my way
through endless visions, crying when the pain was too intense to bear
in silence.

My hair stuck to my tears as I retched, trying in vain to force the
poison from my body. Whether it was sleep, unconsciousness or
death, something had to take me from this nightmare.

'I know it hurts, treasure,' a voice murmured. 'But you have to
learn, don't you?'

The room spun like a carousel, twisting until I could barely hold on. I bit a pillow to stifle my screams. I tasted blood and knew I must have bitten something else – my lip, my cheek, my tongue.

Flux never wore off. Even if you vomited, it worked itself into the organs, spread like poison in the blood. The pain washed over me in wave after wave.

'That is enough. We need her alive,' a new voice said. 'Get the antidote at once.'

The antidote. I might yet live. I tried to blink away the rippled haze, the visions and distorted things, but all I could see was the candle.

'Let me out,' I said faintly.

'Bring water.'

The lip of a glass clashed on my teeth. I took deep, thirsty gulps.

'Please.'

Two burning eyes looked into mine, and suddenly, the nightmare stopped. I plunged into a sweet black sleep.

When I woke, I lay on my stomach, my throat roasted. It was such a severe pain that I was forced to come to my senses, if only to seek water. I realised with a start that I was naked.

I managed to roll on to my side, tasting dry vomit in the corners of my mouth. Shivering uncontrollably, I reached for the æther.

There were other dreamscapes here.

It took a while for my eyes to adjust. I was sprawled on a single bed. To my right was a barred window with no glass. The floor and walls were made of stone.

A bitter draught sent goosebumps racing all over me. My breath came out in tiny clouds. I drew the sheets around my shoulders, swallowing.

A door was ajar in the corner. I could see light. Testing my strength, I went to it, my ankle protesting.

Beyond was a simple bathroom. The light stemmed from a single lamp, revealing a rusted tap on the wall. It was perishing to the touch. When I turned the valve beneath, a deluge of icy water drenched me. I knocked it the other way, but the water refused to heat up.

Despite my situation, I was desperate to wash, if only to clear my head. My hair felt greasy, my body slow and fragile. Bracing myself, I tried again, dipping each limb under the crude excuse for a shower. My joints ached. My skin hurt. A sharp pain lingered where the dart had gone in, and somehow I had strained my neck.

There were no towels, so I used the bedsheets to dry off, then wrapped myself in one. When I tried the main door, I found it locked. I blew on my numb fingers, wishing for a heat pad.

My shivers weren't just from the cold. I was naked and alone in a dark cell, barely strong enough to stand, and these might be my last hours. Nobody knew what happened to voyant prisoners – none had escaped to tell the tale – but there were rumours of water torture.

I had to be in the Tower of London. The æther was oddly quiet, if so, but my sixth sense was still as weak as the rest of me. All I knew for sure was that my father was not in this building.

Harbouring a voyant was misprision of treason. Was he already dead?

They had needed him enough to pluck him from a war zone. Surely they would spare his life.

Against my will, I slipped into a fitful doze, curled against the back of the bed. When the door crashed open, I snapped awake.

'Get up.'

A light appeared. I blinked at the sight of an old paraffin lamp. Holding it was a statuesque woman, with polished bronze skin, impeccable posture, and black hair tumbling in loose curls to her waist.

I blinked again, harder. It might have been the lack of strong light, but her face seemed ageless. I was confident she was no younger than me; neither was she elderly. Otherwise I had no idea.

I noticed three odd things about her. First, her eyes were yellow. Not the kind of amber you might call yellow in certain lights – no, these were *yellow*, tinged with green, and glowed like candle flames.

The second thing was her aura. She was voyant, but not a type I had encountered before.

And third was her dreamscape – exactly like the one I been chasing in Seven Dials. I already knew I couldn't breach a dreamscape like this, certainly not in my current state.

'Get up,' she repeated.

Slowly, I stood, clutching my bedsheet like a shield. This had to be some aftermath of the phantasmagoria. How else could her eyes do that?

'Take these,' she said.

I looked at the two pills in her hand. She wore a tailored leather glove.

'Must I give you every order twice?'

I wanted to refuse, to fight back, but the flux had drained me. Besides, I had no power here. With no other choice, I necked the pills dry.

'Cover yourself,' my jailer said. 'If you resist, I will remove your fingernails.' She threw a bundle of clothes at me. 'Pick those up.'

Too unsteady to protest, I did. Black trousers, socks and underwear, including a thin shirt. Ankle boots with low, broad heels. A collared white tunic. Finally, a black gilet, stitched with a small white anchor.

This was a uniform. Wherever I was going, it clearly wasn't to the gallows. Not yet. I dressed in rigid strokes, hair soaking my collar, fingers cramping on the buttons of the tunic.

It was even colder outside the room. The towering woman led me through a labyrinth of stone corridors, past torches burning in wall brackets, too bright after the cool blue streetlamps of London.

She unlocked a door and went inside. When she returned, a seer came after her. He was scrawny, with a mop of sandy hair and signs of flux poisoning: pallor, glazed eyes.

'Move,' the woman said.

He stumbled into step beside me. 'Carl,' he managed, clearly in pain.

I nodded. 'Paige.'

No harm in giving my real name. Scion had got me now.

The woman collected more voyants, all in the same uniform. Three more soothsayers. A few augurs – the second order of clairvoyance, just as populous, who used the raw material of the natural world in their work, from fire and twigs to the human body.

Next came an oracle, who looked intrigued by our situation, and a whisperer with darting eyes. She must be listening to the chatter of the nearest spirits, unheard by the rest of us.

Soon there were twenty of us. Last to join was a palmist with short blue hair, shaking so hard her jaw rattled. Few of them looked older than thirty, or younger than fifteen. All were haggard from flux.

We were steered into a room with a wet floor, lit by a few candles, where several people were already imprisoned. Our jailer loomed in the doorway.

'I am Pleione Sualocin,' she said. 'Tonight you will attend your welcome oration, which will take place in the Residence of the Suzerain.'

A number of wary looks were exchanged.

'You will not look any Rephaite in the eye. You will keep your gazes on the floor, where they belong,' Pleione said. 'You will obey any commands you receive from the Rephaim you encounter.'

The whisperer raised a hand. 'Sorry,' she said, 'but what *is* a Rephaite?'

'I am,' Pleione said. 'You will not speak again without my permission.'

'Fuck that,' said one of the augurs – a tasseographer, to be precise. They used tea leaves to foretell the future. 'Where are we?'

'You are about to find out.'

'What gives you the right to collar us?' he demanded. 'Unless you've got Senshield working early, you can't prove I have an aura, you—'

He stopped. As we all stared at him, dark beads of blood seeped from his eyes. A frisson passed through the æther before he collapsed.

Pleione dealt him a pitiless look. When she lifted her face, I saw that her own eyes had turned a clean blue, like the flame on a blowtorch.

'I trust,' she said, 'that there are no further objections.'

The palmist clapped a hand over her mouth. Pleione left, locking the door in her wake.

At first, no one spoke. I had no idea what I had just witnessed, and apparently, neither did anyone else. The palmist slid to the floor with a weak sound of despair, holding her right arm as if it hurt.

I sat in a corner. Beneath my sleeves, my skin was stippled with goosebumps. It had been a bad idea to wet my hair in this cold place.

A man in his early twenties, bald and tall and broad-shouldered, moved to sit beside me. His large eyes were as deep a brown as his skin.

'Julian,' he said.

'Paige.' I cleared my throat. 'How did you end up here?'

'Believe it or not, I was on my way to buy milk.' Julian breathed out through his nose. 'Did they just get you for your aura?'

'I may also have killed an Underguard.' It didn't sound real. 'You?'

'I may also have killed a Vigile.' He looked weary. 'I only wanted a cup of tea.'

We both glanced at the tasseographer, who lay where he had fallen. He was still breathing, but out cold, his aura fainter than before.

'She just … looked at him.' Julian spoke quietly. 'She was voyant, wasn't she?'

'Of some kind. On that note, I can't get a read on you.'

'I didn't do it with my gift, if that's what you're asking.' He leaned against the wall. 'I shot him with his own gun in the struggle, but he must have called for backup. Didn't take them long to find me.'

He was avoiding my unspoken question. I nodded, letting it slide. His aura did interest me, but some voyants liked to keep their gifts secret.

Icy water dripped from the ceiling and landed on my nose. A crystallist was rocking back and forth, muttering to himself in another language. All the soothsayers and augurs must be losing it without their numa, the materials they used to connect with the æther.

'I can't put a finger on your aura, either.' Julian narrowed his eyes. 'I'd say oracle, but—'

'But?'

'I met an oracle a few years ago, and you're not giving me the same feeling. Are you a sibyl?'

'No,' I said. 'I'm an acultomancer.'

It was a lie I often told. A deflection, but also a test of competence. That type of soothsaying was rare enough that people sometimes believed me, if they didn't have the knack for auras.

Julian arched an eyebrow. Evidently he did have the knack.

'Okay,' he said. 'What did you do, stab your Underguard with a needle?'

'Something like that,' I said.

There was a crash from outside, then a scream. Everyone stopped talking.

'I haven't read *On the Merits of Unnaturalness* in a while,' Julian said, lowering his voice further, 'but surely your aura would be purple.'

'It is purple,' I said.

'It's clearly red.'

'What are you, a painter?'

'Well, no, I just—' Seeing my face, he said gravely, 'Red and purple can be easy to confuse.'

'Yes.'

He took the hint and dropped the subject.

His mention of the pamphlet had left me with a churning stomach. Scion must have taken my backpack, and with it, my annotated copy. I could never have got such a thing without knowing the writer.

Scion would have no mercy on a member of the syndicate.

Even as I thought it, I scanned the room. I didn't recognise anyone, which was probably for the best. Jaxon had many enemies.

'I don't know about you lot,' the whisperer said, 'but I've got no idea what's going on.' Her eyelid twitched. 'Where are we?'

'Must be a new wing,' said a soothsayer.

'What?'

'It can't be,' Carl croaked. 'Why would they flux us just to move us around?'

'To make us easier to torture,' a medium said, her gaze distant and blank. 'That'll be why we're here. To be interrogated.'

A clouded ringing filled my ears. I talked a big game on the streets, but I had no idea how strong I would be if they put me on the waterboard.

The oracle spoke: 'Where do you think we are, exactly?'

That earned him several frowns.

'The Tower of London,' the medium said. 'You really don't know where you've been locked up?'

'Wait,' I said. 'How long have *you* been locked up?'

'I lost track after three years.'

'Three.' A hoarse laugh from the corner. 'Lucky for some. Try nine.'

Something wasn't adding up. Scion didn't put voyants in prison – not to our knowledge, at least. Anyone who was detained was executed without trial. There was no need to store us.

'When were you caught?' I whispered to Julian. 'Do you remember?'

'About two weeks ago, I think.'

'We're not here to be tortured. They're ending it,' an augur said. 'We're in for the swing today, and I'm glad.'

'No.' A taut voice, another soothsayer. 'We've all seen hanged voyants. They're never dressed like this.' She pulled at her gilet. 'We've been ... chosen for something. I think they've pressed us into the NVD.'

Julian nodded, his face clearing. 'There could be a shortage of volunteers.'

'As if we'd ever stoop to rubbing shoulders with those spine-less bastards,' the first augur muttered. 'Better to hang now and be done with it.'

'Speak for yourself,' the oracle said.

There was a long silence, broken only by the palmist, who was trying to stifle her sobs on her sleeve. She sounded heartbroken.

Someone else was in a bad way. A boy with freckles and a wispy fringe, so pale he almost looked bloodless. I had failed to notice him because he had no aura.

'What is this place?' He could hardly get the words out. 'Who are all of you?'

Julian furrowed his brow. 'You're amaurotic. Why have they taken you?'

'I'm what?'

'Probably a mix-up.' The oracle sounded bored. 'Tough luck, kid.'

The boy looked as though he might faint. He lurched to his feet and yanked at the bars.

'Please. I'm not meant to be here,' he shouted. 'I'm not unnatural, I swear!' He was almost in tears. 'I'm sorry. I'm sorry about the stone!'

'Stop it,' I hissed. A few people swore at him. 'Do you want to be next?'

He sank back to the floor. I guessed he was about fifteen. I was reminded of a different time, when I was both surrounded and alone.

'Hey,' I said, gentler. 'What's your name?'

'Sebastian Pearce,' he said. 'Seb.' He shifted closer to me. 'Are you really ... unnaturals?'

'I'll do unnatural things with your entrails if you don't stop flapping that jaw of yours, rottie,' a voice sneered. 'Ever heard of a splanchomancer?'

Seb cringed.

'He's being dramatic,' I said. 'I'm Paige. This is Julian.'

Julian gave me a bemused look. Clearly it was my job to make small talk with the amaurotic. Seb glanced between us like a nervous rabbit.

'We're not going to hurt you, Seb,' I said. 'Where are you from?'

Seb hesitated. 'IV-1.'

'Nice area,' Julian said gamely. 'Whereabouts?'

'Richmond.'

Seb wrapped one arm around his knees. His stained lips shook with cold.

'Tell us what happened to you,' I said.

He glanced at the others. I couldn't find it in myself to blame him for his fear. From the second he could understand words, he would have been told that voyants were the source of all evil.

'One of the other students planted something in my satchel. A stone,' he said. 'The Schoolmaster saw me trying to get rid of it and called the Vigiles to assess me. It took hours to convince them I was innocent. A week later, on my way home, two strangers followed me. I heard a gunshot, and— and then I think I must have fainted. I was sick.'

I wondered about the effects of flux on amaurotics. The physical symptoms might appear, but probably not the phantasmagoria.

'That's awful,' I said. 'I'm sure this is all a terrible mistake.'

Seb perked up. 'Then they'll let me go home?'

'Probably not,' the oracle said.

The sound of footsteps silenced us. Pleione pulled open the door.

'Follow me,' she said.

No one dared protest. We stepped over the tasseographer as we left.

Pleione led us outside. The air was cold enough to snap, all our surroundings smudged by mist. Seb stuck to my side. *Head down, eyes open*, I told myself. Nick had taught me that rule; I would follow it here.

We walked over grey cobblestones, wet after a night of rain, reflecting the glow of the streetlamps – a pale glow, not blue. It took a moment to realise they were gaslights. The buildings were nowhere near the height of those in London. Julian fell into step beside me as Pleione led us onward. We soon found ourselves in a bustling town.

This street was significantly wider than the first. Not a car or a moto in sight – just a long line of ramshackle dwellings, winding drunkenly from one end to the other. Thin walls propped up scraps of corrugated metal, clothes drying on lines between them.

Larger buildings flanked the slum, grand remnants of ages past. In sharp contrast to the shacks, they were clean and stately, with ornate façades – carved limestone, wooden doors, pointed windows lit by candles. Some were crenellated, like the castles of the monarch days.

Scion had sent us back in time.

About halfway along the street, a group of figures waited on a stage. Hundreds of lanterns flickered around them, illuminating their ornate masks. A violin sang below the boards – voyant music, the sort only a whisperer could perform, luring the nearest spirits.

Looking up at these people – actors, mimes – was an unruly audience. Every member of that audience wore a red tunic and a black gilet.

'Welcome,' someone called to us. 'Everyone, it's the new crop!'

Rowdy cheers and whistles erupted. Above, the performers began to dance. All of them were clairvoyant; in fact, almost everyone was clairvoyant – the dancers, the spectators, most of my group.

This was no back-alley gathering of thieves.

The performance went on for a while. Not all the spectators were paying attention. Some were talking among themselves, others jeering at the stage. I was sure I heard a shout of *cowards*.

Everyone in my group looked just as baffled as I felt. Either my brain was still drug-addled, or this was some kind of voyant cult.

After the initial dance, a woman in a winged mask stepped on to a high platform, her dark hair slicked into a tight bun. She jumped and seized two purple drapes that hung from the rigging above. Weaving her legs and arms around them, she climbed nimbly before unravelling into a pose, earning a smattering of applause.

Looking past her, I took the chance to study the street. This was definitely not the Scion Citadel of London. Old buildings, gas lamps, cobblestones – it was as if centuries had rewound.

I knew exactly where I was.

In 1859, on the first of September, the university city of Oxford had burned to the ground. At the time, the tragedy had been pinned on the Carrington Event, a geomagnetic storm of unprecedented magnitude. The story had never made sense to me, but there was no point in questioning Scion.

What remained of the city was a Type A Restricted Sector. Because of some indefinable contamination caused by the storm, no one was allowed to set foot there. Scion had wiped it from the maps.

According to Jaxon, a journalist from the *Roaring Boy* had tried to drive to Oxford once. He had never returned. The *Roaring Boy* – a penny paper, already on thin ice – had vanished a week later.

Pleione turned to look at us. In the dark, her eyes were as bright as the gas lamps.

'Come,' she said. 'You do not want to be late for the oration.'

We followed her, stupefied.

She brought us to a pair of lofty iron gates. Two men let us pass. Both bore a resemblance to Pleione – same yellow eyes, same daunting stature, same faint metallic sheen. Pleione sailed into a large courtyard, where other people joined us, dressed in white or grey.

We filed into a stone building, forbidding in its grandeur. Pleione led us down its corridors, illuminated by flickering chandeliers and candelabras.

Our journey ended – or began – in a cavernous room where bookshelves swept up to a plaster ceiling, packed with beautiful old tomes. The décor was baroque, the dressed stone floor like a chessboard, arched windows lining one of the walls. Pleione shepherded us into rows. I stood between Julian and Seb.

This room was a melting pot of voyants, from augurs and soothsayers to mediums and sensors. As far as I could tell, the oracle was the only person from my order.

Pleione went to stand on a low platform with a balustrade. She joined the end of a line of tall figures, presumably her fellow Rephaim (whatever that meant), who had the look of statues on display in a museum.

All of them wore dark clothing in a style that reminded me of the Tudor portraits I had seen at the black market – though a touch more practical, bordering on military in their cut. They almost looked human, but those dreamscapes and yellow eyes told me otherwise.

One of them – a pale, expressionless woman – finally approached the balustrade.

'If you paid me all the money in London,' Julian said out of the corner of his mouth, 'I couldn't even guess what she was going to say.'

The room slowly fell silent.

'Let's find out,' I whispered back.

4

THE FORGE OF THE ANCHOR

'Welcome to Sheol I, formerly known as the University of Oxford.'

The speaker was about six and a half feet tall. Her argent face was perfectly symmetrical – a long, straight nose, high cheekbones, hooded eyes. The candlelight ran through her thick hair, which gleamed like spun gold, falling unadorned to her waist.

'Nashira Sargas is the name I bear here.' Her voice was cool and low, resonant enough to fill the room. 'I am blood-sovereign of the Rephaim and Suzerain of the Republic of Scion.'

'Is this a joke?' someone muttered.

I wanted to ask the same question. So far, nothing here appeared real.

In keeping with the monarch look, two of the very tall figures wore livery collars, including Nashira Sargas. Hers was gold, studded with amber.

'First of all, I must apologise for your harrowing journey, especially if it began in the Tower of London,' she said. 'After being sedated, you were placed on a train and taken to our Detainment Facility. Your clothing and belongings have been confiscated.'

As I listened, I watched her, probing the æther. Her aura was especially strange, simmering like water on the boil.

'No doubt you are surprised to hear that this city is still populated,' she continued. 'According to Scion, it was quarantined due to contamination. This was a lie. It was so that we, the Rephaim, could make it our home on Earth.'

My face must have been a picture. She could only have been speaking for a minute, but I already felt unmoored from reality.

'Most of you here are clairvoyant, capable of interacting with the æther,' Nashira said. 'You commune with spirits, and in return, they may offer you their guidance and protection. But when these drifting spirits grow too great in number – too cowardly or stubborn to leave, to meet their unmaking in the last light – it places a significant burden on the æther. Some time ago, this burden finally became too heavy, shattering the ethereal threshold.'

Julian looked torn between laughter and trepidation. Seb swayed on the spot.

'When the ethereal threshold broke, the Netherworld was overrun by hostile creatures named Emim,' Nashira said. 'They feed on flesh and spirit, devouring both without remorse, and they do not hear reason. Their arrival caused the Netherworld to fall into decay, forcing us to abandon it.'

The whisperer let out the quietest of nervous chuckles. 'How am I still this high?'

'Shh.'

'In 1859, we crossed the veil to Earth and negotiated with the human government of England,' Nashira went on. 'Together, we agreed on a new way of living, to ensure that Earth would not also fall to the Emim. We established the Republic of Scion.'

Silence filled the room.

Nashira Sargas had our attention.

'When we arrived here, we found you vulnerable. Only a small number of humans are clairvoyant; still fewer have marginally useful abilities,' she said. 'We might have simply let the Emim overrun your world, to avenge the loss of ours. We might have killed you all. Instead, we showed mercy. Here in this city, a bargain was struck. You stand in the very forge of the anchor.'

I looked at Julian, who blinked, hard.

'Earth requires custodians with more wisdom than human-kind. Over eons, you have caused untold suffering,' Nashira said. 'You have fought and killed one another with abandon – not only saddling your realm with restless spirits, but ruining ours. You cannot be allowed to continue. Where you failed to protect this world, we will not.'

She levelled her gaze on my line of prisoners. I lowered mine, just in case.

'Some of you were detained by humans in our employ. They are called red-jackets.' She indicated a line of men and women, clad in scarlet tunics and black gilets. 'Since our arrival, we have taken many clairvoyants under our wing. We train you to destroy the Emim. This city acts as a beacon to the creatures, drawing them away from the amaurotic population.'

No safer place. The motto rang with new meaning. *No safer place.*

'When the Emim breach these walls, red-jackets are summoned to repel them. Such breaches are announced by a siren. There is a high risk of mutilation.'

There is also, I thought, *a high risk that this is all in my head.*

'We offer you this fate as an alternative to what Scion would offer: death by hanging or asphyxiation, or a short life as a Vigile.'

In the row behind me, a girl whimpered. She was hushed at once.

This was ridiculous. Scion was trying to make us think we had lost our marbles. Either that, or Jaxon had paid all these people to play some elaborate trick on me. I wouldn't have put it past him.

'London is our primary source of clairvoyants,' Nashira said. 'Scion ensures that you are recognised, relocated and rehabilitated, away from the amaurotics, who despise you. This is the truth behind the anchor.'

I forced myself to consider the possibility that all of this was real. I understood almost none of it, but if Nashira Sargas *was* telling the truth, Scion was no more than a puppet government.

The girl behind me cracked. With a desperate sob, she made a break for the door.

She stood no chance against the bullet.

Screams erupted everywhere. In the chaos, one of the Rephaim thundered, 'SILENCE.'

His pipes would have put an organ to shame. The hall fell silent at once.

The killer was human, wearing red. He holstered his revolver and clasped his hands behind his back. Two other guards took the body by the arms and towed it outside, leaving a smear of blood.

'If any more of you wish to run, now is the time,' Nashira said. 'Be assured, we can make room in the grave.'

Nobody moved an inch. If there had been any suspicion left that this was a game or hallucination, that bullet had shattered it.

In the fraught silence that followed, I risked a glance at the other Rephaim.

One of them was looking at me.

He must have been examining me for some time. His gaze cleaved straight to mine, as if he had been waiting for me to look, watching for a flicker of dissent.

Like Nashira, he wore a livery collar. His skin was a warm dark gold, setting off his flaming eyes. He was the tallest of the Rephaim, with brown hair, short and roughly cut. A strange aura enfolded him, overshadowed by the others in the room.

He was the single most beautiful and terrible thing I had ever laid eyes on.

I snapped my gaze back to the floor, shaken. Distantly, I realised Nashira was still talking.

'Clairvoyants have developed great strength over the last two centuries. You have learned to endure Scion,' she said. 'Over ten years, we select a certain number of you for enrolment in for our penal colony. We call these decadal harvests Bone Seasons. Yours is the twentieth.

'The clairvoyants among you will now be assigned an identification number and a Rephaite keeper. Seven of my companions will welcome humans into their residences this Bone Season.

'Your keeper will be your master in all things. Their duty is to train you for your tests, during which your value to our cause will be judged,' Nashira said. 'Should you disobey or displease your keeper, you will receive the yellow tunic of a craven.'

I know it isn't my place — you've told me so — but I think you should consider the University.

43

My lips quaked into a smile. This might not be the University of Scion London, but it sounded like I would be taking exams.

'Those of you who are amaurotic – that is, the few of you who have no idea what I am talking about – will be put to work in our residences,' Nashira said. 'Since amaurotics reap the greatest benefits from Scion, it is only right that some of you should join our long campaign against the Emim. You are here to serve.'

Seb was starting to look very unwell.

'If you do not pass your first test, or if you should thrice earn the yellow tunic, you will be sent to Beltrame the Overseer, who will mould you into a performer,' Nashira continued. 'Performers exist for our entertainment, and the entertainment of those loyal to us.'

I soon understood. Those people on the stage had been the cowards, the failures.

A few people were crying now; others stood in rapt horror. Nashira didn't appear to notice.

'Those of you who adapt to this system will be rewarded. Those who do not will be punished,' she said. 'This is your life now.'

This proved too much for Seb, who fainted. Julian sidled around me to help me prop him up, but he was still a dead weight.

Seven of the Rephaim stepped down from the platform. 'These Rephaim have offered their services as keepers,' Nashira said. 'They will now decide which of you to take under their wings.'

The giants began to survey the room, walking between the rows. The tallest – the one whose gaze I had met – stayed on the platform with Nashira and the others, who must be there as observers.

'It can't be true,' I said in a whisper.

'Look at them.' Julian barely moved his lips. 'They're not human.'

'There is no such thing as a Netherworld.' I shut up for a moment when a Rephaite passed. 'There's here and the æther. That's it.'

'Rotties can't sense the æther, but it's real. Who's to say there isn't more?'

A wild laugh bubbled up inside me. I managed to restrain it. I had imagined many reasons for voyants being taken, but nothing like this.

Across the room, a Rephaite stopped in front of Carl. Her clothes were particularly spartan, down to her sturdy boots and the plain cut of her doublet.

'XX-59-1,' she said, 'I lay claim to you.'

Carl swallowed. Once his new keeper had pointed him towards one side of the room, the Rephaim returned to their circling, like flimps sizing up wealthy marks. I wondered how they were choosing us.

After a few minutes, the whisperer joined Carl. Pleione claimed the oracle. One by one, we were picked like fish at the market.

A male with an angular face chose the palmist. She wept in panic, gasping 'please' to no avail. Julian was taken not long after – 26. He shot me a worried look and went with his new keeper.

They got to 38. Finally, there were only a few of us left: the amaurotics, a polyglot, and me.

The polyglot – a small boy with cornrows, probably no more than twelve – was led away by Pleione and given the number 39. Now I was the only voyant.

The Rephaim looked to Nashira. My spine pulled tight.

The one who had been watching me stepped forward to stand at her side. They seemed to have a silent conversation before she crooked a finger at me.

So much for keeping my head down.

Seb was still unconscious. Noticing my predicament, one of the amaurotic men took him from my arms. Every eye was on me as I walked across the marble floor, my footsteps echoing, too loud.

I stopped in front of the platform. Nashira watched me, one hand on the balustrade. She wore black leather gloves, as they all did.

'What is your name?'

'Paige,' I said.

'And where are you from?'

I lifted my chin. 'Ireland.'

A murmur passed through the room.

'I see,' Nashira said. 'Your aura is intriguing. Tell us what you are.'

'I don't know.'

Head down, eyes open.

'A mystery, then. I have good news for you,' Nashira said. (I highly doubted it.) 'You have caught the attention of my consort – Arcturus, Warden of the Mesarthim. He has decided to be your keeper.'

The other Rephaim exchanged glances, expressionless.

'It is rare that he takes an interest in a human,' Nashira told me. 'You are fortunate.'

I didn't feel especially fortunate. I felt like death warmed over.

Arcturus looked down at me. A very long way down.

'XX-59-40.' His voice was deep and soft. 'I lay claim to you.'

As he spoke, I looked right into his eyes, even though I shouldn't. I wanted to know the face of my enemy.

'It is done,' Nashira said. 'Those of you who remain will be escorted to Amaurotic House. The rest of you will go with your keepers to the residences.' She clasped her hands. 'You have been spared the wretched fate of other clairvoyants in Scion. Embrace your new lives, and you will reap many rewards. Together, we will make sure that there is no safer place than Scion.'

With that, she departed, shadowed by two of the human guards.

Arcturus started to leave. From his purposeful stride, he was used to people hurrying to clear a path for him. When I didn't come at once, he waited.

Everyone was staring at me. My head spun as I followed my new jailer.

The first red of dawn had dusted the sky. Arcturus swept through the gates and turned left. I barely managed to keep up with him.

'You are my tenant now,' he informed me. (What a nice word for *prisoner*.) 'Should you pass your tests, you will live with me on a permanent basis. If you fail, I may decide to evict you. You should try to avoid that fate. The streets here are not kind.'

They couldn't be much worse than London.

'You should know that we sleep by day. There is a strict curfew,' he continued. 'You must be indoors from sunrise to dusk.'

When he led me past an old sign reading CATTE STREET, I took note. I needed to learn the layout of this city as soon as possible.

'Your silence concerns me.' Arcturus stopped. 'Do you understand what I am telling you?'

'I'm not allowed to speak without permission,' I reminded him.

'I will grant you that privilege.'

'I'm fine, thanks.'

Arcturus returned my unflinching gaze. His eyes held a dead heat.

'We are stationed at the Residence of Magdalen.' He turned his back on me again. 'I trust you are strong enough to walk.'

'I can walk,' I said curtly.

'Good.'

Arcturus strode on to another gaslit street, this one named Magdalen Walk. From the hush and stillness, the sinister performance had come to an end.

As I trailed after him, I spotted a group of voyants standing under a streetlamp. One woman caught my gaze, but she was quick to look away.

'You lot,' a red-jacket barked at them. 'Back to the Rookery. The Bone Season does not exempt you from the curfew.'

They melted into the shadows at once. Arcturus ignored the disturbance, but glanced back to make sure I was still following.

Magdalen was from another time, another world. Imposing and magnificent, it boasted tall chimneys, Gothic arches, and a bell tower with turrets, and that was just what I could see from the street.

Deep chimes rang out as we approached a wooden door. THE RESIDENCE OF MAGDALEN was carved into the lintel, flanked by lanterns. I had less than no idea why Arcturus pronounced it *maudlin*.

He used an iron knocker to rap on the door. It opened to reveal a man with brown skin and grizzled black hair, who bowed and let us inside.

'Warden,' the man said, once the door was closed and bolted. 'Welcome back. I trust the Bone Season brought a promising crop.'

'Yes. This is my new tenant,' Arcturus said. 'Her number is XX-59-40.'

The man gave me a guarded look. He was probably in his early fifties. His grey tunic and lack of aura marked him as an amaurotic.

'Very good, my lord,' he said. 'I'll inform the night porter.'

Arcturus led me across a courtyard, into a stone passage. It was open to the cold on one side, making the torchlight flicker. I

47

followed him up a flight of steps. At the top, there were more steps to the right, leading to a door. He unlocked a larger door on our left.

Beyond lay a room with a high ceiling, befitting the lair of a giant. The walls were pale, with dark and polished wainscoting. A gramophone played 'Gloomy Sunday' from a stand in one corner.

The furnishings were beautiful. Thick red curtains framed the oriel windows. A daybed and a couch – also red – faced each other beside a crackling fire, accompanied by a wing chair. A low table stood between them, set with two goblets and a decanter.

At least my aura would fit in with the décor.

Arcturus walked ahead of me. I watched him return the key to his belt.

'The Founders Tower,' he said. 'This is where you will live.'

As he spoke, I dared to skim his dreamscape – ancient and strange, hardened by time. I recognised those defences, their impossible layering.

The stranger in the æther had definitely been one of them.

Arcturus turned to me, possibly sensing what I had done. Or perhaps he was admiring his prize.

'Come here,' he said.

I walked to him, stopping a short distance away. He was a clear foot taller than me. To look him in the face, I had to crane my neck.

I still met his gaze without hesitation. Let him see every ounce of my hatred for him. Now the initial shock had faded, I was fuming.

'You do not have the sight,' he observed. 'That may prove to be a disadvantage here, unless you have some means of compensating.'

His accent was that of most Scion officials, classic Inquisitorial English. You could have cut glass on those consonants. It was a measured voice, betraying next to no emotion.

Then again, he might have none.

'I must leave soon.' His face was cold. 'Do you have any questions?'

I looked around. 'I've all this to myself?'

'No. This is my parlour. Until your room is ready, you may sleep here.'

'Where *is* my room?'

'In the southwestern attic adjoining the tower. Anything else?'

Magdalen clearly had no shortage of rooms. If he had installed me in his own quarters, he must want to keep a close eye on me.

'No,' I said, my voice sounding distant to my own ears. 'No, this all seems perfectly simple.'

'Very well.'

He went to a display case. I watched his every move, like the good thief I was.

'I will be away until tomorrow.' He took out a short glass. 'You should acquaint yourself with the city in my absence. Should you hear the siren, return to the Founders Tower at once. If you steal or touch or otherwise meddle with anything, I will know.'

'Yes, sir.'

The *sir* just slipped out.

Arcturus poured water into the glass. He presented it to me with a green tablet.

'Take this,' he said. 'Take another at dusk, along with the red and white pills. You will find them in the middle drawer of my desk.'

'What if I refuse?'

There was a long silence.

'It was an order,' he said. 'Not a request.'

'I've met people like you before. The sort of people who like to throw their weight around,' I said softly. 'You don't scare me.'

'Then you are a fool.'

My jaw clenched.

If I meant to survive this place, I would have to pick my battles. I washed the pill down. Arcturus took the glass from my hand.

'One more thing,' he said. A tremor shot down my spine. 'You will address me by my ceremonial title – Warden. Is that understood?'

'Yes.'

I forced myself to say it.

'We will begin your training upon my return.' He made for the door. 'Sleep well.'

'I don't know what you are,' I said, 'but know this.' I met his eyes once more. 'You brought the wrong voyant in here.'

Arcturus regarded me for a moment. Without another word, he closed the heavy door behind him, leaving me alone in the shadows.

The key turned in the lock.

5

THE ROOKERY

13 March 2059

A bell roused me from a deep sleep that evening. For a drowsy moment, I thought I was in my old room in Islington, a long weekend of nothing ahead of me – away from work, away from Jaxon.

Then I saw the ceiling. I sat up, heart pounding, hair wild around my face. I was still in the opulent parlour, on the daybed.

The Rephaim, the halls and the dancing; the origins of Scion. Somehow, all of it was real.

I hadn't meant to doze off, but the flux had left me weak and tired. The small of my back ached. Rubbing my stiff neck, I drank in my surroundings. Arcturus – Warden – was nowhere to be seen.

His gramophone was sorrowing away. I recognised 'Danse Macabre' immediately, my pulse quickening – Jaxon listened to it when he was in a sour mood, usually over a glass of vintage wine. I switched it off and pushed the drapes from the nearest window.

The last blue light was leaving the sky. Across the parlour, a writing desk stood by a leadlight. A note had been left on it, penned in black ink.

Wait for the bell.

The bell must lift the curfew. Beside the message, I found a floor plan of Magdalen. I noted the names of the buildings, the rooms.

Next, I had a look around. A chess table stood in the alcove formed by a window, ready for a new game. Apart from the main door, there were two others, both locked. One was most likely for a bedchamber; the other led on to the roof of the cloister. The former had a few wooden stairs leading up to it.

The main door was newly unlocked. Once I had picked up a candle, I exited the parlour and crossed the landing, taking the steps to a bathroom with plastered stone walls. The bath itself was enormous, made for someone of great height. A mirror shone above the sink, polished to perfection. There was a concerning lack of toilet.

I set the candle down in its holder and turned one of the brass taps on the sink. Hot water rushed out. With a sigh of relief, I washed my face and neck, leaving the pristine towels where they were.

I held my own gaze in the mirror, thinking.

The Rephaim had struck their deal in 1859. That was long before the fall of the monarchy in 1901. Queen Victoria had been allowed to reign until her death. Had she known she would be the last monarch?

Lord Palmerston had been the Prime Minister. He must have paved the way to Scion out of fear, trying to save the world. What I still didn't understand was why the system targeted voyants. The Rephaim blamed all humans for the loss of their home. Why were we paying the price?

Even stranger, the Rephaim *were* voyant. So far, they all had auras. I couldn't wrap my head around this arrangement.

My priority was to get out of here. Until then, I would learn what I could. For now, it was probably in my best interest to play along.

Tonight I planned to check on Seb. I could almost hear Jaxon laughing at me, but Seb wouldn't last a day on his own. Once I had found him, I would look for Julian, who seemed to have a level head on him. It might pay to forge an alliance or two.

On my way out of the bathroom, I glanced up the rest of the steps. Those must lead to the attic.

Back in the parlour, I laced my boots and opened the middle drawer of the desk. Inside were three blister packs of pills. I popped one of each – red, white and green, none of them labelled.

The city was full of things I didn't yet understand. These pills might be there to protect me from something: toxins, radiation. Maybe I should take them. Once Warden returned, I would have no choice.

For now, I washed them all down the sink. No matter what happened to me in this place, I refused to blindly obey.

The Residence of Magdalen was like nowhere I had ever seen. It could have been a small district, if anyone had cared to fill it. As it stood, I could only sense three other dreamscapes, all human.

I did a lap of the cloister, which surrounded a pristine lawn. As I went, I tried various locked doors, committing each to memory.

Warden was away tonight. I should use the opportunity to explore the residence, but I wanted to be outside. I would survive Oxford the same way I had survived London, by learning its secrets.

Magdalen could wait.

In the Porters' Lodge at the front of the residence, a soothsayer had replaced the man from earlier. Her thin brown hair was pulled into a bun, and her gilet looked warmer than mine.

'Good evening,' she said. 'You must be 40.' I nodded. 'I'm the night porter. Welcome to the Residence of Magdalen.'

'Thank you,' I said, for want of anything else to say.

'It's lovely to have a newcomer to the household. The Warden has never been a keeper before – not once, according to our records,' she said. 'You're very lucky to be training with him.'

'So I've been told.' I eyed her pink tunic. 'If he's not your keeper, who is?'

'Alsafi Sualocin. He suspected I wouldn't survive my second test, so he permitted me to leave Queens to work for the Warden,' she said. 'I'm proud to say this is my twelfth year at Magdalen.'

That was alarming. I hadn't been planning to sit around here for twelve days, let alone twelve years.

'I hope you were comfortable in the Founders Tower,' she added. 'The attic will be ready for you soon. We just need to clear it.'

'No bother.' I folded my arms. 'I'd like to go outside, if I may.'

'Of course.' She opened a thick book. 'Let me sign you out.'

'Am I allowed to go anywhere in Magdalen?'

'Anywhere but the Old Chapel. Otherwise, you can go as far as the gate just east of the lawns. You can also explore the city whenever you like during the night, so long as you sign out.'

'Anything else I should know?'

She considered me. 'Personally,' she said, 'I would stay close to the residences, within the limits of the medieval city wall. You *can* go farther, but if you're alone, you may be questioned.'

'I didn't see a wall when I arrived.'

'The wall itself doesn't exist any more, but the boundary is marked on that map. You'll know it when you reach it. It's where the lamplight ends.' She nodded to a frame on the wall behind me. 'After that point, the city is dark and dangerous. The farther you stray towards the outskirts, the closer you are to Gallows Wood.'

'And what's in there?'

'The Warden will tell you,' she said. 'In good time.'

There was a finality to her tone. I decided not to push my luck.

'I see.' I went to look at the map. 'Any idea where I can get food?'

'Magdalen will provide you with two meals a day if you work hard. For now, use this.' She handed me a small drawstring pouch. 'The harlies always want numa. You can often exchange these for bread and broth in the Rookery, the shanty town on the Broad.'

I shook my head, lost. 'Harlies?'

'The performers.'

I undid the pouch. It rattled with rodent bones and needles, as well as a cheap ring.

These numa were brittle. They would break or degrade. A cruel and clever way to keep the soothsayers in line – perhaps some of the augurs, too. Things like bones and tea leaves must be hard to find.

'Right.' I tucked them away. 'Is there a bathroom for humans around here?'

Now, there was a question I had never imagined asking.

53

'Oh, yes. The nearest is just east of the cloister, adjoining the tool shed. I'd wait until morning, if you can. It isn't heated,' she said. 'The day bell rings at sunrise. Don't be late.'

'Fine. Thanks for your help.'

'You're welcome. Have a wonderful night.'

Well, somebody was brainwashed. I hefted the main door open and left.

A thick fog had descended. It was cold as midwinter here. As I turned up my collar, I wondered what I had got myself into with Warden. His name was said like a prayer, like a promise.

You're very lucky to be training with him.

I would look into it later. For now, I would get some food and find Seb.

There seemed to be no electricity in this city. To my left was a stone bridge, lit by gas lamps on both sides. A line of red-jackets blocked that way to the outside world. When I got too close, they pointed their rifles at me. With their sights trained on my back, I set off to find the Rookery.

According to the map, the Rookery was a short way north. I retraced the steps I had taken with Warden, back along Magdalen Walk.

The next path lay as quiet as the first, leading me to a square I recognised. I passed the Residence of the Suzerain, fighting off a chill.

Several large buildings emerged from the fog. One of them had pillars and a decorated pediment, like the Grand Museum in Bloomsbury. I skirted around its edge, on to the Broad.

The sound of human life strained through the night. I recognised this place. Rickety stalls ran down the street, skeletal and gloomy, hung with dirty lanterns. On either side of these were rows of rudimentary huts, shacks and tents, made of ridged metal and plastic – a shanty town in the middle of a city.

And there was the siren, right by the settlement. An old giant with a rotor and a gaping horn, nothing like the sleek models in London.

The smell of roasting meat drew me into a shack. My stomach was tight with hunger. Plywood tunnels linked the dwellings, patched with scrap metal and cloth. They had few windows; instead they were lit by paraffin lamps and the reddish glow from the cook-fires outside, which leaked in through innumerable cracks.

The people here wore threadbare clothes. None of them looked healthy. These must be the performers, who had failed their tests and been condemned here, probably for both life and afterlife. Most were soothsayers or augurs, from the most common orders of clairvoyance. A few glanced my way, but quickly moved on.

The source of the smell was a large square room, a smoke hole cut into its roof. I stood to one side, trying not to draw attention to myself.

The meat was being served in thin slices, pink and tender in the middle. The performers shared plates of vegetables and spooned gravy from silver tureens. They were hunched over the food, stuffing it into their mouths, licking the hot juices from their fingers.

Before I could ask, a tall voyant pressed a plate into my hands. He was in his thirties, dressed in little more than rags, with a tangle of brown hair. His thick glasses were scratched all over.

'Is Mayfield still in the Archon?'

I raised an eyebrow. 'What?'

'Mayfield,' he repeated, impatient. 'Is he still Grand Inquisitor?'

'Mayfield died a few years ago.'

'Who is it now?'

'Frank Weaver.'

'Oh, him with the whiskers, right. You haven't got a copy of the *Descendant*, have you?'

'They confiscated everything.' I glanced around for somewhere to sit. 'Did you really think Mayfield was still the Inquisitor?'

'All right,' the voyant snapped. 'Don't get on your high horse, oracle. This is our first news in ten years.' He grasped my arm, leading me to a corner. 'Did they ever bring back the *Roaring Boy*, then?'

'No.' I tried to free my arm, but he clung. 'Look—'

'Tell me they never found the Fleapit.'

'She's only just arrived, Cyril. I think she'd like something to eat.'

Cyril rounded on the speaker, a young woman with her arms crossed and her chin tipped up.

'You are an absolute stinking bloody curmudgeon, Rymore,' he complained. 'Did you pick up Ten of Swords today?'

'Aye, when I was thinking about you.'

With a glower, Cyril snatched my plate and scarpered. I made a grab for his shirt, but he was faster than a flimp.

The woman shook her head. She had delicate features, framed by black ringlets. Her red lipstick stood out like a fresh wound against her skin.

'You had your oration last night, little sister.' She spoke with a warm Scottish burr. 'Trust me. Your stomach wouldn't have taken it.' She took me by the elbow. 'Hurry. Come with me.'

I wasn't sure whether or not to laugh at being called *little sister* by this tiny woman. 'Where?'

'I have a place. We can talk.'

After a moment, I nodded. My street instinct told me not to follow a stranger into an unfamiliar place, but she might have information.

My guide touched hands with various people, keeping a sharp eye on me all the while. Her clothes were in better condition than those of the other performers, but she must still be cold in them – a flimsy shirt with bell sleeves and trousers too short for her legs, clearly repaired by hand.

She drew back a ragged curtain to reveal a cramped room, where a paraffin lamp kept the dark at bay. A pile of stained sheets and a cushion served as a bed. Several pots and pans hung from hooks on the wall, and a shirt was drying on a rack.

I sat by an old stove. 'Do you often take in strays?'

'I know how it is when you arrive,' the woman said. 'I was terrified.'

'How long ago was that?'

'Ten years.' She knelt on the other side of the stove and held out a callused hand. 'Liss Rymore.'

After a moment, I shook it. 'Paige Mahoney.'

'XX-59-40?'

'Yes.'

Liss caught my expression. 'Sorry. Force of habit,' she said. 'We do use our names in the Rookery, but we have to be careful.'

Even though her face was careworn, she could only be in her early twenties. She must have been young when she arrived here.

'It's fine,' I said. 'How do you know my number?'

Liss took out a bottle of paraffin and poured a little into the stove.

'News travels fast in a city this small,' she said. 'Your number is on everyone's lips.'

'Dare I ask why?'

'Did you not hear?' she said drily. 'Arcturus Mesarthim has *never* shown interest in training a human. It's the most excitement we've had in a while.' She struck a match, setting a flame in the stove. 'I'll warm up some broth. The others won't share.'

'Why not?'

'They don't like jackets, with good reason.' She set a pot on the stove. 'They'll want to judge your character before they trade with you.'

'But you don't care.'

'I always give new arrivals a chance.'

Liss heated the broth. Once it was steaming, she divided it between two bowls. I offered her my numa, but she shook her head.

'On the house.'

I took a sip of the broth, a thin concoction of oatmeal and shredded leaves. It was gritty, but warm.

'Here.' Liss passed me a hunk of stale bread. 'Skilly and toke. It takes the edge off, at least.'

'Thank you.' I nodded towards the central room. 'There's food in there.'

'A rare display of generosity for the Bone Season,' she said. 'Our usual rations depend on what sort of performing we do. I get more than most, but it's never enough. We're always hungry. Always cold.'

'How do you manage?'

'I forage, myself. Others risk stealing from the residences. I hear Merton is best,' she said. 'You can slip a few eggs from its coops, or scrump apples.' She served herself. 'You could try fishing, if you're patient. Some poach squirrels and pheasants with traps, but that never ends well. Not in the woods.'

So far, stealing from the residences sounded like my best option. It fit my skill set.

'I assume the red-jackets have plenty of food,' I said.

'Aye. They get chicken from Balliol, venison from Magdalen, all sorts. The amaurotics prepare their meals. They sometimes help us, but they've been less willing since December.'

'What happened?'

'In winter, the killing cold blows in, and we can't forage any more. An amaurotic – Nita – took pity on us,' Liss said. 'She used to leave food in a basket at the back of Queens. It kept us strong for weeks, but someone reported her. I've not seen her since.'

'Some humans are loyal to the cause, then.'

'Just like Vigiles. Be careful who you trust.' She moved her feet closer to the stove. 'So you're at Magdalen. What's it like?'

'A gilded cage.'

'It's a very exclusive residence. In all my time here, there's never been more than three humans living there. You've pushed it to four.'

'How many residences are there?'

'Seven that traditionally accept humans. Those are Balliol, Corpus, Exeter, Merton, Oriel, Queens and Trinity,' Liss said. 'The Overseer has the whole of Kettell Hall, which is here on the Broad.'

'And the other buildings?'

'Those are reserved for the Rephs, except when the amaurotics are cleaning them. You saw the Residence of the Suzerain. There's also a storage facility on Fish Street, the House.'

'And what's Gallows Wood?'

'When the Rephs came, the outlying districts of Oxford were demolished, replaced by a forest that now surrounds what's left of the city.' Liss drank some broth. 'Gallows Wood is where the Emim hunt. The red-jackets patrol it to stop them reaching the lamplight. Apparently its far reaches are full of mines and trap pits.'

'And beyond that?'

'I've heard there's a wall. After that, it's probably just countryside.'

'Has anyone ever tried to escape?'

'Yes.'

Her shoulders were tense. I tore off a scrap of bread.

I wasn't surprised no one had succeeded. You couldn't plan a jail-break if you were fighting a constant battle for your next mouthful.

'How long were you in the Tower?'

I glanced up. 'I didn't go to the Tower.'

'Then you must have only been caught a few days ago.' When I nodded, Liss blew out her breath. 'You're lucky. They collect voyants for each Bone Season over a decade.'

'Nashira said. It seems like a bit of a palaver,' I said. 'Why not just send us here as they catch us?'

'It's so they can curate an interesting variety. And the Rephs are good at taming us,' Liss said. 'They know every way to break a human. Even one year in the Tower would break the strongest person. After that, anything seems like a release, even a place like this.'

'What are the Rephs, exactly?'

'None of us really know.' She dabbed some bread in the broth. 'Whatever they are, they never let us forget that humans are inferior. We broke the ethereal threshold, so we're responsible for the Buzzers.'

'Buzzers?'

'Emim. That's what we've always called them,' she said. 'The red-jackets came up with it. They're the ones who have to fight them.'

'How often?'

I was asking far too many questions, but I needed knowledge.

'Depends. They attack a lot more in winter, so you've just missed the worst time of year,' Liss said. 'A single tone from the siren calls the red-jackets to arms. If the tone starts to change, you need to get inside. It means the Buzzers have breached the city.'

'Have you seen them?'

'No, but I've heard stories. The red-jackets like scaring us.' The firelight played across her face. 'They say the Buzzers can devour your spirit – erase you from the æther, as if you never existed. Others say they're skeletons that need skin to cover themselves. I don't know how much of it is true, but they do eat flesh. Don't be surprised if you see a few missing limbs out there.'

It should have unsettled me, but this place still felt disjointed from the real world.

Liss adjusted the curtain. As she moved, a pile of folded purple silk caught my eye.

'You're the aerialist,' I said.

She smiled at me over her shoulder. 'Did you think I was good?'

'Very good.'

'That's how I earn my flatches here. Lucky for me, I picked it up quickly.'

'I think I saw you after the oration, too.'

'I was curious to see who each Reph would choose.' She sat back down. 'This place is already rustling with speculation. That's why I got you in here quickly, before everyone realised who you are. Your aura was … a talking point.'

I nodded without elaborating.

Julian had not believed I was an acultomancer. I doubted Liss would, either. The lie was even less likely to work on a soothsayer. Passing myself off as an oracle was my best shot at secrecy.

'Well,' Liss said gently. 'Are you going to make me guess?'

I tilted my head. 'Can you?'

Perhaps I could trust one person with the truth. Liss had been here for a long time. I needed her to tell me whether to hide or use my gift.

'I can try.' Her fingers drummed on the floor. 'Your aura is red. That makes me think you're an oracle – but I hear oracles have come here before, and Arcturus Mesarthim never took an interest.'

I saw the idea taking root in her mind.

'You have to be something else. Something unprecedented. You have to be—' The realisation dawned. 'A dreamwalker.'

I nodded once more. Liss sank back as if her stomach was punctured.

'Well,' she said, 'that solves it.'

'What?'

'Why he took you under his wing. Nashira must already suspect what you are. She wants you protected by her own consort.'

'Why would she care?'

'You won't like this.'

I waited.

'Did you notice that aura of hers?' Liss asked. 'She doesn't just have one ability. She walks several different paths to the æther.'

'I've never met a voyant with more than one gift.'

'This place has its own rules.' She pulled her knees up to her chin. 'Nashira has five angels.' (Another impossibility.) 'This is just a theory, but we think they used to be voyants, and that she can use the gifts they had in life.'

'Not even binders can do that.'

'Exactly.' Liss shot me a perturbed look. 'If you want my advice, give no inkling of what you are. If she sees for sure … you're done for, Paige.'

I kept my expression neutral. Three years in the syndicate had hardened me to danger, but here, I would have to keep my wits sharp.

'I know how to hide what I am,' I said. 'I did it for eleven years.'

'It'll be harder here. They'll test you to expose your gift. That's what the tunics mean. Pink after your first test, red after the second.'

'Did you fail yours?'

'By choice. Now I answer to the Overseer.'

'Who was your keeper?'

Liss breathed out through her nose, her jaw tight.

'Gomeisa Sargas,' she eventually said. 'The other blood-sovereign.'

'Was he at the oration?'

'No. He lives in London now, but I imagine he'll visit soon, to hear about the Bone Season. Nashira shares her power with him.'

'Arcturus is her consort.'

'Yes, but he's not a Sargas. That's what *blood-sovereign* means,' Liss said. 'Only their family – their blood – can rule. Arcturus is from a smaller family. His conjugal title is *blood-consort*. Like a prince consort.'

'But he's also the Warden.'

'We *think* that means he's the head of his family. Not that I've heard of many other Mesarthims.' She nodded to the pot. 'More skilly?'

'I'm fine. Thanks.' I watched her slide our bowls into a tub of water. 'It can't have been easy to live with a Reph. But it doesn't look easy to live out here, either.'

'It isn't,' she said, 'but I refused to give up my humanity.' She glanced at me. 'Rephs aren't human. No matter how much they look like us, they've got nothing here.' She tapped her chest. 'If you ever mean to earn their trust, you'll have to cut away your kindness.'

Before I could ask, the curtain was torn aside. A lean male Reph stood in the doorway.

'You,' he barked at Liss. Her hands flew to her head at once. 'Get up and dress, lazy filth. And with a *guest*, I see! Are you a queen?'

Liss stood. All her strength was gone, leaving her small and fragile. 'I'm sorry, Suhail,' she said. '40 is new here. I wanted to explain the rules.'

'40 should already know the rules.'

'She only just arrived. I—' Liss backed into the corner of the shack. 'I didn't think I was performing tonight. Have you spoken to the Overseer?'

'I do not answer to humans.'

'Of course not. Forgive me.'

This Reph didn't have the blank stare that some of the others did. Every crease of his chiselled face bled contempt. He looked as if he was made of dull gold, with a long sheet of hair, platinum blond.

'The other aerialist is injured,' he said. 'The red-jackets expect their favourite jester to replace him. Unless you wish to suffer this evening, you *will* perform.'

Liss nodded. Her shoulders pulled towards her chest, and she looked away.

'I understand,' she said. 'I'll get ready.'

Suhail finally seemed to notice me. He gave me a sneering look before ripping the curtain down on his way out. I helped Liss gather it.

'He seems nice,' I said drily.

'Suhail Chertan.' Liss was shaking. 'The Overseer is always a bit tense under his greasepaint. He answers to Suhail if we do something wrong.'

She brushed at her eyes. Thinking she was crying, I gently took the curtain from her hands. The cuff of her shirt was smeared with blood.

'Hey,' I said. 'Did you cut yourself?'

'It's nothing. He just took a bit of my glow.'

'What?'

'He fed on me.'

I was sure I had misheard her.

'He fed on you,' I repeated.

'Did they forget to mention that Rephs feed on aura?' Liss let me see her face at last. 'That part must have slipped their mind.'

She had bled from both eyes. Just like the tasseographer when Pleione fixed her gaze on him.

'That's not possible,' I murmured. 'That would mean they weren't just voyant.'

'They act like gods.' Liss reached for her silks. 'We harlies are their libations, but you jackets – you don't get fed on. That's your privilege.'

Rephs feeding on aura made no sense. It was a link to the æther, unique to each voyant. I couldn't imagine how they could use it for survival.

But the news was a stark light on this place. This was why they took voyants into their fold; why the performers weren't bumped off if they failed their tests. The Rephs didn't just want them to dance.

This was why *voyants*, most of all, were paying for human error.

'Someone has to stop this,' I said.

'They've been here for two hundred years,' Liss said. 'If it were possible, don't you think someone would have done it by now?'

She had a point.

'I've been here for a decade,' Liss said. 'I've seen people fight, people who couldn't let go of their old lives. They're all dead. In the end you'll stop trying.'

I studied her. 'Are you a seer?'

She wasn't, but I wondered if she would lie.

'I'm a broadsider,' Liss said. (An old word for a cartomancer, street slang of a decade past.) 'The first time I touched a deck of cards, I knew.'

'What did they show you?'

Liss knelt beside a wooden box and took out a tarot deck, tied with purple ribbon. This had to be her favoured numen. She picked out a card and showed it to me.

63

The Fool.

'The first card in the tarot,' she said, 'and somehow I still wound up at the bottom of the pile.' She traced its edge. 'Paige, I wish I could give you some hope, but it's been too long. I've accepted my lot.'

'I've never had my cards read.'

'Perhaps we can change that.' Liss tucked the deck away with care. 'Come and see me again soon, sister. I can't protect you, but I might be able to stop you getting yourself killed.' She gave me a tired smile. 'Welcome to Sheol I.'

Liss gave me directions to Amaurotic House, where Seb had been placed under the questionable care of Graffias Sheratan, the Grey Keeper. She also gave me a bread roll, wrapped in paper.

I had learned a great deal from her. The most troubling revelation was that Nashira could be on to me. If she was a binder, like Jaxon, she might want to turn me into her boundling – a spirit forced to stay and serve.

Not getting to the last light – the end of the æther – was something I had always feared. I hated the thought of being a restless spirit, a clip of spare ammo, for voyants to abuse and trade. Still, that had never stopped me making spools to protect myself, or helping Jaxon bind Anne Naylor, the Ghost of Farringdon, who had been a young girl when she was murdered.

In the end you'll stop trying.

Liss was wrong.

I would prove it to her.

Amaurotic House lay on Fayre Street, outside the heart of the city. I soon understood what the night porter had meant about the boundary. Even a short way north of the Rookery, the streets were almost deserted, most of the gas lamps unlit. I breezed on with all the confidence I could muster, as if I were on my own turf in London.

A few plane trees lined the boulevard. The farther I walked, the darker and quieter it became. A few red-jackets were stationed in doorways, armed with lanterns and pistols. Before long, I heard the inevitable shout: 'You there. What are you doing?'

I stopped.

'My keeper told me to get my bearings,' I called back. 'Can I have a look around?'

'If you insist. Just make sure you're back for the day bell.'

'Got it.'

I quickened my step before the red-jacket could change her mind.

Soon I had found the building I needed. A chained gate was set into its façade, with a lunette reading AMAUROTIC HOUSE. There was a phrase underneath, probably Latin: DOMUS STULTORUM.

Two flaming torches lit those words, contained in iron brackets on either side of the gate. I looked between the bars to see the telltale glint of yellow eyes.

'I hope you have good reason to be near Amaurotic House.'

I stepped back as a Reph approached. Thick dark hair spilled over his broad shoulders, and his lower lip was full and petulant. Like the other Rephs, he could have been shaped from dull metal – palest copper, like rose gold. It made him look invulnerable.

'Just on a walk.' I kept my composure. 'Are you Graffias?'

'Indeed. Graffias Sheratan, the Grey Keeper.' He stopped on the other side of the gate. 'And who is *your* keeper, white-jacket?'

'Arcturus Mesarthim.'

'I should have known.' Graffias wrapped a large hand around one of the bars. 'Perhaps you walked exactly where you pleased in London, but I would not advise straying too far by yourself again. All manner of dangers lurk in this city.'

I believed it. Even with a gate between us, his gaze chilled me to the bone.

'I can handle myself,' I said.

'Can you?'

Rephs' auras were hard to read, but if I were to take a wild guess, I would have said Graffias was an augur. I reached for the pouch.

'Look,' I said, 'there's someone in here I want to see. I can pay.'

Before I could think it through, I offered him the numa. Graffias gave me a look of such hatred, such open disgust, that I flinched. I almost preferred the emotionless stares.

'Fool.' He drew a spool of spirits. 'Get out of my sight, before I call your keeper to discipline you. Do not let me see you here again.'

Without protest, I turned and walked away from the gate, my breath darting out in white puffs. I shoved the numa back into my pocket.

That had been a stupid thing to do. Even if Graffias *was* an augur, he would use numa of the finest quality, not fragile rodent bones.

For one dangerous moment, I had forgotten where I was.

Just as I was about to hightail it back to Magdalen, a quiet voice came from somewhere above my head.

'Paige!'

Above me, a hand reached through a barred window. I released my breath.

'Seb.' I kept my voice low. 'Are you okay?'

'No.' He sounded tearful. 'Please, Paige – please get me out of here. I have to get out of here. I'm sorry I called you unnatural, I'm sorry.'

Graffias had retreated into the building. When I was sure the coast was clear, I climbed up to the window and passed Seb the bread.

'I'll let you off the hook.' I squeezed his icy hand through the bars. 'I'm going to get us out of here, but you have to give me time.'

'They'll kill me.' He unwrapped the bread. 'I'll be dead in a week.'

'What did they do?'

'They made me scrub the floors and clean pieces of a smashed mirror,' he said, biting into the bread. His fingers were cut to ribbons. 'Tomorrow I'm supposed to start work in the residences.'

'What sort of work?'

'I don't know yet. I'm scared to know.' His voice was cracking. 'I want to see my parents. Why did this happen to me, Paige?'

'I think you were just unlucky,' I said.

'Scion was supposed to keep us safe.'

'Scion lies,' I told him. 'Now you know that as well as we do.' His right eye was swollen and bloodshot. 'What happened there?'

'Graffias hit me. I didn't do anything, Paige, really. He said I was human scum. He said—' Seb hung his head, and his lip shook. 'I don't understand why they would be so cruel to us.'

'You don't have to understand. Just survive.' I nodded to the bread. 'Eat that. Try and get yourself assigned to Magdalen tomorrow.'

'Is that where you live?'

'Yes.'

Seb nodded. Now he was calmer, he also seemed drowsy, unfocused. It occurred to me that he might be concussed. He needed a hospital, a doctor, but I doubted the Rephs provided those.

'Thank you,' he said. 'You're kind, Paige. I'm sorry for what happens to unnat—' He paused, swallowing. 'To clairvoyants.'

'Okay. I'll come back when I can,' I said. 'You just keep your head down, Seb.'

6

L A M P L I G H T

I had meant to find Julian, but meeting Graffias had reminded me of how little power I had in this place. In London, I had bent the streets to my will – one mention of Jaxon, and voyants sat up a bit straighter. Here I would be playing by a different set of rules.

I needed more sleep, to sharpen my judgement. Going back to Magdalen still felt like a defeat. Once the night porter had signed me back in, I trudged up the stairs to the Founders Tower.

In the parlour, I kicked off my boots. Before I slept, I would have another look around. There had to be something of interest in here.

Warden had warned me not to touch anything. Trusting my light fingers, I opened every drawer in his desk. I found three pairs of black gloves, a pen and creamy paper, matches. Nothing out of the ordinary.

A linen cabinet stood against one wall, a tall display case by another. Those looked more interesting. When I opened the display case, my sixth sense twinged. One shelf was full of exquisite drink-ware: absinthe glasses, snifters, silver goblets. The others housed a collection of beautiful numa, including a crystal ball.

Now, this *was* a thieves' paradise, for all the good it did me. I wasn't a soothsayer, and I couldn't steal or sell any of this. Still, my education in burglary reminded me to be thorough. I ran a hand around the inside of the display case, checking for hidden treasure.

My fingertips soon caught on something, tucked just out of sight. I brought it into the glow of the candles.

It was an ornate snuffbox – an antique, from the look of it. A delicate flower blossomed on its lid. Inside were two stoppered vials, each filled with something clear and iridescent.

I returned the snuffbox to its place, making sure there were no prints on it. It had been a long shot to think I would find anything useful in here.

A dull pain stabbed into my temple. I closed the curtains and lay on the daybed.

Now the fire had burned out, the Founders Tower was cold. I considered taking some bedding from the linen cabinet, but that would be hard to conceal from Warden, and I wasn't about to die for a duvet. Instead, I huddled against the backrest.

As I started to drift off, I thought of Jaxon. No doubt he was sending voyants to watch the Lychgate, expecting my corpse to appear up there.

Danica and Nick lived double lives in Scion. Maybe they could track me down. Surely there must be a record of transported prisoners somewhere. I held the thought close and let myself sleep.

I woke to the sound of the door opening. By the light of the few candles that still burned, I saw the faint outline of Warden. When he walked towards the daybed, I feigned sleep.

After what seemed like an eternity, he turned away and went across the landing, towards the bathroom. This time, his booted footsteps were heavier, and I could tell he was sporting a limp.

He was in there for a good long while. In that time, I could feel every heartbeat. I listened hard, hearing the distant creak of pipes. When he returned to the parlour, he was naked as sin. I closed my eyes and kept up my act as he unlocked the door to the next room.

Only when his mind had quietened, some time later, did I rise.

From the way he had been moving, he hadn't wanted to wake me. Somehow I couldn't imagine a Reph being that considerate.

Not without reason.

I let in a sliver of light from outside. A lamp shone in the courtyard, beneath a predawn sky. In silence, I padded up the wooden stairs and pushed the door open. The hinges made the slightest creak.

As I had suspected, this adjoining room was his bedchamber. Darkly panelled, it was bookended by two bay windows, grander than the ones in the parlour. It also had its own fireplace.

Beside that cold hearth stood a four-poster bed. Not daring to breathe, I looked between its red curtains.

Warden lay on his side, hair snarled over his brow. I held my nerve. The bedding was up to his shoulders, his face tilted into the pillow.

At first, I couldn't see anything wrong. Perhaps he just wanted to avoid me, which suited me just fine. I had nothing to say to him.

Then I spotted it. A faint glow, leaching through the bedspread.

The æther rang in warning.

He was as still as a corpse. I pushed the curtains farther apart, willing them not to make any sound. Once I was sure he was either asleep or unconscious, I lifted the bedspread. Beneath it, the sheets were soaked in molten light, like the contents of a glow bar, the same greenish yellow as his eyes. I peeled one sheet away, then another.

And there it was. A row of deep punctures on his upper arm, seeping beads of light.

I listened to the old residence, waiting. Surely the night porter had seen him come back in this state. Surely help was on its way. For the first time, I became aware of a clock, ticking on the mantelpiece.

Warden must have used another way into the residence.

The light kept oozing from his arm. It could only be their equivalent of blood. The wounds didn't look bad enough to kill him, but they could be infected. When the Rephs found him like this, I would be the only witness.

If Arcturus Mesarthim died on this bed, I was the prime suspect.

I drew in a long breath. As far as I could tell, I had three choices. I could see what happened, finish him off, or try to save his life.

The second option was tempting. He might not have hurt me yet, but he would. Scion had sent me here in the full knowledge that I had killed before. I could make them regret that decision.

I reached for a cushion, then paused.

He could wake up and break my neck. Even if I succeeded, I would only be executed myself, or thrown to another Reph.

I had to save him, for my own sake.

Rephs looked similar to humans. I would treat him like one – clean the wounds, stem the bleeding. That would buy him time, at least.

Something told me not to touch that strange light. I went to his chest of drawers and found yet another pair of gloves. They were massive, made for hands that dwarfed mine. This was going to be clumsy.

I took off the white tunic, leaving me in my undershirt. I fetched some cloths from the linen cabinet and soaked them in hot water. By the time I set to work, Warden was starting to look grey.

It took a long time. I mopped blood even as it congealed, coaxed grit from his broken skin. At first, I thought he must have been stabbed, but the open wounds seemed too ragged. While I was near them, I sensed the nearest spirits so keenly it almost hurt.

What are you?

By sunrise, I had made a dent. As the bell rang, I used a towel to pad his arm, securing it with a tie-back. It was crude, but it was the best I could do. I lay back down on the daybed, exhausted.

Now it all rested on him.

As soon as I woke, I knew I was alone. I got straight up and rushed into the bedchamber.

I blinked. The floor had been cleaned while I slept, the linen whisked away. The bedspread was immaculate – in fact, it looked as if it had been ironed.

Warden was nowhere to be seen.

Rain trickled down the windows. The fog had thinned. I soon found the note on the desk. In that same elegant cursive, it simply read:

Tomorrow.

71

Some fresh clothes had been left for me, including a new under-shirt. I changed into them and washed my pills down the sink, then curled up on the couch and stayed for a long while, turning the incident over and over in my head. The gramophone played in the background, its crackles mingling with the sound of the rain.

Part of me wanted to stay by the fire, rather than facing this grim, hostile place. Warden hadn't given me any specific instructions. I could keep warm and have a good look around Magdalen.

But whatever Liss said, I couldn't just lie down and accept this. I didn't care if the Rephs had been here for two hundred years or a thousand – I wasn't their soldier, and she wasn't their lunch.

In the Porters' Lodge, nothing seemed amiss. The night porter was reading by the light of a paraffin lamp. Seeing me, she smiled.

'Going out?'

'Yes.' I cleared my throat. 'Is the Warden here?'

'No, he's gone to Oriel. I doubt he'll return until dawn.'

He was alive, then. And the night porter was none the wiser.

'He'll train you in good time,' she said, misreading my face. 'There's no hurry.' She made a note in her book. 'I'm sorry, but Magdalen can't provide you with a meal today. Do you need more numa to trade?'

'Yes,' I said. She handed me a dull excuse for a shew stone, which I pocketed. 'Thanks.'

'You're quite welcome.' She closed the book. 'You're free to go. Just make sure you're—'

'—here before sunrise,' I finished. 'I know.'

I stepped on to Magdalen Walk and drew the door shut behind me. Some way ahead, a pair of red-jackets laughed, one of them holding a lantern. They wore hooded raincoats. Avoiding them, I turned into Catte Street.

In the Rookery, I swapped the stone for a bowl of porridge. It was thick and grey as wet cement, but it would muffle the hunger. I ate under a lean-to, watching the performers murmur and trade.

Now Liss had described her loss of hope, I could see it in all their faces. Their bright clothes were a harsh contrast, like graffiti on a headstone.

'All right?'

I looked up. It was the whisperer from the first night, standing in the greasy light of the nearest lamps, her dark hair scraped into a ponytail.

'Tilda,' she said. 'Can I sit?'

'If you like,' I said.

'Ta.' Tilda slid down the wall to the floor, all limbs. She looked about my age. 'Well. Proper headwrecker, this place, isn't it?'

'You could say that.'

She had a roll-up between her fingers. Lilac smoke trailed from the end, thick with the sickly perfume of purple aster. Seeing me look, she said, 'Want some regal?'

'I'm fine. I was just wondering where you got it.'

'One of the harlies.' She leaned against the wall. 'Probably a bad idea, but you try hearing the dead at all hours, muttering things you don't understand. You'd want a distraction, too.'

'This place isn't enough of a distraction for you?'

Tilda let out a husky laugh. 'Let's see how unhinged it gets. I keep expecting Frank Weaver to pop up and say it was all a big joke,' she said. 'Scion officials must get their jollies somehow.'

'Weaver doesn't have the imagination for something like this.'

'True. At least we're alive,' Tilda said. 'That's more than I expected.' She crossed one ankle over the other. 'They really put the spotlight on you at the oration. Your keeper is important, then, is he?'

'So I'm told. Who's yours?'

'Terebell Sheratan. I'm at Oriel,' she said. I resisted the urge to ask her if she had seen Warden, and roughly how close to death he had looked. 'What part of Ireland are you from, by the way?'

'You wouldn't know it. Why do you ask?'

'Just curious. I had some Irish friends up north, from Scion Belfast.'

I nodded to her. 'You a Scouser?'

'Good ear.'

'What brought you to London?'

'Just looking for a job. Scion mostly uses the north for heavy industry. It's dangerous work – mining, weapons manufacturing, shipbuilding, that sort of thing. Not sure if this is better or worse.'

Tilda took another puff. She had the dab hand of a courtier – someone who used purple aster on the regular. I had never seen anyone tolerate it this well.

'My keeper gave me some pills,' I said. 'Did you get them, too?'

Tilda nodded. 'The little white one is a contraceptive. It will stop your period.'

Now I wished I had taken it. Mine was due in a few days, and having to cast about for tampons was all I needed.

'Okay,' I said. 'The red one?'

'That's a food supplement.'

'And the green one?'

Tilda shook her head. 'You've lost me. I didn't get a third pill.'

My stomach clenched.

'If you bring it to me, I can have a look,' Tilda said. 'I can't promise I'll know it, but I might be able to give you an idea.'

'Thanks,' I said. 'I will.' She was about to take another drag when I spoke again: 'You went with Carl at the oration, didn't you?'

'I don't associate with him. He's already turned nose,' Tilda told me, her face tight. 'That palmist, Ivy – with the blue hair?' I nodded. 'He saw her sneaking out after curfew and dobbed her in, the little scab. You should see what her keeper did to her.'

'Who is her keeper?'

'Thuban Sargas. He scares the shit out of me,' she said. 'Ivy picked a lock and hightailed it, apparently. Our residences are right across from each other. Carl spied her going down Grove Lane.'

'What, and told your keeper?'

'Terebell wasn't there. He ran to the day porter, and she ran to the staff at Corpus. Absolute scum, the pair of them.' Tilda blew out smoke. 'Ivy didn't hide in time. Thuban brought her back.'

'Did he hurt her?'

'He beat her and shaved her head,' Tilda said. 'I don't want to talk about it.' Her lips thinned. 'If that's the price of surviving here, send me to the æther. I'll go quietly.'

Rain pattered on the shelter above us, dripping near our booted feet.

Ivy was either brave or desperate, to have made a play for escape this early. I had to wonder what had been going through her head.

'When we arrived at the Detainment Facility, I was sitting with someone in that holding cell,' I said. 'Do you know where he went?'

Tilda tilted her head. 'The bald guy?'

'That's him.'

'Yeah, he's at Trinity. The main entrance is on the Broad, but if you go down Parks Road, you'll be able to see the gardens,' she said. 'A few people were training out there yesterday.'

'Thanks.' I stood. 'I'll bring you that pill, if you don't mind.'

'Yeah, any time.'

I left her to light up again. Before I headed off, I returned the bowl and spoon to the performer.

Eliza had lost several years to purple aster. Even after Scion used the flower to create flux, the syndicate had never stopped trading in it. There were four types of aster with ethereal properties, each affecting voyants in a different way.

Even before she dabbled in purple, Eliza had been hooked on white, which caused amnesia. Since kicking the habit, she had made me swear never to touch aster. I saw no reason to break that promise.

Still, I couldn't blame Tilda. Having lived with a whisperer for almost two years, I knew it was one of the hardest gifts to carry.

Trinity was guarded on the side that faced the Broad. I went down Parks Road and ended up outside a set of tall gates. Just as Tilda had reported, a group of soaked humans were on the lawn, led by one of the Rephs. They worked by the light of a lamp post.

Julian was in the group. Half of them were holding silver batons, waving them about as if they were conducting an orchestra.

The Reph suddenly rounded on Julian and threw a spirit at him. It must have caught him off his guard – he lost his footing and crashed to the ground.

'On your feet,' she said, her voice carrying. 'Or do you wish to die here, 26?'

Julian shook his head. He slowly rolled on to his side and shuddered.

'Get up.'

He couldn't do it. Of course not – she had just hit him in the face with a furious spirit. She looked down at him with utter disdain before returning to the warm glow of Trinity.

The humans exchanged weary glances before they followed. None of them stayed to help Julian. I pushed the gates, but they caught on a chain.

'Julian,' I called.

He raised his head. After a while, he picked himself up and walked to the gates. His boots and white tunic were covered in mud.

'She loves me,' he said when he reached me. 'Really. I'm her star pupil.'

'I'm sure. What kind of spirit was it?'

'Just a wisp, I think.' He rubbed his raw eyes. 'Sorry. I'm still seeing things.'

'Like what?'

'Piles of burning books. A red sky.'

The wisp had left an impression of its final hours. It was an unpleasant aspect of spirit combat.

'It will pass. Give it a minute,' I said quietly. He nodded and grasped the gate, blinking a few times. 'How are you otherwise?'

'Oh, you know, fine. Just a normal evening with the giants from another world.'

We held it together for a solemn moment, then cracked up at exactly the same time. Wheezing on either side of the gate, we surrendered to the absolute horrifying absurdity of our situation, using our sleeves to muffle our laughter, tears seeping down our cheeks.

'This is … ridiculous,' I managed. 'What is going *on* here?'

'We've gone mad.' Julian wiped his eyes. 'It's the only explanation.'

'Okay. I'm glad we agree.' I sucked in a deep breath, collecting myself. 'Back to your training. What were those batons?'

'They help you learn the ropes of spirit combat, like training wheels. Aludra wants us to know how to make and deflect spools by April.'

'You won't be an expert by April, but it's easier than it sounds.'

'Good to know. Where did you learn?'

'My parents,' I said. 'They were voyant.' The lie came out smoothly, strong and convincing. 'Aludra is your keeper, I take it.'

Julian nodded. 'I don't know why she volunteered. She clearly hates us.'

'They all hate us. Can you come outside?'

'I can try.' He glanced over his shoulder. 'Have you heard how the Rephs sustain themselves?'

'I have. Explains a fair amount, doesn't it?'

'Aludra did it to Felix yesterday. All he did was ask for water,' Julian said grimly. 'He couldn't stop shaking when he came round.'

'They're not supposed to feed on jackets. One of the performers told me.'

'Aludra clearly doesn't care.' He released the gate. 'Arcturus hasn't fed on you, then.'

'No. I've barely seen him.'

Something told me not to mention what had happened in the small hours. All good syndies knew that secrets were a currency, and now and then it paid to let them gather interest for a while.

'I overheard the amaurotics talking about him,' Julian said. 'You're the first voyant he's ever trained.' He raised an eyebrow. 'Sure you're an acultomancer, Paige?'

I gave him a steady look.

'Julian, I'll level with you,' I said. 'I'm not an acultomancer – you knew that – but it's safer for me not to say what I am. If you won't ask about my gift, I won't ask about yours.'

Julian studied me. This close, I could see that he was full-sighted. The half-sighted could suppress their spirit sight, but Julian always saw the æther, layered over the physical world. Whenever I was in front of him, so was the question mark of my aura.

'Deal,' he said. 'Let me ask if I can sign out.'

'Be careful,' I said. 'I'll meet you in the Rookery.'

He disappeared into the residence. It occurred to me that he might never come out.

I waited for him by a cookfire. Craving a hot coffee, I held my hands over the flames.

The performers gave me curious looks. Liss must have told them I was the new tenant at Magdalen. I hoped she had kept my gift to herself.

As I sat there, warming my fingers, I couldn't help but notice the unusual lack of spirits. London was deeply haunted, its streets thronged with the restless dead. Oxford might be smaller, but it was an old city – I should have sensed more than a few wisps and ghosts.

Julian was taking his time. I was about to give up when the main door to Trinity opened, and he stumbled on to the Broad. I went to meet him.

'What happened?'

'Aludra,' he said. 'She said I could get food, but I wouldn't be able to smell it. Or taste it.'

When he moved his hand away from his face, I drew a sharp breath. His nose was red and swollen, blood seeping to his chin.

'You need ice.' I had a closer look. 'The performers might have some.'

'I'm all right. I don't think it's broken.'

'Let's get you some food, at least.'

As we made our way through the Rookery, I kept an eye out for anything I could use to arm myself. Even something crude would do – a sharp hairpin, a shard of metal. Nothing jumped out at me.

If the Emim breached the city, the performers had no way to defend themselves. The red-jackets were their only protection. I glanced at the old siren, ominous above the shacks.

Julian sat on a low stool. I traded the rat bones for skilly and toke, then found a stall offering various herbs. In exchange for my needles, the performer brewed me an infusion of willow bark, which apparently helped with pain. I took the steaming cup to Julian.

'Here.'

'Thanks,' he said, taking a sip. 'It's so cold here. I don't get it.'

Bruises were forming under his eyes. As I sat cross-legged beside him, another performer brought us a cloth and a bowl of water.

'Thank you,' I said, surprised.

She nodded once and walked away. Julian used the cloth to clean up the blood, then moulded it into a cold compress for his nose.

'So,' he said, a little thickly, 'what do we know about the Emim?'

'Nothing on my end. I'm more curious about the tests, to be honest.'

'I've heard what happens in the first one. You have to verify your gift, prove you have control of it,' Julian said. 'Soothsayers and augurs usually have to make a prediction. Mediums have to provoke and survive a possession. You get the picture.'

'Who told you this?'

'The night porter at Trinity. He claimed his prediction in his first test got somebody else brought here. I think he was proud of it.' He drank a little more. 'My guess is they want us to prove our commitment to this place, even if it puts other humans in danger.'

I refused to give up my humanity, Liss had told me. *If you ever mean to earn their trust, you'll have to cut away your kindness.*

'Great.' I breathed out. 'So much for keeping our gifts to ourselves.'

'I want to stay under the radar, too.' Pause. 'We could fail.'

'That's always an option.' I glanced at him. 'What about the second test?'

'The night porter wouldn't talk about that.' His gaze roamed across the slum. 'He wears a pink tunic, so he can't have passed it. The Rephs must need a few of us in administrative roles.'

'Sounds like a cushy job.'

'And inconspicuous.' His face changed. 'Paige, look. Her fingers.'

I followed his line of sight. Opposite us, a woman in her forties was sitting on a bench, talking to a man of around the same age, both of them eating skilly. Three of her fingers were missing or cropped.

When I looked away from her, I soon noticed other signs of violence: an absent hand, claw marks, scars on arms and legs. These people had been gnawed and thrown out like chicken bones.

'The Emim.' I kept my voice down. 'They must have breached the city.'

'Or those performers used to be red-jackets,' Julian said. 'Maybe they lost their nerve.'

'Wouldn't they be wearing yellow tunics if they bottled it?'

'Aludra explained this to us. You get the yellow tunic if you show cowardice or disobey orders, but only for a month. Once you've been humiliated, you revert to your previous tunic.'

'But three strikes, and you're out here in the cold for good.'

'Exactly.' Julian narrowed his eyes. 'No one looks much older than fifty, do they?'

'Not that I've seen. What are you thinking?'

'If there's been a Bone Season every decade since the Rephs came, we should be seeing people in their nineties, theoretically. Why is everyone so young?'

I gave him an incredulous look. 'You think the Rephs want to look after us when we're old?'

'Honestly, no. I just wanted you to say something reassuring.'

'Sorry.' A gust of wind blew my hair into my eyes. 'No, it is a little strange. You'd think some of the porters or amaurotics would be older. Then again, we might just not have seen them yet.'

'Thanks. That was reassuring.' He offered his bread. 'You want this?'

'I'm grand.'

We fell into silence, our laughter already fading into a grim memory. Our new reality might be absurd, but it could still kill us.

In London, the stars were faint, drowned out by electric light. Here they glittered in multitudes, sharp and clear, untouched by our little fires. Seeing my interest, Julian looked up as well.

'Wow.' He released his breath in a flutter. 'At least there's that.'

I nodded, thinking.

Liss had warned me not to let Nashira confirm her suspicions about me. I couldn't see a way to pass my first test without doing that.

To survive, I was going to have to fail.

There was a sudden hush. I looked down to see Carl, hair freshly combed and parted, wearing a pink tunic under his gilet. The performers cleared a path for him as he strolled into the Rookery.

'That was quick,' I murmured. 'I wonder what he had to do.'

Julian finished his drink. 'Whip tomorrow's weather out of a teacup?'

'That's augury. I think he's a soothsayer.'

'His aura looks bluish to me.' He gave me a sidelong glance. 'You're not sighted, are you?'

I shook my head.

Carl had probably never had a chance to prove himself in London. *On the Merits* had placed soothsayers at the bottom of the hierarchy of clairvoyance. Jaxon made no secret of his disdain.

They're a penny a punnet, darling. Pay them no mind.

'They're already trying to earn his favour.' Julian watched a performer offering a shew stone to Carl, the same one I had traded away. 'They must think pink-jackets have sway over the Rephs.'

Carl brushed the woman off, and she retreated, head downcast.

'We can't trust him,' I said. 'Remember the palmist, Ivy?'

'I remember. What happened?'

'She broke out of Corpus. Carl took it upon himself to report her.'

Julian grimaced. 'I hope they go easy on her. She didn't look well.'

Carl kept on with his sauntering. Seeing me and Julian, he flashed a cocksure smile. I toyed with the idea of punching it off him.

Before he could reach us, the oracle stepped into his path, appearing as if from nowhere. From their handshake, the oracle was offering his congratulations. I pursed my lips. Barely two nights in this place, and this pair of fools were already indoctrinated.

'Julian,' I said, 'how many pills do you get?'

'Just one.'

'What does it look like?'

'A red capsule,' Julian said. 'Why, how many do you get?'

Carl distracted me from answering. Now he and the oracle were closer to our fire, I could hear snatches of their conversation.

'—to see the Suzerain. Turns out she's very keen on finding this White Binder,' Carl was saying. I tensed. 'He's a mime-lord, you know, a syndicate leader. She lent me the most perfect stone so I could scry for his location, and of course, I was happy to—'

'Paige,' Julian said. 'Are you okay?'

A deathly cold swept over me.

'Fine,' I said.

Before I knew it, I was striding towards Carl. His eyes popped when he noticed me. I grabbed him by the gilet and marched him away from the oracle, off the path between the stalls. Once I had got him out of sight, I slammed him into a plywood wall.

'Why is Nashira interested in the White Binder?'

Carl stared at me as if I had just grown a second head. 'What?'

'You heard me. What did she want you to do?'

'None of your business.'

He looked clammy and pale up close, strands of hair stuck to his forehead.

'I asked you a question, Carl,' I said, keeping hold of his gilet. 'I'll ask another, while I have you. Did you rat on Ivy?'

'She was out after curfew!'

'I can see why the Rephs rushed you to your test. You missed your calling as a Vigile.'

'I was first to be *chosen*, stupid. We're probably testing in order of number.'

That did make sense. If he was right, I would be last in line.

'I get it now. You're trying to cheat,' Carl said, his tone almost triumphant. 'Well, you can shake and intimidate me all you like, but I'm not telling you *anything* about the first test. It's not—'

He stopped when I dislocated my spirit and forced pressure into the æther, making it quake around us both. My vision prickled as I fixed him with a hard stare, making it very clear it was me.

'I thought you were an oracle,' he whispered. 'How are you doing that?'

I smiled. 'Doing what?'

This was a serious risk. I shouldn't be revealing my abilities, but I needed Carl to spit it out.

'All right,' he gasped. 'Please, just stop it.' I shifted my spirit back into place. 'I saw a pillar. That's it. Just a pillar. I don't remember any detail. Nashira gave me a shew stone, a good one.'

'Why the White Binder?'

'I don't know.' He flushed with sudden indignation. 'The White Binder is a *criminal*. Why do you care what I tell her about him?'

Blood roared in my ears as he glowered at me. I had to fix this, and fast.

'I don't.' I let go of his gilet and sighed, trying to look contrite. 'I'm sorry if I scared you, Carl. I've just been nervous about the tests, and you passed so quickly. I'm a little envious. After they singled me out like that, I really need to impress my keeper.'

I could turn on the charm when I felt like it. Fortunately, the flattery worked.

'Don't worry. That's understandable,' Carl said graciously, relaxing. 'I'm sure you'll pass. You *are* an oracle, aren't you?'

'Yes. That pressure can happen sometimes, before we send visions,' I said. Carl nodded along. 'Congratulations, anyway. Do you know what you'll have to do for your second test?'

'Not yet, but I can't wait. This is a chance for our lives to mean something,' Carl said, with conviction. '24 will see that, too, once she's a red-jacket.'

When I realised he meant Ivy, I knew he was already lost. I forced another smile and walked back into the firelight, towards Julian.

Carl had reason to be proud. He was a good seer. Nashira had told him what she wanted to know, and he had scried it in a shew stone.

She had been his querent. If the æther – a vast network of spirits and dreamscapes – could be compared to the Scionet, then a soothsayer or augur was the search engine, and the querent gave the terms.

Nashira had given just the right terms to uncover a hidden truth in the æther. Carl had glimpsed the sundial pillar at Seven Dials.

I had to warn Jaxon. Whatever Nashira wanted with him, I couldn't let her bring him here. How did she even know about him?

Scion was aware of the syndicate, of course. More than once, undercover Vigiles had been planted among us to root out the Unnatural Assembly. Though they had failed, Scion must be familiar with some aliases. The anchor might even have learned that the White Binder was behind *On the Merits*, an open secret in underworld circles.

But if Nashira was interested in the syndicate, surely her key target should be Hector. Jaxon was just one mime-lord of many.

Jax, what have you done?

Julian raised his eyebrows when I returned. 'What did you say to him?'

'Nothing. Just shook him up a bit,' I said. 'Are you definitely not eating that bread?'

'No. You want it?'

'Seb will. I'll leave it in his cell at Amaurotic House.'

'So they lock up voyants in London, and amaurotics here.' He handed me the bread. 'You shouldn't risk it, Paige. I'm sure they'll feed him.'

'They haven't fed us,' I pointed out. 'Seb might not be able to visit the Rookery.' I pocketed the toke. 'I'm still knackered from the flux. I'll come back tomorrow. Will I meet you here?'

'I'll be here.' Julian glanced at his residence. 'If I can get out.'

Amaurotic House was dark and quiet when I arrived. This time, I knew better than to try my luck with Graffias. Instead, I climbed straight up to the window.

Beyond the bars, the room was empty. There was no fireplace in there, no music. Just a single unmade bed and a wardrobe. Seb must have been sent to one of the residences.

The back of my neck prickled. Suddenly wanting to leave, I took the bread from my gilet and slotted it between the bars, hearing it drop to the floor. I lowered myself back down to the street.

Too late, I was sharply aware of the æther. I turned to see a pair of heavy-lidded eyes, cold and unforgiving, locked on mine.

7

AMONG GIANTS

Warden was standing very still – a statue in the shape of a man. Tonight he wore a black doublet with a high collar, its shoulders trimmed with gold. Its sleeves concealed the arm I had bandaged.

He gazed down at me with no expression. His eyes no longer glowed yellow, but electric blue. I grasped in vain for an explanation.

'So,' he said quietly, 'you dress wounds *and* feed the helpless. How quaint.'

Pure revulsion filled me, laced with fear. I considered running, but then I saw the other four Rephs, all with ironclad dreamscapes.

Graffias had stitched me up. These Rephs had waited for me here, to catch me in the act. When I took up a defensive stance, three of them chuckled. They laughed the way a raven talked – a mimicry of the real thing.

I should have sensed their dreamscapes coming. Tension and fatigue were grinding my guard down, along with my lack of life support.

Warden did not laugh. He looked at his fellow Rephs, then at me.

'Terebell,' he said, 'go to the blood-sovereign. Inform her that we have found my tenant.'

Terebell considered me with steady golden eyes. Her dark hair was short and glossy, curving around her lean face like a hood. This was the Reph who had taken Tilda and Carl into Oriel.

'It will be done,' she said.

She strode ahead of the others, the darkness swallowing her whole.

'You are some way from the residences,' Warden said to me. 'A white-jacket has no cause to venture beyond the lamplight.'

'You told me to acquaint myself with the city,' I said. 'That's what I was doing.'

'Amaurotic House is out of bounds, as you are well aware. The Grey Keeper informed me of your attempt to bribe him,' he said, confirming the obvious. 'He also ordered you not to return.'

'I was checking on one of the amaurotics. Is that a crime around here?'

'Their welfare is not your concern. Since we have business elsewhere this evening, I will overlook your impertinence,' he said, 'but do not expect me to do so again.' He turned away. 'Come with me.'

I was outnumbered and unarmed. Trying to get out of this situation would be suicidal. Surrendering to the inevitable, I followed him.

Warden led me back down the boulevard. The other Rephs walked behind us, keeping a respectful distance. I glanced at his eyes again.

He caught me looking. 'If you have a question,' he said, 'you may ask.'

'Why are your eyes like that?'

'Doubtless you will soon find out.'

I stiffened. 'You're taking me somewhere to punish me, then?'

'No. I am taking you to your first test.' When I gave him a sharp look, he said, 'I did call at Magdalen to collect you. When I saw you were gone, I suspected I might find you at Amaurotic House.'

'I've been here two days. I haven't even done any training.'

'The first test requires none.'

'We're not testing in number order?'

'That is the usual approach,' Warden said. 'You are an exception.'

Of course.

'I have one more question,' I said, keeping my voice low. 'What happened to you last night?'

Warden looked straight ahead.

'I rescind your invitation to speak,' he said.

I almost bit my tongue in two. Patronising, despicable bastard. I should have killed him.

The Rephs escorted me back to the lamplight, to the building where Nashira had turned my world upside down. For the first time, I noticed the gold letters arching over its gates, reading THE RESIDENCE OF THE SUZERAIN. The guards bowed when Warden passed, pressing their gloved fists to their chests.

The gates closed behind us. The steely clang tightened my muscles. My gaze darted, seeking handholds and footholds. Looking for a way out was an instinct I could never shake.

Warden took the gravelled path that wrapped around the oval lawn. Two of his friends went to stand guard on either side of the doors, while a third came to my other side. He was the spitting image of Pleione, down to his well-boned face and raven curls.

Flanked by Rephs, I stepped over the threshold, into an entrance hall with spotless ivory walls. Suhail Chertan waited beside a stone pillar.

'You may remove your tunic,' Warden said to me. 'It will limit your range of motion.'

He framed it as a choice, but I had none here. 'You told me this didn't require any training,' I said. 'Is it something physical?'

None of the Rephs answered. I unbuttoned the white tunic and handed it to Suhail. We proceeded up a set of black steps, where two gates opened to allow us through a gilded baroque screen.

When we emerged on the other side, I turned colder. Several Rephs awaited us in a long chamber. The back wall was a feat of intricate stonework, humanlike figures carved all the way up to the hammer-beam ceiling. A chequered floor reflected the candlelight.

Warden went to one knee and lowered his head. I did the same when a Reph stared me down. Most of them were unfamiliar.

'Arcturus.'

I risked a glance.

Nashira Sargas had appeared. Tonight she wore a set of black robes that covered her to the chin, along with the obligatory gloves. Passing an old wooden chair, she came to stand in front of us.

'I see you have brought our curiosity,' she said. 'Good evening, 40.'

Warden stayed on one knee at my side, gaze downcast. A strange way to greet his partner, but customs might be different in the Netherworld.

'I understand my consort found you close to Amaurotic House. You have taken it upon yourself to feed one of its occupants,' Nashira said. 'The Grey Keeper distributes the amaurotics' rations. Your intervention demonstrates contempt for his authority.'

'Yes.' I heard myself say it. 'He should pick on someone his own size.'

'You will address the Suzerain with respect,' said the one who resembled Pleione. 'Unless she invites you to speak, hold your tongue.'

'Peace, Alsafi,' Nashira said. '40 is new, but she will learn.'

With all my willpower, I swallowed my retort. Nashira gave the smallest nod, and Warden stood. After a moment, I did the same.

'I trust Arcturus has told you why you are here, 40,' Nashira said. 'You may be surprised to be summoned this soon, but your gift is of great interest to us. As was the incident that led to your arrest.'

Warden stepped away from me, while Alsafi left through a side door. Nashira and I were now facing each other across the room.

'Your first test is simple,' she said. 'All we ask is that you show us your gift.'

I glanced at the other Rephs. Surely they didn't want me to fight her.

'I will ask you again,' Nashira said. 'What manner of clairvoyant are you?'

I wet my lips. My best way out of this might still be to feign ignorance.

'I told you at the oration,' I said. 'I don't know.'

'Tell us about your clairvoyance, then.'

A draught blew into the chamber. It cut into my undershirt, leaving me stiff with goosebumps.

If I did nothing, surely they would have to fail me. They might send me straight to the Rookery. I could learn a few circus tricks, keep a low profile, start looking for a means of escape.

Jaxon leaned out from my memory, teaching me how to charm and deceive: *A lie is harder to distinguish when it dances with the truth.*

'I'm sensitive to the æther. I feel it a long way around me,' I said. 'Sometimes I see visions of the future. They give me headaches.'

'Show us,' Nashira said. 'Send us a vision.'

'They come at random times. I don't know how to share them, in any case.'

'How convenient.' Her tone never changed. 'You would have me think you are an untaught oracle. Doubtless this deception has been successful in the past. The differences between auras can be subtle, but no oracle can kill with their spirit.'

Now I was remembering the swoop into darkness. The unbearable pain, as if my own body was punishing me for what I had done.

'I didn't kill anyone.' I held my voice steady. 'It was the poltergeists.'

'Of the two bodies found on the train, only one bore signs of a poltergeist attack,' Nashira said. 'There was also a survivor, whose spirit had been violently dislodged. He, too, was unmarked.'

Scion had conscripted my father for his expertise in forensic pathology. I wondered if they had forced him to examine the bodies.

'They attacked me, too.' I showed her the scars on my left palm. 'See these?'

'Those marks were noted upon your arrival here,' Nashira said, 'but they are not recent. Our eyes can tell, even if yours cannot.'

I fisted my hand at my side.

'You caused two deaths that night,' she said. 'I believe you can project your spirit from your body. For your first test, I would like you to do it again.'

Perhaps I could.

Nashira wanted a dreamwalker for her entourage of angels. There must be something I could do that she had no way to deter, some advantage I could use against her. I could demonstrate my ability in front of all these Rephs, just as they wanted.

To the best of my knowledge, only an unreadable could lock out a dreamwalker. Nashira was not unreadable. Even if her defences were strong, there had to be a crack. If I could find it, I could worm into her dreamscape and give her the shock of her life.

I could kill her.

Before I could encourage her to volunteer, Alsafi returned. He bore a limp figure in his arms, a human with a black bag over their head.

The prisoner was dumped into the wooden chair, and their hands cuffed to its arms. This was an amaurotic. I thought of my father and felt sick to my stomach – but the figure was too small, too thin.

'I believe you two know one another,' Nashira said, just as I recognised the dreamscape. 'Sebastian has been asking for you.'

Alsafi removed the bag.

Seb stirred. His eyes were the size of small plums, his hair hung in reddened strings, and his lips were cracked and swollen, crusted with dry blood.

Alsafi slapped his cheek. Seb managed to look up, blinking in the candlelight.

'Paige?'

His broken voice made my blood burn. I rounded on Nashira.

'What have you done to him?'

'Nothing permanent,' she said. 'That is your task.'

'What the hell are you talking about?'

'Hold your tongue.' Alsafi took a step towards me. 'Or I will relieve you of it.'

'No need, Alsafi,' Nashira said. 'Let her embrace her anger, her fear. Those emotions must have overwhelmed her on the train.'

Their bodies flashed in front of me, the two men on the carriage floor – one hollowed out, one driven mad.

That was my test. To earn my next tunic, I had to kill an amaurotic.

I had to kill Seb.

'No,' I said.

'No,' Nashira repeated.

The word carried in that echoing space, right the way up to its rafters.

'I can't do it,' I said. 'I won't.'

Alsafi did not beat about the bush. His massive hands clamped on my shoulders, and he shoved me towards Seb. My boots squeaked on the polished floor as I pushed back in vain.

'Kill the boy,' Alsafi said, 'or I will have Graffias bring *all* the amaurotics here to die. Scion can always send us more.'

'No.'

'Take the test.'

'I *can't*.' I spoke between my teeth. 'Did you not hear me, Reph?'

Alsafi held me with bruising force. Seb watched dully, blood seeping from a cut on his brow.

I suddenly clawed for Alsafi, trying to rake his face. He jerked back as if my hand was on fire, releasing one of my shoulders. I used my other hand to swipe his knife from its sheath on his belt.

One deep stab was all it took to break his grip. I lurched away from him and stood in front of Seb, the knife clutched in my hand.

'Stay back,' I warned.

Nashira was unmoved. To her, I was already a performer – a human with a head full of confetti and fireworks, here to entertain my betters.

For the first time, I noticed the angels Liss had mentioned, close to Nashira. Only two of her five were here, but they hummed with power. If I attacked her, they would overwhelm me.

Warden stood nearby, his gaze soldered to my face. I pointed the knife at him.

Alsafi lifted a hand to the wound I had just put in his side. When I looked at the blade, I saw a yellowish light at its tip. The same glow that had bled from Warden.

'You are resourceful,' Nashira said. 'Very well. If you refuse to kill the amaurotic yourself, perhaps you will defend him.'

'And you expect us to respect you.' I shook my head. 'State of you all, torturing some frightened kid who can't fight back.'

'If you are what I suspect, then you *can* fight back, 40.'

Seb was crying now. I tightened my grip on the knife, but my hands were clammy.

'I can't,' I said again. 'Just fail me. Send us both to the Rookery.'

'That would be a terrible waste of potential,' Nashira said. 'Aludra, disarm her.'

Aludra Chertan stepped forward. Pale hair sleeked to her waist, not a flyaway or split end in sight. She drew it away from her face, fastening it at the base of her neck.

'This is your last chance, 40,' she said in a silvery voice. 'Kill the amaurotic.'

Even if I had wanted to, I still had no idea how to project my spirit, or I would have done it for Jaxon. Even his barbs and wheedling had never forced it out. Only a threat to my life had worked.

'No,' I said.

Warden came to join Aludra. I planted my feet, taking slow breaths through my nose.

Part of me knew I would lose. I couldn't defeat all these Rephs with a knife, and other than the two angels, which would only answer to Nashira, there were no spirits to spool in this chamber.

But seeing Warden reminded me. When I had cleaned his wounds in the dark, his blood had sharpened my perception of the æther.

Alsafi had the same light in his veins.

I held the blade up to my face and inhaled. The æther enfolded and submerged me like ice water. All at once, I felt calmer. I focused.

With a flick of my wrist, I flung the knife at Aludra. She sidestepped it, but only just. My aim had improved, just as I had thought.

Aludra picked up a candleholder – almost as tall as she was – with unnerving ease. 'You have lost your weapon,' she said. 'Not that it would have helped you. What are you going to do now?'

'Come and find out,' I said.

Aludra stalked towards me. I led her away from Seb. I was leaving him vulnerable, but Warden made no move towards him. His gaze stayed on me.

When Aludra swung her improvised weapon, I ducked. The candleholder hit one of the carvings, destroying its face in a shower of dust. I moved again at once, trying to keep plenty of distance between me and the Reph. If she could wield something that heavy without breaking a sweat, she could also snap me like a twig.

I didn't expect her to throw it at me.

Seb screamed my name as the candleholder soared across the chamber. I dived to the floor. A heartbeat later, the candleholder clanged down, barely missing me. The din rang through the chamber like a stricken bell. Before I could get up, Aludra was on top of me. She lifted me with one hand, bringing us face to face again.

'We know what you are,' she said. 'Your days of hiding are over.'

It came out of nowhere. As I struggled against her grip, a dizziness rushed over me, as if I had been turned on my head. The sickening loss of control before fainting – that was the only thing that compared.

It took me a moment too long to realise. My aura was pulling towards hers, *into* it. Her eyes brightened, turning a livid red.

'Aludra,' Warden said sharply.

She glanced at him. I tasted metal, felt the wetness on my cheeks.

Now I understood.

I understood why their eyes changed.

Aludra released me, and I fell to the floor, my legs giving way at once. I lifted a cold hand to my cheek, finding blood on my fingertips.

'All this to protect an amaurotic,' Aludra said. 'This boy would have seen you strung up by the neck in London. Even if he could move now, do you think he would lift a finger to save you?'

A cool gleam caught my eye. The knife, the one I had thrown at her face, almost near enough to touch. I could put her eye out.

Aludra spotted it. She pinned my wrist with her boot, then leaned down to pick up the knife.

'A pitiful display,' she said. 'You are not even fit for the Rookery.'

'I quite agree,' Nashira said. 'We cannot reform them all, after all.'

'No,' Seb choked out. 'Stop it, please. Paige!'

Aludra knelt and held the blade under my jaw. Jaxon, Nick, the others – none of them would ever know why I had disappeared.

The knife bit hotly into my skin.

And suddenly, I was in the æther.

In my spirit form, I saw without eyes. A silent void, studded with starry orbs. I knew that each one represented a dreamscape. It would be suicidal to attack Aludra – her mind was very old, very strong – but her arrogance had thinned her defences.

I flew into her.

She wasn't prepared for how it would feel. That was how I got so far. I cut straight to her abyssal zone, the second layer of her mind.

Aludra rallied quickly. Her defences leapt back up. I was thrown out with the force of a bullet, and then I was back in my own body, my head in agony. I fought to breathe, staring at the ceiling.

I had done it again.

My hand went straight to my throat. Aludra had only left a small cut. Beside me, she was lying on her side. Blinded by pain, I lurched to my feet – a hunted animal, surrounded, scrabbling out of a trap.

The chamber leaned around me. The Rephs were disembodied eyes, all the candles blurred and quivering. When Seb called my name, I turned on the spot. It tapped into a memory, to hear someone calling like that.

Finn, don't leave me.

I took a few drunken steps, only to lurch into Warden. He caught me by the arm. If he was human, I might have thought he was steadying me, but I recoiled from him, panic flooding my body. Almost against my will, I tried the same attack. This time, I didn't even reach the æther. I buckled to the floor and stayed there.

Sorry, Liss.

Nearby, Aludra looked up at Nashira, nodded once. Nashira gazed at me.

'So it is as I thought,' she said softly. 'You are a dreamwalker.'

Silence reigned for some time. Finally, a Reph spoke: 'Congratulations, blood-sovereign.' I closed my eyes. 'It has been a long search.'

'Indeed,' Nashira said.

Alsafi approached me. I was in so much pain that all I could do was let him drag me up, my legs shaking. Warden came to my other side.

Nashira now turned her attention to Seb. His terrified stare snapped towards her.

'Thank you for your service to our cause.' She stopped beside the chair and touched his ashen face, almost tenderly. 'We are grateful.'

Before he could say a word, she twisted his head, the movement so quick I almost missed it. His neck crunched in her grasp.

'No!'

The denial ripped out of me. I tried to run at Nashira, heat writhing in my blood, only for Warden and Alsafi to grab my arms, holding me back.

'You *monster*,' I snarled at Nashira. 'Who the fuck gave you the right?'

'You did.' Nashira turned to face me. 'You could have killed him yourself, 40. Had you not taken him food, he would not be here.'

I cursed blindly at her, kicking and thrashing with all my strength, my hair lank with sweat.

'I ought to give you a yellow tunic for your cowardice. But I will assume you were telling the truth – you did not know how to project your spirit,' Nashira said. 'Not without the right persuasion.'

Alsafi was about to dislocate my shoulder. Warden had a lighter hold on me, but his grip was still unbreakable. I dug my fingers viciously into his upper arm – the one I had bandaged, the one that must still hurt. He tensed at once, and I dug harder, loathing him.

'I will destroy you,' I gritted out. 'You see now what I can do. I swear I'll bring every one of you down. You and your anchor—'

'Suhail,' Nashira said. The Reph in question emerged from the side door. '40 has passed her first test. Let us congratulate her.'

'With pleasure,' Suhail said.

Alsafi threw me to the floor. I tried my utmost to get up, to reach Seb – he was just about clinging to life, I could sense it – but now I was being held down on the floor, and Suhail was there, and I finally saw it, the hot glow of it, as merciless as the light in his eyes.

'XX-59-40,' Nashira said, 'you are bound in life to the Warden of the Mesarthim, and in death to the Suzerain. Henceforth, you will renounce your name, and serve only the Rephaim.'

With those words, pain seared into the back of my shoulder. I couldn't help but scream. Seb slumped in the chair just as I passed out, and his spirit gave one last flutter, untethering.

8

DENIAL

There was a storm in my dreamscape. I ran in circles, driven from its heart. Caught in the dark, my spirit was stumbling, lashed by windblown red petals.

Outside, in just as thick a gloom, my body was in agony. Nashira had got her proof of my gift; now she could only be killing me for it.

This must be a flux overdose. I wondered what it would be like, to witness my own death from the inside – to be trapped in my mind when it vanished from the æther, leaving me disembodied for good. No dreamscape could hold its shape in a corpse.

Paige, can you hear me?

The voice came from outside. It faded, and I was running again, trapped in the circles of the mind where no other spirit could tread. I glimpsed my sunlit zone in the distance – the only place I would be safe – but each time I tried to run to it, I was forced back into the shadows. That place should have been the eye of the storm. Now it was in turmoil.

All living things had a dreamscape. Of the many concepts Jaxon had taught me in the early days, it had probably been the hardest to grasp. Where the brain controlled the body, the dreamscape housed and nurtured the spirit. It was a haven, the strongbox of memory. Mine took the form of a field of red poppies.

Even amaurotics could glimpse their dreamscapes, though only in their sleep, in shades of grey. As for voyants, we could enter ours consciously – wander our minds, bask in their colours. Most could stray no farther than the sunlit zone, the centre.

I could go anywhere.

Now I could see flashes of the world outside my body. In my mind, I grew calm, watching as the storm receded. I lay down in my flowers and waited for the end.

In the Founders Tower, the gramophone was warbling 'Did You Ever See a Dream Walking?' – one of my blacklisted favourites. From what I could feel, I was back on the daybed. Someone had put me in a pair of shorts, propped me on my side with cushions, and tucked a sheet around me, leaving my shoulders bare.

My eyes cracked open. The fire was out, and only candles lit the parlour.

As I gazed at the ceiling, my heart started to pound. I had a vague memory of a violent struggle, and two excruciating pains, one after the other. Now the back of my right shoulder burned with a ferocious heat, and my left thigh felt swollen and strained.

I turned my head. It was too dark for me to make out the time, but I could see Arcturus Mesarthim. He sat in the wing chair, decanting medicine into a silver cup.

My lips trembled. I could still feel his grip on me, holding me back, stopping me reaching Seb as he died. I doubted he cared about the pointless murder, or the other humans enslaved in Amaurotic House. Even his dealings with his consort seemed mechanical.

He must have sensed my hostile gaze, because he looked up from his work. His eyes had settled back to a steady apple-gold.

'His spirit,' I forced out. 'Did it leave?'

'No.'

Seb had died in a state of utter fear and confusion. If no one had said the threnody, he would linger – still afraid, still alone, still a prisoner.

'You were branded,' Warden said quietly. 'You must be mindful of the wound.'

'What?'

The word escaped me as a whisper. My breathing turned ragged as I twisted to look over my shoulder, reaching for the pain with one hand, clutching the sheet with the other. A shudder of denial racked me as I found the raw numerals, burned into my skin.

'You'll suffer for this, Reph.' I hissed the words between my teeth. 'I meant what I said. You don't know who you've crossed.'

Warden flicked his gaze over my face, like he was trying to read an unfamiliar language, which only stoked my anger. He must understand why I was distraught.

'Suhail overheard your last threat. He took umbrage,' he said. 'To punish you, he injected you with flux, but his knowledge of human anatomy is wanting. The needle entered your femoral artery.'

I got the sheet off my leg and saw the mottled skin of my left thigh, the slew of dark purple that stained it. When I applied the slightest pressure, I had to strangle my own scream.

'Suhail acted rashly. He has been reprimanded,' Warden said. 'A paramedic was called from our outpost at Winterbrook. She removed you from immediate danger.' He picked up the silver cup and brought it to me. 'All you need do now is drink this.'

Several amber bottles stood on the table. I looked at them in a haze of pain.

Maybe Nashira *had* tried to kill me, using Suhail as her executioner. Either it hadn't worked, or she wanted me to die a slow and painful death. Her consort was well placed to finish me off.

It could be poison in that cup. Even if it was medicine, he wasn't offering it to me out of kindness. I clamped my mouth shut.

'Your condition may deteriorate,' Warden said. 'Is that what you want?'

'Our lives clearly mean nothing to you,' I rasped. 'Why do you care if I die?'

'You are not ready.'

'Seb wasn't, either.' My throat was in agony. 'Whether you're trying to kill me or save my life, I won't help you. Or your consort.'

He narrowed his eyes a little.

'Very well. I will not force you.' He placed the cup on the table, out of my reach, and returned to his chair. 'Inform me in your own time if you wish to live.'

'Get fucked.'

Warden gave me a measured look. I turned my head away, my sight blurred.

I couldn't tell you how long I lay there, weak and burning up. All I could think was how much he must be enjoying this. Now it was him with the power again; him watching me suffer and sweat.

The clock ticked on the mantelpiece. At some point, dawn broke, and the day bell rang.

Warden stayed right in his chair.

Apparently he could sit very still and do nothing for hours. He left just once and returned with a basin, which he placed beside the daybed.

My thigh looked strained and shiny, like a blister on the verge of bursting. I pressed the tender skin and kept on pressing, harder and harder, until stars burst in my vision. I had hoped it would knock me out, just so I could have a short bout of relief. Instead, I threw up. Warden watched me cough acidic bile into the basin.

He wanted me to beg for death. I would not give him the satisfaction.

The daylight faded into dusk. I heard the night bell ring.

If Aludra let Julian out, he would have no idea where I was. I could only think of this because the pain – inexplicably – had gone.

So had the sensation in my leg.

Fear chilled my spine. I tried to move my toes, rotate my ankle, but nothing happened.

'If you wait any longer,' Warden said, 'you may lose your leg, if not your life.'

I would have gladly spat at him, but the vomiting had dehydrated me. When he brought me the cup again, I shook my head.

'Do not be a fool,' Warden said, softer. 'This medicine will ensure your recovery. Take it, and you will be able to stand by midnight.'

My willpower was waning. If I died now, I would never be able to get even with Scion – not just for this, but for everything.

In the end, survival instinct overcame my pride. I reached for the cup, but my fingers had no strength. Warden tipped it to my lips. It stung to do it, but I drank. He nodded as I took a little more.

'Good.'

I mustered a look of contempt. Once I had I drunk the medicine to the dregs, I slumped back against the cushions and slept.

By the time I came round, it was half past eleven. A fire burned in the hearth, but not my skin, and the swelling in my leg had gone down. When I realised I could move it, I let out all my breath.

A clean undershirt was folded beside me. With the sheets over my legs, I eased it on, tensing as it brushed the back of my shoulder.

When Warden stepped back into the room, I looked hard at him.

'I treated your wounds. I'm sure you don't like being in my debt,' I said, hoarse. 'If you want to repay me, tell me what happened to you.'

His face might as well have been a mask.

'Hypnagogic hallucinations can appear for several days after an episode of phantasmagoria,' he said. 'They are easily confused with reality. I would advise you not to pay them any heed.'

I smiled.

'Okay,' I said softly. 'If that's how you want to play it, Reph.'

His sleeve might be hiding the evidence, but it was there. I had something for my arsenal now. A secret I could turn against him.

All I had to do was find out why this was something he needed to hide.

'You are in no fit state to leave the residence tonight, but you may go to the Porters' Lodge,' Warden said, his tone clipped. 'The night porter will provide you with medical attention.'

'I don't see my clothes.'

'Your new uniform was delivered this morning.' He went to the linen cabinet and withdrew a tunic. 'You have been promoted. Congratulations, Paige.'

That was the first time he ever said my name.

9

STAINED

Warden watched me take my pills. I swallowed the red and white ones, but held the third between my teeth. As soon as I left the Founders Tower, I plucked it out and slipped it into my pocket.

The night porter was ready for me. She sat me on her chair, sterilised and dressed my shoulder, and took my temperature with a glass thermometer.

'Keep your shoulder as clean as possible,' she said. 'I'll leave a salve and dressings in your quarters.'

'I want to go out.' I gazed at the wall, unblinking. 'Do you have more numa?'

She looked sceptical. 'Did the Warden say you could leave?'

'Yes. To get something to eat.'

'You're still feverish. It's not safe out there.'

'He watched them do this to me. I'm not safe in here, either.'

Without commenting, she handed me another pouch of numa. I drew on my new tunic and left before she had signed me out.

It was hard going. Magdalen was only a short way from Catte Street, but as I reached it, I almost blacked out. On top of the pain, I hadn't eaten. I leaned against a wall until the feeling passed.

Carl hadn't mentioned the branding. Then again, he had looked ill. No doubt the Rephs had already convinced him it was necessary.

The city looked just the same as before, yet I was stained. Instead of white, I wore sickly carnation pink, to match the anchor on my new gilet. The fit of laughter seemed like it had happened in another life.

If they had killed a child in the first test, what would they do to me in the second?

How much blood would be spilled before I was red?

There had to be some way out, even if I had to dance around landmines. Anything was better than being moulded to fit this place.

The Rookery was calm tonight. I limped into its passages, my leg weak and heavy, searching for Julian or Tilda. Each time a performer glimpsed me, their face went blank, their head down. My tunic now served as a warning. It proved I had betrayed my own.

'Paige?'

I stopped, my leg shaking. Liss was leaning out of her room. She took one look at my pink tunic before her expression darkened.

'Liss,' I started.

'You passed,' she said stiffly. 'What did you do?'

'The Rephs got Seb.' For the first time, my voice quaked. 'They wanted me to kill him with my spirit.'

'Kill him,' she whispered. 'Where is he, Paige?'

'He's dead.'

Liss gave me a look of pure betrayal, then closed her curtain. I let myself sink to the ground, too shaken and drained to defend myself. So far I had made a grand total of two allies in this hellhole, and one of them now thought I had killed someone in cold blood for a tunic.

Perhaps I should have stayed at Magdalen for the night. But then I would have been trapped in the same building as Warden, and I couldn't stomach any more of him tonight.

'Sebastian Pearce,' I murmured, trying to call his spirit. 'Seb?'

Not even a twinge from the æther. I might be missing part of his name – or someone had already bound him, putting him beyond my reach.

The curtain seemed to judge me. The rip in it had been carefully sewn. I closed my eyes, trying to ignore the ache in my thigh.

Three years in the syndicate had taught me the importance of a gang. Julian was a solid first link, but he and I were still new to this place. We needed someone who knew it to its deepest roots – someone like Liss. Whatever it took, I had to prove myself to her.

With an effort that left me coated in sweat, I got up and headed for the cookfires. Julian might turn on me once I had told him about Seb, but I hoped he would hear me out.

Halfway there, I smelled aster in a shack and sensed Tilda. She was sprawled among a few delirious performers, head propped on a cushion, smoking. Minding my leg, I knelt beside her.

'Tilda,' I said. 'You okay?'

'Oh, hello.' She blinked hard. 'Are you real?'

'Last I checked.'

Tilda laughed. Her aura jerked and shifted as the aster warped her dreamscape. 'Give me a second, Irish,' she said. 'Still reigning.' She rubbed her bleary eyes. 'Get me a drink of water, will you?'

'From where?'

'There's a barrel outside. They collect rain in it.'

I checked the performers' breathing on my way out. Much as I understood their urge to get high as a skyscraper, this place was dangerous and confusing enough without ethereal drugs in the mix.

The rain barrel was running low. A few chipped teacups had been left on rusty hooks beside it. I filled one and took it back to Tilda. She sat up and managed to take a few sips.

'Right,' she said, with conviction. 'I'm dethroned.'

'Are you?'

'Well, abdicating.' She knuckled her eyes again. 'You passed, then. What happened?'

'You just have to show your gift. The Rephs are going to call you soon,' I said. 'You can't let them find you like this.' She nodded. 'I brought the pill, the green one. Could you take a look?'

'Yeah. Give it here.'

I fished it from my gilet. Tilda raised it to eye level, scrutinising it from every angle. She ran her thumb over it, then split it and crushed one half between her fingers, smelling and tasting the residue.

'It's herbal,' she concluded. 'I couldn't tell you which herb, mind.'

'Do you know anyone who could?'

'Maybe.' She dropped her head back on to the cushion. 'Duckett, the man who grows the aster – he might be able to tell you. The password to his shop is *specchio*.'

'Where is it?'

Tilda had already dozed off. I wondered what Suhail would do if he caught them.

The Rookery had many small rooms, most of which were shared by two or three performers. It must help them survive the biting cold. It was frigid enough now, in March – I couldn't imagine this place in December. Liss was unusual, to live by herself.

There were no hygiene facilities, no medical supplies, and little bedding. They had been left to scratch out a life in any way they could.

Sniffing the shop out took a while. It was hidden behind several curtains and false walls. I only found the path after questioning a wiry performer, who introduced herself as Nell. She warned me of coercion and high prices, but pointed me in the right direction in exchange for the dried rose petals from my pouch.

When I found the shop, I also found the young polyglot I had seen at the oration. He was sitting on a cushion, reading a book that looked older than both of us put together.

'Hello,' I said.

'Hi.' A pure, sweet note. 'You found us.'

A boy who could speak the language of spirits. It was a rare and strange ability, one of the hardest to conceal from amaurotics.

'Just about,' I said. 'You went with Pleione, didn't you?'

'Yes. I'm Joseph,' he said, 'but you can call me Jos.'

'Paige. I'm told someone called Duckett lives here.'

'I found the shop yesterday, when I was exploring. He said I could guard it when he's away.' His right eye was sticky, clearly infected. 'He's in there now. Do you have the password?'

I nodded. '*Specchio.*'

Jos stood up. He pulled the last curtain aside for me, and I went through.

Duckett had made his nest in the very heart of the Rookery. His shop was two adjoining shacks, one of which had been transformed into a modest house of mirrors. He sat on a battered leather armchair, gazing into the glass. The mirrors betrayed his speciality: catoptromancy.

When I entered, he raised a monocle to one eye. He had the misty stare of a voyant who had scried too much.

'I don't believe I've seen you before,' he remarked. 'In my mirrors *or* my shop.'

'I arrived a few days ago,' I said.

'Ah, the Bone Season. Who owns you?'

'Arcturus Mesarthim is my keeper,' I said. 'If that's what you mean.'

I was already sick of that name – hearing it, saying it.

'My word.' The seer lowered his monocle. 'So *you* are his mysterious tenant.'

'I'm not that mysterious,' I said. 'You're Duckett, are you?'

'My number is 10.' His face was deeply lined, his hair grey and receded. 'But yes, the performers – my assistants – call me Duckett. I no longer remember whatever name I had before.'

'10.' I paused. 'What's the rest of your number?'

'XVI-19-10.'

It took me a moment to parse the code. 'You've been here forty years?'

'Oh, yes. I am the oldest human resident of this city. Once I was a soldier, and then I was an acrobat. Alas, these bones are too frail now.'

'Why did you become a performer?'

'Now, now. Beyond introductions, I give nothing away for nothing.'

'Fair enough.'

His stock was displayed on shelves and a table. I was briefly reminded of the black market in Covent Garden, which offered all manner of wares: numa, moonshine, trinkets from the free world, anything outlawed by Scion.

There were some numa here, but Duckett sold other ways to survive. Not just things a voyant needed, but what any human did.

There were clean sheets, plump cushions, matches and tweezers, rubbing alcohol, soap, paraffin, canned heat, bandages, sewing kits, tools and nails, toothbrushes – even prescription medicine.

No weapons, of course. Not even a penknife or a pair of scissors.

'Quite a stockpile,' I said. 'Where did you get all this?'

'Here and there.'

'I presume the Rephs don't know about it.' I picked up an old tinderbox. 'You're clearly not in need of numa. What do you trade in, Duckett?'

'Favours,' he said. 'In exchange for what you need, I might ask you to fetch more supplies for my shop, or carry a message, or run some other errand. A simple and beneficial exchange.'

I cast my eye over the antibiotics. Some of those could be lifesaving. 'I see,' I said. 'What would I have to do for information?'

'That depends on the information you seek.'

I put the remaining half of the green pill on the table.

'I hear you grow the regal they're smoking out there. I assume you know a fair amount about drugs,' I said. 'Can you tell me what this is?'

Duckett rose to look. He used his monocle to peer at it, then picked it up, his thick fingers shaking. 'For this,' he finally said, 'I will give you anything you like from the shop, free of charge.'

'You want to keep it?'

'Oh, yes, if I may. After forty years, I thought I had seen everything this city has to offer, but this is unfamiliar. Where did you get it?'

'I'm sure you'll understand that I can't share that, Duckett. Just like I'm sure you wouldn't tell me where you grow your aster.'

'A wise decision.' He set the pill down. 'If you bring me whole ones, I will trade each for an item. No errands necessary.'

'Tell me what it is, or I walk away.'

Duckett held the pill near a flickering lamp. 'I can tell you that it is an herbal tablet, and that it is harmless,' he concluded. 'Is that enough?'

'It's something,' I said. 'Three items in advance, and you've got a deal.'

'Done. You are a shrewd negotiator.' He put the pill down and returned to his chair, steepling his fingers under his chin. 'What else are you?'

'I'm an acultomancer.'

'You'll have to forgive my ignorance. *On the Merits of Unnaturalness* was published long after I came to this place – I've never seen a copy. I remember a time before the seven orders,' Duckett said. 'Remind me, what does an acultomancer do?'

'My numa are needles. I cast them and interpret the patterns.'

He chuckled. 'A pretty lie. Does it ever work?'

'Sometimes.'

'Not on me. With age comes experience in such things, and I sense you do not rely on a numen. It seems we have a very interesting crop this decade.' A smile tempted his mouth. 'You are the envy of us all, living at Magdalen. A beautiful old residence, with a most selective master. What do you make of the Warden?'

'I would have thought that was obvious.'

'Not at all. There are a variety of opinions on our overlords.' Duckett ran his thumb over his monocle. 'The blood-consort is considered by many to be the most … striking of them.'

'Well, I don't base my opinions of people on that sort of thing.'

'You agree, then?'

'He can look however he likes. I'll still find him repulsive.' I picked up some canned heat, then put it down. 'You say you're the oldest human in this city. How did you survive this long?'

'No more information, I'm afraid. Our deal is cut.'

'Fine. I'll take my items.'

Duckett watched me consider his stock. I chose a thick fleece blanket, a box of aspirin, and a dripper bottle of fusidic acid.

'I certainly hope to see you again soon,' he said. 'It was good to do business with you, 40.'

'Paige,' I said curtly.

I walked out of the shop. His gaze stung my back.

A man deprived of power who had found a way to make his own. The performers must be knocking on his door all night in winter.

His questions had felt like an interrogation. Why he had seen fit to remark on how Warden *looked*, of all things, I had no idea. Then again, forty years in this prison would unhinge the sanest person.

If he had been in here that long, I must have little hope of finding a way out.

As I left, I tossed the fusidic acid to the polyglot. He looked up at me and tilted his head in question.

'For your eye,' I said.

He blinked. I kept walking.

When I reached the right shack, I rapped my knuckles on the wall.

'Liss.' No reply. I knocked again. 'Liss, it's Paige.'

When Liss pulled the curtain aside, I stepped back. She carried a small lantern.

'Leave me alone, Paige,' she said tightly. 'I don't talk to pinks or reds. I'm sorry. You'll have to find other jackets to—'

'I didn't kill Seb.' I offered the blanket and the aspirin. 'Look, I got these from Duckett. You can have them. Just let me tell you what happened.'

She looked from the items to my face. Her forehead creased, and her lips thinned.

'You'd better come inside,' she said. 'Your friend is here, in any case.'

Liss had found a tired Julian by the fires. After he said he was looking for me, she had taken him in for a bowl of skilly and liked him enough to let him doze off. He stirred when I came in with her, and stayed awake for long enough to hear about the test, his eyebrows rising when I finally told him what I was.

My voice never wavered as I recounted it. Part of me wanted to cry it out, but Jaxon couldn't abide tears. Even here, I felt that he could sense my every move; that he would soon know if I broke from his mould. Safer to remain within it, cold and unmoving.

After I had told the story, Liss made an infusion. While Julian nodded off again, she handed me a steaming cup.

'Drink this,' she said. 'It will help.'

'Thank you.'

She sat beside me. Her face was swollen, her neck bruised. I sipped in silence.

'You can stay until dawn, if you want. Both of you,' Liss said. 'I shouldn't have shut you out like that, Paige. It's just that … after the first test, most jackets only come here to gloat. I couldn't bear it.'

'It's fine.' I glanced at her. 'I'd still like to be friends, if you would.'

'I'd like to try. We could all use friends here.'

The brand still throbbed on my shoulder, and my thigh still hurt badly. Even if I escaped this place, I could never forget last night.

Julian snuffled in his sleep. Liss had given him some of the aspirin.

'It was good of you to bring those supplies.' She covered him with the new blanket, voice low. 'What did you have to do for Duckett?'

'Give him one of my pills,' I said.

'We get the pills, too. Why would he ask for one of those?'

'Because I get a green pill, and I don't think anyone else does.'

'That's odd, but if Duckett is interested, you should take advantage,' Liss said. 'He's as cruel as the Rephs, after years in this place. He forces us to jump through hoops for every item, even if we're desperate. We're his entertainment as much as theirs.'

'Is the medicine real?'

'We think so. Most of it is expired, but it's the best we can get.'

She passed me a knitted blanket. I watched her gingerly touch her cheek, where a bruise was rising.

'Liss,' I said. 'Who did that?'

'Gomeisa. He called me for a reading.' She poured more water into the pot. 'Rephs don't often ask us for predictions, but I've never been wrong, and he knows it. It's why he still calls me. He just doesn't always like what I tell him.'

'I'm sorry.'

Liss shook her head. 'It doesn't happen often. He left this morning.'

'What did he ask you?'

'I'd tell you if I could, but there's a code of honour among some augurs and soothsayers. We don't share our querents' futures,' she said. 'I hate Gomeisa, but I'll not lower myself for him.'

'I understand. Were you his only human?'

'I was the same as you, with a keeper that had never chosen anyone before. When I refused the test, Nashira gave me a yellow tunic. Gomeisa was so disgusted, he branded me himself and threw me straight out here. I didn't get a second or third chance.'

109

'I tried to refuse, too. Now I have a target on my back, and Seb is dead.'

'They'll use other amaurotics in the tests. Maybe performers, too. A few of us could disappear before this round is over,' Liss said. 'But I don't want to think about that. Let's have something to eat.'

She reached over to the wooden box where she kept her valuables, taking out a pot of instant coffee, two cans of beans, and three eggs.

'I've been saving the coffee for a while. It's the last of what Nita got for me,' she said. 'Cyril stole the eggs from Oriel. He owed me. I think we should have a late breakfast, the three of us.'

'Don't waste it on us, Liss. We can get food at our residences.'

'Not straight away. And coffee is nicer with company.' Liss smiled at me. 'Besides, there are new amaurotics to help us, and Scion will have sent food to restock the kitchens. We can afford to eat like queens.'

'May a king join the banquet?'

Julian was sitting up. Our voices must have woken him.

'Of course.' Liss gave him a nod. 'How are you feeling, Julian?'

'Better.' He touched his nose. 'Thanks for the aspirin, Paige. Sorry for dozing off after that story. I can hardly keep my eyes open.'

'You're grand,' I said. 'I'm not feeling especially awake myself.'

'That's why we need coffee,' Liss said. 'Is Aludra not letting you sleep, Julian?'

'Not much,' he said, his voice still thick. 'She made us train with those batons until noon. We're allowed to ignore the curfew within the residences.'

'Where does she keep you?'

'An old wine cellar under the hall. She says we can only have our own rooms once we've all learned to spool. Ella and Felix don't have a clue, so we're sleeping on the floor for a while.'

'If it gets too much, you can join us out here,' Liss said. 'Being a performer is tough, but it's easier than patrolling Gallows Wood.'

I wrapped myself in the blanket. 'Have you seen a Buzzer?'

'From a distance, when they've got into the city. I've always found a place to hide.'

The water roiled and steamed. Liss poured it into three mugs and mixed it with the granules. I took a grateful sip. My last coffee had been snatched between errands on the day I was arrested.

'I'll keep at it for now,' Julian concluded. 'I might as well sharpen my spirit combat. I've let myself get rusty over the last few years.'

Liss nodded once.

'Some people do find it harder out here,' she said. 'I used to share this place with a friend, but she couldn't bear the shame of being a performer. After a bad winter, she convinced her keeper to give her one more chance. She's been a bone-grubber ever since.'

'Bone-grubber?'

'Our name for the red-jackets.' A flicker of sorrow crossed her face. 'Stay at Trinity for now. You'll be fed if Aludra approves of your progress.'

'So far, she thinks we're all useless.'

'If it helps,' I said, 'I managed to knock her over during the test.'

'That does help, actually,' Julian said.

Liss stared at me. 'You hurt a Reph?'

'Only a little,' I said.

'She'll not forget that in a hurry, Paige. Aludra and her family are vicious.' She put another pot of water on the stove. 'Julian, you mentioned batons earlier. I don't remember that from my training.'

'I was telling Paige about them yesterday. I don't know how, but they have ethereal properties,' Julian said. 'You can use them to exert control over the nearest spirits, to help you practise spooling.'

Liss frowned. 'I don't like the sound of that. Can amaurotics use them?'

'Even if they could, they wouldn't touch anything unnatural.'

'They do employ night Vigiles,' I said. 'Scion has always dabbled in hypocrisy. It doesn't really surprise me that its founders are voyant.'

'But they built an empire that hates us.' Julian chewed his cheek. 'The Rephs could have done the opposite – honoured clairvoyance, not vilified it. We could have worked together as equals. And why did they feel like they had to do all this in secret?'

'I doubt we'll ever know their reasons for doing anything,' Liss said shortly. 'But I can't see why they would broadcast their presence.'

'Why not?' I said. 'Julian is right. If they're so sure of them-selves – if they're so mighty, and we're so weak – why the need for secrecy?'

'They believe we're inherently violent and cruel. I doubt they want anything to do with us, beyond what they see as necessary.'

'They're violent and cruel, too,' Julian said. 'Don't they see that?'

'I'm sure they do,' Liss said. 'They just think we deserve to be treated that way. That's why they didn't bat an eyelid when they murdered Seb.'

'Poor Seb.' Julian glanced at me. 'Warden and Nashira are consorts. They must be able to feel *something*, if not guilt.'

'Well, I've not seen them show it,' Liss said. 'Not in ten years.'

We finished our coffee. Liss passed us each an egg, and we ate them out of the shells.

'I was thinking,' Julian said. 'What did the Rephs do for aura before they found us?'

Liss was starting to look tired. 'I don't ask questions like that.'

'Knowledge is power, isn't it?'

'Not necessarily. Knowledge is dangerous. Once you know something, you can never be rid of it. You have to carry it, always. Even if it pains you.'

'Unless you take white aster,' I said, scraping out the last of the egg.

'Even then, it's somewhere in your dreamscape. Just … buried, tucked away.' Liss held out a hand. 'Here, give me your shells. I'll powder them later.' Seeing our furrowed brows, she gave us a thin smile. 'You can eat them. Helps keep your bones strong.'

We handed them over.

'You've been here ten years,' Julian said. 'Do you ever think about fighting back, Liss?'

'Every night,' she said, 'but there's no point in it.'

'How do you know?'

'Because all the Rephs would do is kill me, and I won't give them my life just yet,' Liss said, low and embittered. 'Is it not enough they've stolen everything else – my freedom, my pride?'

Julian and I traded a glance, neither of us knowing what to say.

'I know what you both must think of me,' Liss said tightly. 'I've got no backbone. I'm a doormat.' Before we could protest, she cut across us: 'No. I don't blame you. When I first came here, I held on to the hope that I would escape. And then I learned about Bone Season XVIII.'

I waited, cold all over. Liss looked between us, her face hardening.

'Are you sure you want this knowledge, Julian?'

After a moment, Julian nodded.

'Duckett is the oldest human in this city. I'll tell you why,' Liss said. 'Twenty years ago, the prisoners here planned to rise up against the Rephs. At that point, there were far more of us than you see now. When Nashira was informed, the humans were thrown out of the residences, the doors were locked, and the Emim were allowed into the city. Only Duckett escaped the slaughter.'

That was not what I had expected her to say.

'That seems—' Julian shook his head. 'Surely not everyone was involved.'

'She didn't care. The first humans from my Bone Season arrived in a deserted city,' Liss said. 'Scion had to post Vigiles here to support them.' The pain in her eyes aged her by decades. 'I can tell you're both fighters, but you need to accept what's happened to you. Scion could have executed us, but instead, they sent us here. I promise you, death is the only way out.'

Her voice quaked on the last sentence. Julian rubbed a hand over his head.

'Sorry.' Liss dropped her gaze. 'I didn't want to scare you this soon.'

'No,' I said. 'I'm glad you did.'

It was true. Now I knew exactly how high the stakes were in this place.

'Let's talk about something else,' Julian said. 'Where did you used to live, Liss?'

She gave him a guarded look. 'Inverness.'

'I've always wanted to go there. Why did you come south?'

'My parents were caught distributing seditious pamphlets. My father was arrested.' She drew a sheet around her shoulders. 'He escaped on his way to the New Tolbooth, but we had to go into hiding.'

Scotland no longer formally existed. Like Wales, it had been absorbed into Scion England. The Scots still found ways to resist.

'We could have gone to my aunt in Edinburgh, but my father was too proud to ask for help,' Liss said. 'He spent all our savings to get us to London, hoping we could join the syndicate, but soon, none of the mime-lords or mime-queens wanted us.'

Jaxon might have been to blame. After all, he was the writer who had made soothsayers undesirable.

'Because of *On the Merits*, I assume,' Julian said, voicing the same thought.

'Partly, but my mother was amaurotic. I don't remember the specifics, but one of the mime-lords said he wouldn't accept us with her in tow. When Dad argued with him, he put out word that we were Scion informants. After that, no one would touch us.'

That sort of petty blacklisting was common in the syndicate. It wasn't always successful, but it hit new arrivals the hardest.

'Once the money ran out, we had to earn a living without crossing the syndicate,' Liss said. 'Its couriers were everywhere. They would force my father to move on if they saw him, but they didn't usually expect a child to be busking. I earned most of the money.'

I didn't trust myself to speak.

'When I was ten, my parents got lung fever. After that, I was on my own,' Liss said. 'One night, a woman approached me and asked for a reading.' She took her cards out and ran her thumb over them. 'I was only eleven. How was I to know it was a sting?'

Julian grimaced. 'How long were you in the Tower?'

'Two years. I was thirteen when I got here.'

I cleared my throat.

'Where did you live, Julian?'

'Morden,' he said. 'I've always tried to blend in with the amaurotics, so I never bothered with the syndicate. I had a couple of voyant friends, but we didn't do proper mime-crime. Just séances.'

Liss looked ready to drop. She barely knew either of us, and the conversation had gone to dark places.

'I'm exhausted,' I said. 'Shall we get some rest while we can?'

'Good idea,' Julian said.

Liss gave me a small nod. She blew out some of her lamps before we all got as comfortable as we could. I rested my head on my arm.

I couldn't sleep. The pain in my shoulder was sharper than ever, and Bone Season XVIII played on my mind. If Nashira reacted that strongly to dissent, it was no wonder Liss didn't want to fight back.

A terrible sound pulled me upright. It cranked and creaked, working itself up into a tremendous scream. My body reacted to it at once: a prickling in my legs, a thumping heart. Julian jolted awake.

Footsteps thundered through the passages. Liss was up at once, pushing her deck of cards into a pocket.

'You have to go,' she urged. 'Run straight back to your residences.'

'Come with us.' I stood. 'Just sneak into one. You're not safe in—'

'Do you want to get a slating from Aludra, or the Warden?' she shouted over the siren. 'I've been doing this for years. I'll be fine. Go *on*, both of you!'

Julian only hesitated for a moment. I didn't know what Warden would do to me if I was slow in returning, but from her track record, Aludra might just kill Julian for the same transgression. We ducked out of the shack and ran.

10

PORT MEADOW

I was slower than usual. By the time I passed the Residence of the Suzerain, my run had turned into a limp. Several red-jackets were standing guard outside its gates, armed with rifles and flamethrowers.

Magdalen was the farthest residence from the Rookery. It stood between the shadow and the lamps. When I was halfway there, the siren changed. A Buzzer must have breached the city.

I almost fell against the door. Moments after I knocked, the night porter appeared, her face drawn. She pulled me inside and slammed the door shut.

'You weren't supposed to be out there.'

'Sorry.' I caught my breath. 'He didn't hurt you, did he?'

'Of course not.' She shot me a hard look. 'Go straight to the Founders Tower.'

I left her to secure the door, noticing its iron bolts and drawbar. Still breathless, I crossed the first courtyard and stumbled into the dark cloister, where I stopped, my skin beading with sweat.

Behind the thick stone walls of the residence, the sound of the siren was duller. Beneath it, I heard someone running along the other side of the cloister. I wanted to check the æther, see if I could sense the Buzzers, but my head still ached from attacking Aludra.

Liss would be fine. She must have heard that siren many times. I took a moment to collect myself, then faced the steps to the Founders Tower.

The parlour door was unlocked when I arrived. I sidled inside and stepped quietly on to the flagstones.

Not quietly enough. Warden was in front of me at once, eyes flaming.

'Where have you been?'

'Outside,' I said stiffly. 'Why, where have you been?'

'I ordered you not to leave.'

'You said I was in no fit *state* to leave. You should be more specific.'

I could hear the insolence in my own voice. His expression never changed – all his displeasure was confined to his eyes.

'You will speak to me with the proper respect,' he said, 'or you will not be allowed to leave at all.'

'I'll let you know if you earn my respect.'

Warden stared me down. I was playing with fire, but pain and fatigue had snapped my restraint.

When I refused to either apologise or avert my gaze, he walked past me and shut the door. My heart beat roughly, my hair clung to my clammy brow, and my leg shook, but I stayed upright.

'You are fortunate that the Emim did not catch you in the open.' He turned the key and tucked it into his belt. 'Since you are not at your full strength, they would have made short work of you.'

'If you want me at full strength, you might consider feeding me.'

'Magdalen is not impregnable. The Emim have been known to enter the grounds and cloisters,' he said, ignoring me. 'As soon as you hear the siren, you are to return to this parlour with all haste. You will not tarry for any reason. Is that understood?'

I just looked at him coolly. He leaned down so his face was at my level.

'Do I need to repeat myself?'

'I'd rather you didn't,' I said.

He straightened to his full height, which was considerable. I braced myself.

'The night porter had to wait for your return before she could secure the main entrance,' he said. 'You endangered all the residents of Magdalen by leaving in your condition. You also lied to her.'

'It's not her fault. I wanted to leave.'

'What you want is irrelevant to the Suzerain. She expects your training to begin tonight. Now you have fewer hours of recovery.'

'I won't take another test,' I said. 'Just send me to the Rookery. I'll juggle.'

'Not with your gift. The Suzerain would not see you as a performer, existing only to entertain others. You have greater potential,' Warden said. 'Refuse to train with me, and she will use another human to compel you. I assume that is not what you want.'

I set my jaw. *A few of us could disappear before this round is over.*

'The attic is now ready for you.' Warden held out a key. 'While there is an Emite in the city, I advise you to lock the door.'

'Will it keep you out, too?'

'I have my own key.'

'Of course you do.' I snatched the key. 'Since we've separate quarters now, who's going to save you if you're injured again?'

'I have addressed this matter with you.'

'I wasn't hallucinating.'

'Go to the attic.' His eyes flared. 'I will rouse you at dusk.'

'I want some water,' I said, just to annoy him.

'Take it, then.'

I chose the nicest glass from his cabinet, then picked up the pewter jug on the table. The room felt smaller, the air charged.

'Before I go, I have a question.' I poured. 'What is the green pill?'

'That is my concern,' Warden said.

'I'm the one taking it.'

'And I am the one who gives the commands.'

I should have left him to bleed out. Jaxon really would be howling at the state of me. *Honeybee, you just don't have the sting in you.*

Give me time, I thought.

Warden stood aside, allowing me to pass. I made a point of catching his gaze before I brushed past. He made a point of locking me out.

I really hadn't thought he could get any more uptight.

Across the landing, I took the steps to the top and opened the door to the attic. The room had one small window, low down. The bed was simple, with a fleece blanket on top of the sheets.

I turned up the paraffin lamp by the bed. This room had no fireplace, and a draught was whispering from somewhere. It was still better than sharing even a hairline of my personal space with Warden.

Just as I had downstairs, I checked every corner and nook. I soon realised the window had been put in where a fireplace had once been. The old chimney went up a long way, but it had been sealed fast.

As well as a nightstand, there was a narrow closet for my uniform. Beside it, another door stood open, leading to a rudimentary bathroom. No window in there, but it did have a toilet and sink.

As promised, the nightstand was stocked with dressings and salve, along with some hygiene supplies: soap, comb, a toothbrush and paste, a frayed towel. As I scrubbed my teeth, I thought of Julian in his dark cellar, Liss in her cold shack. It might not be a hotel in here, but it was secure, and I had some privacy. I could sleep without fear that someone would steal from me.

Of the three of us, I was in the best position to resist. If I wasn't fighting to survive, I could devote my attention to the matter of escape.

I couldn't see any nightclothes. Once I was down to my undershirt, I dimmed the lamp and got into bed, each movement pulling at the tight skin of my shoulder. I curled into a ball for warmth.

I should have been out like a light, but I found myself skimming the edge of sleep, thinking of the past. I thought back to the first time I met Nick – Nicklas Nygård, who had introduced me to Jaxon.

Nick, who had once saved my life.

The year after we came to England, my father and I had been granted permission to leave the citadel for a few weeks. We had gone by train to the village of Arthyen, in the region formerly known as Cornwall, to visit a woman named Giselle, who my father said was an old friend. I never cared to ask him why he had old friends in England.

Giselle lived on a cobbled hill in a house with a roof that hung over the windows. The surrounding land had reminded me of Ireland – wild beauty, untamed nature, everything Scion had taken from me.

I had not adjusted well to London, or to my new school, where the other children took pleasure in tormenting me. I had learned words like *kern* and *boglander*, which were hissed at me in corridors, scrawled and shoved into my satchel. Not once had the teachers stepped in to defend me, even when I was sure they had seen. They ignored me in class, leaving me confused by half my lessons.

Scion welcomed countries that joined the fold by choice. But if one of its targets dared to fight back, its people were for ever stained. At nine years old, I was being punished for the Molly Riots.

The trip to the countryside was a reprieve. A summer holiday before I was thrown back to the wolves. At night, I would gaze at the stars, and I would miss my grandparents so terribly it hurt. My father had never explained why he left them in Ireland.

He had promised me we could visit the coast. I longed for open water – to breathe in the salt air of the sea, the glittering road that stretched to the free lands. Ireland lay over it, calling me home.

In the end, he was too busy with Giselle. They talked deep into the night. I would often hear their murmurs, but I never tried to eavesdrop. All I had wanted, in those weeks, was to be left alone.

London was dangerous for voyants, but the countryside was no idyll, either. Far from the Westminster Archon, amaurotics grew nervous, suspicious. They made a habit of watching one another, eyes peeled for a crystal ball or shew stone, waiting to call the nearest outpost – or take justice into their own hands. Even if you avoided being caught, there was no work. The land needed tending, but not by many hands. They had machines to farm the fields. No wonder voyants were drawn to the citadels.

At first, I hadn't liked to leave the house. The people of Arthyen talked too much, looked too much, reminding me of school. Giselle was almost as unnerving. She was a stern and bony woman, with beady eyes and a ring on every finger.

But then, from her rooftop, I spotted a haven – a poppy field, a pool of red beneath the iron sky. Every day, when my father thought I was playing upstairs, I would walk to that field and explore for hours, watching the poppies nod their heads around me.

It was there that I had my first real brush with the æther. At the time, I had no idea I was voyant; only that I was different. Unnaturalness was still a story to a child of nine, a bogeyman with no clear features. I wasn't yet a dreamwalker. I had sensed the æther since I was young, not knowing what it was, but no specific gift had manifested.

That day, everything changed.

Once more, I had gone to the poppy field – but for the first time, I wasn't alone. There was a woman there. I didn't see her, but I felt her watching me. I sensed her in the poppies, in the wind; I sensed her in the earth and in the air. I sensed her like I would a splinter trapped under my skin – out of sight, but sharply present.

I stretched my hand out, hoping to greet her. For a moment, I was colder than I had ever been, as if I had fallen through ice.

And then I was suddenly on the ground, bleeding. The woman had been a poltergeist – an enraged spirit, one that could touch the corporeal world.

I could see it again. A young man walking from the poppies, as if he had been waiting there – tall and pale, with a kind face. Seeing my injuries, he wrapped me in his overcoat and carried me to his car.

My name is Nick. You're safe now, Paige.

In the dark, I dreamed. I dreamed of poppies struggling from dust. I had rarely seen colours when I slept before, but now flowers bloomed in my mind, red as blood. They sheltered me, shedding their petals, blanketing my fevered body.

When I woke, I was propped in a bed with starched sheets, my hand bandaged, the pain gone. The blond man was there, smiling at me.

Hello, Paige.

I asked him where I was.

You're in hospital, he said. *You had an accident.*

Are you a doctor?

I am, but I don't work at this hospital. I'm just here until your parents arrive. Can you tell me who they are?

I've just one, I told him.

Nicklas Nygård, a transfer from Stockholm, had saved my life that day. He had weighed the risks of taking me to a Scion hospital, invented a story to explain the wounds, bribed a nurse, and watched over me as my clairvoyance awakened.

Later, I learned that Nick had accepted a position at the same research facility where my father worked. During his probation, he had been working virtually, to adjust to life in England before he put his nose to the grindstone. I never did find out why he was in that poppy field.

When my father had arrived to pick me up, Nick had seen me to the door. I remembered him kneeling in front of me, taking my hands.

Paige, listen to me. This is important. He had spoken in a low voice, his face grave. *I've told your father you were attacked by a dog.*

But it was a lady.

That lady was invisible, sötnos. Some grown-ups – most – don't know about invisible things.

But you do, I said, confident in his wisdom.

I do. But I don't want other grown-ups to laugh at me, so I keep it secret. He looked me in the eyes. *You must never tell anyone about her, Paige. Promise me.*

I still had scars from the attack, clustered on my left palm – a collection of short grey cuts, colder than the rest of me. I hid them with a glovelette in the citadel.

I had made good on my promise. For seven years, I held the secret close. All that time, I wondered where the days had taken Nick, and if he ever thought of that little Irish girl from the poppy field in Arthyen.

After those seven years, my patience was rewarded. Nick found me again.

If only he could find me now.

I drifted in and out of the memory. Perhaps Warden was right, and all the flux was giving me hallucinations. As the hours ticked away, I listened for a footstep, or the echoing melody of the gramophone. All I could hear was the same thick silence.

At some point, I must have fallen asleep. Fever still burned through me, and I wrenched awake every so often, my vision bursting with pictures of the past, my shoulder ablaze under the dressing.

A knock on the door woke me. I opened my eyes to pitch darkness, disoriented. A moment later, the lock clunked, and a candle appeared. When I saw Warden, I backed into the headboard.

'I'll thank you to *wait* after you knock,' I snapped.

'I did.' He placed a pressed uniform at the end of the bed. 'The night bell will ring erelong. Get dressed and join me downstairs.'

Before I could fume at him, he was gone.

There was nothing else for it. Braced against the chill, I pushed the sheets off and sat up, not quite sure if I had slept or not.

With a shudder, I peeled the dressing off my shoulder. The wound was damp, so raw that even the air felt like steel wool on it.

I washed as best I could. Once I had patted my shoulder dry and dabbed it with salve, I covered it with a new dressing. Next came the clean uniform. I fastened the gilet and tied my bootlaces.

My leg, at least, felt stronger. I managed the stairs with relative ease.

Warden was in his parlour, leafing through a novel. I recognised it – Jaxon had a third edition at the den. *Frankenstein; or, the Modern Prometheus* by Mary Shelley was banned in Scion.

'I presume you are ready,' Warden said, seeing me.

'Sharp one, aren't you?'

'Hm.' He set the book aside. 'What does your dreamscape look like, Paige?'

The directness of the question caught me off guard. In the syndicate, that was something you only shared with trusted friends.

'A poppy field,' I said, wary. 'Why?'

'I was curious.'

'Right. Any chance of something to eat, now your curiosity is satisfied?'

He looked away from me, into the fire.

'Go to the Porters' Lodge,' he said. 'I will meet you there.'

After a moment, I did as he said, my stomach grinding with hunger.

I reached the Porters' Lodge just as the bell rang, ending the curfew. The night porter noticed me and removed her reading glasses.

'There you are,' she said. 'Bear with me.'

If she was angry, she didn't show it. Instead, she walked out. After a few minutes, she returned with a small bowl of porridge, thicker than skilly.

'For training.' She handed it to me with a spoon. 'You'll need it.'

'Thank you,' I said.

She returned to her work. I ate the warm porridge with caution, half expecting her to snatch it from my hands. By the time Warden arrived, I had scraped the bowl clean and given it back.

'Good evening, Gail,' he said to the night porter. 'I am bound for Port Meadow.'

'Of course. I'll sign her out.'

I glanced at him. It piqued my interest that he called us by name in Magdalen.

As soon as I thought it, I shook my head. The bar was on the floor.

'Do not open the door for anyone but me.' Warden took a lantern from a bracket. 'The creature may still be loose in the city.'

'No one will go in or out,' Gail said. 'What time do you intend to return?'

'No later than midnight.'

She nodded and opened the door for us, letting in an icy gust of wind.

Warden took me along Magdalen Walk and made a right on Turl Street. We passed the Rookery, which was almost deserted, before taking the long thoroughfare that ran past Amaurotic House.

The performers must still be in hiding from the Buzzer. I reached for the æther, but couldn't sense anything out of the ordinary.

'That book you were reading, *Frankenstein*,' I said. 'It's blacklisted.'

'Yes,' Warden said.

'So is the music on your gramophone.'

'Indeed.'

And those were the only answers I got. I blew out my cheeks and trudged after him.

Once we were past Amaurotic House, Warden continued along the same wide path, ignoring a brighter one to our left. The red-jackets kept to their posts and said nothing.

'Walton Street is the only illuminated way to the training grounds,' he told me. 'While you are a pink-jacket, you are not to use any other path without me.'

I looked over my shoulder at it. 'Why aren't we taking it now?'

'To familiarise you with the city. When you are a red-jacket, you will be expected to know the streets well enough to patrol them.'

Warden led me well beyond the lamplight. The moon was new, leaving us with nothing but the lantern. As we neared the outskirts, the buildings started to look derelict. Scion must not have wanted to spare the money to look after them.

He turned left on Observatory Street. It was lined with old terraced houses, all crumbling. From the look of it, this district had been a slum when the Rephs took the city. I sensed ghosts nearby, along with a pair of weak poltergeists. Warden showed no fear.

By that point, we had been walking in silence for a while, giving me no distractions from the many aches in my body. My breath smoked from between my lips.

'I don't suppose,' I said icily, 'I could have a coat at some point?'

'They are not provided in the spring.'

'This is not a normal spring.'

'If you say so. I feel little cold myself.'

The quilted doublet and cloak must help. I shoved my hands deeper into my pockets.

Keeping us cold must be meant to weaken us, like depriving us of food. If you were cold and hungry, you had no room to develop notions.

'You know,' I said, 'it doesn't seem as if Scion has too much respect for your consort, letting half this city go to rack and ruin.'

'It would be a waste of resources to maintain the outskirts,' Warden said. 'A modest central district is easier to preserve and defend.'

'Whatever helps you sleep at night.'

'I sleep by day.'

He was still expressionless. I wondered what, if anything, made him tick.

The training ground stretched ahead of us. Oaks and pines grew up to its boundary, needled with rime, blocking any glimpse of the outside world. That must be the edge of Gallows Wood.

A fence surrounded the meadow, at least thirty feet high, topped with coils of barbed wire. I read the rusted notice on the sally port:

PORT MEADOW — FOR TRAINING ONLY

USE OF DEADLY FORCE IS AUTHORISED

The deadly force in question seemed to be a Reph. His pale face reminded me of white gold, while his hair – smoothed into a pony-tail – was more like brass in tone. In both ways, he resembled Nashira.

Ivy stood a short way from him, stooped and shivering. The buttons had been removed from her tunic, forcing her to hold it shut against the bitter cold. Her shorn head was bowed, her lip split.

Warden approached the sally port. A moment later, I went after him. When we were close, the other Reph swept into a bow.

'Behold the concubine,' he said in a deep voice. 'What brings you to Port Meadow?'

'I am here to instruct my tenant,' Warden said. 'The blood-sovereign should have informed you, Thuban.'

'Patience, concubine.' Thuban Sargas wore a cloak, but no livery collar. 'What is its number?'

'XX-59-40.'

'Is it sighted?'

'No.'

Ivy caught my gaze as the questions continued. She was scrawny as an awl, her collarbone protruding. On the first night, she had been in tears, but now she looked resigned, her dark eyes dull and weary. We both just came up to our keepers' shoulders – I must look as frail as she did, in comparison.

I didn't recognise her from the syndicate. Still, if she had broken out of Corpus in a heartbeat, she must have a few skills up her sleeve.

'These questions serve no purpose. I can only assume they are meant to waste my time,' Warden said, snapping me back. 'Such pettish conduct does not befit a Sargas. I am sure my consort would agree.'

Thuban curled up the corner of his mouth. The smile fit badly on his face, as chilling as the laughter on the night of my test.

'The red-jackets lost track of the Emite,' he said. 'Since it may return tonight, your training session is restricted to one hour.'

'Very well,' Warden said.

Thuban glanced down at me. I only just remembered to lower my gaze.

'I hear this creature sees fit to insult and threaten the blood-sovereign.' He tilted his head. 'Did you punish it for showing your consort such disrespect, Arcturus?'

'Suhail took it upon himself to act in my stead,' Warden said. I bristled. 'I assure you that she has suffered for her insolence.'

'You should not be complacent.' Thuban motioned to Ivy. 'This one has already tried to escape. As you can see, I have humbled it. Next time it leaves Corpus without permission, I plan to break its legs.'

Ivy stiffened. I suddenly wanted to hurt Thuban. He reminded me of the worst brutes of the syndicate, whose only currency and power lay in violence.

'Humans require a firm hand,' Thuban said. 'If you wish, I can help you discipline yours.'

'Nashira entrusted this one to me.' Warden stepped forward, so I was behind him. 'If you doubt her judgement, you should express it to her. In the meantime, I will execute her wishes.'

Thuban looked up at him, his eyes roaring blue.

'Do not go too far,' he said at last. 'Stay within my sight, concubine.'

Warden strode past him without a backward glance. I went after him.

Until that moment, I hadn't suspected any conflict among the Rephs. To see a crack after less than a week – well, that was promising.

Warden led me through the sally port. Behind us, Thuban turned on his heel and struck Ivy. She caught herself on the fence and looked after me, jaw tight, eyes glinting.

I didn't want to train, but I would make this lesson count.

Warden took long strides. I dallied some way behind him, surveying Port Meadow. This was as close as I had ever come to Gallows Wood.

Before the treeline, the meadow was divided into arenas. The central one – the largest – had watchtowers on either side and smaller pens around it, presumably for individual training. I took note of the unusual fences between them, toothed with small icicles.

Warden waited for me by a shallow pool. Its frozen surface was smooth as a mirror, good for scrying. Wisps and shades – the most predictable types of spirit – were drifting all over the place, waiting to be drawn into combat, but none of them strayed beyond the enclosure. Only ghosts usually stuck to one place.

'The fences,' I said slowly. 'They're not electric, are they?'

'No.' Warden started walking again. 'Your scientists have recently begun to develop hybrid technology, which combines our expertise with yours. These fences are powered by ethereal batteries, which each contain a poltergeist – a spirit that can interact with the corporeal world. The friction generates ethereal energy.'

'Never heard of it.'

'All information about hybrid technology is highly classified.'

Of course. That amount of hypocrisy would hardly go down well.

'Poltergeists can escape physical constraints,' I said. 'How could you trap one in a battery?'

'With a skilled binder or a willing poltergeist. Something of an oxymoron,' he said, seeing my sceptical expression, 'but I trust your first week in this city has opened your mind to the impossible.'

I could give him that. Even if I had been unconscious for some of it, this week already seemed like a year.

'Our counsel also led to the invention of Fluxion 14 and Radiesthesic Detection Technology,' Warden said. 'Scion is close to perfecting the latter.'

'I know,' I said. 'Scarlett Burnish takes pains to remind us.'

So the Rephs were responsible for Senshield. Danica had never understood how Scion had developed it, given their aversion to unnaturalness.

Warden chose the largest of the individual arenas. A clock was mounted on its gate. I stood at a safe distance, keeping my guard up.

'To turn you into a fighter worthy of our garrison, I must first assess your existing skills,' Warden said. 'Tell me what you can do, and be truthful, so I may train you accordingly. We know you are a dreamwalker. Attempting to deceive me will not serve you now.'

'I can sense the æther at a distance,' I said. 'About a mile.'

'Impressive. What else?'

'You know.' I was already losing patience. 'You've seen my records.'

'I am aware that you killed an Underguard.'

'I killed two.'

'No. One was found in a state of unresponsive wakefulness,' Warden said. 'Scion chose to euthanise him.' I pressed my lips together. 'You botched your attack on Aludra, too. You can project your spirit from your body – but from your lack of endurance and grace, it has not been long since you discovered this.'

'The train was the first time,' I said.

Warden nodded. 'Your dreamwalking is raw, unhoned. I intend to improve it.'

I raised my eyebrows. 'Do you, now?'

'Yes.'

Nashira had killed Seb to punish my disobedience. For now, I had no choice but to go along with this.

It could work in my favour. I needed to control this ability, before I disembodied someone else by accident. If Warden thought he could help me, so be it. I could take his knowledge and turn it against him.

Warden unfastened his cloak and hung it up under the clock. 'Tell me,' he said, 'do have you any combat experience?'

I folded my arms. 'Spirit combat, or the other kind?'

'Either.'

'Both,' I said.

'Good,' Warden said. 'I want you to fight me.'

I almost laughed, then realised he was serious. 'I'm not going to do that.'

'I confess myself surprised by your reluctance.'

'Believe me, I'd relish it, but I'd lose. You're a giant, if you hadn't noticed. No, if I was going to attack you, I would ambush you,' I said. 'A nice stab to the kidney to get you down to my level, then a knife to your neck. You wouldn't know what hit you.'

'Stabbing your opponent in the back would be dishonourable.'

'Oh, that's rich, coming from you.'

'Very well.' He turned away. 'I trust you will defend yourself.'

When he faced me again, he was holding a knife. I tensed rigid.

'When those Underguards detected you, you must have believed your life hung in the balance. Your spirit responds to danger.' He levelled the blade at me. 'Allow me to provide it.'

'Don't you—'

He threw the knife. I twisted to avoid it, hearing it clatter on to the concrete.

'You have quick reflexes,' he observed.

I flicked a curl from my eyes, teeth gritted. 'Were you trying to hit me?'

'Perhaps.'

He looked towards the watchtower and raised his hand in a clear signal.

Something flew past my ear. I recognised the whistle of a flux dart. Before I could even flinch, a second came my way. I gave in to those quick reflexes and ran.

Another dart had me turning south. The fourth almost hit me in the shoulder. They were herding me towards the ethereal fence. My sixth sense quivered. By the time I was six feet away, I was nauseous.

Now multiple darts were crisscrossing around me, driving me towards the boundary. I stumbled on a wedge of cement and fell into the frozen wires.

My vision turned white, then red. Goosebumps broke out all over me, and fractured memories stuttered before my eyes – the memories of the poltergeist, a murder victim. A deafening *bang* shook my every bone. I saw a spill of blood, bone shards. My stomach gave an almighty heave. I hit the ground and retched.

When I came to my senses, my body felt uncoordinated. I crawled and lurched away from the fence, blinking away grisly impressions.

Warden was waiting for me. I retrieved his knife, my fingers almost too numb to grip it.

'All right,' I said, breathing hard. 'If you want a fight, let's do it.'

'I would not stoop to sparring with a craven like you, human.'

I shook my head. 'You told me to—'

'You are not a worthy opponent.' Now his voice was cold as steel. 'You hid your gift in your first test. Now you run from me. The yellow tunic is too good for you. I should have you beaten.'

The anger was as sudden as it was blinding. I ran at him, driving my good shoulder into his trunk.

I might as well have charged a statue. Not only did Warden not budge an inch, but I was the one who went reeling back, winded.

'As you conjectured earlier, you cannot best me with your bare hands,' he said. 'Play to your strengths, or you will fail.'

I grasped my shoulder, shaken. 'Are you made of stone, or something?'

'Unlike you, I am no weakling.' His eyes burned. 'Small wonder you could not save Sebastian.'

And just like that, I felt myself sever. The ghastly pull from that day on the train – spirit rending from skin and bone, the agony before release.

A dreamwalker can cross the æther, Jaxon whispered. *She alone can be discarnate …*

I shed my body and flew at Warden.

My spirit went slashing into his mind. Like a knife through taut silk, I cut through his defences, entering the darkest circle of his dreamscape.

As soon as I was there, I regretted it. I was straining against formidable strength, barriers I had no means of breaking. The light of his centre was so far away, and I was already exhausted. Like an elastic band stretched too far, I snapped back across the æther.

My heart fluttered. My cheekbone hurt. I drew a shallow breath, got my bearings. When I opened my eyes, I was sprawled on the ground.

Aludra had buckled when I attacked her. Warden was still upright, but I had rattled his composure. The light in his eyes flickered.

'Very good,' he said. 'Better than I expected, given your injuries.'

I tasted blood. 'You were trying to make me angry.'

'It seems to work as well as fear.' He took another blade from his doublet. 'Try again.'

'Are you—' I could hardly catch my breath. 'Are you joking?'

'By no means.'

'I *left* my body. Without life support,' I ground out. 'I also fell on my face.' I touched my throbbing cheekbone. 'I can't just … do it again, you idiot.'

'Think of your spirit as a muscle, tearing from its natural place,' Warden said, unmoved by the insult. 'The more you use it, the stronger it will become, and the better your body will handle the shock.'

'You don't know anything … about dreamwalking.'

'Neither do you, as we have established. Walk in my dreamscape, I challenge you.'

I rose with caution, finding my balance. I seemed to have avoided a concussion.

'I know what Nashira is. Now she knows what I am, too.' I clutched my chest. 'Does she really just want me to be a red-jacket?'

'What else do you think she wants?'

I fell silent. If I admitted what I knew about the angels, I might get Liss in hot water.

'Nashira has plans for you,' Warden said, 'but you should first concern yourself with mine. I chose you. Your progress reflects on me. You will not shame Magdalen with your incompetence.'

'That isn't going to work again.'

'Then embrace your own rage.' He pitted his gaze against mine. 'You must despise me – your jailer, your tormentor. I did not intervene to save Sebastian. Seize your chance to punish me for that, if nothing else.'

132

My fist clenched. I thought I could resist until my fingers protested. They ached from the strain of cleaning his arm – that act of mercy he refused to acknowledge. A mercy he had not shown Seb.

Two guards entered the pen. I held my whole self in place, body and spirit. Warden waited, hands behind his back, as the red-jackets stacked cushions between us.

As soon as they had shut the pen, I let my spirit fly.

In the hour we spent on Port Meadow, I barely dented his dream-scape. Even when he dropped his defences, I couldn't get any farther than his hadal zone, the outermost ring. His mind was just too strong.

He goaded me the entire time, always in the same callous voice. At first the needling did its job, but the closer we got to the end, the less his insults provoked me. By then, I had a crushing migraine.

In the last few minutes, he threw another knife, taking me by surprise. Though he aimed wide, the sight of the flying blade was still enough to set my spirit loose again. I woke on the pile of cushions.

In all, I managed a dozen jumps before my vision darkened and the migraine grew unbearable. I crumpled.

Warden knelt in front of me. The ground was cold under my palms.

'Let me guess,' I said, once I was confident I could speak without throwing up. 'You're going to tell me I'm pathetic.'

'Quite the opposite. You did well.'

'Keep your praise. You're forcing me to do this.'

'It is necessary.'

I tried to stand, but the migraine was sickening in its intensity, bringing hot tears to my eyes. Warden held out a gloved hand.

'Allow me.'

If he left me on the meadow, I would freeze before dawn. Not for the first time, I was going to have to swallow my pride. I took his hand.

Warden helped me back to my feet. When I promptly keeled over again, he hooked my knees over his arm and lifted me against his chest. My eyes throbbed as he opened the enclosure.

'I need life support,' I slurred. 'If you want me to do that again.'

'I can request it,' Warden said, 'but the decision lies with Nashira.'

'You might as well bury me now, then.'

'That would be self-defeating. We still have far too much to do.'

He walked towards the sally port. I closed my eyes, hating every moment of being in his arms.

Thuban had gone a short way from his post, but watched us leave. When Warden approached the sally port, Ivy fumbled to let us out.

'Thank you, Ivy,' Warden said as he passed. Ivy stared after him.

He carried me through the haunted outskirts. I almost dozed off in his arms, my heart flapping like a bird with a gammy wing. Nick would be aghast to know how hard I had just pushed myself.

Warden set me down at the end of Observatory Street. 'Can you manage from here?'

'Yes.'

'You touched the ethereal fence,' he said. 'Show me your hand.'

After a moment, I did. The thin mark had turned milky, my fingertips grey.

Warden took out a glass vial and tipped a clear droplet into my palm, spreading it over the mark. Before my eyes, it melted away, leaving no trace. I snatched my hand back.

'What was that?'

'The nectar of a certain plant,' he said. 'A plant from the Netherworld.'

I watched him tuck the vial into his doublet. His breath didn't cloud in the cold, as mine did, but for just a fraction of a moment, there was something human in his face – something pensive, almost sad.

He caught me looking, and it vanished.

'You must rest for a few days,' he said. 'We will return to Magdalen.'

I was too tired to argue with him. This time, he let me walk at his side.

The training had been unexpected. I had steeled myself for rampant brutality, but Warden had never laid a finger on me. No doubt this restrained approach was a trap, designed to lower my guard.

Liss had been confident that Nashira wanted my gift. To get it, she would have to kill me. Perhaps the idea was for me to die fighting the Buzzers – but that seemed unlikely. If she was some manner of binder, she would need to be close to my spirit to catch it.

I would get to the bottom of this. Even if it had been gruelling, I had only been here a few days. I could afford to bide my time.

Warden took me on a long route back to Magdalen, avoiding the Rookery. When we reached Carfax Tower, he stopped. A red-jacket was on the corner of Fish Street, pacing with folded arms.

When she saw us, she quickly composed herself. Shadows hung under her bloodshot eyes.

Warden crossed the street. 'You should not be alone with an Emite loose,' he said to her. 'Where is the rest of your company?'

'They're close, my lord. We're fine.'

'Whose blood is that?'

Her lips parted. She looked down at her tunic, seeing the hand-print on her shoulder, darker than the red fabric.

'There can be no secrets in this city,' Warden said quietly. 'Better to make a clean breast of it now.'

With a defeated look, she led us into the backstreets.

In a doorway, two more red-jackets were crouched beside one of their own, a cryomancer in his forties. His hand had been ripped and twisted from his arm, as if it had been caught in a machine. One of the other men was trying to stem the blood with his tunic.

'Shit,' I murmured.

Warden surveyed the scene. 'What happened?'

'We split up to look for the Buzzer. He found it in Wheatsheaf Yard.' The woman dashed sweat from her brow. 'The other companies have already chased it back to Gallows Wood.'

'Why have you not taken him to Exeter?'

'He ran, my lord. A few people saw him,' one of the men said. 'He's already been yellow twice, but he shouldn't have been on his own. It's our fault. We were just … working out what to do.'

Warden seemed to consider.

'Nembus will evict him,' he concluded. 'Nonetheless, he has been loyal.'

They all waited. The injured man was trembling, his face slick with sweat.

'Take him to Oriel. The porter there may be able to help,' Warden said. 'But you cannot hide this from your keepers. By dawn, you must report to Exeter and inform Nembus.'

'Yes, my lord.'

The three of them lifted their friend from a pool of blood. Together, they started moving him towards the nearby Residence of Oriel.

'He needs a paramedic,' I said. 'Can't you call your outpost?'

'Nembus will not deem a coward worthy of treatment,' Warden said.

'As charming as the rest of you, then.'

He answered me with a chilling look. I desisted.

Warden left the backstreets. I shadowed him, trying to tamp down the migraine and the fresh disquiet. I had seen maimings in London, but nothing like what had befallen that cryomancer.

'What have we here?'

We stopped. Two men had just emerged from Catte Street.

'Ah, 40. What a pleasure to see you again,' one called, his voice tinged with amusement. 'The pink tunic suits you very well.'

When he came into the light, it took me a moment to recognise him. The medium who had led my arrest, the one who had chased me across the rooftops. He wore thick greasepaint now – red mouth, black eyebrows, chalky face – and carried that same pistol in a leather holster on his belt. I clenched a fist at my side.

The other man was the oracle. He had a shaved head and mismatched eyes – one dark and piercing, one hazel. His tunic was the same colour as mine.

'Congratulations,' the medium said to me. 'I knew you were a diamond in the rough. We all follow your progress with great interest.' He flashed me a smile. 'Allow me to formally welcome you to the city. I am the Overseer.'

'You vile bastard.' I started towards him. 'If you hurt my father—'

'Stand down,' Warden cut in. 'And hold your tongue.'

I stopped about a foot away from the Overseer, who smirked. 'I understand your father works directly for the anchor,' he said. 'I do hope he won't face too harsh a judgement for your nature.'

My fist tightened. Even if Scion spared my father, his career would be in shreds. That had been his only protection. There was no room in London for an Irish man with an unnatural daughter.

'This is 12, a new tenant at Merton.' The Overseer drew the younger man forward. 'As you can see, he is as quick a study as 40. Earlier this evening, he was confirmed to be a talented oracle.'

Warden glanced at me, then back at the young man. It didn't surprise me that the other jumper had also been fast-tracked.

'The Suzerain was wise to test him swiftly,' the Overseer said. 'I hear the visions were spectacular.'

'I hope to serve the Suzerain for a very long time,' the oracle said. 'I'm grateful to her for clearing my eyes. In all my visions, I never saw a purpose for myself. Now I have a path laid for me.'

Either this man was an excellent liar, or he meant it. From his easy smile and the hands in his pockets, you would think he was comfortable here.

'I see,' Warden said.

'You ought to hurry back to Merton, 12,' the Overseer said. 'Give Pleione my regards.'

'I will,' the oracle said. 'Thank you for your hospitality, Overseer.'

He made himself scarce.

'How fortunate that our paths crossed,' the Overseer said smoothly to Warden. 'If I may be so bold, I had been hoping to extend an invitation to the dreamwalker. By your leave.'

Warden just looked at him.

'This September,' the Overseer said to me (apparently taking the frigid silence as permission), 'a party will be held in honour of the twentieth Bone Season, to celebrate the two hundred years since the arrival of the Rephaim.'

'You refer to the Bicentenary,' Warden said.

'Precisely. During the festivities, the Great Territorial Act will be signed.'

That didn't sound good. Before I could hear any more, a vision flashed in front of me.

Nick was an oracle. He received visions from the æther, but he could also form and send them himself. 12 had the same ability. I glimpsed a clock at noon or midnight, then a flight of steps I knew.

'Get to the point, Overseer,' Warden said. I blinked the picture away. 'There are matters that require my attention in Magdalen.'

The oracle had stopped on the corner of Grove Lane. He raised his eyebrows at me. When I gave him the slightest nod, he walked away.

'Of course,' the Overseer said, his voice as soft as oil. 'I have written a masque for the Bicentenary, which requires many participants. I wondered if 40 might like to join us, as our guest of honour. I was impressed by her strength and agility on the night I captured her, and my rooks could use some inspiration. Perhaps you would permit her to learn one of the performing arts alongside her combat training. I daresay she would make a fine dancer.'

I was about to tell him where to stick his dancing when Warden did it for me, in as many words: 'As her keeper, I forbid it.'

I looked up at him.

'She is not a performer,' Warden said, 'and unless her conduct forces me to evict her, she remains in my keeping. I will not allow her to be paraded like a common seer. The oracle may be our first in decades, but a dreamwalker is another matter entirely.'

The Overseer managed to keep his smile up. No doubt he was used to being rebuffed.

'Very good, my lord,' he said. 'Goodnight.'

Once he was gone, Warden said, 'Do you know the oracle?'

'No,' I said.

'He never took his eyes off you.'

'Probably just interested in my aura,' I said. 'Isn't everyone?'

Warden looked hard at me, then walked on. I followed him towards the flickering lights of Magdalen.

II

BIRDS OF A FEATHER

When we got back to the Founders Tower, Warden sat at his desk, writing. I sat by the fire for a while, just so I could warm up. He let me.

I watched a candle burn to nothing. Once I had got a glass of water, I plucked up the nerve to ask if I could retire to my quarters. He gave me a curt affirmative.

In the attic, I applied the salve and a fresh dressing. My head was in agony. I extinguished the lamp and tucked myself in.

I slept badly for the rest of the night. Some time after dawn, I woke up and vomited, barely making it to the toilet in time.

Just a few days ago, I had been convinced I would never dreamwalk. Now I had proven I could do it several times, given the right conditions – but at what cost, I didn't know. I had no life support.

Jaxon would be delighted. He would certainly approve of what Warden was doing – forcing me to reach my potential, regardless of my reservations. Had Nick not been there to temper him, Jaxon would likely have done the same.

I splashed my face and rubbed the stubborn pain in my temple. My hair was a greasy tangle, my stomach raw. Once I was sure I wouldn't be sick again, I rinsed my mouth and crawled back into bed.

If this is a gift, I thought, *why does it hurt as much as it does?*

The bell woke me at dusk. All I wanted to do tonight was curl up tight and lick my wounds, but the oracle clearly had something to say. Still hurting, I dressed and slowly went downstairs, finding the parlour silent. Another note lay on the desk.

You have a fortnight to recover. There is a painkiller with your usual pills. If you can, research the Emim.

He was already preparing me for my next test. I took my pills, then sat and dozed by the fire, watching the mantel clock. Just before midnight, I left.

The painkiller had blunted my pounding headache. When I requested more numa, Gail handed me a dull pearl and a few tin rings.

Warden was elsewhere in the residence. I could sense him somewhere above ground level.

It was crisp outside, the air misted with rain. I went straight to the Rookery, which had returned to its usual capacity. Finding her shack deserted, I looked for Liss, imagining the worst.

'She isn't here,' a voice called. 'She's practising at the Camera.'

Nell was standing by a fire, her dark curls in a bun on the top of her head.

'Okay,' I said. 'Do you know when she'll be back?'

'Not until dawn. I'll tell her you stopped by.'

'Is everyone all right?'

Nell nodded. 'I don't think anyone got hurt this time, other than bone-grubbers.' She stifled a harsh cough. 'One of my friends is an anthomancer. Do you have any more of those rose petals?'

'Not today. I'll tell you if I get some.'

'Thanks.'

Another voyant was overjoyed to see a pearl for the first time in years, even if it was small and flawed. He filled a mug with skilly for me and promised I could have a serving every day for a week.

For once, it was all I wanted. Forcing some of it down, I headed for the building the map named as the Townsend, the pillared sentinel of the Old Library. It was next to the Fell Theatre, where the performers apparently put on plays and masques.

The oracle sat on its steps. When he spotted the mug, he lifted an eyebrow.

'Are you eating skilly?'

'Apparently,' I said. 'Why, are you hiding a pantry somewhere?'

'I cut a deal with a rottie. She skims a few scraps off the red-jackets' food.' He held out a hand, which I shook. 'David Fitton.'

'Paige. I assume that was an act yesterday,' I added. 'Nashira clearing your eyes, and all that.'

'Surprised a voyant knows how to pretend to be something he's not?'

'No,' I said truthfully. 'You almost had me convinced.'

'Good. If you haven't got anything better to do, I thought I'd take you for a walk.'

'Like a dog?'

David huffed a mirthless laugh. 'I feel like one here, trained to obey.' He stood. 'If anyone asks, we're researching the Emim.'

'I got the same instruction.'

'I think we can assume the second test has something to do with them.'

'I'm surprised they're shoving us through them so quickly. I thought they would give us more time,' I said. 'If only to fight among ourselves.'

'What I'm about to show you may help you understand.'

'I didn't realise this was a walking tour.'

'Unless you're a red-jacket, we have to make our own fun here, Paige.'

The Old Library was sealed on all sides, every window and door boarded. We left its shadow, needled by cold rain. I was going to have to find something to pad my clothes in the Rookery.

David gave me enough space that our auras never touched. He was about two inches taller than me, long in the arms and thick in the torso.

'We'll match our auras soon.' He tapped his tunic. 'Strange to have you around. I'm used to being the interesting one.'

'I'd prefer not to be this interesting sometimes.'

We walked down Catte Street, entering the deserted Radcliffe Square. Through the fog, I saw its centrepiece, the large drumlike building with a leaded dome, which stood opposite the Residence of the Suzerain. A dim and tawny light shone through its windows.

'That's the Camera, if you didn't know,' David said. 'The Overseer told me the harlies train at height in there – tightrope, trapeze, that sort of thing.' He shook his head. 'I don't know how they stand it.'

'Why *were* you with the Overseer?'

'He waylaid me after my test and invited me for dinner at Kettell Hall. Pleione let me go,' he said. 'Beltrame seems to hold the highest rank among humans. Better to keep him on side, isn't it?'

I frowned. 'Why would he invite you for dinner?'

'I imagine I looked like I needed it.' He indicated the back of his shoulder. 'He's probably just unwinding, now the Bone Season is over for a decade. And he likes us. Me and you, I mean.'

'I doubt that. He detained me himself.'

'Exactly. He's been trying to root out rare voyants, but he hadn't found many before we appeared.'

'So he's a procurer.'

'He curates the voyants the Vigiles put in the Tower,' David said. 'He's trying to live up to the legacy of the previous Overseer.'

'What happened to the previous one?'

'Not sure, but he lived in London, not Oxford. Beltrame is on a tighter leash. He's usually only allowed to visit London a couple of days a year, to liaise with the Vigiles.'

'What, and we just happened to run into him on the two days he was in town?'

'No. Nashira let him stay there for the final month of the hunt. Guess he was desperate by that point. He thinks the syndicate is protecting the rarest voyants, making them harder to find.'

Beltrame was right. If I had been on my own turf when I was arrested, Jaxon could have saved me.

'That's why he likes us,' David said. 'He netted two jumpers, including a dreamwalker, at the eleventh hour. We saved his reputation.'

Ours was the seventh order of clairvoyance – the highest, according to *On the Merits of Unnaturalness*. Jaxon prized our abilities even above his own.

I finished the skilly. 'You're not part of the syndicate, then?'

'No. I was only visiting London when I was arrested.'

'Where are you from?'

'Kent.' David smiled. 'You ask a lot of questions, Paige.'

'Isn't that the point of this?'

'Maybe. I also just wanted to meet you. I hoped someone from my order would be a good ally,' he said. 'Birds of a feather, and so on.'

'Depends what you're trying to achieve.'

'You first.'

'I want to get out of here in one piece.'

David cocked an eyebrow. 'You don't want to know more about this place first?'

'Not particularly. It's a prison.'

'You seriously don't care that humans aren't alone – that there's another world we never knew about before?' The corner of his mouth twitched. 'You're a difficult woman to impress, Paige.'

I hung the mug on a finial.

'I care,' I said. 'I'm just not sure it's wise to linger.'

'Then let's help each other. Have you sniffed out anything of interest?'

'Not much.'

'That's fine. I'll start.'

Our destination turned out to be the towering derelict between Magdalen Walk and Radcliffe Square, named on the map as the Vault. Several of its windows had no glass, and the door of the south porch – framed by twisting columns – was charred, with a gap at the bottom.

'There's a hidden balcony on the steeple. The view is great for stargazing,' David said. 'And from what the Overseer told me, you're used to heights.' He ducked under the door. 'Watch out.'

Graffias was coming down the street, leading three undernourished amaurotics. I cursed under my breath and went after David.

Inside, I beheld a scene of destruction. There had been a significant fire in here. Some of the ceiling had collapsed, the scorched beams flattening the pews, and stained glass shimmered on the floor, mingled with dust and ash. I picked my way through the rubble.

Scion forbade all religion, deriding it as unnatural. In London, most places of worship had been converted into Vigile stations or district halls, but you could still find them in this state, left as warnings to anyone who dared to defy the anchor.

'There are stairs,' David called to me. 'Over a hundred, by my count.'

'Fine, but this had better be worth it.'

In my exhausted state, it took me a while to get up all those steps. When I emerged at the top, a high wind caught my hair, whipping it around my face.

David rested his arms on a stone balustrade. The view of the spires was spectacular, even if the dim light made it hard to see too far. Beyond the gas lamps, all was dark, except for those dazzling stars.

'I like this place.' He pulled a roll of white paper from his pocket and used a match to light it. 'Not sure the Rephs even know about it.'

I joined him on the balcony, where the slight glow of the city lit our faces.

'You found yourself a bolthole quickly,' I said.

'Pleione lets me wander. I've spent most of this week exploring the city.'

'Aside from your test.'

'Yes.' He blew out smoke. 'Nashira wanted to know about some criminal, the White Binder. If I will it hard enough, I can sometimes invoke a vision. The æther must have known I really needed something. It sent me a picture of a pillar. I passed it to her.'

'Did you recognise the pillar?'

'No.'

I tried not to show my worry. The sundial pillar was very distinctive.

'Carl was asked to find the same man,' I said.

'They can have my visions,' David said. 'I'm more concerned about the Buzzers.' He tapped his cigarette. 'I spoke to someone who fought them.'

'A red-jacket?'

'A former one. She's a trapeze artist these days, after getting her yellow streak. Her test was ten years ago, so it could be different now.'

'Tell me anyway.'

His gaze became distant.

'Gallows Wood is where the second test takes place,' he said. 'My informant had to work as a team with three other pink-jackets to track down a Buzzer and herd it back into the Netherworld.'

'How?'

'They come through portals.' He drew on his cigarette. 'First, a cleromancer made lots from stones. When she cast them, they pointed west, so the group set off. After a while, they'd found nothing, so the cleromancer tried again. With each casting, the lots indicated a new direction. The Buzzer was on the move.

'The pinks changed tactics. First, the rhabdomancer made a dowsing rod, and that got them a bit closer – but they had been out in the dark woods for hours, in the middle of winter. They stopped to rest, built a fire, and did a séance, calling the nearest spirits to help them.'

I leaned against the balustrade. 'Are there many out there?'

David nodded. 'Over all those decades, more than a few people risked the minefield.'

I hid a shiver.

'As they sat by the fire,' David continued, 'the sound of flies came from the woods. And then, out of nowhere, a monster appeared – giant, bloated like a corpse, letting out these horrific screams. It had scalped the rhabdomancer before anyone could so much as flinch.

'The fire was going out, but my informant could still see it. She watched it rip the cleromancer limb from limb, then behead the medium. All the while, she felt like there was an oil spill in the æther – as if it was congealing around her, stopping her from using her gift. An augur threw a knife at it, but nothing happened.

'About then, the fire went out. My informant could hear the last of the other voyants screaming. Even though it was dark, she rushed to help. She grabbed the Buzzer, smelled the decay on it. Next thing she knew, she was on her back with a shredded arm.'

I thought of the strange wounds on Warden.

'Using the last of their fire, she lit a dry branch and warded off the Buzzer,' David said. 'She ran for her life. The last thing she heard was her teammate, screaming as he was eaten alive.'

We stood in silence for a while. What a way to go.

'I think fire repels them, and that's why she lived,' David said. 'She was lost in those woods all night, but made it back at sunrise. They stopped joint testing after that. We'll be out there alone.'

Now I understood why some of the red-jackets carried flame-throwers. I had a feeling I wouldn't have one when I took my test.

'I assume she failed,' I said.

'Yes. Her keeper gave her a yellow tunic. She passed the second time, but she lost her nerve twice while she was a red-jacket.'

'The Rephs are clearly stronger than us. Why send a bunch of puny humans to fight?'

'Sometimes a keeper does go, apparently, to observe from a distance. They don't want too many of us to get eaten,' David said. 'But keeping us terrified keeps us in line. Why not let a few people die horribly every so often?'

He dropped his cigarette and crushed it out with the toe of his boot.

'I don't understand why the Buzzers come here,' I said. 'What stops them attacking anywhere else?'

'They could be drawn to the Rephs.'

'Why, because they're from the same world?'

'No idea. Just guessing.'

I fell silent, grinding my jaw.

'You've got more questions,' David said. 'It's fine. I've missed parlour games.'

'There was an uprising here.' I glanced at him. 'Know anything about it?'

'Yes.' David nodded towards the door. 'Let me show you.'

We moved to stand in a small room, where he lit a torch, mounted in an iron bracket on the wall. Its light revealed a stone memorial, surrounded by humble offerings: candle stubs, acorns, dead leaves and straw, and the spidery yellow flowers of a witch hazel.

'It began on Novembertide,' David said, his voice low. 'A group of Rephs hatched a plot to overthrow the Sargas family. Their plan was to destroy Nashira and evacuate all the humans to London.'

I raised my eyebrows. 'Rephs going against their own?'

Liss had never mentioned that.

'So the story goes. Since there were so few conspirators, they needed a lot of humans on side,' he said. 'But someone betrayed their plans: XVIII-39-7. One weak link, and it all came tumbling down. Nashira had the perpetrators tortured in the House – hence the only name they're known by now, the scarred ones.'

'And the humans were killed.'

'All but Duckett.'

'Was he the traitor?'

'No. He hid during the carnage, then pleaded for his life. Other than him, rumour has it there were two others – the traitor, and a child.'

'Why would Scion send children here?'

'Easier to brainwash. That new polyglot can't be more than twelve,' David said. 'Duckett swears the child lived, too. He was the one who cleaned up the corpses – one of the grisly terms of his survival.'

'But the Buzzers eat flesh.'

'Not the shoulder, apparently.' David tapped the spot where he was branded. 'Duckett claims he never found the girl. But this says otherwise.'

He crouched beside one of the offerings. A stuffed toy, limp and dirty, with buttons for eyes. Around its neck was a note. I picked it up and held it to the light.

XVIII-39-0

'Those flowers look fresh,' I murmured.

'Probably the harlies,' David said. 'I doubt the Rephs involved are still here.'

A deep hush descended. I laid the toy back among the flowers. 'I think I've seen enough,' I said.

David walked me back to Magdalen. There were several hours left until dawn, but the training had taken a heavy toll, and all those stairs had put my body through the wringer. I needed to sleep.

When we reached the door to the Porters' Lodge, I turned to David. The lanterns cast a strong light on his face, revealing freckles.

'Thank you,' I said. 'For the information. And for showing me the memorial.'

'Just keep it to yourself. A gift from a fellow jumper.' He gave me a calm look. 'I'll give you one more question. If I can answer it, I will.'

I thought about it. 'Out of curiosity, why are they called Bone Seasons?'

'Ah.' He leaned against the wall. 'Well, one meaning is obvious, but the word *bone* used to be thieves' slang for something good or prosperous – from the French, *bonne*. For the Rephs, it's the Good Season, the Season of Prospect. Of course, we see it the other way.'

'And you learned all this in a few days.' I raised my eyebrows. 'You're good.'

'I know.' He gave me a brief smile. 'I should get back to Merton.'

A strange instinct was rising in me. I watched him start to walk away.

David clearly knew the value of a secret, just as I did. I had pocketed my fair share this week, but nothing like what this man had up his sleeve. He had shared them with a stranger, apparently for nothing.

And secrets were like coin. They could be counterfeited, laundered. Debts could be claimed later, when you had no way to pay.

'You could have lied to me about all this,' I said. He stopped. 'How do I know you haven't?'

'I have no reason to lie to you,' David said. 'You'll just have to trust me.'

'I'm not sure I do.' I sauntered up to him. 'Less than a week, and you've uncovered a secret not even my contact knew. You clearly got it from Duckett, an eyewitness – but he gives nothing away for nothing. What favours are you doing him in return?'

'Let's just say I'm good at finding things. And getting people talking.'

'Yes, like your new friend Beltrame. If he likes us both the same, he has a funny way of showing it,' I said. 'He invited me to dance, to debase myself. But you got a fancy dinner in Kettell Hall.'

'Drop it, Paige,' David said quietly. 'Just take the knowledge.'

'In exchange for what?'

'I told you. It's a gift.'

His face and voice were getting stiffer. I was on to something.

'You must have agreed to do something big for Duckett. You wouldn't just share a secret like that,' I said. 'Not unless it served you.'

'Paige, I don't blame you for being cynical, but I'm just trying to help.'

'Duckett is interested in my keeper. Maybe he asked you to get him some inside knowledge.' I moved closer. 'I could inform the Warden that I think you're trying to spy on him. I'm sure he'd be very grateful. Or you could just tell me why you've taken such an interest, David.'

David clenched his jaw. His throat worked, and he took a deep breath.

'You're overthinking this,' he said. 'I wanted to build trust, but not because I want to spy on you.'

'What, then?'

In answer, he took a step forward and cupped my elbow. His aura washed against mine.

'I would have liked to be subtler,' he said. 'This place is going to grind us down, Paige. I'm here if you ever want company.'

His eyes were so close, I could see my reflection in them. I looked exactly as nonplussed as I felt. When I realised what he meant, I pursed my lips.

'Did you just tell me all that,' I said coolly, 'on the off-chance that I might want to meet up for a ride at some point, David?'

'I wouldn't have brought it up like this.'

'Thank you, but I'm fine.' I folded my arms, brushing off his hand. 'If that's something you want, you should ask someone else.'

'I will. See you around, Paige.'

149

He left without a backward glance. I watched him disappear into Rose Lane before I knocked on the door to the Porters' Lodge.

Gail let me in. 'You're back very early. I'll come up to light the fire when I'm free.' She clocked my face. 'Are you all right?'

'Fine,' I muttered. 'Just dealing with the local joker.'

'What?'

I marched across the courtyard without answering, slowing halfway when my leg protested.

Nobody had their head on straight here. First Duckett and his bizarre remarks about Warden, and now David. My face burned.

He really could have shared those secrets just to tug my heartstrings. If so, I couldn't blame myself for not anticipating it. By and large, Eliza was the one who got that sort of interest, not me.

But something about the whole thing did feel strange. My instincts were rarely wrong, and before I had doubted and pushed him, David had barely spared me a glance. The change had been jarring. He had also looked faintly relieved when I turned him down.

Whatever his motive, I would investigate his claims. His revelation about the scarred ones was the most significant, but even if it was true, it might not help. Any rebellious Rephs would have been expelled from the city, if not executed.

In the Founders Tower, I found no sign of Warden. I rinsed the green pill away, took the others. I knew better than to use his bath, but I seized the opportunity to steal hot water from his sink.

In the attic, I made a reckless attempt to wash my hair with soap. As I fought to untangle it, I searched for the source of the draught, to no avail. I collapsed back into bed, defeated.

I really wanted my old life back.

Over the next fortnight, I fell into something like a routine. The training had done such a number on me, I could barely muster the will to go up and down the stairs to the attic, but I still went to the Rookery every other night, to check on Liss and Julian.

On the nights I stayed in Magdalen, I explored its unlocked rooms. I found an icehouse, a dining hall, a library of books written in French and Greek. A small grove lay just north of the lawns; I spotted a herd of deer from a distance.

After years in central London, this silent place disquieted me. Magdalen was a beautiful shell, abandoned even by its ghosts. If I stopped inside it, it felt as if nothing else could be moving. Gail saw me off whenever I left, but in two weeks, I didn't see either of the other residents, whose names were Michael and Fazal. We were like figures in a dollhouse, all in different rooms.

Warden barely returned in that fortnight. When he did, I was always in the attic. Sometimes I could sense him elsewhere in the residence.

He must have told someone to feed me. Every time I woke, fresh bread or a bowl of porridge waited in the parlour, along with a tiny cup of medicine for my leg. Those morsels of food only deepened my hunger. One night, I took a lamp to the dining hall and walked between its long tables, imagining them piled high with a feast.

I was becoming part of Magdalen.

For all I wanted to escape, it had accepted me.

On the second of April, thick fog swathed the city again, blurring the gaslight. As usual, I went out, my pockets rattling with numa.

In the Rookery, I traded a pair of scratched dice for toke. Julian was training, while Liss had been summoned to perform at the Fell Theatre. I sat on a bench in Radcliffe Square and bit into the stale bread.

As I sat there, I watched David pass, engaged in conversation with the Overseer. He was definitely off my list of potential allies.

Fortunately, neither of them saw me. Once I had finished the toke, I returned to Magdalen, heading straight for the Founders Tower. I expected to find it empty.

What I found was blood.

12

D I S T R A C T I O N

2 April 2059

The first drop was on the steps. My sixth sense abruptly sharpened, and I looked down to see a glowing spot, right next to my boot.

A trail of mud and blood led me upstairs. I followed it into the parlour, then up to the bedchamber.

Warden was out cold. He had attempted to draw the curtains around his bed. Now one of them lay on the floor, along with his boots and a black jerkin.

As I waited for any sign of life, I picked up the jerkin, finding it heavier than I had expected. From what I could tell, squares of metal had been sewn into the lining, but they hadn't saved him. Half the fastenings hung loose, while the others were gone.

'Warden,' I said.

No reply.

I put the jerkin on a chair. Before I decided what to do, I had to check how bad it was.

He was on his back, wearing the remains of a dark shirt. The sheets covered him to the chest, already stuck to him with light. Intending to take a pulse, I reached for the side of his neck, just where it met his jaw.

Before I could, a gloved hand caught my wrist. I tensed as I locked eyes with Warden.

'You.' His voice was thick and raw. 'What are you doing here?'

'I live here,' I reminded him.

'You usually spend more time in the Rookery.'

'Not tonight.' I held still. 'Go on. Tell me this is all in my head.'

Warden released my wrist. I scooted out of reach, my heart thumping.

'You've bled all over the place,' I said. 'What happened to you?'

'Nothing of your concern.' He did his level best to sit up, only to fall back into the pillows, grasping his side. 'Though you may … stay to watch me suffer, if you wish. No doubt you will enjoy it.'

His throat was glazed with sweat. I wanted to give him a tart reply, but instead, I nodded to his shirt. 'You need to get that off the wounds.'

'I am aware.'

'So do it,' I said flatly. His grip on his side tightened. 'Fine. I will.'

'No.'

'Look, I can't stand you, Reph. But if you die, I don't know what will happen to me, and my life has already been turned upside down,' I said in an undertone. 'Patch yourself up or let me do it.'

Warden returned my gaze with defiance, dark circles etched under his eyes.

'If you don't need me, you must think someone else is coming. Where are they?' I pressed. 'Are you sure they'll get here in time?'

His eyes closed.

'Fetch water and salt,' he said, defeated. 'Look in the display case.'

In the parlour, I found a salt cellar and a spoon, along with linen. I set them up on his nightstand. Next, I brought a bowl of steaming water.

'You must wear gloves,' Warden said, trying to sit up again. His movements were laboured. 'It is … strictly forbidden for us to make direct physical contact.'

'Your gloves are too big for me.'

'Do as I say.'

Reluctantly, I did. As I picked up the gloves, I noticed something else in the drawer.

A letter opener.

The sight of its sharp tip gave me pause. Last time, I had decided that saving Warden was in my best interests. Now all that reason was leaving my head, chased away by the gleam of a weapon.

Warden was clearly too weak to stand. This might be the last time he was at my mercy. I had thrown away one good chance to get rid of him. No criminal worth her salt would miss two.

Suddenly the gloves were on, and the letter opener was in my grasp. All the anger I had stowed was surfacing with every breath. Nashira had destroyed my life. I could teach her how that felt. If she was going to execute me, I would take her consort first.

'Do it.'

I paused.

'Cold steel cannot kill the deathless.' His gaze burned into my back. 'Even if you drove that blade into my heart, it would not cease to beat. But if you wish to try, by all means, vent your gall.'

A silence fell, thickening by the moment.

'You're bluffing,' I said, keeping my voice low. 'We both know you couldn't stop me. You can't even clean your own wounds.'

'That may be so, but my point stands. Ask yourself,' he said. 'If weapons of human making could harm us, would we arm the red-jackets?'

I considered that question, the haze clearing.

'If I succumb to these wounds, you will be given to a member of the Sargas family,' Warden said. 'Know this before you make your choice.'

My nape prickled. After a long moment, I put the letter opener back.

There was the Pale Dreamer, rearing her head in the wrong place again. Even flirting with the idea had been madness. I hated Warden, but he was the lesser of two evils. Thuban would snap me in half.

'If I help you,' I said, 'will you forget this?'

'You stayed your hand,' Warden said. 'There is nothing to forget.'

'Good.'

I returned to his bedside. Slumped against the headboard, he reached for his shirt, pulling it away from one broad shoulder. I soaked a cloth and leaned in to examine the slash there, which ran under his collarbone. It reeked of something rotten and metallic.

'Either you've somehow wrestled a bear,' I said, 'or this was the work of a Buzzer.'

'As the performers call our enemies of old.'

I sat on the edge of the bed. 'You didn't wake up last time.'

'Those were puncture wounds.'

'This slash is still quite deep.' I looked closer. 'It needs stitches.'

'For the time being, purging with salt will suffice.'

'You'll bleed out.'

'No. It is a corruption in my body that imperils me at present. Rest assured, the salt will help.'

'If you say so.' I glanced at his drawn face. 'Will I start, then?'

Warden gave me a nod.

I squeezed hot water into the laceration. His muscles hardened, and the tendons of his hand pushed out, visible through the back of his glove.

'Sorry,' I said, then regretted it. I should be savouring this chance to make him feel our pain.

Warden watched me blot the wound. His blood seeped like honey. The way it sharpened my senses was distracting and calming at once.

As I wet the cloth again, I remembered the first time he came back in this state. I looked towards the window. The curtains were open.

'Tell me about yourself,' Warden said.

I stilled. 'What?'

'You heard me.'

'As if you're interested in my life.'

'I am, else I would not have asked.' He was remarkably calm, all things considered. 'Should you pass your second test, you will stay with me for good, unless I see fit to evict you. I know the crime that brought you here, but I trust there is more to you, Paige Mahoney. If not, I made a poor choice in claiming you.'

'I never asked to be claimed.'

'True.'

The glow in his eyes had faded. I kept flushing the wound, not bothering to be gentle.

'You are Irish,' Warden said. 'From which region?'

He really was keen for a chat. I doubted I had a choice in the matter.

'Munster,' I said. 'I was born in Clonmel.' I soaked and wrung the linen. 'My father worked in Dublin, so my grandparents raised me on their dairy farm. We had a quiet life until Scion invaded. Come to think of it, I have your consort to thank for that.'

'Yes. The Sargas deemed Ireland ripe for the taking. Inquisitor Mayfield enacted their will. He wanted to live up to the legacy of the Balkan Incursion, which brought four territories into Scion.'

'I know.' I dealt him a hard look. 'I can't get this one any cleaner. Where next?'

Warden loosened the ties of his shirt and drew his other sleeve down some way, revealing several more slashes. This was going to take a while.

'You have known war, then,' he said. 'How did you come to be here?'

'You must know this,' I said, impatient. 'It's in the database.'

'Humour me.'

From the way he was looking at me, I could almost convince myself he cared. I dipped a new cloth and held it to his skin.

'My father was a forensic pathologist. He did a lot of work for the Gardaí,' I said. 'Scion conscripted him during the second year of the Molly Riots. They wanted him to help research the root cause of unnaturalness, among other things. By that point, it was obvious that Ireland was fighting a losing battle, even if the rebels didn't know it. Cathal Bell arranged our safe passage to London.'

Saying that name was difficult. It burned like poison in my craw.

'I see,' Warden said. 'Did your father know you were clairvoyant?'

'I imagine he does now.' I dabbed along the first mark. 'He's amaurotic. He thinks it's an illness.'

'That must have been difficult.'

'Yes.' I sat back. 'Are these wounds necrotic?'

'In a sense.'

'Then salt isn't going to help. Half your arm needs debriding.'

'That would be the case if I were human.' He never took his eyes off me. 'So you were forced to come to London. What of your grandparents?'

'They stayed behind.'

Warden regarded me. I kept my face just as blank, even as my chest ached.

'You have mentioned one parent,' he said, once I was on the lowest slash, near the crease of his elbow. 'Do you have another?'

I should have expected this. It had always been an interrogation, couched in false curiosity. He was lulling me into letting my guard down.

'My mother died when I was born. Placental abruption,' I said. 'In case you were thinking of getting her, too.' I put the cloth down. 'Where now?'

Warden glanced away. I followed the blood to a new source, realising.

'Right.' I pushed my curls back. 'You need to take your shirt off.'

'I cannot move enough to do that.'

'I'll have to cut it, then.'

'Do as you will. I will clearly not be wearing it again.'

With a nod, I retrieved the letter opener. When I had it, I sat back down and pulled the front of his shirt taut. Turning the blade, I let the tip rest at the hollow of his throat.

Warden watched me, apparently undaunted. Brushing aside the loose ties below his collar, I sliced the shirt. The gloves and the dull edge made it hard, but I managed to get down to his last rib.

All the while, I avoided his gaze. I was close enough that I should have been able to hear and see him breathing, but Rephs must only need aura.

I started to peel the shirt away from the remaining wounds. His muscular chest was split open, the skin raked as if with a pitchfork.

Rephs were strong. If he was this hurt, surely humans stood no chance.

'These are the last,' he said. 'I believe.'

I scrunched more linen into the water. 'Did the Buzzer rip that armour off you?'

'Yes. No armour can withstand them for long, but I suspect it was expressing its displeasure at my attempt to thwart it.'

'They're intelligent, then.'

'To a degree.' His pupils dilated. 'Perhaps you will indulge another question. When did your gift first make itself known?'

I wished I could end this farce and tell him my life was none of his business, but our proximity gave me a chance to look for weak spots on his body.

'When I was nine, a poltergeist attacked me,' I finally said. 'In the months after it happened, I had a recurring dream – at least, I thought it was a dream. I saw a field of red flowers. The farther I ran, the darker it became. Every night I would go farther.'

I started on the lowest gouge, which ran along the solid muscle of his waist, right beneath his chest. He no longer tensed under my touch.

So far, he looked human. Other than his eyes, the only difference was that dull sheen to his skin. Then again, I could only see so much of him. Even in this state, he wore those gloves.

'One day, I was at the edge of the field. In the dream, I jumped,' I said. 'I stepped over the edge, and everything went dark. I woke up in intensive care. Apparently I had sleepwalked out of my room, then just … stopped breathing. My father rushed me to hospital. I was home the next day, and it somehow got buried. I really don't know how I wasn't detected.'

'Your medical files show no record of that incident.'

'Well, thanks for that invasion of my privacy.'

I pressed hard on the wound. A rough sound scraped his throat.

'Perhaps I deserved that,' he said.

'You did.' I hooked my hair behind my ear again, the gloves making it difficult. 'I must have slipped out of my body. After that, I was afraid of the void. I never went near the edge again.'

'Until the night of your arrest,' Warden finished. I nodded. 'The poltergeist gave you the scars on your palm.'

'Yes.' I moved to the next slash. This one was deeper. 'I think it woke my gift a few years early. I've heard that can happen.'

'Hm. And from whom did you hear this, I wonder?'

Now I was treading dangerous waters. I couldn't let on that I was involved in the syndicate.

'I've had voyant friends,' I said offhandedly. 'Most of them went to the gallows.'

'I see.'

'Speaking of which,' I said, 'did you ask Nashira about my life support?'

'She denied my request. My consort is confident you can make do without it.'

'I suppose we'll find out.'

Warden was mercifully silent as I cleaned the rest of the gashes. By now, his hair was stuck to his forehead, sweat pouring off his skin. I tried not to think about the life support. Instead, I distracted myself with the task at hand, which took all my concentration.

Once I was done, I got a towel from the bathroom and bundled it against his side, holding it in place with a bolster. With sore hands, I took off his gloves and placed them on the nightstand.

'That's as much as I can do,' I said. 'I'll ask the porter to send a message to Nashira.'

'No,' Warden said.

There was a long silence.

'You're her consort,' I said. 'She'll want to know you're hurt.'

Warden held my gaze. I stood and walked to the bay window.

'Both times you've come back like this, there's been fog. You didn't want to be seen.' I glanced at him. 'Whatever you're doing, you're not supposed to be doing it, are you?'

He pressed the wadding to his wounds as best he could. 'She may question you about me,' he said. 'Perhaps not yet, but soon.'

I went back to him, my boots loud on the wooden floor, and leaned against the bedpost with a smile.

'Well,' I said. 'That's interesting.'

Warden clenched his jaw.

'You have a talent for finding me in delicate situations,' he said. 'If not for your quick thinking on the first occasion, and your presence here now, I would have succumbed. I owe you a debt.'

'I gave you my reasons. Never think I'm helping you out of the kindness of my heart.'

'If you truly wish to hurt me, you could report this to Nashira.'

'Or you could owe me a favour. For the debt,' I said, 'and to keep me quiet.' I dropped the smile. 'Make it a good one, and I might be persuaded to keep my mouth shut about your … excursions.'

159

Warden suddenly looked as if he were seeing me for the first time. I thought I saw a flicker of utter repugnance in his eyes.

Either that or grudging admiration. Hard to tell on a face like that, carved and emotionless.

'So you are an opportunist,' he said. 'How venturesome of you, to blackmail your keeper. One might question the wisdom of it.'

'Set me free, and I'll have no reason to rat on you.'

'Name another price, and I will weigh the cost of paying it.'

I should have known my freedom was too much to ask.

'I'm not convinced you'll be around to pay it, at this rate.' I folded my arms. 'You don't look any better. What do you need?'

'You have wits enough to know.'

When I realised what he meant, I stepped back. 'Don't even think about it.'

'Do not fear. Your rank as a pink-jacket prohibits me from feeding on you,' Warden said. 'We afford this courtesy to humans who conform. Instead, give me your solemn oath that you will keep these events to yourself. In return, I will grant your favour.'

His jaw was locking. I made him wait some time for my answer.

'I don't know how much my oath is worth to you, solemn or otherwise,' I finally said, 'but I won't tell anyone.' I turned away. 'Don't sleep too easy, Warden. I'll start thinking of my favour.'

'I would expect nothing less, Paige.'

He really did hate me. I could hear it in his voice, tight with dislike.

In the parlour, the clock struck the hour. Before I could march out of the bedchamber, Pleione Sualocin swept into it, a man in grey behind her. They both stopped dead at the sight of me.

At first, I thought the man was amaurotic, from his tunic. Then I noticed his gentle aura – the aura of an unreadable, a voyant whose dreamscape had collapsed and regrown with thick armour. I slowly looked over my shoulder, disgust rising in my gut.

'You may go,' Warden said.

So that was why he could last without my aura. I went back to his bedside and leaned in close, looking him straight in the eyes.

'Next time,' I said softly, 'I hope you bleed to death in the fucking woods.'

Warden raised his chin. I walked out.

13

AFTER THE POPPIES

17 April 2056

I first met Nick Nygård when I was nine. The next time I saw him, I was sixteen.

It was the balmy spring of 2056. At the Ancroft School in Bloomsbury, the students in my year group had an important decision to make. We could stay on for another two years and apply to the University of Scion London, or jump ship and look for a job.

To convert the undecided, the Schoolmistress had organised a lecture series from 'inspirational' (her word) speakers, with talks held every week during our last compulsory year. Some of them were former Ancroft students, while others had flown in from elsewhere in Scion. All of them had at least one degree.

I had no intention of going to the University. What else London could offer a young Irish woman, I didn't yet know, but anything was better than two more years at Ancroft.

It was a grand building on Russell Square, formerly a hotel, with its own coffeehouse and roof terrace and a famous student orchestra. To everyone else in London, it was a perfect school. To me, it was a glorified prison, reminding me I would never belong.

That day, some of the teachers shepherded my year group into the lecture hall, all in our black suits and starched white blouses. Emma Briskin, head of chemistry, stepped up to the lectern.

'Good morning, everyone,' she said. 'Today marks the last of our inspirational lectures in the sciences. Many of you excel in this field, and Ancroft looks forward to your long and successful careers.'

Even with the windows cracked, the hall was sweltering. I crossed my arms and slouched in my seat, wishing this could be over.

'Our speaker today is from Sweden. He transferred from the Scion Citadel of Stockholm, finished his medical training in London, and now works as a lab technician at the Special Organisation for Research and Science, colloquially known as SciSORS.'

That was where my father worked.

'Now, please give a warm Ancroft welcome to Dr Nicklas Nygård.'

It couldn't be him.

Surely it couldn't.

He arrived on the stage to a storm of applause. My saviour from the poppy field was just as I remembered him, except for the tailored suit and pomade. When he reached the lectern, he smiled.

'Good morning, everyone.'

'Good morning, Dr Nygård,' we chorused.

'Thank you for having me here in Bloomsbury,' Nick said. 'I know it's too nice a day for a lecture, so I won't take offence if you fall asleep.'

That got some chuckles. Most of the speakers had been dry as baked sawdust.

Nick took a sip of water and set out his notes. His gaze flicked up and caught on mine. The slightest frown creased his forehead.

He smoothed it away and hitched up his smile. 'I'll start at the beginning,' he said. 'Why science, of all the disciplines of Scion?'

I felt welded to my seat. My fingertips were tight on its arms.

'In a way, it started with words,' Nick said, glancing at me again. 'The words *scion* and *science* both come from Old French. When I was studying English, I forged a link between them in my head. I learned *scion* comes from a botanical term, referring to a part of a plant that is cut away and grafted to new roots ...'

Suzette leaned towards me. 'He looked at you,' she whispered. 'Didn't he?'

Behind us, Clara Barnes scoffed under her breath. 'Who would ever look at her?'

For once, I could ignore the barb. Seven years of wondering had just come to an end.

'My father works in the same place,' I murmured to Suzette. 'He might recognise me.'

'Oh, Paige.' Clara dug her knee into the back of my chair. 'Do you really think someone like Dr Nygård associates with kerns?'

Suzette frowned at her. I ignored her again, my jaw clenched.

Nick delivered an engaging lecture. He spoke about his life with enthusiasm, cracking jokes as he went. He told us not only about his long career in bioscience – he had been a child prodigy, enrolling at university when he was fifteen – but also his love for his adopted citadel. At the end, Clara was first to raise a hand.

'Yes,' Nick said, gesturing to her.

Clara stood. 'Dr Nygård,' she said, 'how long before we eradicate unnaturalness altogether, do you think?'

'I really couldn't say, but we're trying.'

I barely heard the remaining questions. As soon as the applause started, I almost ran from the lecture hall.

Nick Nygård was my only hope. There had never been a dog in Arthyen. I needed him to tell me what had flayed me open there. I needed him to tell me why the scars were always cold.

I needed him to tell me this before it was too late.

I was the first student to burst into the corridor. Nick emerged from the lecture hall through another door, accompanied by the Schoolmistress. When he saw me, his eyes brightened at once.

'Hello,' he called. 'Did you have a question?'

After a hesitation, I walked towards him. Of course the Schoolmistress had to be there.

'I just—' I held my nerve. 'Your speech was very inspiring, Dr Nygård.'

'Thank you,' Nick said. 'What's your name?'

'This is Paige Mahoney,' the Schoolmistress said, putting her usual stress on my surname. She gave me a glacial look, taking in my untucked shirt and loose collar. 'Your uniform, Paige.'

Evelyn Ancroft had resented my existence from the first day I arrived. Her goal in life was to mould the finest denizens in Europe, and Scion gave her piles of money to do it. I was the only flaw.

Ancroft was known for both its academic excellence and its watertight security. After our arrival in England, my father had convinced someone in Scion to override the usual entry requirements for me, in order to protect me during and after the Molly Riots.

He had not accounted for Evelyn Ancroft. Or how long the hatred of the Irish would endure.

'Ms Gildon would like a word with you, Paige,' she said, while I tucked my shirt in. 'Your arithmetic has been clumsy of late.'

'Paige was brave to come to see me, Schoolmistress. I'd like to see if she has a question,' Nick said. 'Some students are too shy to put their hands up.'

'That's very generous of you, Dr Nygård, but Paige has never shown much interest in the sciences.' She took him by the elbow, lowering her voice: 'A kern case – orders from on high. These brogues make up their own minds as to how much work is necessary.'

And then, against my will, it happened. My head gave a sharp throb. A slow pressure built at the front of my skull, darkening my sight.

'You're bleeding, Schoolmistress,' I said.

'What?' When she looked down, blood dripped on to her crisp white shirt. 'Oh, for goodness' sake. I do apologise, Dr Nygård.'

Nick glanced at me, face wary, and offered her a handkerchief.

'Perhaps you should sit down, Schoolmistress,' he said. 'I'll join you in the conservatory.'

'Yes, of course. Thank you.'

As soon as the Schoolmistress was gone, Nick turned to face me, his smile disappearing. Other students were spilling into the corridor.

'I'll meet you tomorrow at four,' he said in an undertone. 'Coram Street. Can you make it?'

'I'll be there,' I said.

He gave me a nod and was gone. I was left to cradle my books, my hands clammy, my heart pounding. Suzette came up to me.

'Well?' she prompted. 'Does he know Colin?'

'No.' I cleared my throat. 'I just wanted to ask him something.'

'Let's not pretend you'll be at the University, Paige.' Clara shouldered past me. 'Some people were born to lick the bottom of the pot.'

Clara Barnes was lucky that I let her walk away.

I didn't sleep on Monday night, fearing he might not come back. On Tuesday, I endured my classes, unable to concentrate. When the bell rang, I forced myself to walk calmly out of the gates, but sped up as soon as I left Russell Square.

Something unusual had happened that morning. I had daydreamed about a silver car. The picture had come to me during my French lesson, leaving me nauseated. Now that very car was parked in Coram Street.

Nick wore sunglasses today. I got into the passenger seat and faced him.

'Tell me what happened in Arthyen,' I said, winded from walking so fast.

'If you really want to know, I will,' Nick said, his tone careful. 'But the truth might scare you, Paige.' Seeing my expression, he breathed out. 'Let Colin know you'll be home by seven. I'll drive you.'

I sent my father a message, telling him I was doing my homework with Suzette. He replied to say that he would leave my dinner in the fridge.

Nick drove me east through the citadel. I wanted to bombard him with questions, but I could hardly think straight, let alone speak. After a while, Nick said, 'You never told Colin what happened, did you?'

'How do you know?'

'We cross paths at work.' His hands tightened on the wheel. 'Paige, what I'm going to tell you – you won't understand it all in one day.'

'I've waited years,' I said.

'I know.'

As a child, my grandparents had often caught me staring at nothing. Sometimes I had felt tremors when certain people went past me.

Now I wasn't just sensitive. I could hurt people. Something was emerging from me, forcing its way into the light. In the end, someone would see.

'I should have got in touch sooner,' Nick said, as if he could read my thoughts. 'Does the Schoolmistress always treat you that way?'

'Yes.' I glanced out of the window. 'That's her third random nosebleed.'

'I can help you control it. I can keep you safe.'

'I believe you,' I said. 'You saved my life.'

Nick parked his car near Seven Dials. We sat in a quaint coffeehouse in Neal's Yard, where I tried my first brew. I secretly thought it tasted like mud, but Nick had already paid, so I drank.

'Paige,' Nick said, 'you know about unnaturalness.'

'It's a little hard to avoid,' I said drily.

He cracked a genuine smile.

'I don't want to frighten you,' he said, 'but you're showing signs of it.'

After a long moment, I nodded. Part of me had always known.

Still, Irish *and* unnatural. That was a hell of a combination in Scion.

'I would never turn you in,' Nick said quietly. 'We can talk safely here. The owner, Chat, is a good man.'

'I was young in Arthyen, but I remember it. There was no dog, was there?'

'No.' Nick sipped his coffee. 'Paige, I've brought you to here to see a friend of mine, who wants to meet you very much. I trust him.'

'Is he … like me?'

'He is. I am, too,' he said. 'You saw my car before you got to Coram Street. Even the plate was identical, wasn't it?' I stared at him. 'That's what I do – my unnaturalness. I can make people see things.'

'But you work for Scion.'

'To bring it down. Over the years, I've learned to be careful,' he said. 'You've done well to not be detected so far.'

'I don't go out at night.'

Nick nodded. I drank some more coffee, if only to warm my fingers.

'Ah,' Nick said. 'There he is.'

I looked over my shoulder. A man strode into the coffeehouse.

He slotted a cane into the coat stand. Tall and fine-boned, he was probably in his late thirties, with waxen skin and short dark hair. He wore a gold cravat, pressed trousers, and a black embroidered waistcoat.

You could have sharpened pencils on his cheekbones. His lips were pale and petulant. As he approached, they tweaked into a smile.

'You must be Paige,' he said, his voice deep and slightly amused. 'Jaxon Hall.'

He snapped out a hand. I shook it, intimidated.

As soon as our fingers touched, I felt the faintest of vibrations, as if a cold draught had wafted from him. It was very similar to what I sensed from Nick. Jaxon took the seat opposite mine.

'If this is a spurious case,' he said to Nick, arching an eyebrow, 'I will be crestfallen.'

'It's not.'

When the waitron came, Jaxon asked for nothing but a glass of blood mecks, an expensive substitute for red wine. Nick ordered soup for us both.

All the while, Jaxon observed me.

'Nick told me the story of how you first met,' he said. 'He also informed me that you can inflict certain … medical abnormalities on other people.' His gaze was cool, intrigued. 'Is that correct, Paige?'

I glanced at Nick.

'Jaxon doesn't work for Scion,' Nick said. 'I promise.'

'Don't insult me,' Jaxon said, with disdain. 'Farther from the anchor than the cradle from the grave.' He took a sip of his mecks. 'Not that those two states are far apart, but you understand my meaning.'

I wasn't sure I did.

'Sorry,' I said. 'Are you talking about the nosebleeds?'

'Yes, the nosebleeds – fascinating.' He clasped his hands on the table, his eyes alive with a sort of agitated intelligence. 'Anything else?'

'Headaches,' I said. 'Sometimes migraines, if I'm angry. Once I think I made someone faint.'

'And how do you feel when it happens?'

'Tired and sick, mostly.'

'I see.' He sat back, scrutinising me. 'How old are you?'

'Sixteen.'

'Old enough to leave school, then. Do you plan to apply for the University?'

'No fear.'

'You seem very sure. Then again, I doubt I would have cared for higher education in Scion. Alas, I was denied the chance to go to school at all. Without a degree, it can be hard to find well-paid work in the citadel.'

'I'll take my chances. I'd rather die than spend one more year in that place.'

'Brave girl.' The corner of his mouth pulled up. 'Do you have any idea what clairvoyance is, Paige?'

I shook my head.

'It is one of the gentler and prettier names for the noble art of unnaturalness, as named by Scion,' he informed me. 'One who practises it is properly called a clairvoyant. Do you speak any French?'

'Yes.'

'Translate for us, if you please. Two words, *clair* and *voyant*.'

'Clear seeing,' I said.

I might not like arithmetic, but I excelled at French.

'Precisely,' Jaxon said. 'A clairvoyant is one who sees clearly, perceiving truths that lie beyond the reach of the five senses. Truths hidden from others.'

'Hidden where?'

He blew out the candle in the middle of the table.

'In the æther.'

I watched him through the trailing smoke.

'The æther,' Jaxon said, 'is the source of all spirits – ergo, the cradle of being. We come from it; we live our lives alongside and within it; in death, we pass back into it, shedding our physical selves for good. It is knit with the living world, as much as air – a realm, invisible to most, thronged by the spirits of the dead.'

He had just uttered more treason than I had ever heard in my life.

I was drinking my first coffee with a pair of unnaturals.

'Paige,' Nick said. 'Are you all right?'

'I'm fine, but … sorry, I don't think I fully understood any of that.'

Jaxon pursed his lips.

'The æther is essentially a different plane of being,' Nick clarified. 'Only people like us – clairvoyants – can sense it.'

'Not merely sense it, but *use* it,' Jaxon cut in. 'Forgive him, Paige. Dr Nygård tends to understate.'

'I'm trying not to overwhelm her, Jax.'

'Nonsense. She deserves to know what clairvoyance truly is,' Jaxon said. 'And rest assured, it is a marvel, Paige – not an affliction or a vice, as Scion would have you believe.'

A man with one hand brought our food on a platter. I dipped a slice of bread in my tomato soup, mostly for something to do with my hands.

'Scion says the first unnatural was the Bloody King,' I said. 'He was a murderer.'

'Edward was an unpalatable character, by all accounts. He might well have been Jack the Ripper,' Jaxon conceded, 'but I doubt the man was clairvoyant – rather a drunk and convenient patsy, framed to end the monarch days, and to clear a path for the Republic of Scion.'

'Scion used him as an excuse?'

'Yes, my dear.' He gave me a catlike smile. 'Harden yourself to the notion.'

'We're like anyone else, Paige. We do good and bad things,' Nick told me. 'Even if he was clairvoyant, his actions don't reflect on all of—'

'Don't lie to the girl. We are most certainly not like *anyone else*,' Jaxon chided. 'We are clairvoyants, Dr Nygård. We are the keepers of truth, the guardians of the future; the bridge between the living and the dead, the mundane and the divine.'

All the hangings on the screens. Everything that had happened in Ireland. If Jaxon was telling the truth, all that blood had been spilled for a lie.

'If you—' I took a slow breath. 'If *we* aren't evil, why do they hunt us?'

Saying that *we* covered me in goosebumps. That word was like a tight embrace. At first, I felt trapped and afraid – it was too intimate, too much – and then it warmed and steadied me. I let myself sink into it.

'We don't know,' Nick said.

Jaxon lit a cigar with a match. Now my curiosity was layered thick, muffling any trepidation.

'Tell me more about spirits,' I said.

'Gladly,' Jaxon said. 'When we die, we abandon our bodies. Ideally, we go to the heart of the æther, where most voyants believe a lasting death is found – but some choose to linger as drifters, of which there are various kinds. We can barter them, bind them, call them for help.'

'You're talking about real, dead *people*. You can just pull their strings, and they'll dance?' I pressed. 'Why would anyone want that?'

'Oh, they cling for many reasons – to settle old scores, to haunt their killers. To stay with their loved ones, I suppose,' he said, giving his cigar a wave. 'All voyants can feel their presence, but we use them in different ways. They have knowledge of what is, and what is yet to come.'

As I listened, I ate a little of the bread, though it had as much taste as a wad of wet cotton.

'Let us dig a little deeper.' Jaxon tapped my hand with a fork. 'Behold your earthly, mortal form – the cage of flesh and bone that lets you walk upon the corporeal plane. Within this cage, your spirit dwells.' I hung on his every word. 'Now, if your brain is the seat of your physical self, consider the dreamscape your spiritual house.'

'Jax, enough,' Nick said, weary. 'We have plenty of time to—'

'Wait,' I said quickly. 'Do you mean my poppies?'

Nick paused. 'Poppies?'

'I've seen them in my sleep since Arthyen.'

His face softened.

'Perceiving your dreamscape is not quite sleep,' Jaxon said, watching me with fresh interest. 'But your instincts are right.'

I nodded. 'Do only voyants have one?'

'Oh, no. Even birds and beasts have a dreamscape; all embodied creatures do. It serves as both sanctuary and strongroom – a locus amoenus, if you will.'

I had no idea what he meant, but I was still enthralled.

'Now, voyants can see our dreamscapes at will, learn to retreat into their depths; we also see them in colour,' Jaxon went on. 'Amaurotics can only glimpse theirs in their dreams, and only dream in shades of grey.'

'Amaurotics?'

'The dullards, darling. The normals and naturals, beloved by Scion.'

'If they both have dreamscapes, how do I distinguish one from the other?'

Jaxon smiled again. 'She asks the right questions, Dr Nygård. Would you like to tell her?'

'Our connection to the spirit world is called an aura,' Nick said. 'It manifests as a kind of light around a person, usually just one colour. That's how you can tell a voyant from an amaurotic.'

'I've never seen one,' I said. 'Neither of you have one.'

Nick took a sterile cloth from a packet, wiped his hands, and reached for his eyes. I watched as he peeled off a pair of contact lenses.

'Can you see, Paige?'

His eyes were pale wintergreen. The right pupil was shaped like a keyhole.

'Some of us have the spirit sight,' Nick explained. 'We can see auras – even spirits. Having this hole in my iris makes me half-sighted. I can blink away the æther when I want. Jaxon is full-sighted.'

Jaxon widened his blue eyes for me. He had the little holes in both.

'You can't turn it off,' I said, hedging a guess.

'Quite right.'

I nodded, reassured. 'I'm still voyant, even though I don't have those.'

'Yes,' Nick said. 'You just can't see auras.'

'Unsightedness is somewhat rare, but not a disadvantage. Without the sight to help you, your sixth sense will be working harder,' Jaxon said, clearly pleased. 'Now, Nick is an oracle, while I am a binder. Concentrate, now, Paige – can you feel any difference between us?'

'Jaxon,' Nick said in despair. 'This is too advanced. Even you can't always distinguish between voyants.'

Jaxon tutted. 'Killjoy.'

I finished my coffee. It tasted worse cold.

'The woman in the poppy field,' I said to Nick. 'That was a spirit.'

Nick nodded. 'A violent spirit called a poltergeist. It's a class of breacher, which means it can affect the living world. That's how it hurt you.'

'Then she did this to me. She made me this way.'

'No, Paige.'

'The poltergeist may have woken your gift early. Nick tells me it happened when you were nine,' Jaxon said. 'Usually an aura takes longer to sharpen.' He drew on his cigar. 'But you were always one of us. You would have come into your own either way.'

I glanced between the two men again.

Nick mustered an encouraging smile. Jaxon looked at me as if I were a lost valuable he had just recovered.

'Okay,' I said. 'What kind of ... voyant do you think I am?'

'That is what I would like to find out,' Jaxon said. 'Over the years, I have classified seven orders of clairvoyance. I believe you may be of the highest order – a dreamwalker, rarest of all. Perhaps the only one.' He leaned across the table. 'And I would like to offer you a job.'

'What sort of job?'

'The sort that will teach you to master your gift. The sort that will protect you from Scion. Honest work is hard to find,' Jaxon said, with a mischievous glint in his eye, 'but dishonest work is far more enlivening.'

'Scion is everywhere,' I said. 'Won't it be dangerous?'

'Every day.' Nick nodded. 'But we'll have each other.'

'And riches aplenty,' Jaxon said, silken. 'To cushion our woes.'

My heart thumped at my ribs. A job lined up before I had even left school.

'I hear your father is amaurotic. We'll make sure he believes you're doing something else,' Jaxon added. 'Something comfortable and sensible.'

Nick nodded again, solemnly.

I had lived in fear of myself for so long. I had lived in fear of Scion. For over a decade, I had fought to survive the anchor; to be as small and unnoticed as possible, so it might not crush me altogether.

Jaxon was offering me more. If there was any chance that I could live – any chance I could grow into what I was, embrace it – then I had to take it.

'I've just the one question,' I said.

'Go on,' Jaxon purred.

'How much do you pay?'

Jaxon Hall smiled until the corners of his eyes crinkled.

'Nick,' he said softly, 'I do believe you may have found our fourth of Seven Seals.' He clinked my glass. 'To you, Paige Mahoney.'

I smiled back.

14

A GREAT EMPTINESS

For a long while, Warden and I maintained a chilly silence. He never ordered me to train. Every night, I would leave Magdalen as soon as the bell rang, ignoring him. He didn't stop me. I almost wished he would try – frankly, I was in the mood for a fight.

Pleione had served that unreadable up like a nice cup of mecks, to be drained at his pleasure. Warden might pretend to take an interest in my life, but humans were just things to him. I had been a fool to save him once, let alone twice.

Warden was stealing out to fight Buzzers. I didn't know why it mattered, but it must.

Unfortunately, I had no proof. I had searched in vain for even a speck. The floor had been scrupulously cleaned, the bedding changed. Warden could safely call my bluff.

My first attempt to outflank my keeper had officially gone down in flames. I would take it on the chin and win the upper hand another way.

As the days passed, my resentment of him kept simmering. Each time I glimpsed him, I was tempted to sell him out, with or without evidence. All that stopped me was a greater hatred of Nashira.

The attic was getting colder. I refused to ask Warden for help, so I handled it as best I could, wrapping myself up tight in the bedding.

By day, I dreamed of the past, memories dripping into my sleep. The flux must have sprung a leak in my dreamscape. Jaxon had never said that was possible, but nothing else made sense. When I woke from hazy dreams of Seven Dials, I would hug my knees to my chest and wait for my heart to slow down, tasting salt.

I had given up hope that the others were coming. It had been too long. Jaxon would go to great lengths to protect me, but it would never cross his mind that I could be in the lost city, of all places.

No, he would assume I had been executed. The Pale Dreamer was dead.

Three weeks into giving Warden the silent treatment, I woke suddenly, not knowing why. For once, my sleep had been dreamless.

I listened. It was raining hard; the clattering on the roof must have roused me. Still groggy, I covered my head with the pillow.

A drop of water landed on my arm. Groping for the lamp, I turned the flame up and squinted at the ceiling. Another drop splashed on to my nose, making me blink.

Of course. First a leaky dreamscape, and now a real leak in the roof. As I moved my bed out of the way, I imagined the water rotting the rafters, collapsing the whole tower on top of Arcturus Mesarthim.

Spring came late in this prison. It brought a watery sun, but no warmth. A few April showers blew in and froze, leaving the cobbles slippery with ice. Tilda took a fall and sprained her ankle.

The ice silvered the lost city. More than once, I got up before dusk to wander on the lawns of Magdalen – to see the copper sunlight on the frost, hear the ground crunch and crack underfoot.

Once I glimpsed Warden from a distance, on a solitary walk of his own. When our eyes met, I headed in the other direction.

One clear evening, Liss made a rare excursion to the outskirts, armed with a basket and a lantern, taking me and Julian with her. We met in the Rookery and walked north on Walton Street.

'Terebell lets me forage,' Liss explained, 'but she isn't on duty too often. Tilda said she's there tonight.'

'Tell me her nickname is Terrible,' Julian said.

Liss smiled. 'No, she's actually quite decent, for a Reph – I've never seen her raise a hand to a human. She mostly keeps to Oriel.'

In Port Meadow, Terebell Sheratan stood alone, guarding the sally port. When she gave us a curt nod, we followed the outer perimeter of the ethereal fence, our boots sinking into thick mud.

After a while, we slowed to watch a group of red-jackets running laps in the central arena. Another Reph sent a spool to chase them. The way she was dressed struck me as particularly martial.

'Merope Sualocin,' Liss said. 'Balliol.'

Julian blew into his hands. 'Dare I ask what they're all doing?'

'Group exercise. It's not just spirit combat they need in Gallows Wood.'

'Trinity has a gym and grounds. I see people exercising all the time.'

'Merope does regular drills and assessments to make sure no one is slacking off. You'll start them with her soon, so she can bring you up to snuff. After that, it's your responsibility to stay there.'

'Speaking of which,' I said, 'any word on your first test, Jules?'

Julian shook his head. 'Layla refused to take hers a few days ago. She's still at Trinity, but Aludra gave her a yellow tunic.'

'Good for her. In the Rookery, we see it as a sign of courage, not cowardice.' Liss glanced at me. 'Still no training, Paige?'

'Just the once,' I said.

'I find that very odd. It's been weeks.'

'If they have all the time in the world, why rush?'

Everyone agreed the Rephs were immortal – or more durable than humans, at least. Duckett swore that none of them had aged a day in forty years.

'Well,' Liss said, 'unless they want to retrain us harlies, they need more red-jackets.'

'Their life expectancy must be short,' Julian said.

'The Rephs do try to keep them alive, but you've seen what the Buzzers can do. Trinity and Queens definitely need more soldiers.'

'Can I ask how many people were in your Bone Season?'

'That's a layered question. It was chaotic, to put it mildly.' Liss kept walking, and we followed. 'After the Novembertide rebellion, the Rephs had no human tributes. From what I've heard, Scion rounded up some voyants and Vigiles and sent them to hold the fort, then bulked up the garrison over several years.'

'That must have unnerved Scion,' I said. 'Nashira broke the terms of their arrangement.'

'I doubt anyone cared. By 2049, it was business as usual. They sent the standard tribute of voyants and amaurotics – a long hundred, including me. That year was the official start of the Bone Season.'

Julian nodded. 'So that's how some people have been here longer than ten years.'

'Aye, even if their numbers say otherwise.'

Liss paused to cough from her chest. Julian and I gave her worried looks.

'Sorry,' she said. 'There's yet another cold in the Rookery.'

'Here.' I offered my canteen. 'I got it from Duckett.'

'Oh, thank you.'

Julian held the lantern for her. 'If you were a late arrival, how are you number 1?'

'The original 1 was dead by the time I arrived. Gomeisa gave me her number.' Liss drank. 'Since things were back under control, the support Vigiles were transferred to a new outpost, Winterbrook.'

'Nashira must have been rattled, to shake things up that badly.' I pocketed my hands. 'Liss, did you ever hear about any Rephs being involved in that rebellion?'

She frowned. 'What makes you ask that?'

'David heard a rumour. It might explain why she came down so hard on the rebellion.'

'I've not heard that myself. Why would they revolt against their own?'

I had wondered the same.

'I think she just wanted to wipe the slate clean,' Liss said. 'I don't know how future Bone Seasons will look, but yours was smaller than we expected.'

I exchanged a glance with Julian.

From what I could sense, about three hundred of us were imprisoned here. In contrast, there were between thirty and sixty Rephs at any given time. Some only visited for a few days before leaving.

I wasn't fool enough to think our numbers would even the odds, but our Bone Season *had* been small, considering how many people must have been killed on Novembertide. Even with Gallows Wood shrinking it, Oxford was too big for this skeleton army.

The Rephs were holding on to the bare minimum of humans. Just enough of us to keep the city running. I didn't know exactly what that meant, but it was interesting.

Gallows Wood was made up of thick Scots pines and knotted oaks, interspersed with birch and horse chestnut. Liss lit two oil lamps for me and Julian, then pulled on a pair of mittens and unhooked a pair of blunt clippers from her belt.

While she tackled a jumble of nettles, I went up to the trees and plucked moss from a trunk. This was the closest I had ever been to the forest that surrounded our prison. It looked unremarkable, but I could have sworn the night was colder at its edge.

There had been a few sirens over the last few weeks. Each time, by a stroke of luck, I had already been in Magdalen.

'I need chickweed, if you see any,' Liss called. 'Do you know it?' I nodded. 'I wish I could get willow bark. It's so good for headaches.'

Julian picked a few dandelion leaves. 'Why can't you now?'

'A cold spot formed near the old willow. I can't risk it.' Seeing our confusion, she said, 'I'd better let Warden and Aludra tell you about that.'

I brought her the moss. 'If Warden ever deigns to speak to me again.'

Liss took it. 'Did something happen?'

I almost told her. It would feel good to betray him, but a secret like this could be dangerous. Better not to involve Liss and Julian, for now.

'No,' I said. 'He's just a dryshite.'

Julian grinned, while Liss laughed herself into a coughing fit. It was so unexpected that I smiled, too. I had rarely seen her cut loose before then.

We stayed there for a while, looking for hedge garlic and bitter-cress. I sniffed every leaf, hoping to find the herb in the green pill.

A terrible sound rose from deep in the woods. Julian and I both held still as it screamed on and on, splintering the air, then dwindled, leaving a faint echo. My whole body prickled with chills.

'Time to go.' Liss rose with her basket. 'Come on. I'll make us dandelion soup.'

As Julian trained harder with Aludra, he had less and less time to visit the Rookery. Liss was often on the stage. In their absence, I spoke to some of the performers from the previous Bone Season.

None of them knew a way out of the city, of course. According to Cyril, a cartomancer had once broken into a sewer in a desperate attempt to leave.

'The Overseer made her use her own *cards* in performances,' he said in a hushed tone. 'She did flourishes with them, that sort of thing.'

'I remember her,' Guy said gruffly. Other than Duckett, he was the oldest human in the city, a tailor from Leeds. 'Beltrame would let other voyants bend and scratch her cards. That was her last straw.'

'He's vile,' I said. 'Does that sort of thing happen often?'

'No, but she was at Corpus. Thuban always finds ways to torture his tenants, even if he evicts them.'

'As soon as they realised where she'd gone, the Rephs sealed her in,' Cyril said. 'Her bones must still be down there now.'

'Likely.' Guy gave me a stern look. 'Learn from this, Paige. Trying to escape leads to nothing but trouble.'

Guy was a dactylomancer, a voyant who used rings to reach the æther. In exchange for a whole pouch of them, he bulked up my gilet with bird feathers.

Most of the performers were resigned to their fates. This prison had stood for two centuries. In that time, to their knowledge, not one person had escaped.

Still, three years as a criminal had taught me to think I could get out of anything. Thanks to Jaxon, I also had a strong belief that I was exceptional.

So I started my own long search of the city. I climbed to several rooftops to consider it from above. I explored as many buildings as I could break and enter, finding most of them unfurnished or burned out. The amaurotics cleaned a few of the locked buildings, presumably so they would be ready for visiting Rephs.

It worried me that they were out in the world, doing who knew what.

I also ventured beyond the lamplight, eluding the guards. Gallows Wood shaped and surrounded the city; I wanted to see how.

To the south, the trees came up to a flood meadow behind the House. To the north, I could walk no farther than a marshy path called Trap Lane. To the west and east respectively, Scion had grown the forest up to the banks of two rivers, the Acheron and the narrow Cherwell. The Cherwell ran past Magdalen and coursed up to Divinity Gardens, a walled park reserved for the Rephs.

Most of Gallows Wood had high fencing around it, but there were gaping holes and weaknesses. I spotted two more sirens.

During those solitary excursions, I never set foot in the forest. Once I understood its boundaries, I stopped going to the outskirts and turned my attention back to the lamplight.

The Old Library was my greatest temptation. Fronted by the Townsend, it was a grim and ponderous building, waiting for an age of free thought to return. One entrance had no boards, but it was locked.

I did like a challenge.

Duckett had no screwdriver in his shop, so I traded my pills for a few lengths of scrap wire. Liss lent me a pair of tongs when I asked. With these makeshift tools, I returned to my room and began to make lockpicks.

I worked on those picks every day for a week. Once my set was ready, I waited.

My chance came on a night of heavy rain. I went alone to the Old Library. With the wind gusting around me, I broke the padlock with a brick. Next, I used my picks, working until my fingers hurt and I was drenched from head to toe. The lock was old enough that I soon got inside.

The Old Library had been stripped. In the early days of Scion, there had been thousands of biblioclasms, scouring all traces of unnaturalness or dissent from literature. Now these grand book-shelves stood empty. The dust in here was so thick it scratched at the back of my throat.

I carried a handheld lamp, one of my acquisitions from Duckett. A short way into the library, I put it down and dried my hands over its flame. This was the last item he had given me in exchange for the green pills. Apparently he was satisfied with his stockpile.

I refused to run pointless errands for anyone. If I needed any more of his items, I would find a way to steal them.

While the storm raged, I explored. Only a few books remained, packed tight on a shelf. I picked one up and traced its title: *The Turn of the Screw*. With care, I leafed to a random page, reading its small print.

> *The terrace and the whole place, the lawn and the garden beyond it, all I could see of the park, were empty with a great emptiness.*

I closed the book. All that risk and finicking, all for a great empti-ness. Still, I was clearly the first person to have set foot in the Old Library in a while. A place to hide, or store things, could be valuable.

As a last resort, I opened each book and skimmed the foxed pages, searching for notes. When I came up empty-handed, I went flat on my stomach and slid a hand into the space under the shelf.

My first reward was a small glass jar. I opened it to find black ink, which smelled of marzipan. Next came the dip pen. Now scenting a reward, I reached as far as I could.

And there it was.

A leather-bound diary, splayed on the floor. I brought it out and blew dust off it.

My hopes had been too high. Someone had torn the pages out, sparing only the flyleaf. In the corner was a blurred sketch – some-thing that could once have been a face, now smeared and disfigured. A tiny message was scrawled beside it. I held it to the light of my lamp.

> *How long will they haunt me for what I have done?*

The crabbed writing gave me a shiver. The traitor could have written this. I wished there was a bibliomancer in the city, so they could try using this book as a numen.

Sitting with my lamp, I took a bit of stale toke from my pocket and gnawed it. It had been a while since I was last on my own. To my irritation, Warden had stopped disappearing. He was always reading or writing in the parlour, which meant I could never sit by the fire.

His injuries were still a mystery to me. Clearly he was fighting the Buzzers – but why keep that a secret when they were the enemy?

Why hide it from his own consort?

Pleione had brought him the unreadable. She must have known he would get hurt. Whatever he was doing, he was doing it in her confidence.

Warden had a secret, but I had one as well. I was hiding my link to the voyant underworld – a nest of traitors Nashira would want to burn away. I would live with his silence so he would fail to notice mine.

Somehow I drifted off on the floor, my head on a stack of books. Even in London, I had never slept enough – Jaxon had always over-worked us.

A rough shake brought me back to reality.

'Paige!'

Liss was in front of me, eyes wide. I rubbed mine, confused by the brightness.

'What?'

'You overslept,' she hissed. 'It's nearly ten in the morning. Warden sent the red-jackets to look for you.'

Now I was wide awake.

'You're lucky they didn't find you before I did,' Liss said, taking my arm to drag me up. 'You're not supposed to be in the Old Library.'

'I picked the lock.' I scraped my hair back. 'Liss, it's fine. Warden ignores me.'

'He's ignored you because you've kept your head down. Now you need to beg forgiveness. Even then, he might punish you.'

'I won't beg him for anything.'

'You're going to have to swallow that muckle great ego of yours.' Liss glared at me. 'Grit your teeth and beg. You need to live.' She grabbed my hands, staring. 'If he sees ink on you, he'll know where you've been. Come to my place first. We'll get this off.'

'Liss, no. You'll get in—'

'Better they find you with me than realise where you really were,' Liss said firmly. 'We'll get you out quick. There's a secret way you can use.'

I kicked the diary back under the bookshelf, hiding the evidence. We ran down the steps, back into the open.

In the Townsend, Liss held me back. Once the coast was clear, we ran towards the edge of the Rookery. Liss forced two plywood boards apart, and we squeezed into a crawl space, thick with dust and rat droppings, emerging in the passage by her shack.

Julian waited inside, a bowl of skilly on his knee. He looked up when we ducked inside.

He was wearing a pink tunic.

'Jules,' Liss said, despairing. 'Why are you here?'

'Aludra sent me to help find Paige,' he said, raising his eyebrows. 'Apparently the reds were having trouble by themselves.'

'Glad to give them something to do.' I sat beside him. 'Happy to see me?'

'If only to remind me to get myself an alarm clock from Duckett,' he said drily.

'They'll check the Rookery again soon,' Liss warned. 'Jules, you should go.'

Julian stayed where he was, toying with the stiff button at his throat. I gave him a nudge.

'Do you want to talk about it?'

'Aludra took me to Nashira a few days ago.' He glanced at me with tired eyes. 'She asked me what I was. I don't know for sure, and I told her so. They brought an amaurotic into the testing chamber and told me if I tried to hide my gift, this woman—'

I nodded.

'I panicked,' Julian said, looking grim. 'I guessed making up a vision was my best way to get us both out alive, so I said I was a hydromancer.' (Whatever Julian was, he was not that.) 'I'm not sure if Nashira believed me, but she played along. She filled a basin and told me to look for somebody called Antoinette Carter.'

I frowned. 'Toni Carter?'

Julian frowned back. 'You know her?'

'Not personally.'

'Should I know who she is?'

'She was a celebrity in Ireland before the Dublin Incursion.' I kept my tone steady, casual. 'My aunt used to watch her chat show.'

'The mighty Suzerain,' Julian said, sceptical, 'is trying to find a chat-show host?'

'That's what I'm telling you.'

'For ... a chat?'

'Carter used to tell her guests' fortunes. She would predict the outcomes of elections, break the news before anyone else. Either she was a gifted fraud, or she was voyant. She was also outspoken against Scion.'

'She's a fugitive now, then?'

'Unless she's dead, yes.'

Jaxon had told me most of this. I barely remembered, being so young when I left.

After the Molly Riots, Carter had gone into hiding. She had been linked to a pamphlet called *Stingy Jack* in Dublin, which had condemned our conquerors. Jaxon had got wind of it and taken an interest.

All this could still be connected to him. Last spring, he had paid our local jarker to establish contact with Carter. I had never heard the outcome. Leon was good at his job – he must have associates in Ireland – but it could take weeks or months to get a message across Scion.

Jaxon had never explained why he wanted to meet Carter, but I could guess. Her gift had intrigued him, even from afar. He could never resist his instinct to sort every voyant into a neat box.

'So she told you to find Carter,' I prompted Julian. 'What did you tell her?'

'I repeated what Carl said. I'd run into him,' he explained. 'He couldn't help but brag about the pillar he saw. I gave Nashira the same description, with a few tweaks so it wouldn't sound identical.'

'Carl was scrying for a mime-lord, not Antoinette Carter.'

'Well, it still worked. I passed.' When he saw my face, he frowned again. 'What is it?'

Liss came back with a tin bucket of rainwater, saving me from having to answer.

'Let's get that ink off,' she said. 'Julian, can you stop them coming this way?'

'I can try.'

He gave me a quick look, then got up and left. Liss offered me a bar of soap.

'It's paraffin wax,' she said. 'Let's hope it works.'

'Thank you,' I said.

I scrubbed at the ink, rinsing the grey suds away in the water. It was stubborn. Seeing my predicament, Liss handed me a brush with hard bristles. I tried to thank her, but suddenly my throat felt tight.

Liss had been abandoned by the syndicate, her family left to starve on the streets. If she ever learned who I was, she would never speak to me again.

Because I wasn't just any mollisher. I served the White Binder, the man whose pamphlet had sown resentment and pain among voyants. The creator of a hierarchy that dumped her on the lowest rung.

'Paige,' Liss said, watching me, 'you need to be more careful.'

'I know,' I said.

'No, you listen to me.' She moved to kneel in front of me and grasped my elbows tight. 'I've been training for the Bicentenary. If Nashira is going to kill you, she'll want to make a spectacle of it, to keep us browbeaten for another decade. Why not then?'

It made sense.

'If I'm right about her intentions,' Liss said, 'you only have a few months to build your strength, to give yourself a chance that night.' Her dark gaze drilled into mine. 'Just do your training and stop antagonising Rephs. Will you promise you'll do that for me?'

I glanced away, clenching my jaw.

'I don't know how you've done it for so long,' I said. 'Ten years, Liss.'

'Probably the same way you survived London.' She raised an eyebrow. 'Don't tell me an Irish lass never learned to bite her tongue.'

'Maybe that's why I can't do it again here.'

'I'm not saying it isn't hard.' Liss moved one hand to grasp my shoulder. 'You and Julian are my first new friends in years. I don't want to lose you. Promise me that you'll do everything you can to live.'

From the catch in her voice, she meant it. I felt worse than ever for keeping my secret.

'I promise,' I said. 'I've no intention of dying here.'

'Good. If your hope is alive, so are you.' She handed me a cloth. 'You'll need to take that passage out of here. Go straight back to Magdalen. Grab that shawl in the corner and use it to cover your tunic.'

She went to get rid of the soapy water. I headed the other way.

The passage took me back outside. I hid from the people gathered on the Broad, all blinking in the daylight, and sprinted down Turl Street, past Exeter, hoping nobody would look out of its windows.

Another derelict building loomed to my left. With my back pressed to it, I glanced on to Magdalen Walk. It was deserted. Not a good sign – I would stick out.

There were dreamscapes on all sides. The red-jackets must have fanned out to search for me. I drew the shawl over my hair and covered my tunic. Holding my nerve, I strode towards Magdalen.

Warden was there. I sensed him. I quickened my step, steeling myself for pain. He must know that I had no leverage and no protection. If he wanted to punish me, I had no way to stop him.

'What have we here?'

I stopped. A Reph had stalked out from the Porters' Lodge.

'Suhail,' I said, stunned.

The æther had failed me. He was right there, yet there was no trace of his dreamscape.

Just one more impossibility.

'You look better than when I saw you last, 40,' Suhail said. I took off my threadbare disguise. 'I understand I almost deprived you of a leg. Even with both intact, it appears you cannot find your way back to your residence. Where were you?'

'I'll tell Warden,' I said. 'He's my keeper.'

'Arcturus has waited since sunrise. I am confident he can wait longer.'

He stepped towards me. I stepped back.

'Aludra is my cousin. You dared to walk in her dreamscape,' Suhail said. 'I intend to answer this insult to my family.'

'You already punished me for that. As you've pointed out, I almost lost my leg.'

'That was for your insolence to the blood-sovereign.'

'Yes, and I hear she was pissed off about it.' I kept backing away. 'I was taking a test, Suhail. Warden didn't punish me.'

'Perhaps Arcturus has grown tired of you. He has not trained you in weeks, to my knowledge. I suspect he intends to evict you from Magdalen,' Suhail said. 'I would be happy to relieve him of you. Clearly you require a stronger master.'

Just then, a group of red-jackets came sprinting down Magdalen Walk. They must have seen me from Exeter. Julian followed with Guy and a sober Tilda, who wore a yellow tunic.

'Paige,' Julian called. 'Are you all right?'

'Don't interfere.' A red-jacket lifted her baton in warning. 'No names.'

Suhail considered the small crowd before fixing his gaze on me again. I willed him to let it go.

'Perhaps it is well that we have witnesses.' Suhail raised his voice to the others: 'Hours since the day bell, and none of you could locate 40. Exeter Company, how do you explain yourselves?'

'We came as soon as we saw her,' one of the red-jackets said. 'Forgive us, my lord.'

'Not yet. Observe as I deal her punishment now,' Suhail said. 'You will meet the same fate soon, when I inform your keepers of your failure.'

He turned to strike me. Like a blade on a spring, I snapped out to meet him.

Suhail had not expected me to attack him in broad daylight. Aludra must have described her experience to him, but *knowing* something – that was different from *feeling* my spirit coming towards him, colliding with his dreamscape. I had the element of surprise.

It had been too long since I had dreamwalked on Port Meadow. I couldn't hold out. Jolting back to myself, I found my back cushioned by a chest, strong arms steadying me. Julian had managed to break through the line of red-jackets and catch my body.

I blinked away a storm of flashing lights, grasping my chest. My heart kicked at my palm. When my vision cleared, I stared.

Suhail Chertan had fallen to the ground.

The other humans stood in silence, frozen in shock. As we all gaped at him, Suhail rose and towered over us, his eyes flickering like fire.

'Now you've really done it,' Julian croaked.

I nodded, swallowing.

The red-jackets leapt back to life. They wrestled Julian away from me, abandoning me to my fate. Tilda and Guy both shouted in protest as Suhail bore down on me and gripped me hard by the nape.

'You,' he said, his eyes turning red, 'have just made your last mistake, 40.'

He wrenched me into Magdalen.

15

DEATH WISH

24 April 2059

The day porter stared as Suhail passed, his hand tight at the back of my head, my hair twisted around his fingers. My head was pounding, my cheeks streaked with blood. I was forced up the steps of the Founders Tower, tripping and banging my shins all the way.

When Suhail reached the parlour door, he knocked with his fist, rattling it on its hinges.

'Arcturus!'

Warden came in moments. Suhail let go of my hair, taking a fair amount with him. Caught on the landing between them, I had never been so aware of my own mortality, my own brittleness.

'Suhail,' Warden said.

'Your lost property.' Suhail shoved me at him. 'She will not say where she was hiding.'

Warden looked at us both in turn. The evidence was clear as glass: red eyes, bloody cheeks.

'You fed on her,' he said. 'My tenant is a pink-jacket, Suhail.'

'She forfeited her privileges when she chose to attack a Rephaite.'

'I was defending myself,' I said to Warden. 'He was about to—'

'No one allowed you to speak, 40.' Suhail clamped a hand on my shoulder, right where he had branded me. I gritted my teeth. 'Not only has she set the city in an uproar, but she dared to use her spirit against me, in plain sight of other humans. It felled me.'

'Release her, Suhail,' Warden said, very softly.

After a moment, Suhail let go, but I was confident I would have bruises where his fingers had been. Warden leaned down to my level.

'Did you do this?'

His voice was as soft as before. I nodded, just the barest movement of my head.

'You seek to corroborate my account,' Suhail said, his face tightening. 'You would trust this scrap of rotting meat over your own?'

'I only wished to see if she would lie,' Warden said. 'It appears not.'

'Even she cannot deny her disobedience.'

'Neither will you be able to deny yours to Nashira.'

Suhail managed to wind his neck in. I allowed myself a stab of satisfaction.

Warden looked hard at me. His gaze touched on my face, the dust on my clothes, and my loose curls, awry where they had been yanked.

'An eventful return to Magdalen,' he said. 'Is this also your doing, Suhail?'

'She deserves a rough handling for her insolence,' came the sour reply.

'She is not yours to handle. You almost killed her in March. Nashira will not be pleased that you failed to control yourself a second time. Such displays of temper are beneath your dignity.'

'Your approach to discipline has failed,' Suhail shot back, flaring up again. 'Over a month in this city, and she remains untamed. She is obstreperous, insolent, and sees fit to defy her betters in public. Will you allow a human to tarnish your name further?'

'Remember who I am, Suhail.'

Warden never raised his voice, but he could make it dangerous. It sent goosebumps all over me.

'Be assured,' Suhail said, 'that none of us have forgotten.' I felt his red eyes on me. 'I may be moved to mercy if you show remorse, 40. Kneel before your betters and beg for our forgiveness.'

In the silence that followed, as I turned around to face him, I did consider doing it. *Just do your training and stop antagonising Rephs*, Liss had said. All I had to do was stroke his ego.

As it happened, I didn't feel like doing that.

'Take your forgiveness, and your mercy,' I said to him, with soft relish, 'and shove them both where the sun doesn't shine.'

Before I could so much as breathe, Suhail grabbed my hair again and flung me down the steps. I tried in vain to protect my skull as I went crashing head over heels, landing hard on my ribs at the bottom.

I *really* needed to learn to shut up.

Fazal, the day porter, came running to my side. He must have followed us as far as the cloisters. 'Are you all right?'

'Don't get involved,' I rasped. 'Suhail is coming. Go, quickly!'

He retreated at once. I braced myself as Suhail appeared, his expression thunderous. Before he could strike, Warden was there, blocking his arm. I looked between them, too winded and shaken to move.

'I will discipline her in private,' Warden said, his voice so low I could barely hear it. 'Have the Overseer deal with the commotion.'

They stared each other down. Suhail wrested his arm free and left without another word, his footsteps echoing through the cloisters.

Warden looked at me, dishevelled and bleeding on the floor. I tensed again, but all he did was offer a hand. I got up without it, straightening my tunic.

In silence, he went back up the stairs. This time, I kept my mouth shut and followed him.

He directed me into his parlour. Even by day, it was swathed in darkness, heavy curtains drawn against the morning light. A fire roared in the hearth, and the gramophone chirped out 'Mr Sandman' – unusual in the morning, when Rephs were meant to sleep.

Warden went to the bathroom, returning with a bowl of water and a cloth. He placed them on the low table, locked the door, and sat in his wing chair. I waited for my sentence, still unsteady.

'Come here.'

I moved to stand in front of the chair. He looked up at me; only a short distance – even sitting down, he was almost my height.

'Do you have a death wish, Paige?'

I said nothing. I refused to allow him the satisfaction of scaring me.

'A strict curfew is maintained to keep the peace in this city,' Warden said. 'It is a simple rule. Why were you unable to return by sunrise?'

'I fell asleep. I was tired.'

'Since no one could find you, I will assume you entered a prohibited area,' he said. 'By now, you should have adjusted to sleep inversion. Unlike many keepers, I have provided you with a bed.'

'If you'd bothered to check, you would know there's a leak in the attic. It's freezing.'

'A leak.' He narrowed his eyes. 'How long has it been since you noticed this?'

I shrugged. 'A few days.'

'Magdalen is an old residence. The timberwork in the attic dates to the medieval era,' he said curtly. 'A leak may have already caused irrevocable damage. Why did you not inform me sooner?'

'You've a key to the attic. I thought you'd notice.'

'I was attempting to respect your privacy.'

My brow creased.

'Sit,' Warden said, still cold as stone. 'Your aura will renew itself.'

I sank on to the couch, too sore to protest. 'Are you hurt?'

'I can't believe you just asked me that.'

'I will rephrase the question. Do you require medical attention?'

I took stock of myself. My bones ached where I had been thrown around like a doll, and half my ribs felt bruised, but nothing seemed broken.

'I don't think so,' I said.

'Good.' He nodded to the bowl. 'If you wish to remove the blood.'

'Why?' I said. 'Does it give you a twinge of guilt to see me like this?'

'I take no pleasure in it.'

My eyes had stopped bleeding. I dipped the cloth in the hot water and wiped my cheeks.

'Gail will see to the leak.' Warden clasped his hands. 'You must be hungry.'

Of course I was hungry. No amount of bread or porridge filled the gnawing hollow in my stomach.

'No,' I said.

'I find that difficult to believe.'

'Don't ask me a question if you won't accept my answer, Reph.'

Perhaps I did have a death wish.

Warden considered me with a frank and level intensity, as if he could see past my eyes, straight into my dreamscape. It was disquieting.

His own eyes burned on a low flame. The firelight drew out the structure of his face – the solid line of his jaw, his strong cheekbones. He could have risen from the ashes of the monarch days.

'If you wish,' he said, 'I can have a meal brought up for you.'

'You've barely looked at me for weeks. I honestly thought you'd forgotten I existed,' I said. 'Why do you suddenly care if I eat?'

'I left instructions that you were to be provided with breakfast.'

'Was a second meal too much for you?'

'Given its small number of humans, Magdalen does not have a great deal of food in its larder,' Warden said. 'As to my indifference, perhaps I hoped an interval would teach you patience. It seems not. Your restraint is still lacking; your pride continues to cloud your judgement. It was foolish of you to attack Suhail.'

'I know you don't like me. You resent me for threatening you. I understand,' I said coolly. 'But I will not stomach a lecture from you.'

'You have no choice.'

I stared him down.

'There is another reason I have not summoned you to train,' Warden said. 'From what I have observed, yours is a taxing gift. It places a significant burden on both your body and your spirit. I am loath to overstrain you at this stage. In any case, you were plainly not in the frame of mind to spend time in my company.'

'Trust me, I'm never going to be in that frame of mind,' I said, 'but we have to train eventually. Should we not get on with it?'

'Are you so eager to wear a red tunic, Paige?'

'No, but I don't want to lose any more of my strength.' I raised my eyebrows. 'Suhail will punish the red-jackets for not finding me today. If they corner me for payback, I need to be able to hold my own.'

'I doubt they will accost you. These are not the streets of London.'

'You can't be everywhere.' I searched his face. 'I'm not taking my second test, am I?'

'Why do you say that?'

Liss had given me a secret. Now was the right moment to confront him with it.

'Nashira has guardian angels,' I said. 'I heard they used to be voyant. That she can use the gifts they had while they were alive.'

'There are many rumours in this city,' Warden said. 'Some older than others.'

'I'd like you to confirm this one. You're her consort,' I said. 'If anyone knows, it's you.'

Warden settled back in his chair.

'I might be the only living dreamwalker,' I went on. 'I think she wants me for her ... collection. If so, I don't know why you'd bother training me to be a soldier. That's why you really stopped, isn't it?'

'You are astute.' Warden held my gaze. 'I will confirm your rumour, Paige. Nashira does intend to execute you for your gift.'

Liss had warned me only this morning. Hearing it from him still chilled me.

'Nonetheless,' Warden said, 'I am obliged to continue your training. My consort wishes to understand your abilities, as well as their potential repercussions. Although you are already powerful, you have only just begun to unlock your gift. Before you die, Nashira requires it to be as strong and mastered as possible.'

It took me a moment to understand: 'She lets the fruit ripen before she plucks it.'

'Yes.'

'And your job is to ripen me.' I huffed. 'You really are made for each other.'

He was as expressionless as ever, but one hand tightened on the arm of his chair, stretching his glove across his knuckles. For the first time, I had struck a nerve. I tucked the observation away.

'That's the reason she wouldn't approve the life support,' I murmured. 'She doesn't care if I get hurt, as long as I make progress.'

Warden rose. I tensed, but all he did was pull a long cord by the fire.

'I intend to continue your training in three days,' he said, returning to his seat. 'It will be difficult. Do you have any objections?'

'What, to being readied like a lamb for slaughter?'

'You said you wanted to train.'

'To *survive*, not to die.'

'Nashira still expects you to take your second test. If you wish to survive that, you will train with me. You will also attend weekly physical drills on Port Meadow,' he said. 'Magdalen does not have a dedicated gymnasium, but I will set a room aside for your use.'

'Assuming I survive any of this without life support,' I said, 'let's say I pass the second test. Will I have to fight the Buzzers?'

'That is not the only duty of a red-jacket. You will be exempted from patrol. Instead, you will concentrate on your dreamwalking.'

'Of course. I'd hate to be anything less than a perfect sacrifice.'

I should be more afraid than this. Nashira meant to bind me for eternity.

But holding some degree of fear was my default state in Scion. Over time, I had learned to live with it. Jaxon had made sure his mollisher had nerves of steel. I used them now to look daggers at Warden.

A knock broke the silence. A clean-shaven man in a grey tunic entered, looking as if an old master had brushed him into being. His hair was a dark gold, his features chiselled, lips and cheeks as pink as petals. He could have been a living muse, or a model.

He carried a silver platter, which he set with care on the table. Everything about him was fastidious, down to the polished buttons on his tunic. As soon as I got a closer look at his face, I recognised him.

The unreadable Pleione had brought for Warden. He gave me a curious glance.

'Good day, Michael,' Warden said. 'Would you like a drink, Paige?'

I was tempted to ask for something illegal – real wine, perhaps – but I had to keep my wits about me.

'No, thank you.' I addressed the unreadable, who gave me a nod and a smile before leaving. 'So he's your personal vending machine, is he?'

'Michael manages this residence. He has lived here for the last six years,' Warden said, 'since I received him as a gift from Nashira.'

'How romantic.'

'Not especially.'

'You didn't have to feed on an unreadable, of all people,' I said coldly.

'I will not justify myself to you, Paige. Think what you will of me,' he said. 'I am content.' He nodded to the platter. 'Do eat.'

'I'm looking at an accomplice in my own murder. I might well lose my appetite.'

'If so, you will have let your anger overcome your good sense yet again.'

Just to prove him wrong, I moved the platter to my lap and took off the cloche.

The sight was torture. A basket of wholegrain bread with butter. A bowl of pearl barley, tossed with pine nuts and field beans. A pair of poached eggs, split open to spill hot gold yolks, served on a bed of chopped potatoes and tomatoes.

Warden gave me a nod. Now I wanted to throw the plate on the floor, for the sheer pleasure of defying him.

Except that I was losing weight. Stress and hunger were taking their toll. I could see more and more of my hip bones and ribs. I was tired and short of breath. In London, I had been fit as a fox.

Liss had made me promise to survive, and I owed her that much, for the dark secret I was hiding from her. I had to get my old strength back, or I would stand no chance.

I used the spoon to scoop up some barley. From the first mouthful, relief flooded my body. The beans were soft and warm, the nuts sweet.

Warden left me to savour the meal. When I was finished, my stomach ached, fuller than it had been in weeks.

Six weeks in this place. Already my old life felt like a distant memory.

'You are learning,' Warden said from his desk.

'I'm not going to thank you for the bare minimum,' I said. 'I do hope you're not expecting it, Warden.'

'Michael is the one you should thank. I do not eat, but I understand he is a talented cook. Should I give him your compliments?'

I laid the cutlery down.

'You can,' I said. 'It was very good.'

'Hm.'

Warden sat on the daybed, so we faced each other across the table.

'You are a prisoner in this city,' he said, 'but you have a choice. You can train with me in good faith, or you can resist at every turn, hindering your own progress. I ask you to give careful thought to this decision, Paige.'

'Fine,' I said shortly. 'Is that all?'

'Not quite.'

Rephs were supposed to avoid eye contact with humans, yet his gaze had come straight to mine, as it always did. I raised my eyebrows.

'You said that you would never be in the frame of mind to spend time in my company. Since we live together, that will not do,' he said. 'If you choose to commit to training, I have a condition.'

'You'd better not be asking me to like you, Warden.'

'No. I am asking you to tolerate me, as I must tolerate you. To that end, once a month, I would like you to join me for supper.'

'Absolutely not,' I said.

'If we are to cohabit in peace, we must attempt to reconcile our differences. A shared meal seems a reasonable setting.'

'And if I refuse?'

'I would prefer that you came of your own accord,' Warden said, calm as you like, 'but if I must stipulate it, I am willing.'

'Do you have to *work* at being this irritating, or does it come naturally to you?'

'No amount of petty insults will change my condition, Paige.'

'And no amount of tea and biscuits will buy my obedience.'

'I seek your forbearance and dedication. In return, I will tailor your training to compensate for your lack of life support. I will be mindful of your welfare.'

'Why bother?'

'This is my offer,' Warden said. 'I have already named my price.'

'Nashira can't approve of this,' I said, forcing down my fury. 'You call me by name. You barely even scolded me for attacking a Reph. Now you're inviting me for supper. I've been tarnishing your good name all over the city, and if anything, you're rewarding me for it. What is your game, Arcturus Mesarthim?'

'You will have to trust me. Just as I have trusted you to keep my secret.'

'Are you going to tell me why you've been fighting the Buzzers?'

'Perhaps I will, when you join me for supper.'

My aura had recovered. I was starting to feel the æther again, a faint prickle of awareness.

'I'd like to sleep on it,' I said. 'You still owe me that favour, Warden.'

'I have not forgotten.'

We both stood. Even after weeks of living alongside him, his height remained daunting.

He opened the door to the landing for me. It was such a courteous and unnecessary gesture that I looked at him with suspicion.

'I should not have adjourned your training for as long as I did,' Warden said quietly. 'I have been preoccupied. Forgive me.'

The apology came as such a surprise, all I could do was stare at him. After a long moment, I nodded and went to up to the attic.

Gail came straight up for a look at the leak. She put a bucket down to catch the raindrops, then left me to my thoughts. I rubbed my hands over my paraffin lamp, focusing on the æther. Suhail was on the prowl outside; I could sense him patrolling Magdalen Walk. For the time being, I was stuck in the residence.

I got into bed, minding my fresh bruises from the stairs. As I lay there, I considered the offer.

Accepting it would be a serious risk. If I worked with Warden and failed to escape, I would have colluded in my own downfall, granting Nashira a powerful weapon. Without life support, there was every possibility I could experience a lot of pain first, even if Warden went easy on me. Little as anyone knew about dreamwalking, any fool could tell it was dangerous.

But my gift *was* a part of me. Perhaps it was a matter of pushing through a pain barrier. Besides, learning to dreamwalk might be the key to finding a way back to London – or lasting just long enough for London to find me. Jaxon might have given up by now, but Nick would keep looking.

Getting my gift up to scratch might just increase my chances of escaping – or surviving – the Bicentenary. Even now, I could floor Rephs. From the looks on the humans' faces today, that was unprecedented.

Nashira wanted me because I had a power she lacked. That gave me the upper hand. While she thought I was honing it for her, I was safer than most. No one could hurt me without risking her displeasure.

Warden was offering to train me as if I still had a future. If he kept to his side of that bargain – if he allowed me to set my own pace – then I might yet leave this place unbroken, with my sanity intact.

The mandatory supper was irritating, but I could spin it to my advantage. He clearly meant to gain my trust, but two could play that parlour game, and I had just as much to win.

Thuban Sargas had called him *concubine* – a word I had never heard before then, loaded with contempt. I could discover what it meant. Suhail, too, regarded him with obvious disdain. I could find out why.

Long before the night bell tolled, I knew what I was going to do.

Warden was still in the parlour, poring over some papers by candlelight, a goblet within reach. When I stepped into the room, he looked at me.

'Have you come to a decision, Paige?'

I kept my distance.

'I'll train with you in good faith,' I said. 'But I have a condition, too.'

'Name it.'

'If you want me to line my own coffin, you can do me the courtesy of not being a bastard about it. So whatever your consort happens to think, you will treat me with respect.'

'Nashira is not my keeper.' He inclined his head. 'I accept.'

'Good.' I breathed out through my nose. 'And I'll have your wretched supper.'

'I am pleased to hear it. Would a Thursday evening suit?'

'I'll have to check my calendar.'

He kept as straight a face as I did, but his eyes glowed in a way I had never seen before.

16

POSSESSION

Weeks passed in the lost city. Still there was no thaw. Every few days, I trained with Warden on Port Meadow. Each time, I was able to project my spirit. Each time left me drained and shivering.

Warden kept his word. Rather than goading my gift out of me again, he was patient and measured in his approach. Between sessions, he let me take whatever time I needed to recoup, following my lead. Only when I was ready did he take me for another session.

It soon became apparent that the more physical discomfort I was in, the harder it was to dreamwalk. He taught me to detach my thoughts from my body, so it was easier for my spirit to slip away from it; how to shut out the hunger, the cold. The groundwork involved a lot of breathing and sitting, but that was fine by me.

Each time we trained, at least one Reph observed us. I tried not to notice.

As promised, Warden set up a small gym for me. When I wasn't in there, I was on the training grounds, running laps with the other pink-jackets, sticking with Julian. Merope was merciless.

In the meantime, I did some research on Warden, or tried. None of the performers I knew could guess what *concubine* meant.

'The Rephs do use odd words sometimes,' Cyril said, adjusting his old glasses. 'They have their own language. I'm not sure certain things translate exactly, so they use whatever fits best.'

Guy grunted. 'They talk like monarchs.' He was roasting a perch over the cookfire. 'Your keeper most of all, Paige.'

'I noticed,' I said. 'I don't think I've ever heard their language.'

'They only speak it among themselves.'

I finally decided to comb the Founders Tower. Despite the amount of reading he did, Warden didn't seem to store his books in his own quarters. After giving up on the parlour, I found a modest stack in his nightstand, including *A Dictionary of the Republic of England*. Leafing to the right section, I found no trace of the word I needed.

The sound of footsteps had me shoving the dictionary back into place. Michael came in with a sling of firewood. I hitched up a smile and gave him a hand.

Liss kept on with her training as well. Most nights she was at the Fell Theatre or the Camera, preparing for the Bicentenary. Though our paths often crossed in Radcliffe Square, she was usually too exhausted to speak. I left food in her shack whenever I could.

The Overseer gave her the occasional week off. One night found us washing clothes and bedding – a hard job here, done by hand with lye. I sat down by a fire and mucked in with the performers.

In the spring, they did their laundry by a stream near the Detainment Facility, the Sleepwash. It stemmed from a river that flowed through Gallows Wood, which they called the Acheron – but I had a gut feeling that it was, in fact, the Thames.

Naturally, I had sketched a plan to build a boat, only to find out that someone had already tried it. According to Nell, their body had floated down the Sleepwash a few days later, riddled with bullets.

That was all the proof I needed that the city had a defensive wall around it. Even I wasn't fool enough to think I could get past that. Scion would have spared no expense to keep its secret contained.

As I scrubbed a shirt over a washboard, I glanced at the stars and thought of London. Jaxon must still be raging over the loss of his dreamwalker. I might have given up on the idea of a dramatic rescue, but I still hoped Nick would come across a breadcrumb. If not, Danica might be able to access my arrest record.

The Sleepwash was frozen for some of the year, but now it was spring, it was thawing at last. Some way upstream, a few people bathed in the icy water. The Rephs seemed to tolerate this event, but they watched us.

'Thanks for your help,' Liss said to me. 'I miss washing machines.'

She had let her ringlets fall out, so her black hair swept down her back. Her feet were bruised from the silks, one of which she was rinsing.

My clothes were cleaned and pressed for me. I had found a scullery while I was exploring, complete with a mangle, a flat iron, and other tools. Michael seemed to deal with that sort of thing, while Gail maintained the buildings and Fazal did the gardening.

'Jos,' Liss called. The polyglot looked up from his washboard. 'That's enough, now.'

'I want to help,' Jos said. 'I can do it, Liss.'

'Not until it has a good soak in the bucking tub.'

She held out a hand. Jos brought her the shirt, and she placed it in her own basket.

'Thank you,' she said, and gave him a splash. He ducked away with a laugh. 'Go on, away to the Rookery. Get the skilly while it's hot.'

'Okay.'

Liss smiled and went back to cleaning her silks.

Everyone here loved her. If this were London, Jaxon wouldn't have spared her a glance.

On the Merits had changed the underworld. Not just changed it, but revolutionised it. Before its publication, voyants had never really been categorised – not in London, at least.

His radical ideas had spread like a plague. Factions and rivalries had formed; street wars had broken out. Appalled by the violence, the Spiritus Club – his publisher – had withdrawn the pamphlet from circulation, and Jaxon had formally renounced the hierarchy, stating that all voyants stood on equal footing against Scion.

Still, the grudges had lingered; the orders had stuck. Everyone used his names for their gifts. Jaxon had even coined the word *dreamwalker*.

'You look deep in thought,' Liss said, snapping me out of it.

I forced a smile. 'Just thinking of London.'

'Ah.'

Her friendship was keeping my head above water. Even if the deception churned my stomach, I would keep my past to myself, for now.

'Jules tells me you've been training hard,' Liss said. 'Merope has a reputation.'

'Don't they all.' I wiped my brow. 'All I've heard about the second test is that Buzzers are involved. Do you know anything else?'

'No. You're meant to be unprepared, so everyone who takes it is sworn to secrecy.' She drew the silk from the water. 'I'd expect it any day. Just in case it comes as a surprise.'

'Warden doesn't strike me as the spontaneous sort,' I said, wringing a shirt.

'Never think you can predict them, Paige.' Liss did the same to her silk. 'Remember – they might look like us, but they're nothing like us. Do not let your guard down.'

Suhail observed us from the Detainment Facility, standing beside Aludra. For once, I played it safe. I kept my head down and my gaze on the ground.

Late in May, Warden proved Liss right. He took me by surprise. When I came down from the attic, ready to train, he presented me with a black coat.

'I thought you didn't issue these in the spring,' I said. 'It's nearly June.'

'You have done well in your training.'

'Well, thank you for the treat.' I pulled it on and buttoned it up. The lining was thick and warm. 'You'll go harder on me now, won't you?'

'In a manner of speaking.'

His posture seemed different, though I couldn't quite put my finger on how. He secured his cloak and reached into his doublet.

'Gail tells me the leak in the attic was a sign of a more serious problem. The roof needs extensive repairs,' he said. 'While she carries out this work, you may return to sleeping on the daybed.'

Once I might have chafed at the idea of sharing his quarters again, but the attic was still uncomfortably cold. This way, I could sleep by the fire.

'All right,' I said.

'There is another matter.' Warden held out a familiar green pill. 'I know you have not been taking these, Paige.'

'Do you, now?'

'Yes. Have you been disposing of them, or selling them to Duckett?'

'If you want me to take that pill, you'll tell me what it's for. No one else gets it.'

'You are not them.'

'What are you going to do, personally force it down my throat?'

He tucked it into a silver pillbox, eyes flaring. 'I will give you time to reconsider,' he said, returning it to his doublet. 'For now, follow me.'

Michael waited for us in the cloisters. He handed an iron lantern to Warden.

'Hello, Michael,' I said. 'How are you?'

He gave me a brief smile and a nod. I had yet to hear him utter a word.

Warden led me to the gate east of the lawn. 'We are not going to Port Meadow,' he said, taking a key from his belt. 'This is Water Walk, my private retreat. From here, we will go some way beyond the lamplight.'

'Why?'

'You have proven yourself capable of leaving your body, but you will not improve if we repeat the same exercises. I wish to try a new approach.'

Water Walk was lit by nothing but the moon and stars. The darkness thickened as we lost the faint torchlight from Magdalen.

In spite of myself, I stayed close to Warden. The Rephs might send humans to do their dirty work for them, but he was the one with the track record of surviving the Buzzers. He led me off the path, over a rotten bridge, then strode into a tangle of wet undergrowth, leaving me to trudge in his wake, up to my knees in weeds.

'Warden,' I said, 'how far are we going?'

He ignored me.

My boots and socks were already sodden. He was taking me into the untamed meadows behind the residence, which were cradled by the River Cherwell. They were called the Fields of Mercy, since they stood between the lamplight and Gallows Wood.

Warden clearly wasn't feeling merciful today.

'You're pissed off about the pill,' I guessed, fighting to catch up with him. His legs came all the way up to my waist. 'Just tell me what it is.'

'It is necessary,' Warden said.

'Oh, catch yourself on. I managed without it before I had the misfortune of meeting you,' I bit out. 'Would you kindly slow down?'

He deigned to stop. I caught up after a few moments, breathless.

'You win.' I held out a hand. 'Give me the pill.'

Warden regarded me. 'What changed your mind?'

'You're clearly in a foul mood. I don't want you taking it out on me.'

In the silence that followed, he seemed to weigh my sincerity, then removed a tablet from his pillbox. I washed it down with a swig from the hip flask he offered, taking another sip for the bitterness.

'There.' I thrust it at his chest. 'I'd ask if you were happy, but I doubt it.'

Warden took it and kept walking. 'Do you think me incapable of joy?'

'Since you have one facial expression and one tone of voice, I really can't tell.'

'Perhaps you lack perspicacity.'

'Perhaps you lack a personality.' (I neither knew nor cared what *perspicacity* meant.) 'If you ever do learn to imitate joy, I'll thank you to not show it anywhere near me. I can't imagine you get your kicks from anything pleasant.'

'You need not trouble yourself,' Warden said coldly. 'At present, I can imagine no circumstance in which I would feel any joy around you.'

'I take that as a compliment.'

'Good.'

He really was out of sorts, stooping to petty jabs with a human. I found I liked being a thorn in his side.

We kept going for what seemed like hours, though he did me the honour of walking at my pace. Thanks to the coat, I was snug enough, though I wished I had gloves as well, and my boots were still leaking.

When Warden stopped, I almost walked into him. Ahead of us, a small log shelter stood among the weeds. He opened its door and held up his lantern. It took a moment for my eyes to adjust.

In the shelter, a deer – a doe, specifically – was tethered to a post. As soon as she saw Warden, she flicked her tail and long ears.

'That ... isn't quite what I was expecting,' I admitted.

'May I ask what you were expecting?'

'Just about anything but a deer.'

'This is Fionnuala,' Warden said. 'Nuala, for short.'

'That's an Irish name,' I said, after a pause. It meant *white shoulder*. 'Gaeilge is outlawed in Scion. Why would you call her that?'

'For its beauty.'

Warden released the worn collar from around her neck. Nuala butted him with her nose. I waited for her to bolt, but she just stood there, gazing at him. When I noticed the white patches on either side of her neck, I had to smile.

He spoke to her in an unfamiliar language, stroking her throat. She was mesmerised. As I listened to his voice, something in me hummed in answer.

A few months ago, I might have found it strange to see a giant and his adoring deer. Now it was just another night in Oxford.

'She has a penchant for apples,' Warden told me. 'You may feed her, if you wish.'

When I nodded, he tossed me a green apple, which I barely managed to catch. 'Did you just ... produce an apple from nowhere?'

'Perhaps.'

Nuala turned her gaze on me, nose twitching.

'Gently,' Warden said.

I took a game step forward and held out the apple. Nuala gave it a few delicate sniffs. Warden spoke to her, and she snatched it.

'Forgive her.' He patted her neck. 'We have yet to refine her manners.'

'I see yours are coming back.'

'Hm.'

It wasn't an apology, but I decided to let it go. Nuala gave my hand a lick.

'She's beautiful.' I stroked her. 'Why isn't she at Magdalen?'

'Animals are only permitted in the city as livestock. The fallow deer at Magdalen are reared for venison and buckskin. To spare her that fate, I brought her to these fields.'

'Dare I ask *why* you saved a random deer?'

'For company. And for you.'

I smiled thinly. 'Is this your way of telling me that I need to be tamed?'

'Not at all.'

Warden walked back outside, letting Nuala run towards the River Cherwell. He sat on the crumbled remains of a wall, facing me.

'You are a dreamwalker,' he said. 'What does that mean to you?'

'We've been over this several times, Warden.'

'Indulge me.'

I sighed. 'I can sense the æther for about a mile outside myself.'

'Yes. That is your foundation, your starting point – a heightened sensitivity that even Rephaim do not possess,' Warden said. 'Your silver cord is flexible, allowing you to dislocate your spirit from the middle of your dreamscape – an act that widens your perception.'

'Yes.'

'Perhaps, before you even knew what you were, you could hurt people. Perhaps you could put pressure on their dreamscapes, causing nosebleeds and headaches.'

I frowned. 'How could you possibly know that?'

'I am entertaining a theory.' Warden held my gaze. 'Something changed on the train. No doubt you feared you would be executed. For the first time in your life, that power inside you broke into the world.'

'So it did.' I perched on the wall, keeping my distance. 'Did you suspect before I even arrived?'

'Nashira received an urgent report that an Underguard had been killed – bloodlessly, without a single mark on his body. She knew it must be the work of a dreamwalker,' Warden said. 'What is the next stage of your gift?'

'Leaving my body,' I said. 'I can push my spirit into the æther without my cord breaking.'

'And the next?'

I said nothing.

'You forced your spirit into Aludra. You have done the same to me. Even when you fail to break into a dreamscape, you can collide with it,' Warden said. 'What is your intention?'

'I don't always have one. It just happens,' I said. 'In that case, I was trying to hurt Aludra.'

'And when you enter a dreamscape, where do you instinctively aim?'

'The sunlit zone.'

'Indeed. The seat of the spirit. What could happen if you reached it?'

There was a tense silence, broken only by the reedy screech of an owl. I turned away to look at the moon, which sat in a smoking cup of cloud.

'You're talking about usurping a spirit,' I finally said. 'About … possession.'

'Yes.'

My unproven ability. A theory.

Jaxon had broached the subject not long after I started working for him. He had invited me to propel my spirit into his dreams-cape, to see if I could take control of his body. The idea had shaken me. At the time, I had barely known how to broaden my percep-tion of the æther. Nick had stopped him asking me again, but only for a while.

Maybe I could have done it. Maybe I could have seized his body and stubbed out that wretched cigar – but it frightened me, that I had that potential. Even with the promise of a pay rise, I had been too afraid to try.

'I've never done it,' I said. 'You can't make me do it, either, regardless of our agreement.'

'It would be a formidable weapon,' Warden said.

'Let's say I can learn. You think I want to hand that sort of power to Nashira?'

'You agreed to practise with me in good faith. Do not do it for her, but for yourself.'

'I won't be able to possess you. Reph dreamscapes are too strong,' I said. 'So far, I've caught you all by surprise, and you all slammed me back out.'

'I do not expect you to possess me.'

'What, then?'

Warden looked across the field. I followed his line of sight. The doe took a long drink from the river, then scuffed a hoof against some flowers.

'Nuala,' I said.

'Yes.'

I rarely dealt with animal dreamscapes. When I had joined the syndicate, the challenge had been tuning them out. In the early days of scouting for Jaxon, they had been an overwhelming distraction: the birds flying over the citadel, the rats scurrying in its sewers, the insects.

It might not even be possible for me to fit my human spirit into an animal dreamscape. It might drive me to insanity, or hurt the deer, or both. Would she be able to resist my infiltration, or let me straight in?

'I don't know,' I said, after a moment. 'She might be too big to control.'

Warden rose. 'I will find something else.'

'I hate to keep reminding you that I don't have an oxygen supply, but I'm going to do it again.' I stood as well. 'I've never even *tried* to possess anyone. We have no idea what it will do to me.'

'So far, your heart is coping,' he said, even as he walked away. 'Our training sessions would have killed other humans, but your body seems built to handle your gift.'

'You're still gambling with my life.'

'I will not allow you to leave your body for long.'

'Nashira really has ruffled your feathers.' I strode after him. 'Hey, if you insist on doing this, you realise she could possess *you*. You'd trust her with your body when you can't even tell her you're fighting the Buzzers?'

He turned to face me. I stopped, arms folded.

'There are reasons,' he said. 'Only trust that I want you to reach your full potential.'

I held that flaming gaze, trying to read him. Their faces really did ward off emotional guesswork.

'Fine,' I said. 'An insect or a rodent, then. Or a bird.'

Warden gave another nod and left, pursued by a deer. I waited for him by the broken wall.

Nuala wandered back after a while. By then, a deep chill had set in. My breath came in clouds as I huddled against the wall, rubbing my raw hands together.

'Hello,' I said. 'Did your apple dealer get lost, Nuala?'

She looked hard at me, then folded herself down like a clothes rack.

'Oh, are you joining me?'

Nuala laid her head in my lap with a huff. As I stroked her velvety ears, I tried to imagine *being* this deer – running on four legs, living wild in the night.

Scion had done all it could to beat the wildness from me. Perhaps that was the reason I worked for Jaxon. Not just to belong, but to bask in my freedom.

Nuala closed her eyes, content. After a pause, I tested the water. I leaned against the wall before I dislocated, letting my awareness drift.

The dreamscape next to mine was thin and fragile as a bubble. Humans could build layers of resistance – as they aged, or as life callused them – but animals lacked that emotional armour.

I gave her dreamscape the lightest of nudges.

Nuala let out a snort of alarm. I shushed her, feeling a twinge of guilt.

'It's okay.' I stroked her neck. 'I'm sorry. I won't do it again.'

The deer tucked her head back into my lap, but she was quivering. She had no idea it was me who had hurt her.

By the time Warden returned, I was still against the most uncomfortable wall in the world, warmed by Nuala. She blinked up at him.

'You took your time,' I said. 'Did you go to Edinburgh?'

'Not quite. I have found you a host.'

He sat on the wall. Nuala let me up, and I joined him. His skin had more of a sheen by moonlight.

His gloved hands were cupped. When he opened them a little, I looked down to see a pale butterfly, or a moth. It was strange to see hands of such strength used so gently.

'A common brimstone,' he said. 'They rest among the leaves at night.' He raised his gaze to mine. 'Are you willing to attempt a possession?'

'I can try.'

His eyes glowed hot as coals. With one hand, he unclasped his cloak and spread it on the ground for me. After a long moment, I lay down on it.

As I got myself settled, he sat beside me, still holding the butterfly. It always bothered me, to have to leave my body vulnerable.

Warden glanced at me. His eyes were usually like dying embers. Tonight, they were bright enough to cast a slight glow on his cheekbones.

'I will keep watch,' he said.

With a nod, I closed my eyes and took deep, slow breaths. Little by little, I relaxed my body, releasing the tension I stored in my jaw and neck, tuning out the chill. Once I felt as if I could float, I withdrew into my dreamscape and walked my spirit to the edge of the poppy field, where it was darkest. The æther waited just ahead.

I jumped. For the first time, I imagined my silver cord as a harness, keeping me safe.

The butterfly was a grain of salt beside the marble that was Warden. I slid into its dreamscape. There was no reactive jerk, no sudden panic from my host.

I found myself in a world of dreams – a world of stained glass, each splinter aglow. The butterfly spent its days among flowers, and all of their colours had fashioned its haven. Since they weren't voyant, I had thought animals would be like amaurotics, with grey dreamscapes. This kaleidoscope was unexpected.

Rephs had expansive minds, from what little I had seen of them, but here, each step took me into a new ring: hadal, abyssal, midnight, twilight. Even without a mouth, I could feel myself smiling. My spirit longed to walk like this, in strange lands. It had wanderlust.

I was formless here; I saw only a blur when I looked down. When I came to the sunlit zone, I spied a tiny spirit. As I approached, it skittered away.

Now for the real test. If Jaxon had worked this out correctly, stepping on to the right spot would allow me to take control of this body.

As soon as I entered the circle, the sunlight brightened, blinding me. The dream world shattered like a diamond, glinting with rainbows.

For a moment, there was nothing.

Then I was in a private hell.

Panic registered first. My arms and legs had disappeared. I was crushed by my own body, screaming with no lips or voice. When I tried to breathe, nothing happened. When I tried to move, something gave a spasm, as if I were in my death throes.

I had to get out. With a heroic pull, I threw myself clean out of the dreamscape and back into my body. I snapped upright, gasping in panic.

'Paige?'

'Fuck.' I touched my face. 'Never again.'

'You are safe,' Warden said, his tone steady. 'Tell me what happened.'

'I did it.' I wrenched my coat open, my chest heaving. My heart was boxing at my ribs, protesting the latest insult. 'I'm not meant to be in that sort of body. I don't ... know how to exist as a ... butterfly. Do they even have lungs?'

'No.'

'Fuck,' I said again. 'That was stupid. I could have forgotten how to get out.'

It took me a while to collect myself. I blinked away stars, my head pounding. When Warden offered me his flask, I took a few delicate sips. I had almost thrown up on his polished boots last time we trained.

'I apologise,' Warden said, his voice low. 'For my lack of patience with you, and for my carelessness. I should not have made you do this.'

His second apology. My retort died on my lips, blunted by confusion.

'No,' I said, looking away. 'You shouldn't have.' I held my own arms. 'I won't possess an animal again. You can punish me all you like. I don't care.'

'You will not be punished. I gave you my word.'

'Good.' I moved to lean against the wall. 'How long did I last?'

'It was your first possession. I saw you move its wings.'

'How long, Warden?'

'A few moments.'

I huffed. Jaxon would have cracked a rib laughing. 'Is that what my second test will be like?'

'No, but it proves how far you have come. You are ready to try for your red tunic.' Warden opened his hand, and the butterfly fled into the dark. (At least I had managed not to kill it.) 'Can you stand?'

My knees were shaking. Seeing the state of me, he lifted me into his arms. I didn't protest. It really took it out of you, puppeteering the fauna.

Warden carried me into the dark. Above me, his eyes were the only light.

Magdalen soon appeared before us, lit by its lamps and flaming torches. How dark the world looked in the shadows beyond it; how warm and inviting the light in its windows, glowing as if to beckon us home.

17

SURVIVOR

1 February 2046
St Brigid's Day

'Hurry, Paige. We're almost there.'

Finn pulled on my hand. I was six years old, and we were in the congested heart of Dublin, surrounded by shouting people with placards.

'Finn, I don't like this,' I said, but he ignored me. He had ignored me since we got here.

We were meant to be at the cinema, that crisp February morning in 2046, when the winter sun spilled white gold on the Liffey. I had been staying with Aunt Sandra, who had taken me off my grandparents' hands while they dealt with the black mould on the farm. That day, she had told her son to look after me while she was at work.

You shouldn't be going in today. Finn had looked sullen. *We should all be in Dublin.*

Unlike you students, I can't take a day off to go shouting at politicians. Aunt Sandra swung on her coat, her face hard as steel. *If I hear you took your cousin there, I'll not be held responsible for my actions. Do you hear me, Finn Mac Cárthaigh?*

Bell is courting a tyrant. He wants to hand us to the English on a platter. He's meeting Mayfield, Finn had said, furious. *You've nothing to say about that, Mam?*

The Taoiseach won't negotiate. You know he'll keep us safe. She had picked up her keys. *I don't have time to argue with you. I'll be back at seven. Paige, you have a good day, won't you?*

Yes, Auntie Sandra.

As soon as she was gone, Finn had got me into my coat and gumboots and buckled me into the car. As he drove from Dún Laoghaire, he promised we could see a film and have lunch, but first he needed to meet up with his university friends by the statue of Molly Malone.

'Today we make history, Pip,' he told me, squeezing my mittened hand.

I wrinkled my nose; history was for school. I loved Finn – he was funny and clever, and he spoiled me when I came to stay – but I had seen Molly plenty of times. I knew all the words of her song off by heart.

Finn had driven as far into the city as he could, only to find the streets thronged with thousands of people. Abandoning the car, he had taken me into the crowd on foot. Now he was on his phone, shouting over the din.

'I'm here.' He let go of me to jam a finger in his ear. I clung to his jacket. 'Where are you?'

I looked up at the angry people. They were shouting, chanting, all crushed together. I could read some of the words on their signs, but there was one I didn't know, which was everywhere: SCION. Messages flashed past, high in the air, Gaeilge and English mixed together: DOWN WITH MAYFIELD. AXE THE ANCHOR. ÉIRE GO BRÁCH. REMEMBER THE BALKANS. CATHAL THE SASANACH. DUBLIN SAYS NO.

'Finn,' I said tearfully, 'what's happening?'

I spoke in Gaeilge, which got his attention.

'You're fine, Paige.' He sounded impatient, but stopped to pick me up, still on his phone: 'Wait, I can't hear you. Laoise, are you there?'

A deafening chant began: 'SCION OUT! SCION DOWN!'

'Ah, fuck it—' Finn hung up and joined in: 'SCION OUT! SCION DOWN!'

We were near the statue now, jostled by the crowd. When I saw Molly, tears of fright jolted into my eyes. There was a bag over her head, a rope around her neck. Her baskets were overflowing with flowers.

'Finn, I want to go *home*,' I pleaded, but my voice was too small. 'I want Auntie Sandra.'

'SCION OUT OF DUBLIN TOWN!'

I still couldn't understand why everyone was shouting. An elbow knocked into me. People were looking at their phones in confusion, holding them skyward. I held fast to Finn.

'Kay,' Finn bellowed. He put me down, ignoring my pleas. 'Kay, over here!'

Kay pushed through the crowd. I had always loved her. She had beautiful hair – a dark auburn that shone like copper and curled like mine. Finn had given her a Claddagh ring, which she wore on her left hand, with the heart pointing away from her body.

Today she was dressed all in black, and her pale cheeks were painted green, orange and white. Like Finn, she studied at Trinity College.

'Finn,' she called, reaching us. 'I thought I'd never find you. My phone's not working.'

'I thought it was just me.' He pulled her close. 'Where's everyone else?'

'Oscar and Anjali went ahead. Antoinette Carter is giving a speech,' Kay said over the din, 'but there are so many people there. I'm afraid—' She was cut off when someone crashed into her side. Finn swore at the culprit and pushed him away. 'Temi is over at Leinster House. She says there's a rumour Cathal Bell will speak at noon.'

'What about Laoise?'

'Not here. There was a roadblock at—'

'Kay,' I piped up, 'what's going on?'

When Kay saw me, she stared, her mouth falling open. 'Finn,' she said, 'why in God's name have you brought Paige here?'

'What?'

'Take Paige home, now!'

'There's no one home to look after her, Kay. I'm not missing this for the world,' Finn said hotly. 'If these bastards get in, we'll never get them out.'

'Finn, she's six! This could get violent.' Kay grasped my hand. 'Sandra would be ashamed of you, exposing her to this. Come on, Paige—'

'No.' Finn snatched my other hand. 'I want her to be here.'

'Finn!'

My cousin knelt in front of me and pulled off his peaked cap. Beneath it, his hair was tousled. Finn was the spitting image of my father, and now he was just as serious, his hands tight on my shoulders.

'Paige,' he said, 'do you know what's happening?'

I shook my head, holding on to Kay.

'A bad man has come here from over the sea,' Finn told me. 'A man named Mayfield.'

'Is he from England, like Mammy?'

'Yes, from London. He wants to bring other bad people here, to lock us up in our city and hurt us. We won't be allowed to speak Gaeilge any more, or watch the films we like, or go outside Ireland. They'll rip down our buildings and burn our books, take everything that makes us ourselves,' Finn said, his voice roughening. 'And people like you, Pip – they don't like you.'

I looked into his eyes, knowing what he meant. Finn had caught me staring at invisible people. 'Why does Molly have a bag over her head, Finn?'

'Because the bad people do that when they hate other people for no good reason. They put bags over their heads and ropes around their necks, to kill them.' He pulled hard at his own collar. 'Even little girls, like you.'

'Finn, you're scaring her,' Kay objected. 'Let me take her to—'

'This man, Mayfield,' Finn said, 'we've come here to tell him to go home and take his notions with him. We don't want to be part of Scion.'

'SCION OUT! SCION DOWN!'

My eyes hurt. A bubble filled my throat, but I refused to cry. I was brave. I was brave, like Finn. I didn't want the bad people to hurt us.

'SCION OUT OF DUBLIN TOWN!'

Finn put his cap on my head. 'We have to stop them, Paige.' He smudged a tear from my cheek. 'Are you going to help me stop them?'

I nodded.

And then came a sound I had never heard – a sound like a drill, louder than all our voices put together. Kay turned to look as a scream rang out. I saw her lips form my name. Her dark eyes widening in fear.

The sound came again, and she fell to the ground.

And then my world exploded.

I woke with gunfire echoing in my ears.

My skin was slick and cold. I lay as if paralysed, my heart pounding like artillery. I could still hear the screaming, thirteen years later. I could see Kay – and Finn, howling as he tackled her killer, bare hands and rage against a rifle. The crowd had devoured them, leaving me alone.

I never saw my cousin again.

It had taken me years to understand what happened that day. The day of the Dublin Incursion, otherwise known as the Imbolc Massacre.

The *Courier* had broken the story. Cathal Bell, the Minister for Foreign Affairs, had invited Inquisitor Mayfield to Dublin. Bell had long advocated for Ireland to join the Republic of Scion. According to the article, their meeting would be held at Iveagh House on St Brigid's Day.

Mayfield had never been in Dublin. Bell had planted the story himself, luring his most outspoken detractors – activists, students, celebrities, even his fellow politicians – to the streets around St Stephen's Green.

The night before, while my aunt tucked me in, Scion had been sending warships into Dublin Bay. The next day, agents of the anchor had destroyed our phone masts while armed soldiers infiltrated the protest.

None of us had been ready for gunfire.

No emergency services, no warnings, no way out.

Later, it had been agreed that the first shots were fired on Grafton Street, right by the statue of Molly Malone.

I must have slipped back to sleep. When I stirred a second time, I tried to get my bearings, a tightness on my cheeks. The memory had been so vivid.

A sharp breeze gusted past. I blinked several times, blind. From what I could tell, I was lying in a tiny shelter, not unlike the one in the meadows behind Magdalen, where Nuala had been. A tarpaulin covered my body, leaving my face and one hand exposed.

'Warden,' I said hoarsely.

There was no reply.

The cold had sunk past the lining of my coat. Shivering with it, I shifted towards the doorway and reached for a weight in my left pocket, finding a torch. Its beam revealed a long clearing, encircled by old trees.

My breath caught. I rummaged in my other pocket and pulled out a small envelope. I recognised the handwriting and broke the wax seal.

Nashira has decreed that you must take your second test. I wanted you to have more time to recover from your first possession, but my cautious approach has tested her patience.

It had been nine days, but my head still ached from possessing the butterfly. I kept reading:

Gallows Wood surrounds our city, hiding many perils. Your task is to find your way out by sunrise. A marker awaits you on Cherwell Meadow.

The case to your left contains vital equipment. Use your gift. Trust your instincts. And do me this honour: survive the night. I am sure you would rather not be rescued.

Good luck, Paige.

I crumpled the note, trying to think. The last thing I remembered was coming down from my room, ready for training with Merope. Michael had been waiting with a cup of tea, of all things. Like a fool, I had drunk it.

'You bastard,' I breathed.

Warden had forced Michael to sedate me, then dumped me in the middle of nowhere. So much for treating me with respect. I should have expected no less of a Reph.

I took a calming breath. This had been inevitable. Nashira was aware that I was ready for my second test, and Liss had warned me it would be a surprise.

Gallows Wood creaked and rustled. I reached for the æther. There were no dreamscapes in the vicinity, which meant I was over a mile out. For now, my gift wouldn't help as a compass. I wasn't a rhabdomancer, capable of fashioning a dowsing rod to find a path. I wasn't any kind of augur, which would help in a forest, where there were twigs and leaves, even flowers.

I soon found the reinforced case in the shelter. Inside was another envelope from Warden.

Be careful with the darts. The acid inside is highly corrosive. Use the flare only in an emergency. It will summon the red-jackets to your location, but you will fail your test.

Avoid the ice. Do not go south.

I shone my torch into the case. Warden had left me a flare gun, a flip lighter, a combat knife, a syringe of military-grade adrenalin, and three pressurised silver darts labelled FLUOROANTIMONIC ACID, with an air rifle to shoot them. No firearms.

Of course he hadn't deigned to give me a flamethrower or a proper rifle. Clearly some robust protection was too much to ask.

Lastly, there was a wristwatch. Its hands glowed blue, showing me that it was almost half two in the morning. The sun would rise around five.

I had wanted to fail the first test, but I meant to pass this one. A red tunic would give me the authority to support the performers, including Liss.

My breath came in billowing clouds. Unless I wanted to freeze here, I had to get moving.

A small backpack was folded inside the case. I strapped the watch to my wrist. With my hood pulled up and my coat fastened to the chin, I carefully loaded one of the acid darts. The combat knife went into a sheath on my belt, the syringe into my pocket, and the rest into the backpack.

I got up. As I took my first step out of the shelter, something crunched. My torch revealed a line of tiny white crystals, which had been poured around my starting point. After a hesitation, I crouched to rub my fingers in it, then tasted it.

Warden had left me in a circle of salt.

I held still, trying to think. Jaxon thought salt could potentially be used for divination, along with sand and dust – but even if it was true, I was no augur, and Warden knew it. This couldn't be for me.

I could picture him now, watching the clock like a hawk. He would expect pride to hinder me again.

He had no idea what I had survived. I would remind him not to count me out just yet.

His note warned me not to go south. He might be throwing me a bone, telling me I should head north. I searched the sky for the pole star.

Dense woodland lay in that direction, thick and overgrown. I was about to set out when I glanced over my shoulder. The forest looked more navigable on the other side of the clearing – firs and pines looming tall, but spaced wide. That path would lead me away from the city.

Do not go south.

It could be advice, or it could be a warning. Either way, I was curious.

Oxford was northwest of London. If I went south, I was heading in the right direction. I might just reach the very edge of the Rephs' domain – and even if I couldn't escape, I could see what sort of barrier was there.

Wind rushed through the leaves. It was now or never.

I turned and headed south.

Heavy rain had softened the earth, leaving it spongy and damp. My boots made no sound as I trekked between the massive pines, sometimes breaking into a jog. A strange mist wreathed their trunks and wove a thin blanket over the ground. I willed my torch to hold out. I had never been afraid of the dark, but after nearly three months of living in close quarters with Warden, this degree of isolation was chilling. I wasn't used to this silence, this stillness.

These pines had grown for two centuries, hiding the city from prying eyes. I wondered if the journalist from the *Roaring Boy* had seen them, before he was run off the road. Perhaps his car had been dumped here. Perhaps his corpse as well.

Coming this way might have been the wrong choice. The farther south I went, the higher my risk of failing the test. As I walked, I checked the branches, searching for surveillance cameras. Drawing a deep breath, I picked up my pace. I needed to leave myself time to backtrack.

Suddenly I stopped, remembering what Liss had told me.

The red-jackets patrol it to stop them reaching the lamplight. Apparently its far reaches are full of mines and trap pits.

Warden could have been warning me not to venture into those reaches. The clearing must be a last safe point before the mine-field. I stayed where I was, ears pricked. I pointed my torch at the ground.

Other voyants had tried to escape. Perhaps the test included resisting the temptation. I almost turned back, but a mulish determination pushed me on.

The Rephs could be sowing fear of these woods to stop us glimpsing the edge of their city. If I didn't take a few risks, I would never see my gang again. I would never reclaim my position as the Pale Dreamer.

I stopped when my torchlight fell on a skull.

Not just a skull, but a skeleton – still in the shreds of a pink tunic, both legs missing at the knee.

My breath caught. I pressed my back straight to the trunk of a pine, my skin turning damp. When I swung my torch to the right, I saw the crater, surrounded by shards of mine casing.

Fuck this.

Warden had told me not to let pride cloud my judgement. For once, I would listen. No amount of clairvoyance would help me navigate a minefield in complete darkness. Knees shaking, mouth dry, I started to inch back towards the clearing, my hand clammy around the torch.

A root came underfoot and floored me. As soon as I hit the ground, I tensed, eyes tightly shut.

A long silence resounded, broken only by my breathing.

I turned to the skeleton, screwing my courage in place. There was a sack under its fingerbones. Checking the ground in front of me, I crawled towards it, prising the sack free. It was dark with dry blood. Inside I found a hip flask, rotten crumbs of bread, and a rusty trowel.

No one could dig their way out of hell.

Finding the skeleton had given me an idea. I dug in my backpack for the lighter. Dreamwalking was useless for now, but I could still call on the dead. Placing one hand on the broken skeleton, I flicked the lighter open, and a clean flame rose. Even though I wasn't a pyromancer, any nearby spirits would be drawn to this tongue of flame, a numen.

'I need a guide.' I tightened my grip on the bones. 'Are you still here?'

For a long time, there was nothing. The flame guttered. Then my sixth sense jolted, and a spirit – a revenant – emerged from the trees. I got to my feet.

I had rarely seen revenants outside burial grounds. They were similar to ghosts, but specifically haunted their own remains.

'Thanks for coming.' I held the lighter out to it. 'I was hoping to see the edge of these woods. Any chance you could lead me through the minefield?'

The spirit rang in negative.

'It's okay. I knew it was a long shot,' I said. 'Can anyone else help me?'

The same vibration, more insistent.

'All right. I won't risk it.' I breathed out. 'Would you help me find the city, then?'

It started to drift the way I had come. Sensing this was the spirit of the dead pink-jacket, I followed. It had no reason to mislead me.

It was a bitter pill to swallow – just like the one I took every night – but north was my only choice. A minefield was too dangerous to risk.

The shelter came back into sight. The wind blew out my lighter, but the spirit clung fast. I took a moment to catch my breath, then set off into the other trees, torch in hand, my guide darting just ahead.

I had lost time venturing south, so I followed my new friend at a brisk clip. Merope was an unapologetic tyrant, but at least her drilling had forced me back into shape. I could hold a jog with relative ease.

The spirit pressed on. My ears and nose smarted with cold, which set my jaw to rattling. I could barely feel my toes. After an eternity, a dreamscape twinged at the edge of my perception. The farther I walked, the more I could feel. I released my breath in a cloud.

'Thank you,' I said to the spirit. 'I can find my own way from here.'

To my surprise, it stuck to my aura, quivering.

'Really, it's okay.'

It stayed exactly where it was. It might be lonely, after all these years.

Just then, an eerie light caught my eye. It was cool and pale, like moonlight, but that couldn't be it. The moon was in its last quarter, not full enough to shine that bright. I strayed towards it, drawn by the æther.

What I found was a perfect circle of ice. White and smooth, it formed a beacon in the dark, surrounded by mist. I took another step, my breath forming thicker clouds. My spirit guide circled me, frantic.

Avoid the ice.

I had an overpowering urge to disobey. I wanted to step on that ice, to hear it splinter and cave in. I wanted it to swallow me into whatever lay beneath. I saw myself sinking into black waters, deep enough to drown.

Come, it seemed to breathe. *Come into the beyond.*

A seam had burst in the æther, opening a door. I rested the toe of my boot on the ice. My sixth sense heightened, but nothing else happened. The ice was both an invitation and a locked door, unyielding.

A gust of wind ruffled my hair, breaking my trance. It carried a smell that tapped into some primal instinct – something physical, animal. It pulled my attention from the æther. My nape tingled. I turned, shining my torch ahead.

It must have been a fox. Now it was tufts of fur on bone, matted with blood, eye sockets brimful of maggots. I buried my nose and mouth in my sleeve.

A cold spot formed near the old willow. Liss picking nettles, watching the wood. *I can't risk it.*

The ice had to be a cold spot. And whatever had killed the fox was out here in the woods with me.

I had just started to leave when a twig snapped.

It must be a guard, a red-jacket on night patrol – except there were no dreamscapes nearby. I heard footsteps, too heavy to be human. I retreated into the hollow of an oak and switched off the torch.

Gallows Wood fell dark again.

The silence pressed against my ears. I could still hear those footsteps, moving closer – and then a wet chewing, the sound of teeth working at a carcass. Something had found the fox. Or come back for it.

Behind me, the spirit trembled. My eardrums were straining to the point that I could hear my watch, the hands chiselling away at my time limit. Even if there was a Buzzer here – and it had to be a Buzzer – I needed to keep heading back. Staying low and quiet, I continued towards the city, each step threatening to expose my position.

Three guttural clicks stopped me.

Every muscle in my body tensed. My lips clamped together, and I froze in place, eyes wide. I took a deep breath and reached for the æther.

Something was very wrong. For the first time, I noticed the complete lack of animals. Not even an earthworm crawled in this area.

The æther should always feel lighter than air. Now it was clotting, as if the cold had spread from the corporeal world and started to freeze it. Within that terrible heaviness, I sensed the inverse of a dreamscape, more absence than presence. A black hole in the æther.

Fear stilled my limbs and tightened my throat. I couldn't get moving until I distracted it. Distantly, I remembered the acid darts. Instinct told me to seek the safety of higher ground, but climbing would make too much noise. I felt along the soil, searching for something I could throw.

Every move I made seemed deafening – every breath, every rustle of my jacket. My fingers closed around a stone. I hurled it towards the black hole.

It hit a tree, then the ground. As the creature loped towards it, I thought I heard a buzzing, like a swarm of flies. It could have been outside or inside my head.

Nausea surged in my gut. Even after the oration, even after what David had told me, I had almost started to believe I would never see a Buzzer.

It was all I could do to keep myself standing. My hands and lips shook; my breathing shallowed. Could it hear my pulse, or smell my fear?

Was it aware of me?

The Buzzer rattled. I needed to leave, but I was light-headed, drained by the thickening in the æther. I slid off my backpack and reached inside, finding the gun with the acid dart. Only when I had it in my hand did I begin to run.

The Buzzer let out a deafening scream, but not a scream like any I had ever heard. It came as if from many throats – like hundreds of people howling in a ballroom, their voices overlapping, all roaring in a deranged cacophony. It set my hair on end and soaked my face in icy sweat.

I aimed into the black hole and fired.

The dart sizzled like hot fat in a pan. This time, the whole forest echoed the scream.

My spirit guide fled. I bolted as well, heading straight for the city.

A weight struck me square between the shoulders. The shock of it pitched me to the ground. Instinctively, I flung out a hand to stop my fall. My wrist bent too far back and broke. I strangled my scream a moment too late.

The Buzzer had just thrown a rock at me. It had enough intelligence to know how to extend its reach. My back ached from the impact.

My torch lay nearby. I grabbed it, shone it on the thing. In the heartbeat I had to look, I glimpsed two white pinpricks of eyes. A body that looked almost human, but somehow both withered and stretched. Had it stood up on two legs, it would have been taller than a Reph.

No sooner was I on my feet than it was on my tail. A rush of air went overhead – its elongated arm, grasping for me. I wove between the pines, hearing its claws scrape against bark, long and sharp as scythes. A dance of death with a grim reaper, seeking its harvest of bone.

My boots pounded. In the jolts of torchlight, I could have sworn I glimpsed dark shapes between the trees, but none of them had dreamscapes. Either I was seeing things, or those were more Buzzers.

Did they hunt in packs?

The flare gun was not an option. I would not fail this test. The memory of my cousin filled me, and hot rage flooded in, crushing the fear.

If I could survive the Dublin Incursion, I could survive Gallows Wood.

One good sprint would get me to the city, but my body was about to give out. The Buzzer moved in great lunges – its limbs cleared far more ground than mine. My agility was all that had kept me away from its claws.

I slewed down an incline, plastering myself in mud. At the bottom, I spotted a fallen tree and crawled inside, buying myself a few precious moments. Shaking with cold and exertion, I loaded another acid dart. Just as the Buzzer found my tree, I took out the syringe and punched the needle through my trousers, straight into my thigh.

A spring-loaded jolt of adrenalin shot into the muscle. Scion military adrenalin was designed to improve performance – not just to help the body function, but to wipe out pain, make you stronger. It would give me the last boost I needed.

I checked my watch, blotting my face. It was almost quarter to five.

Shit.

The Buzzer tore at the trunk. I scrambled out and hit it with the acid dart. This time, I stopped for long enough to see its grey flesh splitting open, steaming. Before it could recover, I launched into a dead run, my heart racing. The adrenalin had no effect on my sixth sense, but it made it easier to focus on the æther, so I could keep tabs on my pursuer.

Sweat drenched my clothes. I passed a rusted sign: USE OF DEADLY FORCE IS AUTHORISED. Good – for once, I was in desperate need of deadly force.

Gallows Wood was thinning. Ahead, I saw the towers of the House.

Warden was there. I refused to be eaten before I could rebuke him for this hellish night.

All that stood between us was a meadow and a rusted fence, which looked as if a toothpick and a wish held it together. It was high, but I sensed no ethereal battery. With no time to find a gap, I started to climb, jamming my boots into small toeholds. The adrenalin was suppressing the pain in my broken wrist, allowing me to use both hands. In the meadow, I could see the marker, the finish line – a flare planted in the ground, flanked by red-jackets. I swung a leg over the fence.

The Buzzer rammed straight into it. I fell off on the other side and hit the ground running. Another crash, and the Buzzer broke through.

David was with the red-jackets. They opened fire with old rifles. I dived to the ground and crawled for my life. The strongest acid in Scion was sizzling in its veins, and somehow the Buzzer was still charging after me.

The marker was close, but so was the beast. I twisted to face it and threw out my spirit, heading straight for the darkness.

Straight away, I knew I had fucked up. Other dreamscapes had defences – others tried to keep me out – but this one was a gaping maw, drawing me towards it. I fought like a fish on the end of a line.

Once you entered a black hole, you could never escape.

I jerked back to myself with a gasp. David lowered a gun with a strange trumpet barrel. A weighted net had flown out to entangle the Buzzer.

'You're welcome,' David said.

Hardly able to see, I planted my boot on the ground and got up, hearing the whole company run forward. With the very last ounce of strength I could muster, I dashed past the flare and collapsed in its fizzing red glow.

'Pass.' Merope looked down at me. 'By the narrowest of margins, 40.'

My own weak laugh was the last thing I heard.

PART TWO

SUMMER

18

MUTUAL TRUST

5 June 2059

There are certain memories that shape the person you become – memories that sink deep roots, changing the way you grow. For me, one of those memories was my escape from Gallows Wood.

The Rephs could be cruel, but they could also understand our pleas for mercy, even grant it. Their ancient enemies were something else. All that thing had wanted was to survive at any cost.

When I came round, it was still dark. Instead of a beamed ceiling, I was looking at a canopy. The gramophone was playing in the near distance. This time it was 'In the Gloaming' – a song I loved, performed in music halls.

My thoughts dragged. I couldn't quite remember what had happened before this. It reminded me of when Jaxon had first let me try real wine. I had the vague sense that I should get up, but the bed was so warm, and my wrist hurt. I drifted back into a drowse.

When I woke fully, the curtains had been opened around me, so I could see the window to my right, the fire snapping nearby. To my left, Warden sat in the bay of the opposite window, accompanied by another Reph. For some reason, I was in his bed.

I watched him, my eyes barely open. He was talking to Terebell.

They weren't speaking English. Their voices were soft and resonant, the words an unbroken glissade, sliding into one another with no stops for breath, more duet than conversation. A few spirits were nearby, almost dancing along. It reminded me of what happened when a whisperer played an instrument, or a polyglot sang.

Warden and Terebell were neither. Then again, none of the Rephs had auras I recognised. This must be the language of the Netherworld.

The two Rephs stood. As I continued to feign sleep, I remembered how I had got here. My fist clenched. The dirt of the forest lined the whites of my nails.

Terebell stopped talking. Her stance was stiff, her face hard. Warden touched her under the jaw – an intimate gesture, one I had never seen from a Reph. She seemed to soften, resting her forehead against his. They stayed that way for a moment, eyes closed, before she left the room.

Interesting.

Warden shut the door behind her. When I shifted on to my side, he looked at me.

'Paige,' he said. 'How are you feeling?'

'Fuck you.'

His eyes burned. 'Better, I take it.'

'You absolute bastard,' I seethed. 'The least you could have done was—'

At that point, I made the mistake of putting my left hand on the mattress and trying to brace my weight on it. I crumpled with a yelp.

'Your wrist is broken,' Warden said, deadpan.

'Yes. Thanks for the warning.' It had been splinted. 'Why am I in your bed?'

'You were cold.'

'Oh, *now* you care.' I gingerly moved my fingers and thumb. 'Nashira clearly doesn't mind how I die. You may as well let me freeze in the attic.'

'You would never have died in Gallows Wood.'

'Could have fooled me. I thought you said I wouldn't have to fight the Buzzers?'

'Nashira wanted you to encounter one. By forcing you to the height of terror, we tested your ability to use your gift under pressure.'

'So she could take notes, no doubt.' I used my other hand to sit up. 'I didn't sense anyone else in the woods. Who was going to stop it from eating me?'

'I assure you that the conditions of your test were tightly controlled.'

'That's a flam and a half. If you think a circle of salt is protection, you're off the cot.'

The slang flew out before I could stop it. Fortunately, Warden seemed oblivious.

'The Emim cannot enter a salt circle,' he said. 'It kept you safe until you woke.'

'Yes, after you had me sedated and dumped on my own in the woods,' I snapped. 'Could you not have just told me the next test was coming?'

'The second test assesses your ability to adapt. An element of surprise was necessary.'

'You think a lot of awful shit is necessary, Arcturus.' I shoved off the covers. 'Excuse me. I'll take the room with the leak.'

'You may not believe it,' Warden said, 'but I am trying to help you, Paige.'

'Go to hell.'

'I already exist on a level of hell.'

'Exist on one that isn't near mine.'

'No. You and I made a deal, and I do not take oaths lightly. It is June,' he said. 'Tonight, you will join me for supper.'

'Fine,' I growled.

I shoved off the heavy bedding. My hair was still full of twigs and pine needles. I was surprised he had let me near his silk pillows, the state I was in.

Then again, his staff was very good at cleaning.

'A bath has been drawn for you,' Warden said. 'Take as long as you wish.'

'You're … letting me have a bath?'

'To warm yourself.'

235

For once, I decided not to argue. I still made a point of slamming the door on my way out, just to rattle his cage.

Several candles flickered in the bathroom. Now Warden mentioned it, I did have a chill. My fingertips were grey, my lips a touch darker than usual.

It took a while to undress with a broken wrist. I craned to look at my back in the mirror. A deep bruise had cropped up between my shoulder blades. I took off the splint, finding the base of my thumb sore and swollen.

A deep, steaming bath awaited me, smelling of lavender. Little by little, I sank into it, savouring every inch of water. Once I was in, I almost shuddered with relief. It had been so long since I had last been wrapped in heat like this.

I let my head fall back, my left hand resting on the side. The windows misted over as I lay there, too exhausted to move. A cake of honey soap, a nail brush, and a jar labelled SHAMPOO had been left for me. Once I had mustered the will to sit up, I scrubbed myself one-handed with the soap and set to work on my hair.

Warden must be trying to butter me up for our supper. I had to keep my wits about me. His consort was still hunting for Jaxon.

I lounged in the bath until it was lukewarm, then rinsed my hair under the cold tap, dried off with a fluffy towel, and slotted my arms into a thick robe, my jaw clenched against the pain in my wrist. Unlike the massive towel, the robe was clearly made for a human. I went up to the attic for my comb and untangled my hair.

Warden awaited me in his bedchamber, where he and Terebell had been sitting. He gestured to the seat on the other side of the alcove.

'Please.'

I sat down. 'Not the parlour?'

'This window has a pleasant outlook. If it is not to your liking, we can use the parlour.'

'It's fine.'

Other than his goblet, the table built into the nook was set for one. I sat with my arms crossed, waiting for him to make conversation.

'Michael is preparing your supper,' he said. 'I trust you feel better.'

'Yes.' I scraped back my wet hair. 'I wouldn't mind having a bath more often.'

'Now you have passed your second test, that might be permitted.'

'I still won't thank you for giving me the most basic of dignities.'

'You are under no obligation to thank me.'

'Good.'

Warden took a sip from his goblet. I tapped my foot.

'Merope tells me you attempted to possess the Emite,' he said. 'You had a narrow escape. Their dreamscapes are like flytraps, ensnaring the nearest spirits – yours included, I should think.'

'I'll add it to the list of things you didn't warn me about, like cold spots,' I said. 'Is that how they get here from the Netherworld?'

'Yes. Cold spots are gateways to our world, but living flesh cannot pass through them.'

'So you can still go there, even though it's decaying.'

'For short periods of time. Sooner or later, we must return.'

'To feed,' I said.

'Yes.'

His eyes were gold tonight. I glanced away from them, out of the window, which overlooked the old tree in the courtyard. It showed no sign of leaves or blossom, but lanterns hung from its branches. Gail lit them at dusk on her way to the Porters' Lodge.

The fire warmed the bedchamber, drying my hair back into curls. In the parlour, the gramophone played 'I Don't Stand a Ghost of a Chance (With You)' – a jazz standard from the twentieth century, blacklisted for the grave offence of having the word *ghost* in its title, even though it had nothing to do with ghosts.

'You seem to like our music,' I said, when Warden refused to break the silence.

His tastes, in fact, were almost identical to mine. I chose not to voice this.

'Very much,' he said. 'Most of my records are from the free world. The quality of music has declined in Scion.'

'You can blame the dedicated censors at the Ministry of Arts. Where do you keep your records?'

'Above this very bedchamber.' He nodded to the ceiling. 'The upper floors have a separate entrance, to which I hold the only key. That is where I store my records, along with most of my books.'

I lifted an eyebrow. 'Should you be telling me this?'

'It is a petty treason. Nashira would simply confiscate my collection if you chose to inform her.' He locked eyes with me. 'One might wonder how you knew my records were blacklisted.'

I should never have given that away.

'The lyrics.' To deflect his attention, I nodded to his goblet. 'That drink illegal, too?'

'Indeed. This is nectar of the amaranth flower, mixed with red wine.'

'I've never heard of amaranth.'

'I used it to treat your wound from the ethereal fence. It alleviates the pain of spiritual injuries, and may heal them, if applied swiftly. I have a limited supply, or I would offer it to you. I suspect it would help you to recuperate from dreamwalking.'

Jaxon would never let me rest again if he got wind of this.

'You're not a dreamwalker,' I said. 'Why do you drink amaranth?'

'Old wounds.'

'From the Buzzers?'

Warden looked at me in silence, his eyes as lambent as the fire.

Michael arrived with my supper just then. He set it down on the table.

'Thank you, Michael,' Warden said. 'Perhaps you would care for a drink tonight, Paige.'

'Will it have a sedative in it?' I muttered. Michael gave me a sheepish look. 'I don't blame you, Michael. I'll take a coffee, if you have it.'

Michael nodded and left. I uncovered the dish, letting out a small cloud of steam. This time, my supper was a pie with a perfect fluted crust, served with a generous helping of gravy, creamy mash and buttered peas.

'This looks nice.' I poured the gravy. 'A bath *and* my first square meal in days. You're spoiling me. Truly, your generosity is unrivalled.'

'You have not even started your supper yet, Paige.' His eyes smouldered. 'Try not to waste all your sarcasm in one breath.'

'I'm impressed you understand it. There was me thinking you were all brawn and big words.' I cut a hefty wedge of pie. 'Don't think that interruption got you off the hook. I've seen a Buzzer now. I want to know why you would ever choose to fight one.'

Warden waited for me to take my first bite, as if he thought he might distract me.

'The red-jackets bear a difficult burden. When I can, I support them from the shadows,' he eventually said. 'I have the strength and means to seal the creatures back into the Netherworld. Their cold spots will always open again, thanks to the broken threshold and the nature of this city, but I can delay their return.'

'But the other Rephs won't risk the corruption you mentioned. That's why they send us.'

'Yes.'

He delivered all this with no emotion. As I ate, I looked at him, my brow creasing.

'Can I be honest with you?'

'By all means,' Warden said.

'I've lived with you for weeks, and I still don't understand you. You go out of your way to help the red-jackets. You're gentler than the other Rephs, but sometimes you look at me as if I'm the bane of your existence. You don't make sense to me.'

'Not understanding does not mean there is no conclusion.' He clasped his gloved hands. 'It simply means you have yet to discover it.'

'You could just tell me.'

'Perhaps I do not trust you, Paige.'

The absolute gall of him.

'Not that I *want* your trust,' I said, 'but I'll thank you to remember that you have all the power here, and I still haven't breathed a word to Nashira.'

'That may be because you have no evidence.'

'I would never give her anything. I don't care if you don't believe it. Think whatever you like of me.'

'Help me form an opinion.' Warden held my gaze. 'You have not only kept my secret. You are holding one of your own, Paige Mahoney.'

'What?'

He rose. I watched him remove a panel from the wainscoting. When he drew something from the hidden nook, I stiffened.

'I believe this belongs to you.' He sat back down with it. 'The night of your arrest, the Overseer mistimed his shot, causing you to fall. The only reason you survived is because your backpack caught on a wire.'

My heart pounded.

'Aludra is responsible for examining our prisoners' effects. Fortunately, I saw your backpack first,' Warden said. 'None of the other detainees were trained to run or climb, as you were. None of them had this.'

He held up *On the Merits of Unnaturalness*. I could feel myself turning grey.

'I should have known,' I said in a whisper. 'You would never give a human a bath or a meal without a return, would you, Warden?'

'This is not an interrogation, Paige.'

He placed the pamphlet on the table.

'Aludra did not see this,' he said, 'but she and a human assistant did make other observations. Aside from the marks on your palm, you also have other scars on your hands and arms, consistent with defence wounds. One of your boots had an improvised pocket for a knife. Your hands were callused, indicating a familiarity with climbing and strength training. You carried a pistol and ammunition that could only have been acquired on the black market at significant cost.

'Your database entry states that you are a waitron at Oxidate, a bar in Holborn,' he continued. 'I decided to test this claim. No regular patrons have ever seen or heard of you. Your employer has continued to pay you, despite your conspicuous absence.'

Bill was a local voyant. In exchange for exemption from syndicate tax, he paid and vouched for me, giving the impression that I had a steady job. I smoothed it out by withdrawing the money and handing it to Jaxon. For three years, that deal had allowed me to live a double life.

Jaxon had forgotten to tell Bill I was missing.

Shit.

'Even if you did work at Oxidate,' Warden said, 'payment for ossistas is low. You could not have acquired an illegal gun after only three years of work.'

'What do you know about the cost of illegal guns?'

'There is also the matter of the phone found after your arrest. Your fingerprints were detected on its surface, but you are not the registered owner. Like the gun, this device must have come from the black market. Either someone purchased these supplies for you, or you have an undeclared source of income.'

I was starting to sweat.

'The device had made just one call, to a public telephone box,' Warden said. 'Why is that?'

'It was a misdial,' I said.

'I doubt it.' The slightest tilt of his head. 'You mentioned having voyant friends. Did any of them belong to the syndicate?'

He had me. At this point, a white lie would serve me better than denial.

'I'm a thief – lockpicking, finewiring, that sort of thing,' I finally said. 'I steal for a local fence. They pay me upfront and sell my spoils at a profit. I'm good enough to have afforded the gun, but I'm small fry.'

'Who did you call?'

'The fence. I hoped they could help me, but it was a long shot.'

'Why does the oxygen bar pay you?'

'I needed a cover to get a travel permit for that section. It's where the best marks are,' I said. 'Bill cleans my record; I don't pick on his customers. He doesn't know I'm voyant. He just likes me.'

Warden looked at my clenched hand, then flicked his gaze up to catch mine.

'I think not,' he said.

I hitched up a smile. 'What, you can't imagine that anyone would like me?'

'You are both too rare and too proud to be a pickpocket. Your gift would have drawn other eyes in the underworld.' He nodded to *On the Merits*. 'You implied there is a hierarchy. The author of this pamphlet may have helped create it. He would clearly have an interest in a gift like yours. We believe he is known as the White Binder.'

Fuck.

Jaxon hadn't written under that name. Warden connecting the two meant he knew a little more about the syndicate than I had anticipated.

'The White Binder would skin a kitten just to shine his shoes with it,' I said. 'You think he would ever stoop to employing a brogue?'

Another lie. No one in the syndicate had ever cared that I was Irish, least of all Jaxon Hall – but if I could make Warden believe it was a hindrance even in the underworld, it might keep him off my scent.

Warden just looked at me. His face held less emotion than a washed dishplate, but I still had a strong notion that he didn't believe a word.

A lie is harder to distinguish when it dances with the truth.

'I did ask to work for him,' I said. 'He turned me down. I tried to nick his pocket watch to prove myself to him, but all I could get was that rag.'

I was building a wall of lies brick by brick, with no time to put mortar on it. Warden was clearly in the mood to give it a tremendous push.

'I understand why you would spin this tale.' His voice was soft. 'What would your friends in the Rookery say, if you did work for a man like the White Binder?'

My body was already so tense, it took the lightest touch to spring it. I snapped out of my seat, my spirit rearing, the taste of blood in my throat.

Warden looked me right in the eyes, daring me.

Michael chose that moment to return with my coffee. Seeing our stances, he placed the tray between us and saw himself out, hands raised.

'You may think I'm some opportunistic lowlife,' I said softly, 'or you might be goading me into becoming one. Either way, I will not turn nose. You can waterboard me, you can beat me senseless, but you will not pry one more word out of me about that pamphlet. Got it?'

Warden stood as well. For a cold moment, I thought he would actually call my bluff and hit me. Instead, he held up *On the*

Merits of Unnaturalness, forcing me to look at it, the cause of my downfall.

And then he threw it into the fire.

'You have no evidence against me,' he said. 'Now I have none against you.'

I stared at it, then at him. 'Why?'

'An overture to mutual trust.'

I walked to the fire. The last of the pamphlet curled up and vanished.

'We still know too much about each other,' I said. 'At this point, you'd be wiser to get rid of me.'

'Perhaps I am not wise.'

Warden joined me by the flames. Our auras brushed, sending a brief shiver through me.

'Nashira holds a feast at her residence at the beginning of each season. I received an invitation for you,' he said. 'It explains why she wanted you to be tested so quickly. She wishes you to join the summer feast.'

'Rephs don't eat.' I glanced at him. 'What does she do at these feasts?'

'She asks questions.'

'You're sure she isn't going to surprise me with a knife to the throat?'

'You will be killed when I deem you ready,' he said, 'but she has requested that I prepare you in time to be executed at the Bicentenary.'

Just as Liss had suspected.

'Put me out of my misery.' I watched the flames. 'How is she going to do it?'

Warden was silent for so long, I thought he wouldn't answer. Finally, he turned to me, one hand on the mantelpiece. The fire crackled.

'What do you know of angels?'

'A class of breacher,' I said. 'A guardian angel is formed by sacrifice. The spirit lingers to protect the person they died to save. An archangel is similar, but stays to protect a bloodline. They're both rare.'

No point in feigning ignorance now.

'Nashira can make a third sort of angel,' Warden said. 'If she kills a clairvoyant, she can not only trap their spirit, but misappropriate their gift. We call these fallen angels. They are bound to remain with their murderer.'

The death I feared – trapped with an immortal binder, used for all eternity.

'She's your consort,' I said quietly. 'No matter what you do to help me, I can never trust you. Not when you choose to be with her.'

'Do not judge too quickly, little dreamer.'

I shot him a quizzical look. 'Who are you calling *little*, Reph?'

Warden made a point of looking down at me from his tremendous height. I defensively stood up as straight as I could, but still got no higher than his shoulder.

'Wait.' I raised an eyebrow. 'Are you trying to tease me?'

'Am I succeeding?'

It surprised me enough that I smiled against my will, hiding it behind my hair.

He could still be trying to break my guard. I had heard the way they laughed – this had to be the same mimicry, to convince me he was human. I couldn't let him win my trust like that, with false promises.

But he *had* burned the pamphlet.

'I'd like to visit the Rookery,' I said. 'Do I get my red tunic yet?'

'Not yet. You have one more test to pass.' Before I could ask, he turned away. 'You should finish your supper and coffee. After that, you may go.'

Now it was summer, the performers were shaking and airing their bedding, drying their clothes on lines they had strung between the shacks. The city was still cold and hazy with fog, but they were trying, as if they could make the seasons matter by sheer force of will.

The Rephs were on to me. They had read my body like a map, down to the nicks I had from fighting off rival gangs and thieves.

But only Warden knew for sure. Without the damning pamphlet, I still had an inch of room to manoeuvre.

Liss was in her shack, wrapped in the blanket I had got for her, cooking one of her foragers' stews. When I came in, she released her breath.

'What happened to your wrist?'

'I fell on it,' I said. 'It's broken.'

'There was a rumour you took your test,' Liss said. 'Did you pass?'

'By the skin of my teeth. Can I join you?'

'You'll get no love from the red-jackets for associating with harlies.'

'I don't care about them.'

Liss gave me a tired smile and patted a cushion. Once I was settled, she offered me a bowl.

'You keep it,' I said. 'Warden just gave me something to eat.'

'He must be pleased you passed,' Liss said. 'You should get plenty of food now, to keep your strength up for patrolling Gallows Wood.'

'He said I won't be stationed there.'

'Where will you be, then?'

'Here, I hope.'

'That's nice to know.' Liss reached for a ladle. 'The red-jackets have been ... confrontational, of late. We're not doing so many shows while we prepare for the Bicentenary. They're getting bored, and when they're bored, they make their own entertainment in here.'

'I'll stop them.'

'Just be careful. The Rephs can always revoke your red tunic.'

'At least I'll have used it for good.' I adjusted my splint. 'How's training?'

'Hard work, but at least it's indoors. Now we've all prepared our routines, we've moved from the Fell Theatre to the Guildhall.'

'Where's that?'

'Magdalen Walk, up near the House. That's where the Bicentenary will be. Beltrame wants us to get used to that space.'

Julian ducked into the shack, holding two cups. 'Paige,' he said, looking relieved. 'I overheard David saying you took your test. Did you pass?'

'Just.' I held up my left hand, snug in its splint. 'With a broken wrist.'

'I'd say you got off lightly, from the injuries we see around here.' He handed a cup to Liss. 'Do you think I should take my test, or refuse?'

'I don't know what yours will be like. I had to get back to the city while being stalked by a Buzzer.'

'Paige, keep your voice down,' Liss said under her breath. 'You're not supposed to tell us.'

'My test was controlled,' I said, quieter. 'You might have to fight or hunt one. If they tell you to do that, I'd get the yellow streak and come out here. It's not worth your life, Jules.'

Julian nodded slowly. 'Why was yours controlled?'

'Nashira wants to execute me herself. Warden confirmed it.'

Liss stared at me. 'He did?'

'Yes. You were right. She plans to kill me for my gift at the Bicentenary.' I drew my knees to my chest. 'If she does it then, I'll have been here for half a year when I die. It's poetic, really.'

'Why?'

'That's how long a farmer waits to send a lamb for butchering.'

My father had told me that, one dark night when despair over-whelmed him. There had been a slaughterhouse a few miles from our dairy farm. It had been knocked down by the time I was born, but my father had walked near it on his way home from school.

'Warden has been training me so Nashira can absorb my gift at its best,' I said. 'He's the one who decides when I'm ready.'

Julian grimaced. 'So if you want to live longer, you need to get him to … like you?'

'Fat chance of that happening.'

Still, Warden didn't seem to hate me quite as much as he once had. By burning *On the Merits*, he had severed my link to the underworld, protecting my privacy. He wanted us to trust each other.

'I'll find you something for your wrist,' Liss said. 'Jules, could I have a few minutes with Paige?'

'Of course.' Julian stood. 'Jos wanted to go looking for berries, anyway.'

'You might find raspberries in the old physic garden opposite Magdalen. It's not usually guarded, but it is overgrown.' Liss passed her clippers to him. 'Make sure you don't go near the glasshouse. Duckett grows his aster there, and he'll not be happy if you tamper with it.'

I lifted an eyebrow. 'Do the Rephs know about it?'

'Aye, I think so. They mostly tolerate Duckett.'

'Noted,' Julian said.

He left the shack. Liss went into her stocks of herbs.

'Still no willow bark, but I did find some comfrey,' she said. 'They call it knitbone.'

Liss set about making a poultice. With care, she soaked the leaves in boiling water, then cut and mashed them as much as she could, slathered the pulp on my swollen wrist, and wrapped it in strips of cloth.

'Leave that on for the rest of tonight.' She touched my elbow. 'How are you feeling about the Bicentenary?'

'I still haven't found a way out of here,' I said. 'My only hope is to fight.'

Liss looked me in the eyes.

'You said you've never heard your cards read,' she said. 'Would you like to see your future?'

'Now?'

'Aye.' She paused. 'Have you ever had any sort of reading?'

'No,' I admitted.

I had been tempted once or twice, but I had never been convinced that glimpsing the future was a good idea. Even though I had met cartomancers before, I had only ever used cards – unclaimed ones – for games of tarock and tarocchi.

'Go on,' I said.

Liss took her deck from its box and placed it between us. This was her favoured numen, one she had used exclusively for years. I could feel the strength of the bond.

'Give me your hand,' she said.

I held out my good one. Liss grasped it. An expression of intense concentration took over her face as her fingers dipped into the deck. One by one, she removed seven cards and placed them face down on the floor.

'I use the ellipse spread,' she said. 'While your aura is in contact with mine, I choose seven cards and interpret them. Not all broadsiders will give you the same interpretation of a card, so don't be too nervous.' She released my hand. 'The first one tells us something about your past. I might get a glimpse of your memories.'

'You *see* memories?'

'Just sometimes.' Liss allowed herself a faint smile. 'Not all of us get visions, but some do. Even *On the Merits* acknowledged it.'

She turned over the first card.

'Five of Cups,' she said, closing her eyes. 'You lost something when you were very small. There's a man with auburn hair. It's his cups that are spilled.'

'My father,' I said.

'Yes. You're standing behind him, speaking to him. He doesn't answer.' Without opening her eyes, Liss flipped the next card. It was upside down. 'This is the present – King of Wands, inverted.' Her red lips pursed. 'He controls you. Even now, you can't escape his hold.'

'Warden?'

'I don't think so, but he is an authority figure – a man shaped by cruelty. His expectations of you are too high. You're afraid of him.'

Jaxon.

'Right.' I cleared my throat. 'Can you see him?'

'I see his wand – a staff of bone.' She was falling into a trancelike state. 'He wears a crown of many secrets, and the shadows are his throne.'

I needed to confess. It was too hard to hold it inside any longer.

After this reading was over, I would tell her the name of the King of Wands.

'Next is the future.' She turned the card, drawing a sharp breath. 'The Devil. This card represents a force of hopelessness, restriction, fear – but you've given into it yourself. Whatever power this person will have over you, you will be able to escape it.'

'Is *that* Warden?'

'I don't know.' She opened her eyes for a moment, offering a smile. 'Don't worry. The next card will tell you what to do when the time comes.'

I looked down at the fourth card. 'The Lovers?'

'Yes.' As Liss closed her eyes again, her voice dropped to a monotone. 'I can't see anything, but there's tension between spirit and flesh. The card has weight. This will be a pillar of your life.'

Her fingers crept towards the next card. I pushed my hair behind my ear, waiting.

I really hadn't expected the Lovers. The Major Arcana wasn't always to be taken literally, but that card did often represent an intimate relationship, from what little I knew about it.

'External influences,' Liss said. 'Death, inverted.' She showed me the skeletal rider. 'Death crops up in most voyants' readings, but not usually in this position.' Her eyes flickered beneath their lids. 'This far ahead, my sight gets hazy. I know the world will change around you; death itself will work in different ways. By delaying the change, you'll prolong your own suffering.'

'Can I avoid any of this?'

'That is beyond our ken,' she said. 'The sixth card points to your hopes and fears.' She picked it up, ran her thumb over it. 'Eight of Swords.'

The card showed a blindfolded woman, bound in a circle of upturned swords.

'I can see you.' Her voice cracked, her skin glowing with sweat. 'You can't move in any direction with ease. You can stay in one place, trapped and stagnant, or feel the pain of the swords. All paths lead to anguish.'

This was a nightmarish spread. I wasn't sure I could stand to see the last card.

'And now the end.' Liss reached for it. 'The seventh.'

The æther trembled.

'Wait.' I caught her wrist, my nerve failing. 'Liss, I need to tell you something.'

'What is it?'

'The King of Wands.' I spoke in a whisper. 'I think it represents my boss.' Liss shook her head, frowning. 'I'm in the syndicate.'

'Okay.' Liss was out of her trance now, her face softening. 'It's all right, Paige. I thought you might be, with your gift. We all do what we must to—'

'No. You need to know who I am,' I forced out. 'I'm not just a member of the syndicate. I'm a mollisher. My mime-lord is the White Binder.'

She stared at me, her lips parting.

'What have we here?'

I let go of Liss. Three red-jackets had just sauntered into the shack. One of them seized her by her other wrist, yanking her to her feet.

'Hello, Silks,' he said. 'Reading for your guest, are you?'

'Emil, I was just—'

'You were *just* using the æther in private,' said another, a woman, with the air of a committed jobsworth. 'You only read for your keeper, I.'

'You know I have no keeper, Kath.'

'Gomeisa still calls you. Your gift is only for his use.'

'Leave her alone,' I said.

They looked at me.

The woman had thick mousy hair, drawn into a bun, showing that one of her ears had been cropped. The two men looked so alike that they could only be twins, sharing the same dimples and blue eyes. The only difference I could see was that one of them was missing half a forefinger.

They were all in their twenties or early thirties, with a good number of scars. None of them were from my Bone Season.

'There you are,' one of the men said. 'We heard you passed your second test. We've been hoping to run into you, 40.'

'Have you, now?'

'Suhail told our keepers that we couldn't find you, that day you missed the curfew. They beat us.'

'And you've been sore ever since.' I sighed. 'Sounds like you've a problem with the Rephs, not me. I didn't beat you.'

'They're good to us.'

'Yes, they sound it.'

Liss shook her head, still restrained by the other man. I stared them all down.

'You don't deserve the honour of a red tunic,' Kath sneered. 'You show up here like you own the place – throwing your special gift around, using it to attack the Rephs. Warden didn't even discipline you, from the looks of it.'

'I didn't ask to come here,' I pointed out. 'Your keeper take that ear off?'

'It was the price I paid.'

'We've been here for years,' one of the men said. 'This is our place.'

I smiled. 'So, what, you're here to put me in mine?'

'You understand.'

'Well, look at you. The big man.' I arched an eyebrow. 'Nashira will crop more than your ears if you kill me. You sure you want to try?'

'We're not here to kill you, brogue,' Emil said, with a short laugh. 'Since the Warden didn't take *your* ear, we thought we'd serve justice ourselves.'

'It's only fair.' Kath unsheathed her own blade. 'It won't hurt for long.'

Hector had tried to intimidate me when I first joined the underworld at sixteen. He had wanted the pleasure of introducing me to its violence. It was only the arrival of a poltergeist that had stopped him.

'Give it your best shot,' I said.

Kath took a step towards me. I stood to meet her, reminding myself to be careful. This woman had been training for a decade. She was tall and strong, and must have survived many patrols in Gallows Wood.

Emil and his brother were both mediums, while Kath was some kind of augur. I had a feeling none of them were going to use their gifts.

They wanted blood.

'Warden isn't here to save you,' Emil said, keeping hold of Liss. 'What are you going to do, 40?'

His brother reached me first, going straight for my broken wrist. Quick as a flash, I jabbed my other fist into the hollow of his throat, making him reel away.

'Oliver,' Emil barked.

He shoved Liss aside and flew at me, grabbing me hard by the neck. Before I could so much as choke, I sliced both my arms upward between his, forcing his elbows apart, and shoved him back far enough to kick him in the chest. A flicker of surprise crossed his face as he went sprawling.

They must think Warden had pampered me for three months. Nick had taught me to fight long before that. My wrist throbbed as I backed away.

This space was too small for a scrap, and I was outnumbered. I ducked a furious swing from Oliver before Kath clutched a fistful of my hair and drove my head into the wall. Next thing I knew, she was on my back, and the knife was at my ear. I managed to roll her off me and pin her, only for her to do the same to me. I caught hold of her wrist, stopping her blade an inch from my cheek.

Kath screamed through her teeth. My arm shook. I reached up and tried to gouge her eye, but her elbow was on my head, the knife at the top of my ear. I felt the hot pull of it through my skin, the blood.

With full intent, I threw my spirit, striking her dreamscape with the force of a clapper against a bell. She rolled off me with a strangled cry.

'Fucking brogue—'

'Oh, get a new one,' I ground out.

'Kath, stop it!' Liss tried to haul her away from me. 'Has Kraz made you this cruel?'

'He's my keeper,' Kath said, glaring at her. 'I owe him this life.'

'He took your ear!'

'And gave me a second chance! I refuse to be like you, living in my own filth, content to be nothing,' Kath spat. 'You're pathetic, Liss.'

Liss lifted a hand to her cheek. I couldn't bear to see the hurt in her eyes.

'We're not done,' I said to Kath.

She stiffened. The moment she rounded on me, I drove my fist straight into her chin, snapping her head to the side.

Kath stumbled and made a grab for my broken wrist, twisting it as she pulled me with her. Eyes watering, I dug my nails into the skin between her thumb and forefinger, my pain so bad I was almost retching.

Oliver was on me next, trying the exact same move as his brother, trying to choke me. I clamped my good hand on the back of his neck and cracked my forehead straight into his nose, drawing a shriek of pain. I tried again to get to Liss, only for Emil to flatten me with a punch to the face, bursting my lip like a grape.

'Paige!'

Julian was suddenly there. From his bloodshot eye and swollen cheek, they must have reefed him before they even reached the shack. Seeing me on the floor, he wrapped a chokehold around Emil.

'This how you grubbers get your kicks?' It was the first time I had ever seen him angry. 'This what you do when you can't laugh at dancers?'

'You're bones, 26,' Emil wheezed. I got back up. 'Wait until Aludra hears about—'

'Tell her. I'd sooner be dead than be one of you.'

Julian yanked him around and socked him upside of the jaw. Jos appeared in the doorway, looking fearful. A few other performers gathered behind him.

'Rymore,' Cyril called.

'Jos,' I said thickly, 'run to Magdalen and get the Warden. Tell him I'm in trouble.'

'Don't even think about it,' Kath shouted at him. 'You find Suhail, do you hear me?'

Jos looked at me, then at Liss, then at Kath. His stare became defiant.

'I'm going to get the Warden,' he said.

'You little traitor,' Emil bellowed as Jos bolted. 'Suhail will deal with all of you!'

Kath lunged at me. Still disconcerted from using my spirit against her, I buckled under her furious charge. Liss came rushing to help, but Kath lashed out with her knife, making Liss yelp. My chest jolted. I shoved myself straight up off the floor, intending to disarm Kath.

'Hurry up, Kath,' Emil snarled, still wrestling with Julian. 'Just do it!'

But Kath had frozen, staring at Liss, whose arm was bleeding. Oliver moved instead, taking me down at the waist. His weight crushed the breath from my chest. As I wrestled against him, a yellow glow flared in the corner of my eye.

The stove. Someone had knocked it over, and flames were racing across the floor.

Liss saw, her eyes widening. Julian and Emil fought in a fury, teeth bared. Unless we could stop this, we were all about to burn to death together. Desperate, I grabbed at Oliver, finding his hand on my shoulder; I tried to roll out from under him, but he was thick with muscle.

A grey haze of smoke was filling the shack. Liss scrambled to gather her cards, scraping the deck back together. Kath got to one of them first.

'Oh, look.' She waved it at me with a laugh. 'I think this one's for you, 40.'

The card showed a man lying flat on his front, staked to the ground by ten swords.

'No,' Liss said hotly, trying to snatch it back. 'That wasn't the last—'

'Shut your trap,' Kath shouted at her. Oliver had me in a head-lock, which I writhed and kicked to escape. 'Useless shitsayer. You think it's so hard to dance for your keep while we're out there getting eaten alive?'

'You didn't have to go back. We had a life here,' Liss said, tears springing. 'Kathy—'

'Shut up!' Kath was beyond anger now, heedless of the spreading fire. 'Every night I'm out in the woods, trying to stop the Buzzers ripping out your worthless throat, all so you can sit on your nancy and play with cards and ribbons. I'll never be like you again, you hear me?'

I used to share this place with a friend, but she couldn't bear the shame of being a performer. After a bad winter, she convinced her keeper to give her one more chance. My eyes stung from the smoke, the frustration. *She's been a bone-grubber ever since …*

Julian hauled Emil outside. 'Paige,' he shouted at me. 'Paige, the fire!'

It was raging now, licking up the walls, the bed erupting into flame. This place was about to go up like a tinderbox.

I risked using my spirit again. Oliver let me go with a scream, as if I had scalded him. I dived for the cards, but Kath got there first. Her boot clipped the side of my head. She seized the deck and let out a joyless laugh. Liss watched her in absolute terror, the fire reflecting in her eyes.

'We are not the same,' Kath hissed at her. 'We will never be the same, Liss Rymore.'

She flung the entire deck into the fire.

Liss let out a gut-wrenching scream. Every hair on my nape stood on end.

The cards burned up like dry leaves. As the images curled, the æther strained. As Liss lunged for them, I finally reached her, catching her wrists.

'It's too late, Liss—'

She had already plunged her fingers into the fire. Weeping in denial, she watched the cards blacken, one numen consuming another.

'Liss, come on,' I said, coughing. 'Come on!'

Kath had frozen again. Liss stared up at her, tears on her cheeks. I pulled her limp arm over my shoulders and towed her out of the shack.

In the Rookery, half the performers were saving their meagre supplies, while others were running for water. Eyes raw from the smoke, I tried to carry Liss, whose strength was already failing. Julian met us in the food shack and lifted her. We shouldered and shoved our way from the settlement and ran towards the Townsend.

'Paige,' Julian called over the din, 'what happened to Liss?'

'Kath torched her cards.'

Julian put her down gently on the steps. Her face was already tinged with grey, her lips with shadow. She choked out heartbroken sobs, her red hands trembling. I cradled her to me. Her small body heaved.

'I'm sorry,' I whispered.

'Paige,' she sobbed out.

I stroked her tangled hair. She had been using those cards for at least a decade; they might even have belonged to her father. Without her favoured numen, she could no longer connect to the æther.

Liss was about to go into spirit shock.

The Rookery was ablaze. Kath stumbled from inside, soot and disbelief on her face. Behind her, Terebell and Graffias appeared. Graffias summoned a huge spool of spirits and sent them into the settlement, while Kath bore down on us, still with the knife in her hand.

'None of that had to happen if you had just taken your fucking punishment,' she said hoarsely to me. 'Get up, 40. I'm not done with you.'

Julian took charge of Liss. I stood, facing Kath.

'I know you've been here for a while,' I said coldly, 'but what happened to you in Scion that you would take that much pleasure in power?'

'I put Liss out of her misery. What is the point of living like her, with no hope, no ambition, nothing?' she burst out. 'She's – she's pointless.'

Kath had barely finished speaking before her nose started to bleed, and her face purpled with an influx of pressure. When she touched her nose and saw the blood on her fingertips, she stared at me.

'Say it again,' I said quietly.

Her brow tightened. 'What are you?'

Before I could show her, Warden arrived in a sweep of black cloak, followed by Gail and a breathless Jos. Gail ran straight for the fire, armed with an extinguisher. Warden saw me and strode towards us.

'What has occurred here?'

My jaw shook. All my pressure was still locked on Kath.

'Stand down,' Warden said to me. 'Temper your spirit.'

I drew a slow breath and managed to settle it, but I couldn't unclench my fist.

Liss was starting to slump over. Julian wrapped her in his arms, cupping her lolling head to his chest. If the Rephs realised she was on the brink of spirit shock, they might see her as a lost cause and kill her.

'Three red-jackets set fire to the Rookery,' Julian said to Warden. 'They wanted to punish Paige.'

'For what?'

By now, a crowd of performers had gathered by the steps. Several red-jackets sprinted from Exeter and Balliol, straight into the burning Rookery.

'Go on, Kath,' I said, my voice dangerously soft. 'Care to tell the Warden to his face why you ambushed his tenant?'

Kath was turning white to the roots of her hair, as if everything she had done was finally sinking in.

'Fine,' I said. 'I will.' I looked up at Warden. 'Kath is of the opinion that you let me off lightly for missing the curfew in April. She thought she'd do your job for you and crop my ear for my offence.'

Warden looked at her. 'Is this true?'

Kath swallowed.

Suhail Chertan now emerged from the Residence of Balliol, along with a hysterical Overseer. Kath suddenly went to her knees before Warden.

'I ask your forgiveness, Warden,' she said, trembling. 'It wasn't my place.'

'Your keeper is Kraz Sargas, is it not?'

'Yes.'

'Fortunate that he is here, else I would be forced to punish your insolence.'

A Reph with enormous muscles to spare had come to see what the fuss was about. He had the features of a Sargas, with golden hair down to his waist. Kath looked as if she might faint; I couldn't blame her.

Kraz Sargas had seen us, too. He approached at a slow pace, adjusting his long gloves. The performers made way for him, giving him a wide berth.

'Arcturus,' he said in a rumbling voice. 'What seems to be the problem?'

'Our tenants have come to blows,' Warden said. 'We should resolve the matter in private, Kraz.'

'Here is as good a place as any.' Kraz cocked his head. 'What have you done, 62?'

'She set fire to the Rookery,' one of the performers shouted. 'She's burned us out of house and home, like they don't take enough from us!'

'It wasn't just her,' Julian said. 'There were two others. They attacked 1 and 40.'

'The famous 40.' Kraz looked at me. 'Since this disagreement is between our tenants, perhaps we should have them fight it out, Arcturus. I believe their kind used to force animals to do battle for their amusement. We could make a new sport out of it – human baiting.'

Warden moved in front of me. I had never seen more fear in the performers' eyes.

'I beg you, blood-heir. It wasn't my idea.' Kath turned to him, desperate. 'It was 16 and 17. They told me the Warden hadn't punished 40.'

'Allow me to be sure I understand,' Kraz said, his tone almost polite. 'You questioned the blood-consort's decision – his authority, by extension?'

'She attacked Suhail,' she said weakly. 'Why should she have a red tunic?'

'It is not your place to have thoughts, 62.' His eyes were a pale yellow, making him look wolfish. 'I gave you a second chance, but a third would be indulgence. Stand up.'

Shaking, Kath did as she was told.

Kraz gave her a soulless look. A moment later, he raised a massive hand and struck her, hard enough that she was dead before she hit the ground.

Gasps and cries went up at once. Some perverse instinct made me step closer to Warden. His gaze snapped to me. I wanted to kick myself.

'There. The matter is resolved.' Kraz clasped his gloved hands in front of him. 'I trust you are satisfied with this outcome, Arcturus.'

'Nashira may not be,' Warden said. 'A decade of training has just gone to waste.'

'A disobedient human is a purposeless one. Surely you would agree.'

Warden replied with a small nod, but I saw the tightening in his jaw.

Kath lay still on the cobblestones. Ten years of toil and suffering in this hell, and her keeper had cracked her skull without a second thought.

'Slovens and cravens,' Suhail roared at us. 'Come and extinguish this fire!' The shaken performers hastened to obey, leaving their possessions by the steps. 'If I find out this was your doing, you will pay for it, 40!'

'Come,' Warden said, softly enough that only I could hear. 'Let us not tempt his ire.'

'Wait.' I went to Julian, breathing in his ear: 'I broke the lock on the Old Library. Hide Liss in there until the dust settles. Keep her alive, Jules.'

'I will.' Julian grasped my elbow. 'Go on, before Suhail makes a scene.'

Liss made a faint sound. Her aura was already starting to flicker. I pressed her cold hand one more time before I followed Warden.

19

TOURIST TRAP

26 August 2057

The fifth and six members of our group were found in 2057, over a year after I joined. It happened during a vicious heatwave, rare in the Scion Citadel of London. One morning in August, a local courier reported two new voyants to Jaxon. Neither of them had declared themselves.

Jaxon dispatched me to deal with it. By then, he had already made me his mollisher. At only seventeen years old, I was a future mime-queen.

I worked myself to the bone for the honour. Jaxon was mellow and charming when pleased, but quick to anger, with a cruel streak – a man as mercurial as the Thames. He was soft on Nick, given his demanding job in Scion – it helped that Nick was generous with his earnings – but Eliza and I were expected to give our whole selves to the underworld.

By and large, I was happy to oblige. I had blossomed in the syndicate, as I never had at school. Jaxon paid me well, and I had my own room at the den. My father had asked me to visit several times, but I kept putting him off. I was tired of pretending to be amaurotic.

As mollisher, one of my duties was to inform new arrivals of their duty to pay the syndicate tax. It had been difficult at first – one seer had already pleaded for leniency – but I soon hardened myself. Jaxon was like a rough stone on the hands, callusing all he touched.

Led by the courier, I found the newcomers in a coffeehouse on Gower Street with a group who were clearly not from Scion. Confirming my suspicions, I tailed them to the Anchotel by Euston Station, where visitors from the free world stayed.

A false alarm. Jaxon sent the hapless courier away with a clip on the ear and a warning not to waste his precious time again.

Nobody expected tourists to respect syndicate law, but the pair had intrigued me. One of them was probably a sensor – relatively common in London – but the other had an aura I had never sensed before.

Jaxon overheard me telling Nick about it. He sauntered in with a glass of absinthe, leaning against the doorway.

'This might be worth a little more investigation,' he said thoughtfully. 'Why would two young voyants risk their lives to visit Scion?'

'They might not know,' Nick said. 'Paige didn't.'

'Perhaps we could enlighten them.' Jaxon had that ambitious gleam in his eye. 'Paige has done her part, Dr Nygård. Your turn now.'

Nick looked sceptical, but nodded.

He soon had some information for us. It pertained to the Grand Conference.

Every five years, the University of Scion London held an event to educate outsiders, inspiring them to embrace the anchor. Eager tourists, politicians, celebrities and investors were invited from all over the free world. They travelled by private charter and basked in luxury for a week. Some of them would continue on the Grand Tour to Paris, Stockholm and Athens.

Scion was seducing them. It wanted them to return to their countries and campaign for conversion, reducing the need for expensive invasions.

At present, the Grand Conference was in full swing. Jaxon despised it. For an entire week, his section was flooded with Vigiles, whose presence disrupted syndicate business. Worse still, there were tour guides on every corner. Scion paid them to keep the visitors on approved paths, avoiding prisons and execution grounds.

On the third day of this, I got up to find Jaxon standing by a window.

'I am offended by the number of witless amaurotics in my eyeline,' he said icily. 'When will they flop back to their own banal lives?'

I joined him. Three laughing men had just emerged from the oxygen bar on the other side of the street. They were easy to clock as tourists – their clothes were bright and loose, unusual in London.

'I could give them all a headache,' I offered.

'Oh, the temptation.' A dark chuckle escaped him. 'No. Don't waste that extraordinary gift on people so unpalatably ordinary, Paige.'

Nick sent a message at midday. The mysterious pair were attending the Grand Conference on a programme funded by a university in Boston.

So far, neither of them had been detained. Then again, I doubted Scion would risk arresting a pair of outsiders, even if they were unnatural.

'Their names are Nadine Arnett and Ezekiel Sáenz,' Nick told us over supper. 'Nadine is the student, and Ezekiel is her guest on the programme.'

Jaxon twirled a chip on his fork. 'I trust you have more than that, Dr Nygård.'

'As if I would dare to rest on my laurels.' Nick cut a sliver of fish. 'I managed to brush past them while they were on a walking tour – close enough to feel their auras. Paige was right. Nadine is a whisperer.'

Jaxon gave me a nod. Whisperers were a kind of sensor. They could hear the voices of spirits and channel their tiny vibrations into instruments.

'A pretty gift,' Jaxon mused, 'but by no means ... groundbreaking.'

'Come on, Jaxon.' Eliza gave him a knowing smile. 'I wasn't groundbreaking, either.'

'Ah, but you are simply exceptional, my dear.'

'Nadine could be exceptional, too. You won't know unless you give her a chance.'

Eliza Renton was our trance medium, a specialist in mime-art. Born within striking distance of Bow Bells, she had worked in an underground theatre on the New Cut until she was nineteen, when she had read *On the Merits* and got in touch with its author, hoping for a new job.

Jaxon had seen her potential at once. Now, two years later, she was his most reliable source of income, standing among the highest earners on the black market. Her forgeries sold for thousands. On top of that, she designed and made all her own clothes by hand. She had clear olive skin, eyes as green as apples, and golden hair she kept in barley curls.

She was never short of admirers – people loved her as much as her muses did – but Jaxon strictly forbade us from relationships that lasted any longer than a night (and that was a grudging caveat), and Eliza respected his wishes. No one was more loyal to Jaxon than his Martyred Muse.

Jaxon narrowed his eyes in thought. Sensors were the fourth order of clairvoyance – less common than mediums. Many of them had left for other citadels during the street wars, making them even rarer.

'Ezekiel Sáenz,' he finally said. 'Could you glean anything from him, Nick?'

'I've never sensed an aura like his before,' Nick said. 'It was somewhere between orange and red, to my eye.'

'A potential fury.' Jaxon raised his eyebrows. 'Now, that *is* interesting.'

The sixth order of clairvoyance, and perhaps the most arcane. None of us had ever met one, to our knowledge.

Nick shared a glance with Eliza. They had both worked with Jaxon for longer than me, and used a language of subtle looks I had yet to learn.

Still, they never left me out, even though Jaxon had passed them both over to choose me as mollisher. Nick went out of his way to make sure I was all right.

Jaxon lit a cigar. He had been scouring the streets for a fury for years, but this must be his first hopeful case. The White Binder didn't just want any commonplace gang – he wanted a box of rare jewels, the cream of the crop, the very best and brightest of voyants. He wanted the Unnatural Assembly to envy him above all other mime-lords.

'It's high time I spoke to them myself,' he said. 'If Ezekiel *is* a fury, I want him for the Seven Seals. I'll take the whisperer as well, if I must.'

I dipped a chip in ketchup. 'You really think you can get them to stay?'

'Did I not persuade you, O my lovely?'

'This is different, Jax. Nadine is at university. She won't want to interrupt that. Besides, they must have families back home, career plans—'

'You dropped your father like the millstone he is, without a second thought.'

'It's not the same. I didn't have to upend my entire life to come and work for you. I just moved to a different part of the citadel. If I wanted to see my father, I could.'

'Well, make sure you don't. I don't want his amaurotic dullness rubbing off on you.'

Jaxon often made jabs at my father. I resented him enough that I could live with it.

'You'd be asking them to stay illegally in an empire that wants them dead,' I said. 'Why would they do it?'

Jaxon steepled his fingers. 'How old would you say the whisperer was, Nick?'

'About the same age as Paige.'

'Then she knows something is amiss. The voices would have come in by now,' Jaxon said. 'She's aware that she is a potential unnatural, but still chose to come here – and to put someone else at risk. Either they came to die, or they crave knowledge.'

'There are only three days of the conference left,' Eliza said, looking just as doubtful as me. 'Won't they need more time to consider it?'

'Not if they have a spark of intelligence between them. What sort of bores would choose a decade of student debt over the underworld?'

'They're not going to stay,' I said.

'Faithless girl. Shall we have a wager?' Jaxon extended a hand. 'If you lose, you do two assignments with no pay. You will also polish my antique mirror.'

'And if I win?'

'I'll pay you double for the assignments. And you won't have to polish my antique mirror.'

We shook on it.

It was fascinating to watch Jaxon take control of a situation. On the whole, he would stay in the den – but when he deigned to emerge from his lair, he was a force of nature.

Within hours, he had discovered that conference guests were allowed to go shopping in Covent Garden for an hour a day without a chaperone. He sent a skilled courier to plant a note on Nadine, inviting the pair to a coffeehouse there, warning her not to let on to Scion.

On the day of the meeting, he dressed in his best, immaculate from his collar to his cufflinks.

'By tonight, we will have two Americans in the Seven Seals, for better or worse.' He pointed his cane at me. 'Be ready to polish that mirror, Paige.'

'In your wildest dreams,' I called after him.

'Voyants don't dream, darling. We achieve.'

The door shut behind him. I shook my head and went back upstairs.

Eliza sketched a design for a dress while I leafed through our files on the local spirits, updating my notes about their haunts. Some of them needed regular attention to stop them causing mayhem. It had been a while since anyone had checked on a nearby poltergeist, William Terriss.

At noon, Jaxon sent us a message by courier:

They are siblings. They are also not American.

'Let me guess.' Eliza glanced up. 'He's already persuaded them.'

I shut the door. 'You really think he will?'

'Jax could sell the sun a candle.' She swept her pencil down the page. 'You'll learn, Paige.'

I kept working. It was another hour before the golden words came in:

The mirror requires elbow grease.

That was the last time I bet against Jaxon Hall.

Jaxon still wasn't sure exactly what Ezekiel Sáenz was, but he loved a mystery. Now he had convinced the siblings to stay, he was confident Ezekiel would bare his soul, and everything would click into place. If not, he still relished the thought of snatching two tourists and whisking them into the underworld. For him, outwitting Scion was a merry game.

We would be doing the legwork, of course. He would just watch it happen, and admire himself for assembling such loyal followers.

Nadine and Ezekiel were due to fly back to Boston on the thirtieth. Before then, we needed to help them disappear. If Scion realised two outsiders had gone rogue in London, it would hunt them down with every resource at its disposal.

At nightfall, the siblings would leave their hotel. That would be hard enough, since Vigiles guarded all the exits, but Jaxon was confident they could do it. It would certainly test their ingenuity.

Next, they would enter the bustling train station at Inquisitors Cross. Eliza had left clothes there – clothes she had made to their measurements, designed to help them fit into London. Both sets included a hat that would hide their faces from the security cameras. They would change in the toilets, then walk to meet me and Nick on Judd Street.

As soon as the pair were safely in the den, Eliza would set the next part of the plan in motion.

Eliza loved beauty, but was always willing to get both hands dirty. She would leave clues near the hotel – some blood and hair, their old clothes in a public bin, a knife slipped down a drain. Scion would relish it. Scarlett Burnish could use the incident to shed horrifying new light on unnatural crimes.

Most importantly, no one would ever come after the missing siblings. We would teach them to blend in, keep them away from the Vigiles.

'I still can't believe Jax convinced them to do this,' I said to Nick. We were in the car he occasionally used for syndicate business, an old guzzler with fake plates. 'Their families will think they're dead.'

'You know what he's like. Jax could convince you to jump off a cliff if you listened to him long enough.'

'Eliza said the same.'

'Same words?'

'No, but same gist.'

'They might not have done well in Boston, sötnos. At least voyants know what they are in Scion. Over there, they must just think they're losing their minds.'

He was right, in a sense. To our knowledge, there was no official policy on clairvoyants outside Scion. We had no legal recognition, no minority status. We only appeared in fiction.

Still, that had to be a better deal than being systematically hunted and killed. Even now, I couldn't work out why they would stay.

Nick parked on Judd Street. We both sipped our coffees.

'You look tired,' I said. 'How's work?'

'No worse than usual.'

'Just quit. You don't need the money. Jax could make room in the den.'

'There's definitely no more room in the den. Besides, it's useful to have someone inside Scion.' He glanced at me. 'Is everything okay with you?'

'It's great,' I said, smiling. 'I'm enjoying it.'

'Jax can be harsh when he's in a bad mood. Don't take it to heart, Paige.'

'I don't.' I paused. 'Is that them?'

Two figures were coming down the street. Nick gave the head-lamps a brief flash, and they quickened their pace. When he unlocked the doors, they got into the backseat and pulled off their hats.

'Hi,' Nick said.

'Hey.' The woman leaned forward. 'I'm Nadine. Please tell me you're Nick and Paige.'

'You're in the right car,' I said.

'Great.' She let out a breathy sort of laugh. 'That was kind of terrifying.'

She sounded American to my ear, but I was no expert. 'You've done the hardest part,' Nick said. 'How did you get out of the hotel?'

'We climbed down from the balcony.'

'Good thinking.' He tilted the mirror. 'You must be Ezekiel.'

'Zeke,' the young man said. His eyes were like black tea, set in a thin, restive face. 'I am happy to see you. We were afraid you might not be here.'

He must be in his twenties, with brittle wrists and skin used to the sun. A strand of dark hair hung over his forehead. He flicked it aside to wipe the sweat from his brow, giving me a glimpse of a vertical scar.

Nadine looked similar enough that you could guess they were siblings. Her skin was a deeper brown, and her hair cut to her collar as if with a ruler, dyed red.

Eliza had designed their outfits with care. Nadine wore a flounced cream blouse, paired with a long twill skirt, while Zeke was in a shirt and dark strides with bracers. A pair of perfect denizens.

'I take it you've both thought carefully about this,' Nick said. 'Your escape might not have been noticed yet. I can still get you back to the hotel.' He glanced at them. 'Once we drive away, there's no going back. We're going to fake your deaths. Your old lives will be over.'

Zeke looked at his sister. She sank back in silence and buckled her seatbelt.

'We're sure,' Zeke said.

'Then let's go.'

As Nick drove, Nadine dug around in her bag and took out a pair of headphones. Without another word, she snapped them on and closed her eyes.

Carefully, I reached for their dreamscapes. Nadine didn't seem to notice. Hers was nothing unusual, but Zeke – well, his was *very* interesting, an opaque presence in the æther. He tensed a little, and I stopped.

'So, Zeke,' Nick said, 'what do you do?'

'For a living?'

Nick nodded. 'Nadine was listed as the student on the programme, and you as her guest. I assume you're not at the same university.'

'No,' Zeke said in a quiet voice. 'Nadine asked me to share an apartment with her while she was studying in Boston. I was in ... kind of a dark place, so I agreed to move there from Mexico, to keep her company.'

He gave no further explanation.

'You're a good brother,' Nick said.

His throat bobbed. Scion had killed his younger sister when they were both in their teens. Karolina was his reason to bring down the anchor.

To give him a moment, I turned to Zeke. He was looking out of the window.

'The streetlamps are blue,' he murmured.

'To calm the population,' I said. 'You'll get used to that kind of shite.' He swallowed. 'What made you decide to come to Scion, Zeke?'

'We needed to ... get away for a while. Nadine saw the programme and applied.' He looked down at his hands. 'I'm glad we came. We've both felt different for years. Now we can learn why.'

Zeke clearly had secrets. Jaxon would not allow him to keep them for long.

'We'll help you.' Nick breathed in, seeming to steady himself. 'What's the official stance on clairvoyance in the States, Zeke?'

'They call it extrasensory perception. They don't want to commit to any stance on it,' Zeke said. 'Scion has invaded five countries and threatened others, so the education programme is very controversial. I think there are four colleges that participate, to give students a chance to see it for themselves.'

I wanted to ask about their family, but something told me to save it for much later. They might have just made the most painful decision of their lives.

'Well, Jaxon is so pleased you're joining us.' Nick offered a smile. 'I hope you'll like it here, even if it's dangerous.'

'You were born in Scion?'

'Yes, in Sweden.'

'What about you, Paige?'

'I was born in the free world,' I said. 'I hated it here when I arrived, but it got better when Jaxon hired me. The syndicate will take care of you.'

'Which country are you from?'

'Ireland.'

Zeke looked at me with sudden understanding. No doubt he had been trying to put a finger on my accent.

I had arrived in London with a strong Tipperary lilt. As the denizens of Scion grew to hate anything Irish, my father had attempted to school it out of me. It was too late for him – his own accent had set deep as dye – but it might still be washed out of a child. He had stopped me from speaking Gaeilge, my first language, the one my beloved grandmother had gone out of her way to teach me.

In secret, I had kept learning, but my accent had soon become a burden. Even at eight, I noticed the looks I got when I spoke, the demands that I repeat myself. I would sit in front of the news every night, imitating the raconteurs, until I could speak like them.

All for nothing, in the end. Nobody at my school had been fooled.

As soon as I left at sixteen, I had finally dropped the act. After eight years of forcing myself to speak in a way that felt stiff and wrong, the sheer relief had left me in tears. Even if my lilt wasn't the same as it had been when I was young, my voice was my own again, and I treasured it.

'I have heard what happened to Ireland,' Zeke said. 'About a year ago, these people managed to escape from Galway and tell their story on the news. It … sounds like it was such a tragedy. I'm sorry.'

'Thank you,' I said.

'They sung a beautiful song about a tree and a meadow. They said it was sung at the end of the Molly Riots, to mourn the people who died.'

'Not just at the end. I left during the second year,' I said. 'I know the song you mean.'

'I would love to hear it again.'

I wished I could bear to share it with him. The last time I had heard it, my family had been gathered in secret in the Golden Vale, remembering Finn and Kay. With no bodies to bury, all we had been able to do was sing and remember, huddled around two empty graves.

'Maybe I'll sing it one day.' I hitched up a smile. 'Do you like music, Zeke?'

'Yes, a lot. I used to be great at the piano,' Zeke said wistfully. 'I love listening to Nadine – she is a violinist – but she doesn't really like to play.'

Nick gave me a worried look. A whisperer who didn't like to play her instrument.

That really was a rarity.

It was only a short drive. Nick returned the car to its garage on Rose Street, and we headed on foot to Seven Dials.

The den was a cosy maisonette above a coffeehouse – three floors, including the garret. Jaxon was a man of fine tastes, but he seemed content with his small home.

For months, I had been learning the ropes of the underworld in this house of golden brick. I had learned about the gangs and their leaders, the trade and auction of spirits, their haunts. Now Jaxon was starting to test my gift.

Not long ago, I had been able to consciously crack my spirit out of place. I had immediately stopped breathing. Jaxon and Eliza had panicked, but Nick had revived me with a syringe of adrenalin to the heart. Even though my chest had hurt for a week, I had glowed with pride when Jaxon congratulated me. The four of us had gone out for supper to celebrate, and Jaxon had ordered life support for next time.

I belonged with these people. They understood the strangeness of my life – a life I was finally beginning to embrace. We had carved out a little world in Seven Dials. We thrived in that world, in defiance of Scion.

Now there were two strangers in our midst. Two brave strangers, willing to abandon their old lives to be part of that world.

Nadine gave the building a wary look. I had expected her to have an instrument case, but there was nothing. Maybe she wasn't a whisperer. There were at least three other strains of sensor she could be.

I used my keys to open the red door. At the top of the stairs was Jaxon, dressed to impress: silk waistcoat, stiff white collar, glowing cigar. He held a small cup of coffee in the other hand. I tried and failed to work out how a cigar and coffee could make a compatible pair.

'Zeke, Nadine,' he said warmly. 'Good to see you again.'

Zeke cleared his throat. 'And you, Mr Hall.'

'Jaxon, please. Welcome to Seven Dials,' he said. 'As you know, I am mime-lord of this territory, and you are now members of my coterie. I presume you left Judd Street in a surreptitious fashion, Nick.'

'No one saw us.'

'Good. Eliza will just need a few things from you,' Jaxon added to the newcomers. 'To help craft the impression that you have been tragically murdered.'

'That's me.' Eliza waved from his side. 'Welcome home.'

'Thank you for your help, Eliza.' Zeke tensed. 'Is that a spirit?'

Jaxon glanced up. 'Yes, that's Pieter Claesz, Dutch vanitas painter – died in 1660. One of our more prolific muses. Pieter, come and meet our new friends.'

'Zeke can do the honours. I'm tired.' Nadine slid her bag off her shoulder. 'I want my own room. I don't share my space. Just so that's settled.'

Jaxon looked at her without blinking, and his nostrils flared. Not a good sign.

'You will have what you are given,' he said. 'Unlike the building you just left, this is not a hotel.'

Nadine bristled. Nick quickly ushered her towards the stairs. 'Of course you'll have your own room,' he said to her, giving me a resigned look over her head. 'Eliza put you with Zeke – we don't have much space – but I'm sure she can arrange something.'

Eliza smiled. 'I really don't know how any of you managed without me.'

'We simply languished,' Jaxon said, still eyeing Nadine.

'We did.' Nick sidled past him. 'Can I get you something to drink, Nadine?'

'Yes, you can, Nick. I will have a glass of your famous blood mecks.' She gave Jaxon a pointed smile. 'I see *some* Europeans know how to treat a lady.'

Jaxon looked as if she had slapped him. Nick steered her into the room we used as both an office and a parlour, shutting the door in their wake.

'I am not,' Jaxon said, with the delicate menace of a wolf holding a doll between its teeth, *'European.'*

Zeke swallowed. I glanced at Eliza, who was clearly trying not to burst out laughing. Nadine had already made at least three missteps.

'I'll make sure nobody disturbs you,' I said to Jaxon.

'Thank you, Paige.' He seemed to recover from the insult, taking a puff of his cigar. 'Do go up to my boudoir, dear Zeke. We should talk.'

Zeke hesitated. 'Your boudoir?'

'On the next floor. The door straight ahead of the stairs.'

With a dazed nod, Zeke went up, stairs creaking beneath his boots. The poor man clearly had no idea what he had got himself into. Before I could speak, Jaxon grasped my arm, drawing me close.

'His dreamscape,' he said under his breath. 'What does it feel like, Paige?'

'I can't explain it,' I said, 'but it's dark and heavy, like—'

'Excellent. Say no more.'

He almost ran after Zeke, his cigar lodged in the corner of his mouth. Eliza leaned against the newel.

'This is going to be interesting,' she said. 'I've no idea where I'm going to put Nadine. We might have to build a false wall in the garret.' She reached for a hat. 'In the meantime, are you interested in helping me create a murder scene?'

'No, but I'll wait up for you. You're sure you can manage?'

'It's just setting a stage.'

She went upstairs. I was left on the landing with a dead artist for company, and as much as I liked Pieter, he was not a man of many words.

It was late, but I wouldn't sleep until Eliza came back. I made some fresh coffee and went to sit in the office, where a painting took pride of place. It portrayed a dark-haired woman in a flowing red dress, gazing into a crystal ball. Jaxon had paid a fortune for it – the last painting by John William Waterhouse, finished in 1902, the year after the fall of the Bloody King.

I cracked open a window and sat down to read the draft of his next pamphlet, *On the Machinations of the Itinerant Dead*. So far, it had told me about four kinds of spirit: guardian angel, ghost, muse and psychopomp.

I had yet to read about poltergeists. The old scars on my palm remained as cold as ever.

Once Eliza had what she needed, she left in dark clothes. Above, I sensed Nadine going up to the garret. Even if it had annoyed Jaxon, her request was reasonable. My room in the den was my sanctuary.

Since he had work in the morning, Nick departed around one, heading for his apartment in Marylebone. Eliza returned about half an hour later.

'Done,' she whispered, removing her gloves. 'I wasn't seen.'

'You're sure?'

'As sure as I can be.' She took off the hat. 'Anything from upstairs?'

'Nadine is asleep, but Jax is still talking to Zeke.'

'Zeke isn't how I imagined a fury. Much quieter than I expected.' She sat down on my bed. 'Jax mentioned they're not American. Where are they from?'

'Zeke is from Mexico. Nadine was studying in Boston, but I think she's Canadian.'

'So they grew up separately?'

'I don't know.'

'I can't wait to hear what life is like out there.' Eliza fanned herself with the pamphlet. 'I won't sleep in this heat. Can I tempt you to come to Psionic?'

'I am never going out dancing with you again.'

'Why not?'

'Did you forget what happened last time?' I said flatly. 'You took one look at that cryomancer and left me to stand on my own in a séance club.'

'Oh, him.' Eliza smiled. 'That was fun. He liked putting ice on his—'

'Whatever it is, I don't want to know.'

'I was going to say *drinks*, Paige.' She winked and adjusted her earrings. 'I do have something else for you to do. Jax wants you to draw your dreamscape.'

'I can't draw. That's your area.'

'Not the flowers. He just wants the basic shape – a bird's-eye view, preferably. We're trying to work out the complete layout of the human dreamscape, but none of us can leave the middle,' Eliza said. 'We think there are at least three rings, but we're not sure. Can you help?'

A sense of purpose filled me to the brim. It was still a surreal realisation, that my gift could be useful.

'Of course,' I said.

Eliza got me a sketchbook and pencil, then switched on her data pad to watch a show. I drew something like a bullseye, with five sections. Once the sketch was finished, I blew dust off it and showed it to her.

'This is the sunlit zone.' I pointed to the middle. 'The place where the spirit is meant to stay.'

'Right. The silver cord is like a safety net or a harness, fixed to that central sanctuary,' Eliza said. 'It stops most voyants from leaving it.'

'But not me.'

'Exactly. Say the majority of us have an inch of string between our dreamscape and our spirit,' she said, measuring with her fingers. 'You have a mile. You can walk to the edge of your dreamscape, which means you can sense far more of the æther than the rest of us. I can only sense aura and spirits at close range. I can't feel the others now.'

I could.

'I probably do have a limit,' I said. 'We just haven't found it yet.'

'That's why we need to be careful. You might be able to leave your body without hurting yourself, or you might not. We'll have to wait and see.'

I nodded. Jaxon had told me about his possession theory, but Eliza was more patient in her explanations.

'What would happen if you tried to leave your sunlit zone?' I asked her.

'The second zone is survivable,' Eliza said, 'but if your spirit enters it, it means something is wrong. Mine kept drifting there after I gave up aster. I was entering my dreamscape to escape from the withdrawal, but I'd often find I was in the wrong place. It was unsettling.'

'But no one can go farther than that.'

'Not that I've heard. If you tried to push beyond that point, I think it would start to really hurt. If you kept going, it would damage your cord and your sanity. It's amazing that you can breeze straight through.'

'I truly am a circus freak.'

'Don't say that, Paige. None of us are freaks,' Eliza said. 'You're a marvel. A jumper.' She took the sketchbook back and examined my drawing. 'So there are five zones. That's interesting.'

'Sunlit, twilight, midnight, abyssal, and hadal,' I said. 'They're quite distinct.'

'Great.' She handed the sketchbook back. 'Add a bit more detail, if you want, and I'll pick it up tomorrow. Jax will love this, Paige. He wants to write a pamphlet on the dreamscape, but he'll need your help.'

'I expect a generous cut of the royalties.'

Eliza laughed. 'I'll tell him.' As she left, she turned to face me. 'Paige, you know what they say about the syndicate – once you get in, you never get out. That will sink in for Nadine and Zeke soon, when they start feeling homesick. Are you sure you're still happy with it?'

'I've never been happier,' I said.

And it was true. Here in this stuffy room, surrounded by forbidden trinkets, I had never felt more like the person I was meant to be. Eliza gave me a smile that was almost wistful.

'Okay,' she said. 'I think I'll pop into the club for a couple of hours. I'll be back before sunrise.'

'Have fun,' I said.

'You can bet on it.'

With a jangle of bracelets, she sidled from my room.

Eliza Renton – a woman who could fake two deaths, then dance until dawn without a second thought. You had to admire her. I started to shade the rings on my sketch, making each one darker than the last.

When my door opened again, I expected to see an enlivened Eliza. Instead, Jaxon appeared, looking almost feverish, spots of pink on his cheeks.

Before my eyes, he downed his entire absinthe. I lowered the sketchbook.

'Jaxon?'

'Unreadable,' he burst out, a wild glittering in his eyes. 'Darling, you have company. Another diamond among stones. Our dear Mr Sáenz is an *unreadable*.'

20

MOMENT OF TRUTH

Magdalen was an ancient building. According to Gail, the former college had been founded in 1458, centuries before Scion. For several hours, I sat in its hold, flinching each time its bells rang the hour.

Warden had taken me back to the Founders Tower, then returned to the Rookery. He had said nothing to me – no reproach, no threat of punishment.

Michael kept checking on me. At three in the morning, he presented me with a bowl of baked chestnuts, with cracked brown shells and velvety white insides, reminding me of midwinters in London. My favourite vendor sold them at the end of Lambeth Bridge.

Half an hour later, Michael brought a cup of sugary tea. I stirred from a doze.

'Thank you.' I took it with my good hand. 'Any time for a break, Michael?'

He shook his head with an apologetic smile.

'It's okay. I know you're busy.' I smiled back. 'Don't let me keep you.'

Michael had already taken my clothes for laundering. I was huddled on the daybed in a spare undershirt, a heavy mantle covering my bare legs.

Warden returned at sunrise. I watched him remove his cloak and jerkin.

'The Rookery is badly damaged,' he said. 'Since the performers need their strength for the Bicentenary, they will be allowed to sleep in the Old Library.'

'Right.' I rubbed my temples. 'Shit.'

'What is it?'

'I broke into the Old Library. Anyone who checks the door will notice.'

'I had the padlock replaced several weeks ago,' Warden said. My brow creased. 'The day you missed the curfew, you could only have been out of bounds. I checked all of the sealed buildings for weaknesses.'

I nodded slowly, even as I questioned why I had told him so readily.

With a padlock back on the door, Julian wouldn't have been able to hide Liss. Not that we could have concealed her condition for long. As soon as she failed to appear for training, Beltrame would have overturned the whole city in search of her.

'The Rookery,' I said. 'Will it be repaired?'

'No,' Warden said quietly. 'After the Bicentenary, the performers will be evicted from the Old Library.'

The implication hung between us. The Bicentenary would take place in early autumn. By then, the killing cold might already be closing in.

'To protect the performers before the Bicentenary, no jacketed humans may visit,' he said. 'As for your attackers, they are forbidden to approach you without supervision.'

'I told you they would come after me.'

'Yes.'

Warden approached the daybed. Flakes of ash were caught in his hair.

'May I see your injury?'

After a pause, I gave him a small nod.

He used his knuckle to lift my chin, brushing my hair behind my ear. Kath had left a graceless cut between its upper shell and my temple.

His touch raised an unexpected chill. It was the gentlest and most intimate I had experienced in a while, softened by the worn leather of his glove. I held still, my knees pressed together, heart beating too hard.

'Michael cleaned it,' I said. 'It's fine.'

'Hm.' He released me. 'You appear to have treated your wrist.'

The dirty poultice was still wrapped around it. The reminder tightened my throat.

'It's comfrey,' I whispered.

'Who gave it to you?'

'Liss, one of the aerialists.' I looked up at him. 'The red-jackets ambushed me at her place. Can I really not go out there to check on her?'

'Even if I could allow it, I think it best that you keep to this residence as much as possible from now on. As you rightly said, I cannot be everywhere. In Magdalen, you are under my protection.'

I swallowed.

Liss had looked at me with the beginnings of betrayal. If she died, I would never be able to explain. It would be the last thing I had ever told her.

Warden sat in his chair and poured himself a generous amount of red wine. 'The summer feast will take place in a week,' he said. 'Until then, you should recover your strength. You have had a strenuous few days, Paige.'

'What about training?'

'You will no longer be training with Merope. Since your position with me has made you a target, I have asked Nashira if I may continue your instruction here, rather than on Port Meadow. I am confident she will agree to this for your safety, if only for the rest of the month.'

Our training sessions had always been watched. Without those eyes on us, Nashira would have no idea of my progress.

'I will try to secure another splint for your wrist,' Warden said, seeing the protective way I was cradling it. 'I assume you lost it in the Rookery.'

'Yes.' It was even more swollen. 'Kath … gave it a pretty good twist.'

'Her death was unnecessary.'

'Who is her keeper?'

'Kraz Sargas, one of the blood-heirs. There are always two – a male and a female, to mirror the blood-sovereigns,' Warden said. 'Should anything befall Gomeisa, Kraz would be his successor.'

'You told me you were deathless,' I said. 'Why the need for heirs, if so?'

'We cannot die of old age, but we are not invulnerable.'

'On that subject, I can't get any sense of *your* age.'

'From a human perspective, I do not know. We are never young, and do not grow old. I was there at the founding of the Republic of Scion.'

It took a moment to sink in.

'If Kraz had forced us to fight,' I finally said, 'would you have been able to stop him?'

Warden looked into the fire. I studied his face, seeking any sign of what he might be thinking.

'No,' he said. 'He is of the blood. Despite my conjugal title, I am not.'

He reached for his goblet. Perhaps I was shaken by the events of the night, but a sudden boldness filled me – something that felt dangerous.

'You drink a lot of amaranth,' I said. 'You said it was for old wounds.'

'I do not believe my health concerns are any of yours, Paige.'

'You said you wanted mutual trust. Can't we be honest with each other?'

'I gave you that opportunity,' Warden said. 'You are no pick-pocket, Paige Mahoney. Until you tell the truth, I will withhold mine.'

Before I could answer, he stood and left, taking his goblet with him. The door closed in his wake, and I was left to wonder how he could be so sure.

For the next few days, I kept to Magdalen. Left to my own devices, I went for long jogs in the grounds, trying to keep my mind off Liss.

Within the halls of Magdalen, nobody observed the curfew. It gave me a chance to soak up the sun. I even dared to climb the steps of the bell tower. At the top, I looked across the misty rooftops, towards the Vault.

David had told me about the scarred ones – the Rephs who had organised the doomed rebellion. Warden took medicine for old wounds.

Arcturus Mesarthim could not be a former rebel. Nashira would never have kept him around, let alone chosen him as her consort. I shouldn't even be entertaining the idea, but whatever *concubine* meant, it was an insult. He acted without her knowledge. He was gentle with humans.

At noon, I went to see the day porter, Fazal. I found him pruning the ivy.

'Faz.' I stopped beside him. 'Do you ever visit the Broad?'

'Not by choice.' Fazal raised a dark eyebrow. 'Why?'

'I can't go there. If you do pass it, could you ask after the aerialist, Liss?'

Fazal shook his head. 'An amaurotic can't get involved,' he said. 'Warden keeps us safe in Magdalen. I won't risk my position here, Paige.'

'I understand.'

I really did. Just as I started to leave, he said, 'I'll ask Gail. She's helping to clear the Rookery.'

'Thank you.'

On the night of the feast, I was permitted to wash again. I was barely out of the bath when Gail used her spare key to enter the parlour.

'Gail,' I said, surprised.

'I won't stay.' She set down a pair of scissors and a comb. 'Just bringing this for your hair. You're expected to look presentable for a feast.'

'Right.' I touched it. 'Faz said you've been working on the Broad.'

'Liss is in spirit shock. The Overseer has convinced Nashira to let her fight through it, or try.' Gail folded her sinewy arms. 'Let's hope she's strong. I can't imagine the pain of that loss.'

Her own favoured numen was a stone she kept in a locked drawer in the Porters' Lodge. When she left, I gazed out of the window.

Spirit shock could last for days or a few weeks. Even if Liss pulled through, she would never read the cards again. She would no longer be voyant.

To distract myself, I combed my hair as best I could, then gave it a trim. It had grown a fair amount. I favoured a bob, but now I kept it long enough to pull into a bun. A stray curl in my eyes could be fatal here.

Gail soon came back for the scissors. I reluctantly handed them over.

Warden took me to the feast himself. I chafed at having to be escorted such a short way, but I knew he was doing it for my sake. The new moon had darkened the city, giving plenty of cover for ambushes.

'You must be nervous,' I said.

'How so?'

'Nashira is probably about to question me. I could tell her anything.' I kept my voice low. 'Even if I have no proof, I think she might be interested.'

Warden looked straight ahead. His eyes were a little greener than usual.

The stars twinkled above the city, making me feel even smaller beside him. When we reached the Residence of the Suzerain, Warden turned to me.

'Terebell will escort you back to Magdalen.' His voice was quiet. 'Do whatever you think best, Paige.'

The gates opened. I stepped inside, shooting him a last glance over my shoulder.

The Residence of the Suzerain seemed even darker and more ominous than it had on the night of the oration. I wondered how many humans had passed through its halls. Alsafi and Suhail flanked me all the way. Even though I had passed my second test, I still wore pink.

'You will treat the blood-sovereign with respect,' Alsafi said to me. 'None of your usual impertinence, 40.'

Suhail gave me a shove. I clenched my jaw, knowing better than to retort.

They led me to an intimate dining hall, lit by candles and a fire. Their flickering light cast odd shadows on the ribbed plaster vaulting overhead. The walls were panelled up to a point, becoming pale stone.

A long table ran down the middle of the room. At the head of this polished table, seated in an upholstered chair, was the Suzerain.

Nashira Sargas sat like a carving, gloved hands folded in front of her. She wore her usual black, her livery collar reflecting the amber glow.

'Good evening, 40.'

I nodded.

'Suhail,' Nashira said, 'wait for the others. Alsafi, stay here.'

'Yes, blood-sovereign.' Suhail lowered his head to my level. 'I do hope Arcturus will return to take you back to Magdalen in good time,' he breathed in my ear. 'If not, I would be happy to walk you there myself.'

'Terebell is taking me,' I said quietly.

'How unsurprising.'

Another odd remark. I squirrelled it away in the mental box of clues.

He stalked back through the doorway, while Alsafi stood guard by the door. I was left in the sinister chamber, facing the woman who wanted me dead.

'Sit,' she said.

I thought about taking the chair at the farthest end of the table – a good twelve feet away – but she indicated the one on her left side, opposite the fireplace. I lowered myself into it, my mouth already dry.

Nashira watched me with intensity. Her eyes were green as burning absinthe.

'I suppose you must be frightened,' she said.

I should be. It was her name that was whispered in the shadows, her command that ended lives. Two of her angels drifted nearby, never too far from her aura.

Tell me who you were, I wanted to say to them. *Tell me how to cheat my fate.*

'Our last meeting was not pleasant,' Nashira said. 'I trust you have had time to reflect on your conduct that night.'

I nodded once, avoiding the trap. I hadn't been given permission to speak.

A bell jar stood in the middle of the table. Beneath the glass was a wilted flower, propped up by a wire stand, petals grey and shrivelled. Whatever kind it had been in life, it was unrecognisable in death. I couldn't imagine why Nashira would have it on her dinner table – but then, she kept a fair amount of dead things hanging around.

I would soon be one of them, if something didn't stop it.

She noticed my interest.

'Some things are better off dead. Would you not agree?' When I kept holding my tongue, she said, 'You may speak freely at a feast.'

'I'm not sure what you're asking me, Suzerain.'

'I hear three red-jackets accosted you. Kraz punished one with death,' Nashira said. 'Arcturus saw it as a squandering of many years of instruction, but we cannot allow you to come to harm, 40. You are worth more than all the others put together.'

There was cutlery in front of me, heavy and silver. The steak knife looked sharp.

'Yet you still display contempt for our authority,' Nashira said. 'Suhail remains quite wroth with you, given your decision to attack and fell him. He has petitioned for me to punish you personally.'

Sitting in her presence was harder than I could ever have anticipated. All I wanted to do was shove the steak knife into her throat.

But I needed to keep a lid on my anger. Any hint of rebellion, and she might decide to cut her losses and kill me at once. I needed to convince her I was tamed, to buy myself as much time as possible – time to help Liss, form an escape plan, and leave before the Bicentenary.

'I didn't mean to attack Suhail,' I said. 'I can't always control my gift.'

'That much is apparent.'

'I'm working on it.'

'Are you, indeed?'

285

'I've understood how lucky I am to be here, Suzerain. In London, I'm just an unnatural and a brogue. Here, I have a place. I have a purpose.'

'Was it my consort who helped you make this realisation?'

'Yes.'

The silence grew and grew. I had no idea whether or not to look at her.

In that silence, I made the grave mistake of looking up, allowing me to see the lines of plaster faces above the windows. Another strange choice of decoration. The nearest was peaceful, wearing the softest smile. A young woman, as calm as if she were asleep.

That was a famous French death mask. The face of a girl who was found in the Seine. Jaxon had a replica in the den. Eliza had made him cover it with a sheet, much to his annoyance. She said it made her skin crawl.

I looked around the room. All of the faces – the people – all of them were death masks. Nashira didn't just collect spirits; she collected faces, too.

Seb could be up there. I dropped my gaze, pressing my lips together.

'You seem unwell,' Nashira said.

'I'm fine.'

'Good. I would hate for you to fall ill at this crucial stage of your training.'

She clasped her hands, allowing me to see the signet ring she wore over her glove, on her forefinger. I had to wonder if it was from Warden.

'Some of the red-jackets will join us soon, but I wished to speak to you alone first,' she said. 'We will have a heart-to-heart, as you say.'

It fascinated me that she thought she had a heart.

'Arcturus has kept me informed of your development. He tells me he has tried his utmost to bring out your gift,' she said, 'but you have yet to attempt a full possession. Is this true?'

'Yes,' I said.

'A pity.'

Warden must not have told her about the butterfly. Surely she would have mentioned it.

He was downplaying my progress.

'Yet you faced one of the Emim and survived,' Nashira said. 'For that reason, Arcturus believes you should be made a red-jacket. What do you think?'

I didn't know what to say.

'How quiet you are,' Nashira said. 'Last we met, you were not so timid.'

'I've learned that it isn't my place to have thoughts,' I said, quoting her cousin.

'Remarkable.' Her eyes were glacial. 'I have a small number of questions for you, 40. They must be kept between us, since they pertain to my consort.'

She may question you about me. Perhaps not yet, but soon.

'You have been keeping quarters with Arcturus in Magdalen,' Nashira said. 'Whereabouts?'

'In an attic by the Founders Tower.'

'Does he ever ask you to come out of it?'

'Only for training.'

'I imagine you have explored his quarters. Is there anything in the Founders Tower that ... troubles you?' she asked. 'Anything out of the ordinary?'

'Not that I recall.'

'Does he ever depart without explanation?'

I thought of his deep wounds. The way he disappeared when fog descended on the city, making it hard for prying eyes see his excursions.

'No,' I said. 'If he did, he wouldn't owe a human an explanation.'

'Indeed. But does he ever seek to speak with you in a personal capacity?'

I shook my head. 'What could I say that would be of any concern to the blood-consort?'

'An excellent point.'

I bit my tongue.

Nashira took something from inside her doublet and held it up for me to see. A tarnished silver brooch.

'Have you ever seen this symbol in Magdalen?'

A flower with eight petals, each tapering to a point. I had seen it before – just once, in the early days, as I explored the Founders Tower.

287

It was shaped exactly like the flower on his snuffbox. The one he kept in the display case, tucked just out of sight.

'You may speak frankly,' Nashira said. 'Arcturus may be your keeper, but you answer to me.'

I lifted my chin. 'I don't understand why you're asking me about him, Suzerain.'

'Earth can be a taxing place. As his consort, I am always concerned for his wellbeing, but he is unselfish by nature. He chooses not to share his burdens with me,' she said, without a lick of discernible fondness. 'Since we live apart, I cannot see them. You must be my eyes.'

As if she would ever involve a human in her relationship issues. She must think I was thick as champ.

'I will ask you once more,' Nashira said. 'Have you ever seen this symbol in the Founders Tower?'

Alsafi watched me from the doorway. I glanced at him, then at Nashira.

This was the moment of truth.

In the heartbeats that followed, I weighed my choices. For months, I had been a pawn in a game with rules I didn't understand. A stick pulled between two dogs that ought to be getting along just fine.

There was a small possibility that Warden had been testing me on her behalf. Something told me that wasn't the case. Surely even she wouldn't expect her consort to put himself in that much danger just to see what I would do.

No, this was my chance to break faith with him. I could tell her everything, from his lenience to the wounds. I could admit to seeing the symbol. I could share my suspicions that he was not wholly obedient to her.

But she would still kill me, sooner or later.

Nashira didn't know I was aware of her murderous intentions. Warden had prepared me for this. Thanks to him and Liss, I knew that all I would gain from betraying him were a few weeks of privilege.

I wanted to know more about Warden. I needed to understand who he was and what he was doing. I thought of his gentle attempt to tease me, and wondered for a moment if it might not have been mimicry.

Impressively, I managed to think all of this in the time it took me to adjust a button on my tunic.

'No,' I said.

Nashira watched me. 'You seem very sure.'

'I am.'

She looked straight at me, into my eyes. I had no idea if I was meant to hold or to break her gaze.

'Of course,' I said, 'if I did see any such thing, I would tell you, Suzerain. I would never want my keeper to be without the love of his consort.'

'I am glad to hear it.'

Nashira gave Alsafi a subtle nod. He pulled once on a tassel, ringing a bell.

'Since you passed your second test, you are now a red-jacket,' Nashira informed me. 'You must be formally introduced to some of your new associates. They are loyal to me, even above their own keepers.'

That must have been my final trial. She had believed me.

I had reached the highest echelons of this city – the inner circle of Nashira Sargas.

A door closed in the distance. A line of red-jackets walked into the room, escorted by Suhail.

'Welcome, my friends,' Nashira said. 'Please, sit.'

There were twenty of them, each well fed and clean as a whistle. They must come to see her in small groups. The veterans were at the front, including 16 and 17, who both walked stiffly. I tensed at the sight of them.

At the back of the line was Carl. The weasel had survived his second test. When he saw me, he looked close to indignation, as did several of the others. They must not have seen a pink-jacket at this table before.

They all sat. Carl took the chair directly across the table from me, while a burly soothsayer with an eyepatch sat to my left. David was a few places away. There was a fresh cut on his head, sealed with a row of stitches.

'Another fine summer begins. Thanks to your efforts, the city has not been breached for several weeks,' Nashira said. 'Having said that, we must never forget the constant threat of the Emim. There is no cure for their brutality. Since the ethereal threshold is broken, there is also no way to imprison them in the Netherworld. You are all that stands between the hunters and their prey. You are the protectors of humankind.'

It was clear from their expressions that they all believed it, with the possible exception of David, who was eyeing the masks. 16 and 17 were wise enough not to look my way, which I appreciated. I was of a mind to chuck all my cutlery in their direction.

'22,' Nashira said. 'How is 75?'

The man in question had a livid case of razor burn. I didn't envy him, trying to shave with whatever dull blade had clearly been provided.

'He's a little better, Suzerain. Thank you,' 22 said. 'No sign of infection.'

'His bravery has not gone unnoticed.'

'He'll be honoured to hear it.'

Nashira clapped. Four amaurotics came through a small door, each carrying a platter and the scent of herbs. Michael was among them, but he didn't meet my eye. I had never seen him outside Magdalen.

Working quickly, they laid out a magnificent feast, avoiding the bell jar. One poured chilled wine into our glasses. A lump blocked my throat.

The platters were laden with food. Beautifully cut chicken, tender and succulent, with crispy golden skin; stuffing with sage and onion; thick, sweet-smelling gravy; cranberry sauce; steamed vegetables and roast potatoes and plump sausages wrapped in bacon – a feast fit for the Grand Inquisitor. When Nashira nodded, the others tucked straight in. They ate with enthusiasm, but without the feral urgency of starvation.

My gut ached. I thought of the performers, living on grease and hard bread, half of them left with nowhere to sleep.

Nashira saw my reservation.

'Eat.'

It was clearly an order. I moved a few slices of chicken and some vegetables on to my plate. Carl gulped down his wine like it was water.

'Watch it, 1,' said one of the women. 'You don't want to be sick again.'

The rest of them laughed. Carl grinned. 'Come on, that was just once. I was still pink.'

'Yeah, leave off him, 6. He deserves a drink.' 22 gave him a friendly punch on the arm. 'He's done well, for a rookie. Besides, we all had a tough time with our first Buzzer.'

There were murmurs of assent.

'I passed out,' 6 admitted. A selfless display of solidarity. 'The first time I saw one on patrol. I would have been killed if not for the rest of my company.'

Carl smiled. 'But you're great with spirits, 6.'

'Thanks.'

I watched their camaraderie in silence. It was mildly nauseating, but it seemed real. Carl hadn't just found a way to survive in this strange new world – he had thrown himself in head first, and he was enjoying it.

To a degree, I could empathise. I remembered the intoxication of belonging. When I first started working for Jaxon, I had been high on that feeling for months. Maybe Carl had never found a place in London.

Nashira was as silent as me. She must take pleasure in this farce. Stupid, indoctrinated humans, learning to love the horrors they faced – all tucked under her thumb, eating her food, grateful for their servitude.

'You're still a pink.' A high-pitched voice came to my attention. 'Have *you* fought a Buzzer?'

I glanced up. They were all looking at me. 'A few days ago,' I said.

'I haven't seen you before.' 22 raised his dense eyebrows. 'Which company are you due to fight in?'

'I'm not part of a company.'

'Well, you're a pink-jacket. You must be joining one,' another man said, frowning. 'Who's your keeper?'

'The blood-consort,' I said.

During the ensuing silence, I took a sip of wine, allowing myself to savour their surprise. The unfamiliar alcohol burned on its way down.

Nobody could drink wine in the citadel. Then again, that was because Scion thought alcohol might turn people unnatural, and that ship had clearly sailed for the present company.

'You're 40,' someone finally said.

'I heard you're a dreamwalker.' Carl narrowed his eyes. 'Is that true?'

'It certainly is.' I offered him a platter. 'Chicken?'

Carl glared at me.

'We have a rarity in 40,' Nashira said. 'One that 16 and 17 almost damaged.'

The brothers tensed. Even their smallest movements looked stiff, as if their clothes were hurting. If not for Liss, I might have pitied them.

'You are both dedicated soldiers. Perhaps it is understandable that you should feel some resentment, seeing a newcomer so cosseted,' Nashira said graciously. '40 receives special treatment because we cannot afford to injure her. I know that 62 was the ringleader – but do not repeat her mistake, or I will be forced to revoke your red tunics.'

'Yes, Suzerain,' they both mumbled. 16 gritted his teeth in obvious agony.

'That applies to all of you,' Nashira said.

They hastened to agree.

Nashira caught my gaze. I gave her a nod of feigned gratitude. She was both the greatest threat to my life and the reason I was theoretically untouchable.

'Since Magdalen has so few humans, 40 will be formally considered part of Queens Company,' Nashira said. 'But she is unlikely to fight. You should consider her as separate from the rest of you.'

A dead woman walking, I thought, against my will.

For several minutes, only the clink of cutlery disturbed the silence. I ate my steamed vegetables.

After a time, the red-jackets made conversation. They swapped patrol stories. They asked each other about their residences, marvelling at the beauty of the old buildings. Sometimes they took a jab at the performers, deriding their cowardice or lack of personal hygiene.

The brothers toyed with their food, occasionally shooting me acrid looks. 30 was pink-faced from the wine, while Carl chewed with excessive force, alternating mouthfuls with sips from his second glass. Only when all the plates were clean did the amaurotics return to clear the table, leaving us with dessert.

Nashira waited for the red-jackets to serve themselves before she spoke again.

'Now you are fed and watered, my friends, let us have a little entertainment.'

Carl wiped the treacle from his mouth with linen. A troupe of performers filed into the room. Among them was a whisperer, who raised his violin to his shoulder and played a lively tune. The others executed graceful acrobatics.

'To business, then,' Nashira said. The diners sat up a bit straighter. 'If any of you have ever conversed with the Overseer, you may know that he is my procurer for the Bone Seasons. For decades, I have been attempting to extract valuable clairvoyants from the crime syndicate of the Scion Citadel of London. No doubt many of you are aware of it; some of you may even have been part of it.'

30 and 18 both shifted in their seats. I didn't recognise either of them, but most of my work had been limited to I Cohort. Carl was open-mouthed.

Nobody looked at the performers. They had their art honed to perfection, and not one person cared.

'As the Suzerain, I seek quality and variety, as well as quantity,' Nashira continued. 'We respect and value all of your skills, but there are many talents we must harvest to enrich our city. We must all learn from each other. It would not do to simply take in seers and palmists.'

I thought of Ivy in Corpus. In May, I had glimpsed her from a distance, in the fog, trailing behind Thuban. I hadn't seen her since.

'40 is the kind of clairvoyant we now seek. She is our very first dreamwalker,' Nashira said. 'We also require sibyls and berserkers, binders and summoners, oracles. All of these would bring fresh insight to our ranks.'

'Personally, I think we could all learn a lot from 40,' David said, raising his glass. 'I'm willing.'

I raised an eyebrow.

In nearly three months, our paths had rarely crossed. If this was his way of trying to win my trust again, he needed to work harder.

'An excellent attitude, 12. We do intend to learn a great deal from 40,' Nashira said. 'That is why I will be sending her on an external assignment.'

The veterans exchanged glances. Carl turned as red as the strawberry tarts.

'I will also be sending 12. And you, 1,' Nashira continued. Now Carl looked elated. David smiled into his glass. 'Of the forty clairvoyants who arrived in March, the three of you have made the swiftest progress. You will go with some of your seniors from Bone Season XIX, who will monitor your performance under pressure. 30, I presume I can count on you to lead them, as you have in previous years.'

30 nodded. 'I'd be honoured.'

'Good.'

Surely *external assignment* couldn't mean what I thought it meant. It wasn't possible.

Carl was on the edge of his seat. 'You're sending us to London, Suzerain?'

'On rare occasions, I dispatch red-jackets to the citadel for assignments that call for specialist knowledge, or where the Vigiles have failed. You are my trusted loyalists. I rely on you to enact my will.'

He swelled with pride.

'In this case, we have a delicate situation to resolve,' Nashira continued. 'As you and 12 are aware, I have been asking recent arrivals to scry for the whereabouts of the White Binder, who leads a group of criminals known as the Seven Seals. This group is part of the clairvoyant syndicate.'

My ribs tightened to the point of pain.

'The Seven Seals include an oracle and a fury,' Nashira said. 'Thanks to focused scrying over several months, we have deduced that they will be convening in London tomorrow night, on the eleventh of June.'

My heart was thumping so hard, I feared someone might hear it. I took a sip of wine to steady myself. It was crucial that I stayed calm now.

'The meeting will take place in Trafalgar Square, which lies on the edge of I Cohort, Section 4,' Nashira said. 'To the best of our knowledge, it will be at one in the morning.'

Carl had seen a pillar in his test. I had feared it was the one at Seven Dials, but it must have been Nelson's Column. That was a small relief – for now, the den was safe – but the detail the Rephs had accumulated was incredible. They even knew we had an oracle.

It sickened me that Nashira had even the faintest knowledge of Nick.

The Rephs really did know how to use the æther to their advantage. Multiple seers and augurs, as well as an oracle, scrying on behalf of a single querent – all of them fixated on a single, powerful desire. Over several months, that would get serious results. Not only that, but the Rephs clearly had a strong affinity with the æther, even more than we did. Of course it would answer their call.

'Tell me,' Nashira said, 'do any of you know anything about the Seven Seals?'

18 was fiddling with the end of her braid, clearly uncomfortable. I avoided her gaze.

'The White Binder is a writer. He published a pamphlet called *On the Merits of Unnaturalness* in the early thirties,' David said. 'It broke us into seven broad orders.'

'We are aware of that,' Nashira said. 'Anything else?'

'No, Suzerain.'

Nashira looked around the table. Her attention inevitably landed on me.

'Surely you were involved in the syndicate, 40,' she said. 'A clairvoyant of your rarity would not have gone unnoticed for so long without protection.'

Warden had definitely not told her about the pamphlet. If he had, I wouldn't be able to deny my connection to Jaxon. I would already be in an interrogation room.

'The gangs are very secretive,' I said. 'There's gossip, but I don't know much.'

'Tell us what you do know.'

I was going to have to offer up a tidbit – just enough information to make her think I was being truthful. Something harmless.

'We all know their false names,' I said. 'I did, at least.'

'And what might those be?'

'The White Binder, the Red Vision, the Black Diamond, the Pale Dreamer, the Martyred Muse, the Chained Fury, and the Silent Bell.'

'The Pale Dreamer is an intriguing name,' Nashira said. (Great.) 'Does it not imply the presence of a dreamwalker within the Seven Seals?'

I dared not speak. Let her think I would never be so foolish as to give her my own alias.

'You worked at an oxygen bar in I-4,' she pressed. 'Is that why you know about them?'

'Yes,' I said.

So she knew roughly where we were based. Or perhaps she had just guessed that from the meeting place, Trafalgar Square. It was a disputed part of the citadel, claimed by Jaxon and Hector.

'Given the rarity of dreamwalkers,' Nashira said, 'I am surprised to hear you may have worked at such close quarters. Surely the White Binder would have employed you, too.'

'No,' I said.

Nashira waited. Now I had to think even faster than I had for Warden.

'The Pale Dreamer is the heir to I-4. She's violent and petty,' I said. 'She would have killed me if she thought she had a rival. The White Binder loves her because she's unique. If he found out some upstart waitron had the same gift, it would threaten her place. I kept out of their way.'

Nashira drank for the first time, from a silver goblet.

'I see.'

Cold sweat dampened my undershirt. I had worked in the syndicate for long enough to know when someone was toying with me.

Nashira Sargas was many things, but she didn't strike me as stupid. Even without the pamphlet, she must have put the other evidence together. There was no way I could have worked on the same turf as another dreamwalker and avoided her gaze for three years.

No, Nashira knew exactly who I was.

'If the Pale Dreamer *is* a dreamwalker,' she said, 'then the White Binder may be hiding some of the most powerful clairvoyants in the citadel. It is rare that we have an opportunity to add such precious jewels to our crown.'

I swallowed.

'Your competence on this assignment is vital, 40. If anyone is capable of recognising the dreamwalker from the Seven Seals, it is a fellow dreamwalker.'

She really was sending us to London.

This was my chance to escape.

'Of course, Suzerain,' I said. 'Do you know why the Seven Seals are convening?'

'A handful of Irish clairvoyants have established contact with the London syndicate. Antoinette Carter is their leader,' Nashira said. 'Carter, whose real name is unknown, has been a fugitive for over a decade. From what the æther tells us, the Seven Seals will be meeting her.'

I had to work hard to control my expression. Leon had pulled it out of the bag.

Antoinette Carter. Thirteen years ago, she had escaped the bloodbath on St Stephen's Green. A fellow survivor – one of the few.

She was coming to London.

How she planned to get there, I had no idea. The Irish Sea was almost impossible to cross, the coastlines guarded by watchtowers and patrol ships. Whatever Jaxon was offering, it must be quite a prize.

Jaxon. At this time of night, he would either be asleep or nursing a glass of sugared absinthe, with no idea his beloved æther had betrayed him.

'It is imperative that a sister syndicate does not form in Ireland,' Nashira said. 'Consequently, this meeting must be averted. Your primary aim is to capture Antoinette Carter. I intend to find out what power she hides.'

I thought back to the night I had been detained. The Overseer had been surrounded by people in uniforms I hadn't recognised. They must have been red-jackets on an external assignment.

That was how they kept the secret of the Bone Seasons. Even the Vigiles must not know.

'The second aim is to apprehend the Seven Seals. The White Binder is a critical target.'

In my lap, my hands were sweating.

'You will be supervised by my consort and his cousin, Situla Mesarthim,' Nashira said. 'I will hold you all responsible if Carter is allowed to return to Ireland.' She looked at each of us. 'Is that understood?'

'Yes, Suzerain,' 30 and Carl said. David nodded, swilling his wine around the glass.

'You will all be free to use your gifts on this assignment. I expect you to show gratitude for the long hours your keepers have poured into your training.' Nashira looked into my eyes. 'You in particular, 40. If you do not attempt to reach your full potential in London, I shall see to it that you never walk the sheltered halls of Magdalen again. You can rot outside with the rest of the fools.'

I forced a nod, knowing she was lying. There was no emotion in her gaze, but there was a great emptiness – an emptiness that rang of hunger.

Nashira Sargas was losing her patience.

21

TRAFALGAR

10 June 2059

I will never forget how Warden looked when I returned to him that night. It was the first time I understood that Rephs could experience fear.

Terebell had walked me to the doors of Magdalen. Gail had let me in, turning as ashen as the fog when she realised what I was wearing.

The red tunic was as warm as a fleece. It came with a raincoat, thicker socks, winter combat boots, a thermal undershirt, waterproof trousers, even tactical gloves. The white tunic was a scrap of paper in comparison.

For the first time in three months, I felt prepared and equipped for this city. I didn't have to brace myself against the cold. I even had a switchblade, which hooked on to my belt. It all made me feel like a Vigile, but I could live with that, if it meant that Nashira believed I was tame.

I climbed the steps and used the iron knocker on the door. When Warden opened it, he went still as stone, taking me in from my face to my reinforced boots.

The trepidation only showed itself for a split second. But I did see it, in that moment – a flicker of insecurity, dim as a candle. I watched him come to the realisation that he might have confided in the wrong person.

'Paige,' he said.

'Warden.'

After a moment, he stood aside. I walked past him.

'How was your inaugural feast?'

'Very interesting,' I said, tracing the red anchor on the gilet. 'You were right. Nashira did ask me some questions about you.'

There was a brief silence. I removed my new belt from over my gilet.

'And you answered them.' His voice was hard and flat. 'So be it.' He bolted the door. 'I must know what you told her, Paige.'

Warden had warned me against pride, but I glimpsed it in him now. He wasn't going to beg. His jaw was clenched tight, his mouth pressed into a firm line. I wondered what was racing through his mind.

Without replying, I went to his display case and opened it. I reached inside for the snuffbox and held it out to him, so he could see the lid.

'What does this symbol mean?'

Warden remained silent.

'Nashira asked me if I'd ever seen it in here,' I said. 'What is it?'

'First tell me how you answered her questions.'

Our gazes locked. Once, I would have taken pleasure in making him wait, just to watch him suffer. Now I wondered if I might be looking at an ally.

'I lied,' I said. 'I told her I'd never seen the flower.'

He watched me return the snuffbox to its place.

'I didn't tell her you vanish in the fog. I denied that you've ever tried to speak to me in a personal capacity.' I never broke his gaze as I spoke. 'I didn't tell her you burned the pamphlet. I didn't tell her about the wounds. I didn't tell her you call me by name.'

His expression changed. I walked towards him until I was close enough to touch.

'In short,' I said, 'your secrets are safe, Warden.'

After a long moment, he went to sit in his wing chair, where he poured his blend of wine and amaranth from the decanter.

'You withheld information from Nashira,' he finally said, 'but you have still been given a red tunic. You must have been very convincing.'

'Well, they do say the Irish have the gift of the gab. It's usually meant as an insult,' I said, 'but I'll take it, on this occasion. I *was* very good.'

'Hm.'

I kicked off my boots, then shed the gilet and the red tunic. Down to my undershirt and trousers, I curled up on the daybed, facing him.

'So you have chosen to protect me,' Warden said. 'You have come some way from wanting me to die a slow death in the woods, Paige.'

'I like you more than your consort.' I helped myself to his wine, pouring a second cup. 'I think I deserve to know what that symbol is, Warden.'

His eyes flickered with the fire. When he said nothing, I pursed my lips.

'Suit yourself,' I said. 'But I have a theory.' I leaned towards him. 'I heard a story that a group of Rephs revolted against the Sargas once. I heard they were the architects of the rebellion on Novembertide. I heard they were tortured in the House.'

'Where did you hear this?'

'If you get to have secrets, I do as well.'

David was strange, but I wasn't about to report him to Warden. He might still be useful.

'You're her consort,' I said. 'That's why I never thought you could be one of them, for weeks.' I held up my goblet. 'But you drink this for old wounds. You've risked keeping a symbol that clearly means a lot to you. Suhail and Thuban treat you with obvious contempt. Most damning of all, your consort doesn't trust you.'

'Surely no relationship is perfect,' Warden said.

I was certain there was a wry note in his voice.

'That brings me to my other theory, which is that you're having an affair with Terebell,' I said. 'I saw you with her. You seem quite … intimate.'

'Terebell is an old friend.'

'A fellow rebel?'

'Tell me again,' Warden said. 'Are you a pickpocket, Paige Mahoney?'

'Among other things.' I held his gaze. 'Are you a scarred one, Arcturus Mesarthim?' When he looked away, I said, 'You'd only be confirming that you *used* to be a rebel. You might not be one now.'

'If I were, more lives than my own would be at stake if I told you.'

'Now you understand why I can't share my whole past with you, either.'

In the long silence that followed, I took a sip of his wine, clearing my faint headache. Warden watched me do it, his fingers drumming on the arm of his chair.

'I hear we have an external assignment,' he said. 'Tomorrow night.'

He was still trying to skirt this discussion. Even now, he wouldn't confide in me.

'Yes,' I said. 'Your cousin is coming with us.'

'Situla is no friend of mine. She will report any misconduct to Nashira.'

'Your misconduct, or mine?'

'Both.' Warden drank. 'It is an interesting coincidence that our target should be the White Binder. Still, since you insist that you have no truck with him ... you should also have no qualms about the assignment.'

'I'd have qualms about bringing anyone here,' I said, keeping my tone neutral.

'Then will you hinder the assignment?'

'Will you punish me if I do?'

'No.'

Even if he had once been a rebel, he might have changed his ways. All of this could still be trickery. The constant uncertainty was forming a knot behind my ribs, making it hard to breathe. My instincts were at war.

I shouldn't trust him, even now, but something in me – my criminal intuition – recognised him as a fellow lawbreaker. All syndies knew their own.

'Nashira may strip you of your tunic, or give you to a different keeper,' Warden said. 'If that happens, I will not be able to help you, Paige.'

'Why do you want to help me?'

Warden looked at me with burning eyes.

'Are you training me to die,' I said, 'or to fight back?'

We were teetering on the brink of a confession. I found myself holding my breath, my chest tight. One of us was going to have to crack.

And suddenly, I knew it needed to be me. I had to be the one to take the risk – to break the deadlock, so we could be honest with each other.

Because if Warden was a scarred one, he had good reason to mistrust me. Twenty years ago, he had tried to save us, and one selfish human – one weak link – had brought the rebellion crashing down.

Warden had no idea if I was cut from the same cloth. If he was going to try again, he had to make sure he was choosing the right allies.

He wanted to trust me. I believed that. But if he learned for sure that I was the Pale Dreamer, he never would. A woman who had served the White Binder by choice – he would be reluctant to rely on my integrity.

He had already guessed the truth, and this assignment would confirm it. I had no plans whatsoever to detain either Jaxon or Carter.

Yet he was still interested, even with his suspicions. Even knowing I was a criminal.

'Say I did work at a higher level of the syndicate – if I was more than just a pickpocket,' I eventually said. 'What would you think about that?'

Warden looked into the fire.

'The syndicate is a blade with two edges,' he said. 'It is rare for us to capture its voyants, which implies it offers a degree of protection. Those who arrive here are often loners, rejected either by the gangs or their own families, or both. That is why they are easy to indoctrinate. They have been mistreated by their own kind, as well as Scion.'

'Because of people like the White Binder.'

'As you say.' He regarded me. 'We treat our human prisoners as inferior, but we acknowledge their clairvoyance. We give them a place, and the opportunity to rise. For many, that is preferable to the streets.'

'You seem to know a lot about this. How, if you don't catch many syndies?'

'Michael was once a polyglot,' he said. 'He knows Glossolalia, or Gloss – our language, the language of spirits.'

So that was its name.

'Like you, he was untaught, alone. He could not always control his outbursts,' Warden continued. 'His parents were so appalled and afraid that they forced him to drink bleach, trying to burn the unnaturalness out. The trauma collapsed his dreamscape. After that, he could not speak.'

It was trauma that made an unreadable. The dreamscape would grow back with layer upon layer of armour, preventing all spiritual attack.

'The Overseer found him,' Warden said. 'He was living rough on the streets of Southwark, having been rejected by the syndicate.' I clenched my jaw. 'Michael told me he prefers Magdalen to London. Though he is treated as an amaurotic here, he still has an aura. I taught him to sign. He may never sing in the way he once did, with the voices of the dead, but he is trying to speak again.'

This was far more than I had expected to hear from this conversation.

'Michael does not mind me telling you this,' Warden said, seeing my face. 'He encouraged it.'

It took me a moment to answer. 'You really taught him to sign?'

'Yes.'

'Why would you do that?'

'Michael is under my protection. You all are, in Magdalen,' he said. 'I do not know what I can do for this world, but I will not let any harm come to you.'

Silence returned to the chamber. Warden placed his goblet between us.

'An Irish girl in the conquerors' stronghold, hiding a power she neither understood, nor knew how to control,' he said. 'A father who could not help her.' I looked away. 'One turn in the path, and you might have shared the same fate as Michael. If you sought protection in the underworld, I am in no position to sit in judgement, Paige.'

'No,' I said softly. 'You're not.'

They might look like us, but they're nothing like us. Liss was in my head. *Do not let your guard down …*

'We should get some sleep,' I said.

'Yes. Gail believes the roof will not be finished until winter,' Warden said. 'While you stay in the parlour, I will give you as much privacy as I can. There is a nightshirt in the linen cabinet.'

I nodded, and he went into the bathroom. Once I heard the water running, I drew on the nightshirt, which tied at the waist with a broad sash. It was cream silk, soft against my skin.

In all our weeks together, Warden had landed one nail on the head: I did have an opportunistic streak. You needed one, to succeed in the syndicate. You picked every pocket that came within reach. You bid high on the best spirits. You left your father and ran away with the first charming stranger to fling you a lifeline, all to seize the day.

Nashira Sargas was a certainty – a guarantee of a few months of safety, followed inevitably by death. She was the deal the night Vigiles made.

Arcturus Mesarthim was a gamble that might not pay off. But I was a chancer.

And he was a chance.

The next day, while I should have been asleep, I was thinking of every possible scenario that could unfold when we reached London. This could be my one and only chance to escape before the Bicentenary.

By sunrise, the parlour was cold. I stirred awake when Warden rekindled the fire. After a pause, he went to the linen cabinet and took out a thick blanket, which he used to cover me. After that, he left the Founders Tower.

I slept uneasily. The clock woke me with a small chime at noon, and I sat up, sick to my stomach.

Tonight I might see Nick again. I might see all of them.

I couldn't let anyone bring them here.

Rain pounded at the windows. I wanted to try to see Liss, but I needed to save my strength. Whatever happened in London, it would be a hard night.

In the bathroom, I splashed my face and fastened my hair at my nape. I dressed in my uniform. Once I was ready, I found Warden's copy of *Frankenstein* and took a seat by the fire. I was a slow reader, but it would kill time.

At six in the evening, Warden emerged from his bedchamber. Instead of the monarch look, he was sporting a black overcoat, like a Londoner. They must have a whole team of tailors working for them.

'It is time.'

I nodded. He locked the door behind us and walked with me down the steps.

'I never thanked you,' he said as we entered the cloister. 'For your silence.'

'Don't thank me yet.' I adjusted my new splint. 'I could still embarrass you tonight.'

'Paige.'

Warden stopped, and I did the same. Even in the dark, the light in his eyes was faint enough that you could almost blink and miss it.

Over the weeks, I had realised that their eyes dimmed as they grew hungry. He must have abstained with intent, to help conceal his nature in the citadel.

'Scion will not allow you to escape,' he warned me. 'If an opportunity appears to present itself, I strongly advise you to resist the temptation. In the unlikely event that you do succeed in eluding the authorities, you will never be able to get back to Oxford.'

'When you escape from somewhere, you don't generally intend to come back.'

'Your fellow humans would still be imprisoned here, including Liss.'

'Don't you dare use her to pull my heartstrings,' I hissed. 'What have you ever done for the performers – for any of them?'

'I help as many humans as I can without raising suspicions.'

'You have all this space, and you brought three people in from the cold?'

'Those in the greatest need,' Warden said, his voice low. 'Fazal was almost killed by Castor Sargas, who once ruled Balliol. Gail has a condition that requires frequent medication. I told you about Michael. I have also done my utmost to protect you by downplaying your progress to Nashira.'

He had never been this frank with me. I waited, not wanting to stop him.

'Magdalen has been my home for two centuries,' he said. 'I have tried to make it safe for you – but I cannot bring every human inside, lest it be taken from me. Nashira has already threatened me with that.'

Jaxon would tell me to harden myself. He would throw every amaurotic and performer into the dirt if stepping on them got me back to him.

'If I stay,' I said after a moment, 'none of us will be any less trapped.'

'Return from this assignment, and I will tell you what I know. I will also tell you the meaning of the symbol you found on my snuffbox.'

'Every time I think you might be honest, you hold back. You can't keep dangling this carrot,' I said under my breath. 'Do you swear it, Warden?'

'You have my word. Do I have yours that you will not try to escape?'

'No,' I said. 'You'll just have to trust me to do what I think is best.'

Warden looked me straight in the eyes. When he strode on, I followed.

Magdalen Walk was deserted. Melting hailstones crunched beneath my boots. When we reached the Residence of the Suzerain, two Rephs escorted us to the oration library, where Nashira waited.

Warden knelt before her. I knelt beside him without being prompted.

At first, I had thought he greeted her like this because she was his sovereign – but none of the other Rephs had to lower themselves. Next, I had assumed they showed affection like this, only to have that dashed when Warden had been so obviously tender with Terebell.

This time, I saw the stiffness of his movements; how he never even tried to lift his gaze. Nashira regarded him as if he were a loyal dog, not her consort. It gave me a hot rush of second-hand humiliation.

Something was off about this relationship.

'Arcturus,' Nashira said. 'I see you have brought our dreamwalker in good time. I am pleased you are both joining this assignment.' (Like we had a choice.) 'Situla will report to me on how you work together.'

Situla Mesarthim was almost as tall as Warden. I could see the family resemblance in their features, though her brown hair was long and plaited, her skin a few tones lighter. Like Warden, she was dressed like a Londoner.

'Cousin,' she said. Warden gave her a small nod. '40, you will treat me as your second keeper this evening. I trust that is understood.'

'I am certain that 40 will behave herself,' Nashira said. 'Rise, both of you.'

Warden stood, looking down a short way at his consort. I got back to my feet.

'You will be teamed with 30 and 1 on this assignment,' Nashira said to me. 'Arcturus will supervise you. Situla will take 18, 12 and 26.'

At first, I thought she meant Julian. A moment later, I realised it must be the 26 from the last Bone Season.

My own counterpart must already be dead. I seemed to be the only 40.

As if David Fitton had been summoned, he emerged from behind a screen. He was dressed exactly like the Overseer on the night of my arrest.

'Evening, 40,' he said.

An amaurotic came to my side. 'This way, please.'

Without looking at David, I followed the woman behind the curtain. David smiled and shook his head, as if I were an amusing child.

The space beyond was a dressing room of sorts. I took off my uniform and donned the one that had been left for me. A fresh undershirt, trousers, then a thicker shirt with long sleeves, made to wick off sweat. Next, the bulletproof armour – a lightweight vest, marked with the red anchor. The final layer was, quite literally, a red jacket.

I pulled on the boots, lacing them tight. I could run, climb and fight in this attire. A small backpack had been provided, which contained a syringe of adrenalin and a medical kit, along with an air rifle and a set of darts.

Flux darts, for hunting voyants.

Once I was kitted out, I emerged from behind the curtain. The human team members had all gathered around a table. Carl beckoned me.

'Hello, 40.'

'Carl,' I said.

He let the name slide. 'How are you finding your new tunic?'

'It fits.'

'I mean, how are you finding being a red-jacket?'

All of them were looking at me now, their faces curious.

'Fantastic,' I said, after a pause.

Carl nodded, pleased. 'It is great. We're glad to have you with us.'

I raised an eyebrow. Carl must have decided that I was a friend worth making.

'I'll reserve judgement,' 30 said, pulling her thick hair from her collar. She was taller than me, wide in the hips and shoulders. 'You newcomers have yet to prove yourselves in London. I'll be keeping a close eye on you both, 1 and 40. You're to follow my orders to the letter.'

'Same to you, 12,' 26 said. 'Take your lead from me and 18. No heroics.'

David nodded.

30 gave me a penetrating look. From her aura, she was a sooth-sayer – a less common one, possibly a cleromancer. If she had been part of the syndicate, she must have clawed her way in. I wondered how many voyants she had helped to detain, and if any of them had been syndies.

'All of you have been issued with an air rifle and flux darts,' she said. 'You're permitted to carry your switchblades for self-defence, but you are not to kill any of our targets. The Suzerain insists they're kept alive.'

Carl looked crestfallen. 'We don't get proper guns?'

'You don't. We veterans do,' 30 said. 'After your third assign-ment, you may be entrusted with a firearm, once you've received specialist training.'

At least they couldn't shoot to kill. Even the White Binder would be powerless against a bullet.

'A Vigile commandant will update us in London,' 30 said, 'but the plan is simple. Our teams will launch a surprise attack on Carter and the Seven Seals. We have no intel on the sort of weapons they might have, or how powerful their abilities are, so I say we hit them hard and fast.'

Jaxon and Nick were lethal in spirit combat. Nick could blind his opponents with visions; Jaxon could wield his boundlings against them.

As for physical combat, Nadine was our best. She was a crack shot, and knew how to fight. Danica could be good at close quar-ters, given her strength.

Zeke and Eliza, however, were not natural fighters. They would be most vulnerable. I hoped Jaxon might leave them at the den, but I knew he wouldn't. He would be far too eager to show Carter his collection.

'Vigiles will be stationed nearby, to catch them if they do elude us,' 30 said, 'but ideally, we need to contain this confrontation in Trafalgar Square, to avoid causing any unrest in London. We render the targets unconscious and get them straight back to our vehicles.'

Warden had been deep in conversation with Alsafi. Now he came to stand with our group, along with Situla and a blond Reph, clearly a Chertan.

'This is Tertius. He will join us,' Warden said. 'Do finish your briefing, 30.'

Tertius gave me a venomous look. At this point, I must have earned the ire of the whole family. 30 nodded, tucking her hair behind her ear.

'Two vehicles will take us to London. They should have just got to Magdalen Bridge,' 30 said. 'If all goes well, we'll be back to our residences by dawn.'

'It must go well,' Situla said. 'If it does not, you will all be held accountable.'

'Come,' Warden said. 'Let us not keep the drivers waiting.'

Carl looked as if Novembertide had come early. He almost skipped after Warden. I was about to follow him when Nashira appeared at my side.

'Suzerain,' I said, unnerved.

'I know who you are.' She spoke quietly enough that only I could hear. 'If you do not bring back a dreamwalker, I will assume that *you* are the Pale Dreamer.'

Before I could reply, she walked away. I took a deep breath and followed Warden.

Two black cars had appeared on Folly Bridge, which the performers called the Brig of Dread. The city guards blindfolded us all before they locked us into our respective vehicles. I found myself in the backseat with Carl, in a heated and upholstered seat.

After three months of living in a medieval building, mostly by fire and candlelight, it was strange to be in a car. It drove away from the lost city.

Nashira couldn't really believe we could apprehend eight voyants and waltz away before dawn. I knew better. I knew Jaxon. This was going to be a brutal clash. I would be fighting on one side and rooting for the other.

Even if I couldn't escape, I had to get word to him. I had to let him know I was alive.

Not long after we left, the car slowed. I looked around. The guards had tied the blindfold too well for me to get a glimpse around it.

'This is our first stop, Winterbrook,' Warden said. 'You may remove your blindfolds.'

Winterbrook, the support outpost. I wished I could get a look at it, but even without the blindfold, I couldn't see much in the dark.

A Vigile was at the door. Even though it was past sundown, she was amaurotic. 'Take off your jackets,' she said, her voice muffled by a helmet.

Once I had, she grasped my arm and pushed up my sleeve. She injected something under my skin, causing a sharp twinge. Carl kept up a brave face as she did the same to him. The doors were shut and locked.

'Warden,' I said, 'what was that?'

He caught my eye in the mirror. I cradled my arm, watching blood seep from the puncture.

'Put your blindfolds back on,' the driver said. 'Next stop is London.'

I tied mine with clammy hands.

It had to be a tracking device. Warden must have been ordered not to tell me.

Now I had no chance of escape. Danica might be able to fry a tracker, but she wouldn't have the right tools on her in Trafalgar Square, if she was there at all. I leaned back in my seat, close to despair.

After a while, I nodded off. Despite my best attempts, I had barely slept the day before. I woke with a sense of confusion when the car stopped.

'We have arrived,' Warden said.

My heart thumped. 'Can I take off the blindfold?'

'Yes.'

I removed it, blinking in the familiar blue glow of London. The car was rolling past Hyde Park, where Eliza and I often went for brisk walks on our breaks in winter, drinking hot mecks and eating roasted chestnuts.

My chest ached. I wanted to get out of this car and run into my citadel. I wanted long and lamplit evenings in the den. I wanted to climb skyscrapers with Nick.

Carl had been jittery for the journey, bouncing his knee and fiddling with his air rifle, but he must have fallen asleep on the motorway, as I had. Before he dozed off, he had let slip that 30 used to be called Amelia. As I had guessed, she was a cleromancer, with a particular gift for dice. It took me a while to remember the exact word: *astragalomancer*. I was getting rusty.

When Carl stirred, I looked at him. His hair needed a wash, and his nails were bitten to the quick, but there were no bruises. Terebell must be treating him well.

'You can take the blindfold off,' I said.

He did, blinking. Seeing me, he hesitated, then leaned towards me.

'Don't try to escape.'

He whispered it.

'They won't let you go. He won't.' He glanced at Warden. 'Oxford is the best place for us. Why would you want to come back to London?'

'Because we don't belong there.'

'It's the one place we *do* belong. We don't have to hide there, Paige.'

'You're not an idiot, Carl. You know it's a prison.'

'And this is SciLo,' he said, his voice hoarse. 'The Rephs let us live. They give us a chance to prove ourselves. All they give us here is death.' When I didn't reply, he scowled. 'Don't think I won't try to stop you running. I won't let you drag the rest of us down.'

'No talking,' the driver interrupted.

Carl slouched back into his seat. I rested my temple against the window, bathed in blue light.

Thirteen years ago, I had thought like Carl. This citadel had been my prison, crushing me in its iron fist. You had to apply for permission to leave. You had to work hard to avoid being caught. You had to fit into the boxes it drew for you: normal, natural, biddable.

It was only when Nick found me again that I had seen its other side. Jaxon had opened the doors to *his* London – an ancient and unseemly beast, abounding with chaos and secrets, all waiting to be unlocked. Scion had pinned it beneath the anchor, but London could not be contained. Entering the underworld had brought me back to life.

And yet I had seen voyants suffer on these streets. I had seen them cold and hungry, spurned by their own kind. The Unnatural Assembly only rewarded those who were useful, and served without question. The rest were thrown out to rot, like the performers in the Rookery.

London and Oxford – two sides of a coin, darkly mirroring each other.

Carl continued to sulk on my right. I shook myself.

I couldn't let him get to me. In London, I was mollisher of I-4. I had a name, a purpose, a place. It was worlds away from the cruelty of the Rookery.

Soon we were in Marylebone, where Nick officially lived. I dared not look up as we passed the luxury apartment block on Thayer Street.

Warden gazed at the citadel. No doubt he had been here before. It chilled me that Rephs had been on the streets, and no one had ever noticed.

Except for me, tracking that strange dreamscape in I-4. Even then, the Rephs must have been looking for Jaxon. I couldn't understand the fixation. To them, he was just one criminal among many.

The driver turned down Bulstrode Street. He was a robust man in wire-framed spectacles and a suit. An earpiece flashed every so often. No doubt Scion paid him well for his silence. It was morbidly fascinating to see its inner workings from this angle. For two centuries, they had guarded the secret, protecting and feeding the forge of the anchor.

In Soho, Warden motioned for the driver to stop on Warwick Street. The man left the car. I sat in tense silence, my heart in my throat. This was my turf. Jaxon owned these streets. Every courier and thief here reported to him. I knew most of them by name.

When the driver returned, he carried a large paper bag. Warden passed it to me. Inside were two hot cartons from Brekkabox, the most popular food chain in the citadel, which served breakfast all day and night.

'For strength,' Warden said. 'You may need it.'

Carl reached straight into the bag and took his share. I opened it again to find a breakfast wrap, a pot of porridge, and a disappointing lack of coffee.

Trafalgar Square was about half a mile away. I took advantage of the stop to probe the æther, my scalp prickling. Thousands of dreamscapes pressed against mine, giving me an immediate headache. I tuned my perception, but it was too hard to focus.

Our car pulled into the courtyard of a building on Suffolk Place, just off Haymarket, namesake of the Underlord. He ruled this part of the citadel personally.

A night Vigile received us with a salute. Warden got out first, opening the door for me and Carl. He was being too courteous towards humans in public.

'Vigile,' he said.

'Warden,' the Vigile said, with a smart nod. 'Please accept my regards from the Chief of Vigilance, the Minister for Internal Affairs, and the Grand Inquisitor. Welcome back to London.' A visor concealed his eyes. 'Can I confirm you have Carl Dempsey-Brown and Paige Mahoney in your custody?'

'Confirmed.'

'Thank you.'

'I expected the Chief of Vigilance to receive us himself,' Warden said. 'Is he unwell?'

'He was called to an emergency. I hope you'll forgive his absence, my lord.'

'Since you appear competent, I may.'

The Vigile turned his visored face towards me. I wondered what had pushed him to turn on his own kind.

'You two should remember that you are still in custody,' he said curtly. 'This assignment is part of your penal servitude, not a night on the town.'

'Shame,' I said.

Warden gave me a warning look.

'If you leave the containment zone,' the Vigile said, ignoring my comment, 'your tracking devices will incapacitate you with an electric shock.'

I kept my expression calm. 'What if our targets leave the zone?'

'You are to desist. We'll take it from there.' He handed me a data pad, which showed a map of the area. 'I recommend you both memorise it.'

The red circle extended almost to the Westminster Archon in the south, and Leicester Square in the north. Seven Dials lay just outside it. I showed Carl.

'To avoid causing a public disturbance, all eight targets must be apprehended quickly,' the Vigile said. 'You should prioritise Carter, the Pale Dreamer, and the White Binder. Vigiles will be in the vicinity, but they will not interfere unless the containment zone is breached.' He checked his watch. 'We have forty minutes until the expected time of arrival. Do not attack until all targets are in Trafalgar Square.'

Carl was looking at the map with obvious worry. He must not know this part of the citadel.

'Once your task is complete, you will return to this building. From here, you will be driven straight back to the penal colony,' the Vigile said. 'If either of you attempts to broadcast its existence or location, you will be shot. If either of you attempts to engage with the public or your targets, you will be shot. If either of you attempts to harm your keeper or a Vigile, you will be shot. Do I make myself clear?'

Well, it seemed reasonably clear that whatever we did, we were going to be shot.

'We understand,' I said, when Carl just swallowed.

'Good.'

The Vigile reached into his utility belt, unpacking a silver tube and a pair of latex gloves. I steeled myself for another injection.

'You first,' he said to me. 'Open your mouth.'

'What?'

'Are you having trouble with the Inquisitor's English?'

He sounded like Evelyn Ancroft. I resisted the urge to make him bleed.

The Vigile stepped towards me and took hold of my chin. I wanted to bite the bastard. He scraped a nib over my lips, coating them in something cold and bitter.

'Shut it.'

With no other choice, I closed my mouth. When I tried to open it again, I found my lips were sealed. My hand flew to them, my eyes widening.

'Just a spot of dermal adhesive.' The Vigile pulled Carl towards him. 'We're not taking any chances, seeing as all you syndies know each other.'

'But I wasn't—' Carl started.

'Shut up.'

Carl was summarily forced to shut up.

'30 isn't glued. Look at her for orders,' the Vigile said. 'Otherwise, stick to your objectives.'

I pushed my tongue against my lips, but they wouldn't budge. This Vigile definitely had some grievance with the syndicate.

Warden reached into his coat and presented us with two full masks, stiff and blank. At night, they would go unnoticed by most denizens.

'Put these on,' he said. 'Are you both ready?'

Carl nodded and donned his mask.

Warden sought my gaze. I looked grimly at him before I pressed the mask to my face, feeling it bond with my skin. With my lips sealed, I couldn't call for help. A tight hood came next, concealing my hair.

Now my only chance of being recognised was for one of the gang to clock my aura. Surely Jaxon would – it was the first thing he noticed about anyone.

He still might not realise who I was. In his mind, I was the only dreamwalker, his peerless jewel. I was also either dead or imprisoned. If he thought he was seeing another one, he might go straight into denial – and even after living with me for three years, there was a small chance he could mistake me for an oracle. He might not believe his own eyes, his own senses. The only way to find out was to get close to him.

Warden put on a mask of his own, making his face even blanker than usual. For the first time, I was glad I was on his side.

Suffolk Place had been deserted, but Haymarket had a few people on it. Tertius met us on the corner of Pall Mall with Amelia and David. Trafalgar Square was now in sight, and we all strode towards it.

'Situla will approach from the other side with 18 and 26,' Tertius said. '12, 30, take your positions.'

Amelia nodded. 'Don't enter Trafalgar Square, 12. It could spook them.'

A bob of his mask was his only reply.

Hector and Jaxon had never agreed on where the line between their territories lay. I had come here many times, to fend off intrusions.

Nelson's Column rose from between its two fountains. Like other major landmarks across the citadel, it was always lit in either red or green, depending on the security level. It was green now; so were the lights in the water, which rippled and churned.

A voyant brushed past me. Glancing at her, I glimpsed an earpiece. A plainclothes Vigile.

After three months away, in a city with a tiny population, so many dreamscapes were overwhelming. I tried again to pinpoint the others, breaking a cold sweat.

When I sensed her, my heart jolted. Looking as best I could through the eyeholes of the mask, I saw a figure sitting on the steps of the Imperial Gallery.

Scion had no idea she existed. Her birth had never been registered. I was willing to bet that no one here knew she was one of the Seven Seals, either.

Eliza had arrived early. I had a wild thought that I could send a ghost across the square to nudge her, but the Rephs would notice at once. If I used my own spirit, I would collapse on the spot.

'Carter will arrive soon,' Warden said, keeping his voice low. 'We must bide our time. Do not allow yourselves to be captured under any circumstances.'

On the steps, Eliza kept sketching, oblivious.

Get out of here. I wished I was an oracle, so I could send her a vision. *Run while you still can ...*

Now I could detect the others. Five dreamscapes approaching from five directions.

Trafalgar Square was surrounded by seven plinths, each housing a tall statue of an important figure in the history of Scion – three women and four men, including Lord Palmerston. Rifle at the ready, Amelia crouched behind Irène Tourneur, the First Inquisitor of France.

Warden led me and Carl to the foot of the seventh plinth, which always depicted the incumbent Grand Inquisitor. Frank Weaver frowned at the square – every detail cast in iron, down to his side whiskers.

A pair of amaurotics were chatting on the steps of Nelson's Column. A voyant approached them with a tin, holding it out for money. They waved him off in annoyance and headed towards Charing Cross.

Eliza watched it happen. Jaxon must have sent her to clear the area. After all, Antoinette Carter was taking an enormous risk by coming here.

Warden glanced down at me. 'Forgive me. I did not know you would be silenced.'

I dismissed his concern with a shake of my head.

'Remember what I told you.' His voice was very soft. 'Remember what is at stake.'

In the distance, Big Ben chimed. Its stately clangs rang out from Whitehall – the unmistakeable music of London. I closed my eyes, listening.

At the first booming strike, Nick arrived on the scene. By the fourth, Eliza had moved to his side. By the sixth, Nadine and Zeke were joining them. In time with the seventh, Jaxon appeared, materialising from the northeast. And last, as the final strike faded, came Danica.

I pressed my back to the plinth, my willpower at breaking point. For almost three months, I had been strong, even if I had also been homesick. Now all I wanted to do was sprint to my strange family.

A hush blanketed Trafalgar Square. Antoinette Carter strode into that silence, coming from the direction of Embankment. She wore a frock cloak, heeled boots, and a brimmed hat. Between her fingers was a cigarette in a silver holder.

When I looked back at Nick, I thought I would burst – into tears, into laughter. Given his day job, he was disguised. I was surprised he had risked coming here at all. A dark wig covered his hair, and he wore tinted glasses. A few feet away, Jaxon was tapping his cane.

I had missed them all so much. It hurt like a kick to the stomach, to be so close and still unseen.

Eliza took a few steps towards Carter. Danica stuck to her side, her stance defensive. A scarf and bowler concealed most of her face.

There was no way she wanted to be here. Jaxon really was keen to impress.

Carter stopped by one of the fountains. I could hardly believe I was seeing her in the flesh. She hadn't brought anyone else to the meeting.

Eliza made a small gesture – three fingertips to her forehead. It was the sign of the third eye, easy for voyants to decipher. When Carter returned it, Jaxon walked towards her, a welcoming smile on his lips. With a smile of her own, Carter grasped his gloved hand in both of hers.

Situla Mesarthim struck first. She had been hiding behind one of the great bronze lions in the square. Almost faster than I could register, she ran at Carter. Warden made towards Zeke, just as Carl sent a nearby spirit hurtling towards Eliza. She crumpled as it struck her dreamscape. As an art medium, muses loved her best, but any spirit could possess her.

Amelia seized her chance. She lunged out and aimed her air rifle at Eliza, only to be tackled by an enraged Nick. David took Jaxon – or *tried* to take Jaxon, in any case (a bold move); Danica lamped him straight away, knocking a spurt of blood from his mouth. Tertius bore down on Nadine, who looked as if she had just seen a corpse rise from the grave. 18 and 26 closed in from the other side of the square.

Danica started trading blows with David, leaving Jaxon as the only one without an opponent to fight. I stepped out from behind the plinth.

Jaxon saw me at once, another masked enemy. He fused six ghosts into a spool and hurled it towards me; I deflected it and sent a flux dart at him, aiming above his head. Jaxon ducked it. Several of his boundlings came soaring from nearby, ready to defend their master.

This was it. I ran straight at him.

Jaxon was livid. Anyone else might have mistaken his pallor and wide eyes for evidence of terror, but I knew otherwise. We had spoiled his plans – plans he had laid for a very long time. Teeth bared, he swept towards me, wielding his cane. It was a weapon in disguise, heavy enough that it doubled up as a bludgeon. He could also pull a blade from inside. I had seen him use it many times, to shed blood and smash bone.

I had always been grateful that I was not the one on the receiving end.

He swung the cane at me. I rolled to avoid it. No sooner was I back on my feet than his fist clipped my cheekbone. If not for the mask, his silver knuckledusters would have broken it. Next, he drove them into my ribs, but my body armour took most of the force. I let him slug me again and again, barely even pretending to fight back. I needed him not just to see my aura, but to sense it, remember it.

When he stepped back, his gaze was hot with bloodlust. He wasn't concentrating on the æther – not yet. Even a red aura couldn't avert his fury. The cane whipped across my shin, and I stumbled, in agony. Its pommel caught my shoulder, my unprotected hip. I realised he might kill me before he recognised me.

The cane barely missed the top of my head. That terrible pulling sensation came, like seams ripping apart, and I hit out at him with my spirit. Now it was Jaxon who fell, floored by the thump against his dreamscape. I clawed myself upright, my cheek pounding, ribs aching. I gripped my knees, hauling air through my nose, unable to gasp.

If I did get away from the Rephs, Jaxon was going to be quite annoyed about this.

A screech caught my attention. Nadine had got away from Tertius and pinned Amelia to the fountain. Nick had taken over. He fired a revolver at Tertius. I watched, my head swimming. Tertius barely looked fazed.

Warden hadn't been lying. Our weapons couldn't hurt them.

Nick fired again. It took a moment to realise it was my revolver – the one I had left in the den, that night in March. The gun I carried on syndicate business.

He had kept a small piece of me with him.

Swallowing, I looked around for Warden. He was stalking after Zeke, who was doing his level best to dissuade him, making spool after spool.

I clenched my fist. Even if my gang wasn't outnumbered, they were out of their depth. Each Reph had the strength of multiple humans – and the resilience of a tank, apparently. I had to help them even the odds.

My broken wrist was throbbing. I pulled out the syringe of adrenalin and slammed the needle into my thigh. After a few moments, all the pain – old and new – dulled to a distant ache. My vision wouldn't settle, but it wasn't incapacitating.

Amelia kicked Nadine back, aiming her rifle. Before I quite knew what I was doing, I aimed mine. The dart hit Amelia in the back. She dropped like a stone.

Nadine whirled around. She hadn't seen me shoot, but now she did see me – not her mollisher, but a masked figure with a dart gun, an agent of the anchor. Without hesitation, she drew her pistol and pointed it.

The best shot in the gang. She would kill me without question, and with ease. Before she could fire, I sprinted across the square and tackled her, taking her down by the waist, straight into the fountain. The water turned luminous red as the security level changed.

Nadine surfaced just after me, hair plastered to her face. I waded back, the water swashing to my knees.

'Take that mask off, coward,' she shouted at me. 'Who the fuck are you?'

I kept my flux gun trained on her, shaking my head. Nadine opened her coat and chose a knife. She had always preferred steel to spirits.

Time seemed to slow. I felt my heartbeat everywhere, right down to my fingertips. Nadine was almost as good with a knife as she was with a gun, and my body armour would only provide so much protection. It left my limbs and throat exposed. In water, I would be slower.

Nadine knew this, and smiled.

She threw the first blade. I lurched away, and it glanced off my mask. Before I could even draw a breath, a longer knife was in her grasp. If she managed to hit the right point on my thigh, I would bleed out.

David chose that moment to appear. Just as Nadine was about to let fly, he put a dart between her shoulders. Her face slackened. She tottered back, swayed, and fell against the edge of the fountain with a splash.

I called her name, but all I could make was a muffled sound, trapped behind my lips. David pulled her halfway out of the water and took her head between his hands. Just as Nashira had done to Seb.

In the heat of the moment, David must have forgotten his orders. He was about to kill Nadine.

I didn't even pause to think. For the second time, I projected my spirit.

I struck the wall of his dreamscape.

And suddenly, I passed through it.

As soon as I was in there, I kept going. Not stopping to see my surroundings, I reached his sunlit zone and shoved his spirit aside. Now I was seeing through his eyes, feeling the solid hammer of his heart. I forced him to release Nadine. I watched myself slip underwater.

The sight tightened my silver cord. It flung me back into my own dreamscape, my own body. Now I was thrashing out of the water, my nose burning, soaked to my skin. Barely able to see, I ran towards David and threw myself at him. We both went crashing to the ground.

My vision turned black for a moment. I lay stunned, my lips trembling as I tried to pull a deep breath in. I had just possessed a human.

I had done what Nashira wanted of me.

Tertius had seen; so had Situla. The eyeholes of both their masks were aglow.

Beside me, David clutched his head, a wordless groan in his throat. I used the fountain to drag myself up, blinking away droplets, my clothes heavy.

Nadine was still fighting the flux. Dazed, she made it to the other side of the fountain and rolled herself out. Zeke was there to catch her. A dart protruded from his side, but he was immune to phantasmagoria.

Not so for his sister. Nadine had only held out for this long because her survival instinct had kicked in. He had to get her out of here.

Carl was circling Antoinette Carter, trying to get a dart in her. Somehow, she was holding her own against Situla, keeping her at bay with spools.

My head was about to erupt. It had been worth it. I did a sweep of Trafalgar Square, assessing the situation. David and all three Bone Season veterans were down, while my gang had only lost Nadine.

Now they had a fighting chance.

'Fury,' Zeke shouted, his voice cracking. 'Get Bell out of here, now!'

Danica was bruised and bloody, but she had always been strongest. She got Nadine over her shoulders and huffed away from the square.

Nick floored Carl with a spool. He was running after Danica when Warden blocked his path. I thought my heart would stop as they squared up to each other – my keeper, pitted against my best friend. A collision of different sides of my life. I started towards them, even as I felt the æther ripple. Nick was about to send a volley of visions.

Before I could get to them, Eliza attacked me.

Spirits flew at me from every direction. Given a choice, they usually sided with mediums. Three of them slammed into my dreamscape. I stumbled, blinded by visions of their memories: towering waves, the blast of muskets, fires raging on the deck of a ship – screaming, chaos – then Eliza gave me a shove, and I fell. I thrust up all my mental defences, while Eliza tried to hold me down.

'Keep at it, all of you,' she urged the spirits. 'You have to buy us time!'

My dreamscape was flooding. Cannonballs ripped through it, and burning wood fell past my eyes. With a huge effort, I forced out the spirits and gripped Eliza by the arm. I squeezed it hard, willing her to understand.

Eliza was drenched in sweat. She must be terrified, to have forced herself to fight that hard – too afraid to distinguish that press of her arm from another cruel hand, or to pay closer attention to my aura. I pushed her away from me and scrambled back, cutting my hand wildly across my throat. I saw her hesitate – just for a moment – before she went for her gun, a pocket revolver.

This was a lost cause. If I were her, I knew I wouldn't stop. I would shoot.

I knew, because I had not stopped to listen to the Overseer.

Warden noticed my predicament. Almost in a single motion, he wove together an intricate spool and sent it flying towards Eliza. It entangled her senses as well as a net. She dropped the gun and buckled.

'Muse,' Nick bellowed.

Warden was still in his way. Now so were Tertius and Situla. He looked between them, his wig awry, my revolver in hand. Hot tears of denial sprang to my eyes. His name burned in my throat. I wanted him to run. Even with his visions, he couldn't fight all three of them.

Nick Nygård stood his ground. I had to help him fight the Rephs.

Just as I rose, I felt the blow coming. I turned just in time to block a bloody cane with my rifle, the jarring force almost disarming me.

'A dreamwalker in uniform,' Jaxon said softly. 'Where did Scion find you?'

My arms were shaking. For a man who rarely left his own home, Jaxon was strong.

'Perhaps you were hidden away in the suburbs. Or in another citadel.' He leaned in close to me, staring into the eyeholes of the mask. 'You can't possibly be *my* dreamwalker. She is dead. If not,

I would already have found her. I have scoured every prison, every dark corner and cesspit of this citadel.' The cane strained closer. 'So who are you?'

Heat pricked my eyes again. He really had looked for me.

Before I could do anything, Jaxon was thrown back by another massive spool, larger than any a human could make. It made him lose his footing. His boundlings retaliated in a fury, shooting towards Warden.

Jaxon lashed out blindly. Instinct jerked my head to the left, and the cane scraped across one side of my mask. I raised my gun, just to ward him off, but a second blow knocked it clean out of my hand.

Danica had installed a blade for him. He could either draw it out fully, or expose the end, like a bayonet on an old musket. The sharp tip flashed across my right arm, cutting through my jacket, deep into flesh.

'Come, dreamwalker, use your spirit!' Jaxon pointed the blade at me, laughing in delight. 'Let go of the pain and fly. Use it to propel yourself.'

Even now, his work came first. I backed away from him, grasping my arm with my bad hand. Already my fingers were covered in blood.

A crowd of amaurotics were on the edge of Trafalgar Square, some of them on their phones. The Vigiles were stopping them from getting any closer.

'Ah, the general public,' Jaxon observed. 'Just as I was enjoying myself.'

Carter ran to join Nick. Her hat was gone, exposing her cascade of dyed crimson hair. Her face was pinched and gaunt, but I remembered it. In desperation, I grabbed Jaxon by the cheeks and shook him as hard as I could. Jaxon stared at me as I tried to say his name.

Antoinette Carter distracted us both.

One moment, she was standing by Nick. The next, the æther drew itself around her, like cloth gathered into a hand. Her eyes rolled back. Even from here, I could feel the change in her aura, an ember blown into a flame. It mocked the blue streetlights of the citadel, the ones designed to soothe the troubled mind. With no hesitation, she physically attacked all three Rephs, hitting them with her fists and boots.

When I had charged at Warden, I had come off worse. Carter was forcing them back. Ten spirits swooped at Situla, not letting her get a hit in edgeways.

'Binder,' Nick bellowed. 'Let's go!'

Jaxon looked at me, and I looked at him. I tightened my grip on his face.

'It's not possible,' he breathed.

Carter spun into a kick that sent Tertius straight into the column. I stared. Situla landed a blow, but it rolled off Carter like water from steel.

And then, with no warning, she took off. Warden swept his gaze across the square, seeing that most of his soldiers were down. Only I was left.

'Stop her,' he called.

The Vigiles were approaching the square. I had to divide their forces and lead the chase away from Jaxon and Nick, so they could get to Eliza.

I let go of Jaxon and sprinted after Carter.

A Vigile let me go past when he saw my uniform. Carter was heading down Whitehall, straight for the Westminster Archon. She was off the cot to go in that direction, but I didn't care. That was the very edge of the containment zone. I needed to keep forcing her there, so she would no longer be my responsibility. She could get away.

Carter had noticed me. I was fast, but she forged ahead. Her battle trance seemed to have fuelled her pace. Situla overtook me, then Tertius. I tried to keep their auras in range as I wove between people and cars.

Whitehall was always busy, even in the small hours. Some way in front of me, a white taxi braked in front of Carter as she crossed the street. She and Situla split around it. I took the straightest course, running up the front of the car and on to the roof, sliding down the other side.

Carter went through a crowd of pedestrians, all waiting for a night bus. Seconds behind her, Situla sliced through the human obstacles. They screamed; I felt one of them die. This would leave quite a mess for the Vigiles.

My legs pumped. If I let up for a moment, Carter and Situla would be out of range. I shed my jacket, then my armour, dropping as much weight as I could. Just when I thought my lungs would burst, we reached the very end of Whitehall.

Westminster. We avoided this area like the plague, so heavy was its contingent of Vigiles. I looked with utter loathing at the Archon, the heart and seat of the Republic of Scion. Had I been in a less life-threatening situation, I would have liked to leave some choice graffiti on those walls.

This was where the puppets danced. Only Haymarket Hector would dare to live so close to it, for the Underlord was the shadow of the Grand Inquisitor. One ruled the surface, and one ruled the underworld.

Situla was only just ahead of me now. When she reached Westminster Bridge, Antoinette Carter turned to face her pursuers. Her skin looked stretched across her bones, like a thin layer of white paint.

'No farther.' Tertius drew a blade. 'Surrender, Antoinette Carter.'

'Do you know what I am, creature?'

The æther quaked.

'I am the voice that heralds the ages,' Carter told him. 'My sisters were the bestowers of truth in ancient times. I warn you not to hinder me.'

Her lips were now as dark as mine, as if her words had stained them.

'Use your spirit, 40,' Situla ordered me.

I stepped forward. Behind me, I could hear sirens and distant cries.

Carter watched me. 'Do I know you?'

She spoke with a richer accent than mine. I wanted to tell her that she didn't know me, but I knew her. That we had both cheated death in Dublin.

Situla lost her patience and sent a flux dart at Carter. It shattered before it could touch her. I tensed as a spirit appeared in front of her, spreading its protection wide, like wings.

A breacher. I concentrated on the æther, trying to identify it. It was something like a guardian angel, but older. This had to be an archangel – a breacher that remained with one bloodline for generations. They weakened over the years, but remained notoriously difficult to banish.

Carter stood her ground. This might be the most powerful voyant I had ever seen. A devastating gift *and* an archangel at her command. I had never imagined that a human could give the Rephs this much trouble.

Situla reached for the nearest spirits, lacing them all together. When Jaxon had first taught me about spooling, he had compared a spool to a rat king – a knot of rodents, entangled by their own tails, stuck together with hair or sap. The more rats in the king, the harder it was to separate them without killing them. And the more spirits in a spool, the harder it often was to deflect.

The Rephs could make spools more intricate than any I had ever seen. Beside me, Situla bound hers as if with mortar, just as Warden had.

Before she could finish the spool, Carter cut her arm towards us, and the archangel rushed forward. Situla flung me in front of her.

A breacher was incorporeal, but it could affect the physical world. I had the sensation of being lifted off the ground by nothing, as if I had taken flight. The archangel launched me towards the Westminster Archon.

The electric shock came at once, searing like white heat under my skin. Screaming inside, I crawled back towards the zone, racked by spasms. My whole body was cold as ice, almost frozen by contact with the breacher. I managed to get back to my feet, my breath coming in clouds.

And then something else collided with me, grabbing me hard before I could fall.

When I saw Nick, I thought I was hallucinating. I stared up at my best friend – still disguised, so close I would have felt his breath on my face, if not for the mask.

Disbelief rooted me to the spot, turning into joy. I was tired, and the line was so close, yet so far away – but Nick was here. He had come for me.

He pulled me across the street. There were columns there, creating a small colonnade that led into the Underground. Thanks to whatever was now happening on Westminster Bridge, distracting both denizens and Vigiles, this colonnade was deserted. All the strength drained from my bones as Nick deposited me on the ground behind a column. His face was ashen, dark circles under his eyes.

He was going to be caught. I tried to tell him to run, to get away from me.

At least he had thrust me back into the containment zone. The pain from the tracker stopped, but another pain now grew in my body. A sticky warmth bloomed under my ribs. I had the distant thought that I probably shouldn't have dropped my armour.

I never did say I was sensible.

'Traitor,' Nick said in a cold voice, the one he used on rival gangs. 'I don't know how you found us, but you failed tonight. We are the Seven Seals, and Scion will not take one more of us. Do you hear me?'

My lips strained against their binding.

He needed to run. The Vigiles would only be distracted for a sliver of time. Soon they would come to collect me, following the tracker.

'The White Binder will not be accosted in his own citadel,' Nick said. 'Let this serve as your reminder never to cross him again, if you live.'

That was when I understood.

Nick had stabbed me.

Of course. All this was still a sort of syndicate business. I had brazenly attacked the White Binder, the mime-lord closest to Trafalgar Square. Such an insult could not go unanswered, even by an agent of Scion.

Nick let me go, leaving the blade where it was. He was going to abandon me. With the last strength I could summon, I nudged his dreamscape.

He stiffened at once. I watched the slow realisation on his face, a flicker of hope, and then denial. His fingertips hooked under the chin of the mask. It took some force to break the seal, to peel it off my face.

When he saw me, he dropped it, gathering me straight to his chest.

'Paige—'

At once, he tried to staunch the bleeding, laying pressure on either side of the blade. Always a medic, even when he was a criminal. I reached for his arm, trying to hold on tight enough for him to know I was happy to see him.

Nick stared at me in absolute shock, tears lining his eyes. 'Paige, I'm so sorry. I didn't know.'

I nodded, understanding.

'We looked for you for weeks. Eliza searched half the North Bank, but—' His words shook. 'We thought they must have killed you. Jaxon almost gave up.' He was turning white. 'Paige, what have they done to you?'

The wound didn't hurt too much. Perhaps the chill had numbed me through.

'Sweetheart, look at me.' Nick grasped my cheek. 'Look at me, Paige!'

I was finding it difficult to look at anything. My eyelids were so heavy. At least I would die in London, with him. Better Nick than Nashira.

He stroked a curl from my brow, shaking his head. Looking at him, I wanted him to carry me to safety again, like he had once before, when I was cold and scared.

I wanted so badly to let him take me back to Seven Dials.

'Paige, don't you dare close your eyes,' Nick said. 'I'm getting you home. Do you hear me?'

All I could do was make the tiniest sound in my throat. A tear seeped into my hair.

There was no way I could tell him, not without my voice. I tried to draw his attention to my arm, where the tracker had been injected – surely he would understand – but he was too distracted by my other injury. Even with the knife in place, blood was leaking from my side.

Nick hated Scion. That was why he had been willing to stab me, beyond his loyalty to Jaxon. He had to know the truth, or no one out here ever would. I couldn't slip away without telling him about the lost city. I had to give the performers a chance. I had to do this one thing for Liss.

My fingers were smeared with blood. I touched my damp side, then reached for the wall and traced the first three letters of its old name.

'Oxford,' Nick breathed. 'They took you to Oxford?'

I let my hand fall.

'It's okay, Paige.' He started to lift me into his arms. 'I'm going to patch you up. I'll fix this.'

A deep exhaustion was setting in, but I still tried to give him the warning. My fingers scratched at his back, and I kept up my faint, desperate sounds.

Nick was too afraid to hear. He turned west towards Canon Row, stopping dead before he could leave the colonnade. Gathering me to his chest with one arm, he pulled a pistol from his jacket and pointed it at something in front of him. A silhouette in the shape of a man.

'There is a tracking device in her arm,' a quiet voice said. 'Scion is watching. If you take her back to Seven Dials, you will doom them all, Red Vision.'

'How do you know me?'

'There is no time to explain. The Vigiles will spare no pains to pursue you, but their priority is to detain Antoinette Carter. You are likely to avoid them if you leave now and make with all haste for Vauxhall.'

'No.' Nick had backed into a wall. 'Paige—'

'Give her to me, and I will see to it that she lives.'

Nick held me tighter, his breathing rough, a tight sob escaping him. I pressed my bloody hand to his chest, so I could feel his pounding heart. My hearing and vision were fading. I didn't have long.

I don't know exactly how long it took Nick Nygård to make his decision. Take me back to Seven Dials, risking the others' lives, or hand me over to a stranger from Scion.

'I'll find you,' Nick whispered. 'Just live.'

He squeezed my elbow and pressed a firm kiss to my forehead, and then he was gone. I was enfolded by new arms, lifted towards eyes like candles.

'I have you, Paige,' Warden said softly.

That was the last thing I heard.

22

CONFESSIONS

Time fragmented into slivers of awareness, interspersed with darkness. Sometimes there were lights, and sometimes voices. I became aware of someone cutting my undershirt. I tried to push away the intrusive hands, but my body mutinied. Distantly, I recognised the smell of disinfectant.

When Jaxon sent Nick to answer an insult, he never aimed to kill. Even a light maiming went against his nature. Still, there was no good place to be stabbed, and Oxford had no hospital. I already knew my chances were slim.

When I woke for the first time, I was on a polished table, a fire to my right. I knew this chamber. I was laid out like a corpse in the Residence of the Suzerain, surrounded by Rephs. Thuban was there; so were Kraz and Alsafi. Nashira loomed on one side, Warden on the other, both speaking Gloss. Nashira glanced down at me, her eyes ablaze.

She was going to kill me now, before I bled to death, and I couldn't lift a finger to stop her. My side and head were in too much pain. I stared up at Warden.

He held my gaze for a long moment. His jaw tightened, and he looked up to speak once more to Nashira. I watched her give him a small nod before I slipped away.

The next time I became aware of myself, that sinister gathering of Rephs seemed like a hallucination. All I knew was pain. My side was in agony, my upper arm on fire. I made a weak sound: half sob, half groan.

'Paige.'

The voice came as if from underwater. I looked around, my vision dark and blurred.

'Michael, bring the scimorphine.' A gloved hand covered mine. 'Hold on, Paige.'

I knew that touch. My fingers hooked between his knuckles. I felt the slow brush of his thumb on my cheek before I slipped back into sleep.

It could have been a century before I woke again. Opening my eyes, I found myself in a familiar bedchamber, feeling as heavy as a duvet. My arm and abdomen were numb, but my lips had come apart, allowing me to breathe in deep. They quivered as I recalled what had happened.

Nick had let me go. I had been in his arms. My chest heaved as I went through it all in my head, remembering the bloody writing on the wall.

Jaxon knew where I was now. They all did.

The gramophone was playing in the other room, confirming my return to the Founders Tower. Lying as still as I could, I ran my tongue over my teeth. All present and correct. My splinted wrist was hurting, and my other hand was attached to a drip. Mindful of the cannula, I used it to shift the bedclothes off.

I was dressed in the silk nightshirt. Sliding it up, I saw the surgical dressing on my left side. My right arm was bandaged and smelled of fibrin gel, used to seal wounds and prevent bleeding.

Other than being stabbed and slashed, I also had deep bruises on my shins and hip, and one side of my face was puffy. Jaxon really had done a number on me. I eased myself on to my right side, huffing.

Something else had changed. I couldn't put my finger on what. My body had clearly taken a beating, but my dreamscape felt different, awry.

Warden was in an armchair, gazing at the fire. Seeing I was awake, he stood.

'Paige.'

The sight of him set off a heavy pounding in my chest. He moved his chair to my bedside, along with a jug of water and a glass.

'The oracle.' My throat hurt. 'Did you kill the oracle?'

'No.'

'What about the others?'

'The Seven Seals escaped, as did Antoinette Carter,' Warden said. 'The assignment was a failure. Nashira was as wroth as I have ever seen her.'

I released my breath, tears soaking my cheeks before I could stop them. A weak laugh escaped me, hurting my side.

Warden waited for me to collect myself. 'Do you need help to sit up?'

After a moment, I took his proffered hand. He placed mine on his upper arm, so I could grasp him for support, then reached around my waist to my back, lifting me towards him with care. I tensed at the sharp pain in my side.

It was strange to be pressed so close to him, even though he had held me before. While he moved the pillows to bolster me up, my fingers tightened on his arm, finding it as solid as iron. Even with all my training, I was fragile in comparison. Once I was settled, he let go.

'So we're back,' I said.

'Yes.'

A faint green stain was dwindling from his eyes. He must have fed on a medium – but not Eliza. She was safe in London, protected by Seven Dials.

'Carter,' I said. 'How did she get away?'

'By jumping into the Thames.'

She had risked her life by doing that, but I was glad she had gone. Whatever power she had, it was too dangerous for Nashira to steal.

'You have quite a collection of injuries,' Warden said. 'Fortunately, the Vigiles had a trauma surgeon on hand. She saved you. I have continued your treatment here, with dacrodiorin and scimorphine.'

Both of those drugs were exorbitant. One was used to accelerate healing, especially after surgery, while the other was a strong painkiller.

'Seems like a waste of resources,' I said, 'given why I'm here.'

'Nashira did consider ending it. You were returned here in a private ambulance after three days in Westminster Hospital. On the first night, she ordered me to move your sickbed to the Residence of the Suzerain.'

It hadn't been a hallucination, then. I really had been laid out on her dinner table.

'After the paramedics left, you developed a mild fever. Nashira planned to kill you that night, believing your injuries might take you first. Tertius and Situla had reported to her that you possessed David – thus, she no longer had any fear of not gaining your gift in its fullness.'

Of course they had told her.

'I renewed that fear,' Warden said. 'I convinced her that you needed to practise the ability you had only unlocked in a moment of dread – to ensure that you had full command of it, and that she would be able to use it at will. I am now confident that she will wait until the Bicentenary.'

'How long has it been since the assignment?'

'A week.'

It was the eighteenth, then. He had bought me about two and a half months.

'Thanks to the dacrodiorin, you should be able to rise when you wish. The paramedics assured me you will be fully recovered by Midsummer Eve,' he said. 'From the day after, I will continue your training.'

'Here,' I said.

'Yes.'

Even if he and Nashira had a cold relationship, she really did seem to trust him to prepare my gift for her. It almost made me doubt myself – but twenty years had passed since the rebellion. Perhaps Warden had been slowly earning her trust back, easing down her guard.

'The Seven Seals were more brutal and powerful than we anticipated,' Warden said. 'Nashira was disappointed to learn that there was no appearance from the Pale Dreamer ... but I wonder if she *was* among us that night. Tertius observed that you chose to attack

337

David. The Vigiles noted that Amelia was incapacitated with a flux dart. One of yours.'

I waited, knowing the inevitable was coming.

'The oracle was the one who stabbed you,' Warden said, 'but this was clearly a case of mistaken identity, given your mask. He tried to save you.'

'You took me from him,' I said.

'He would have exposed Seven Dials.'

'I know. Even if part of me hates you for it.'

'I accepted that possibility.' Warden touched me under the chin, so gently and briefly I hardly felt it. 'Some time ago, you told me I did not know who I had crossed. I would hear you say it. Who are you?'

I lifted my gaze, meeting his.

'Paige Mahoney,' I said quietly. 'But some know me as the Pale Dreamer. For the last three years, I've been mollisher to the White Binder.'

A long silence. The secret I had kept for months, laid in the firelight between us.

'Nashira suspects you,' Warden said in an undertone. 'She is no fool, Paige.'

'Will she interrogate me?'

'Perhaps. She wants very much to find the White Binder – but after you were almost killed, I hope she will be loath to risk your life before the Bicentenary. I will shield you as best I can, but you must be vigilant.'

'I'm a career criminal in Scion. I have to be vigilant,' I pointed out. 'Why is she looking for him?'

'I hoped you might know.'

'I have no idea. Jaxon has a lot of influence, but I don't see why he should concern her any more than the rest of the Unnatural Assembly.'

'Hm.'

It was a relief to be able to talk about the syndicate – to not have to conceal who I was any more, just as it had been liberating to stop pretending I was amaurotic. For better or worse, I had missed the Pale Dreamer.

'You said you wouldn't sit in judgement,' I said. 'Is that still true, Warden?'

'Yes.'

'Even though the White Binder wrote *On the Merits of Unnaturalness*. Even though he created the hierarchy. Even though I worked for him without question, knowing exactly the kind of person he is, and most of the time, I liked it.' I watched him. 'Do you know what a mollisher is?'

'Perhaps something of a lieutenant.'

'Yes. I was his enforcer, his debt collector, his weapon.' I raised a hand to the gauze and padding at my side. 'The Red Vision – the oracle – stabbed me here to punish my insolence, not knowing who I was. It wasn't to kill me. This was a precise stab, meant to nick my liver.'

'It did.'

I nodded. 'I'd either have to bleed to death, or go to hospital, risking arrest.'

'Have you done this to anyone?'

'I haven't stabbed anyone yet. That's not to say I haven't made threats.'

'I believe you are trying to make a point, Paige.'

'You wanted to know who I am. I'm telling you.'

'The Pale Dreamer is not all you are.'

'But she is part of me. I won't deny it.'

Warden detached me from the drip. I watched his hands, their gentle precision.

'I never did understand why you all wear those gloves.' I said it with a thin smile. 'What do you think is going to happen if you touch a human?'

'It is her ruling, not mine.'

'And you disagree with the way she runs things, even though she's your consort, your sovereign. I think you've disagreed with her for a long time.'

'Perhaps it is you who will sit in judgement of me,' Warden said. 'You do not understand why I would choose her as my consort. Is that not so?'

'Yes.'

'Then perhaps you should ask yourself if I did.'

Just as he started to let go of my hand, I grasped his wrist, keeping him where he was. He could have broken my grip with ease, but he stilled.

'I've told you who I am,' I said. 'You gave me your word that if I came back, you would tell me the truth. Are you one of the scarred ones?'

Warden glanced at my hand on his wrist. He lifted his gaze to my face, and I knew.

'Yes.'

I nodded. 'And the symbol?'

'The amaranth, a flower that grows only in the Netherworld. Its history extends to the time before we came here. Now it is a forbidden symbol of rebellion,' he said. 'A rejection of Sargas rule.'

'And you still keep it here.'

'A small reminder of who I once was.'

'Do you want to be that person again?'

'What if I did, Pale Dreamer?'

'Then you would have to be careful. You tried to overthrow her, but one human betrayed your plans. That must have left more than physical scars. I imagine you lost your faith in humanity for a while. It's why you looked so angry when I blackmailed you. You saw a shadow of the human who fucked you over.'

Warden looked into my eyes.

'Perhaps,' he said, 'you do not lack perspicacity after all, Paige Mahoney.'

'Nashira has been testing me. I think you've been doing the same. On Novembertide, you learned the hard way that some humans act in their own interests first. If you try again, you can't repeat your mistake. You've been judging whether I'd be an ally or an enemy, trying to work out if I'm like the traitor – if I'm selfish enough to throw everyone here to the wolves to save my own skin, like him. Tell me I'm wrong, Arcturus.'

The silence was all the answer I needed.

'And you're still not really sure,' I said, 'because now you know who I am, and who I work for, and you can't imagine that anyone like me could be trustworthy.'

340

The gramophone moved on to a new song.

'I feared that, for a time,' Warden said. 'But then I learned something about you, Paige.'

'What?'

'You are a survivor of the Dublin Incursion.'

I couldn't speak.

'Very few were left alive that day,' Warden said. 'When they were, it was intentional. Scion needed eyewitnesses, to tell the rest of Ireland what had happened. To warn them of the bloodshed they would face if they resisted.'

'You can't know I was one of them.' I stared at him. 'I didn't live in Dublin.'

'No, but your aunt and your cousin did. Finn died that day, did he not?'

'Is this in my records?'

'No.'

'Then how the hell do you know?'

Warden stood. He walked towards the hearth and placed a hand on the mantelpiece.

'You have made your confessions. Now I will offer mine,' he said. 'You are right. I needed to be sure that you were not like the one who betrayed us.'

Even as he spoke, my mind was racing.

'You mentioned Seven Dials,' I whispered. 'I never told you I lived there.'

'But I knew.' Warden glanced at me. 'I also know the oracle is called Nick Nygård, and that he works for Scion. I know you were treated cruelly at school. I know your cousin left you during the Dublin Incursion.'

'How long have you known all this?'

'You know how long.'

My heart fluttered as if I had dreamwalked. I was on the brink of passing out.

'What—' I could hardly say it. 'What are you?'

'I can make a person dream their memories.'

My body turned nerveless and cold.

'You're an oneiromancer,' I said faintly. 'Aren't you?'

Warden nodded.

Jaxon had theorised their existence years after *On the Merits* was published, but never proved it. The oneiromancer was the inverse of most voyants. While many among us specialised in foresight, the oneiromancer sought wisdom in the past, finding clear vision in hindsight.

'I've been remembering things since I got here.' I got out of bed, grasping my side. 'I thought I was hallucinating. I thought it was from the flux.'

Warden looked away.

'It was *you*. All that time.' My voice quaked. 'What was in the green pill, Warden?'

'It was a herb called salvia, or seers' sage. It clarifies the memories I seek, and helped open your dreamscape to my influence.'

'All the times you asked me if I was just a pickpocket, you knew exactly who and what I was.' I shook my head. 'Did you enjoy toying with me?'

'I had to see your history for myself, for my allies' sake, before I trusted you,' Warden said, eyes burning. 'Last time, I failed them by not taking sufficient precautions. They were scarred for my error, and almost every human in this city paid for it with their lives.'

My fist clenched.

'Your memories showed me that the White Binder is a strong influence on you,' Warden said. 'But they also reassured me that you are compassionate and loyal, with a good heart and no love for Scion. I saw that you had criminal associates in the citadel, but you never betrayed them.'

'Of course not. They're my family.' I took a step back. 'Your excuses aren't going to work on me. Those memories were private.'

'So are dreamscapes and bodies.'

'You *forced* me to learn possession. Don't you dare try to draw comparisons here, you—' To my horror, fresh heat sprang in my eyes. 'You could have just asked who I was.'

'I did. And you lied,' he said. 'I understand why, Paige.'

I shook my head again, trembling.

'I was so close to trusting you. I don't trust easily,' I said, 'but I was ready to take a chance, Warden. You gave me hope that I might actually get out of here.' I walked right up to him. 'You wanted to know the kind of person I am. I've told you in my own words, and you've seen it. Now you've shown me who you are, too – someone who would violate my privacy to protect himself.'

'It was not only myself I sought to protect.'

'So you'd protect everyone but me, the person you want to risk her neck for you?'

He lowered his gaze, his jaw tightening. An angry blaze flayed my cheeks.

'I will not speak in my own defence,' he said, 'but I apologise for the pain I have caused you, and for breaking your trust. You deserved better.'

My eyes stung again. He waited, perhaps expecting me to say more, but I had nothing left. It was taking everything I had to hold myself together.

'I will sleep elsewhere,' Warden said quietly. 'Michael will take care of you. If you still wish to train with me, meet me in the cloister at dusk on the first of July. Until then, the Founders Tower is yours, Paige.'

He placed his key on the desk and left, closing the door behind him. I sank to the floor by the fire, my hand pressed to my padded side.

He had seen all my loss, all my anger, all my ghosts. The day I had buried for thirteen years. The day I was supposed to die; the day I sometimes wished I had, because then I would have no memory of it. In my mind, I stumbled through those streets again, blood under my boots, my ears ringing in the silence, surrounded by the dead of Dublin.

Scion had left me alive, to tell the world they were coming. I thought of my own cries – the small, broken cries of a lost child – and wept.

23

INTO THE HOUSE

For that first day and the night that followed, I did little but
rest. Gail had made a start on the roof, but I needed to stay
on the dacrodiorin and keep warm. So I slept in Warden's
bed, even though I wanted nothing more from him. I should never
have taken those pills.

Nick wouldn't be able to find me. The gang knew where I was,
but even Jaxon couldn't get past that many outposts, or through
Gallows Wood.

Warden had been my last hope.

For the first time in years, I wished I were amaurotic. I wanted
my life to go back to normal – the way it had been when I lived
with my grandparents, before the poppy field, before the Dublin
Incursion.

But there was no *normal*. There never had been. Normal and
natural were the greatest lies we had ever created – we humans,
with our little minds.

The day bell rang again, as it always did. I removed the drip and got
out of bed, just to distract myself. I had got used to sleep inversion,
but for once, I wanted to see the sun.

In the bathroom, I changed my dressings and washed as much as I could. I combed my hair and cleaned my teeth. Once I was done, I looked at myself in the mirror. My eyes were raw and puffy, my face pale.

Warden played on my mind. I could feel him elsewhere in Magdalen, clearer than ever, as if my sixth sense was more attuned to him.

Now I had space from him, I considered what he had done. I could sympathise with his reasons, even if I bitterly resented him for it. I almost envied his ability to see who could and could not be trusted. No doubt I would have used it, too, if I were an oneiromancer. He had known me for three months, and his allies – whoever they were – for much longer; of course he would put their safety over my privacy, just as I would choose my gang over him. If we did strike an alliance here, it would only ever be a means to an end. A marriage of convenience.

He was even right about my hypocrisy, to an extent. I had violated David in London, snatching his body to help Nadine. In the heat of the moment, I had sacrificed his autonomy and dignity to save my friend. I had acted according to my own moral compass, my own needs.

Still I couldn't shake the sense that what Warden had done was crueller – carried out over time, with intent. I couldn't see memories. He had opened an eye in my dreamscape, watched my past like a film.

I went back to the bedchamber and moved the medicine next to the daybed. Nestled by the fire, I thought back, nursing a slight headache.

Warden had kept my secrets. For weeks, he had known who I was and where I lived, but never told Nashira about Seven Dials, nor reported Nick. She had guessed that I was part of the syndicate, but not because of him. I had accused him of not protecting me, yet that was exactly what he had done.

I still couldn't bring myself to forgive him. I supposed I had until July.

Michael popped in at eleven. Seeing I was awake, he retreated again. I returned to my brooding. When he came back about half an hour later, he pulled the curtains apart, flooding the parlour with golden sunlight. I blinked against the sudden glow.

'Can I help you, Michael?'

He brought in a small trolley from outside. I watched him lay a splendid breakfast on the table in front of me, with fresh coffee and a jug of hot milk to top it off. When I shook my head, Michael frowned.

'I'm not hungry,' I said mulishly. 'I don't want his guilt breakfast.'

Michael pursed his lips. To my surprise, he took my hand, wrapped it around a fork, and stabbed it directly into the pancakes.

'Fine, but I'm eating for you, not for him.'

He smiled. Just to keep him happy, I drizzled honey on the pancakes.

Michael kept a sharp eye on me as he pottered around the room. My first reluctant bite of pancake awakened a punishing hunger. I ate my way through the whole stack, along with two flaky pastries with plum jam, a bowl of sweet porridge, four slices of hot buttered toast, a plate of scrambled eggs, and three cups of coffee. There was fruit, too – raspberries and cream, probably from the physic garden.

Once I was stuffed, Michael presented me with an envelope. I took it.

'Trust him,' Michael said.

It was the first time I had ever heard him speak. His voice was barely more than a whisper.

'I want to,' I said quietly. 'Do you?'

He nodded.

'Does he even have a bed where he's sleeping?'

His gesture indicated that he had no idea.

'Well, if you see him around, tell him I hope he's cold and miserable, won't you?'

Michael gave me a reproachful look. While he cleared the breakfast table, I split the red wax seal on the envelope and unfolded the sheet of thick paper inside. It was bordered with swirling gold. *Paige*, it began:

I know you may never forgive me. I accepted this on the night you arrived – but even if you resent me, know that I sought only to understand you. I wish that you and I had met under different circumstances; that we had been able to become acquainted in good faith, without fear of betrayal. Alas, we have only these circumstances, and this city.

Some apology this was. A little more grovelling would have been nice. Still, I continued to read:

Whether or not you wish to see me again, I urge you to prepare yourself for the Bicentenary. Keep up your strength as best you can, and take the dacrodiorin. I fear my consort intends to make your death a spectacle. You must be able to fight when the time comes. Hone your dreamwalking, if you can. You do not need me for that, Paige. Though you may not have seen it, it was always me who needed you, not the other way around.

Better. I read on, tucking my hair behind my ear.

You said I would protect my allies, but not you. I hope to prove otherwise. As I have been your hope during this long ordeal, so you have been mine. I have left a small gift with Michael. Consider it a token of my gratitude, but use it only if you must.

Just by writing this, Warden was demonstrating his newfound trust in me. It was an intimate and seditious letter; it would be damning for him if I took it to Nashira. Instead, I burned it, knowing that was best for both of us.

'Michael,' I said, 'what did he leave for me?'

He reached into his tunic and handed me the gift. It was a thick glass vial on a chain, about the length of my longest finger, with an ornate gold stopper. Inside, there was some kind of powder, greyish blue.

'Pollen,' Michael rasped.

'Pollen,' I echoed. 'What's the man trying to do, give me hay fever?'

Michael gave me a weighty look. My brow was still knitted by the time he left.

The clock struck one. Reinvigorated by the coffee, I went downstairs, braced for the chill in the cloister, where a door that had been locked was ajar. That must be the way to the private library.

I passed the chapel doors and crossed the courtyard. Fazal was in the Porters' Lodge with a stove, reading the fattest book I had ever seen. He had gained a few grey hairs over the last month.

'Paige,' he said in surprise. 'You should be resting.'

'I'm grand.' I stopped in front of him. 'Faz, you've been here for a while. In your experience, are there usually many guards outside during the day?'

'The Overseer patrols the Rookery, to ensure people are keeping to the curfew. I don't think any of the Rephs go out in daylight. It doesn't hurt them, as far as I can tell – they just prefer to be awake during the night.'

'If I was to sneak out for half an hour or so, would you let me back in?'

'The Warden won't want you going outside, not with your injuries.'

I sighed. 'Faz—'

'You get into trouble every time you go out there, Paige. Not only that, but you drag him into it.'

'I just want to check on Liss,' I said. 'I haven't seen her since she went into spirit shock. I know a secret way to her place. I'll come straight back.'

'No. I'm sorry.'

Accepting defeat, I went back upstairs.

Another two days passed. I slept and did gentle stretches in the Founders Tower, waiting for my body to heal. Nick hadn't known who I was, but I was still going to give him an earful about this, if I ever saw him again. Then again, he would already be furious with himself.

Warden continued to keep his word. He had given up the whole of the Founders Tower.

By the end of the second day, my side was no longer hurting, and the wound had turned into a nice clean scar. I could wait no longer. Fazal and Gail seemed to have agreed not to let me out, but I needed to see Liss.

I waited for Michael to bring my food and medicine. As soon as he was gone, I went to the linen cabinet for my uniform. Inside, I found a new tunic, identical to the others, except it was yellow – the yellow of a sunflower, so bright it could guide ships in fog. A note was pinned to the collar.

Nashira was informed that you left the containment zone. Your red tunic has been temporarily rescinded. Since you were forced out of the zone, I have appealed for her to revoke this decision.

The tunic for cowards. I returned it to the cabinet, shaking my head. Instead, I dressed in my black combat trousers and dark undershirt, then laced up my winter boots. I wrapped the food Michael had brought and tucked it into my backpack from the assignment.

In the hour before the day bell, I left the Founders Tower. I avoided the Porters' Lodge and climbed my way out of the residence, gritting my teeth as my body ached in protest.

The Broad lay quiet. A few lamps and cookfires still burned, lighting the street for the people clearing what remained of the Rookery. The performers' home would be swept away, out of sight of the incoming guests.

Now the Old Library was back in use, the boards had been taken off some of its windows. I squeezed in through an unlatched one. The performers had arranged their remaining possessions on the shelves, each claiming a patch of floor. Keeping out of sight, I looked for Liss.

She lay in a dark corner, covered by a duvet that could only be from one of the residences. Julian and Cyril sat at her bedside, trying in vain to wake her. They both startled when I appeared.

'Paige?'

Julian crushed me straight into his arms. When we parted, I grasped his shoulders.

'What happened?'

He was no longer in his pink tunic. In fact, he was no longer in a tunic at all. 'Aludra stopped me going to see Liss,' he said. 'I broke into her building and set fire to it. I told her it was me.'

'You got yourself thrown out?'

Julian nodded. 'Like you said, it isn't worth my life. And I can be with Liss.'

'You're not supposed to be here,' Cyril hissed at me. 'No jackets allowed until the Bicentenary.'

'I won't stay long.' I passed him my backpack. 'Here. I brought some food.' He grabbed it at once, and I knelt beside Liss. 'How is she?'

'Still fighting,' Julian said.

'How often is she conscious?'

'She wakes up a couple of times a day. Not for long, though.'

Liss was in a fitful sleep. In less than a month, she had grown thin. I touched her forehead. Her skin was icy, even with the duvet.

Now she could no longer connect with the æther, her spirit wanted to abandon her body, to flee to the other side. Like a candle nearing the end of its wick, her aura was starting to gutter and fade. If it disappeared altogether, she would be amaurotic, whether she lived or died.

Some kind of ointment had been smeared on her burned hands. Cyril drummed his fingers on his knee, watching her with an owlish intensity.

'Come on, Rymore,' he mumbled. 'Don't leave us in the lurch for the Bicentenary.'

'You've been away for a while,' Julian murmured to me. Liss turned her head. 'I heard you'd been sent on an assignment. Was it to London?'

'Yes. I was sent to arrest my own friends,' I said. 'I managed to avoid killing them, but one of them stabbed me in the liver. I've been having a great few days.' He snorted. 'Have you been able to get Liss to eat or drink?'

'Enough to keep her alive, but she won't last much longer.' Julian ground his jaw. 'At least Suhail and the Overseer are leaving her alone, for now. Nell volunteered to step in – she's an aerialist, too – so they're satisfied they've got someone to take over for the Bicentenary.'

'Nell isn't as good,' Cyril informed us. 'She falls. Rymore never falls.'

'She's getting weak,' I said. 'This can't go on.'

'But we can't do anything,' Julian said, his voice rough with frustration. 'Even if we find a new deck, there's no guarantee she'll connect with it.'

'We have to try.' I looked towards Cyril. 'There must be an unclaimed deck of cards somewhere in this city. Do you have any ideas, Cyril?'

'The House,' Cyril said, without hesitation. 'That's where the Rephs store a lot of their supplies – confiscated or abandoned numa, and the weapons the red-jackets use in the woods. If a cartomancer died here, the deck would either have been destroyed or sent to the House.'

I nodded. 'Then that's where I'll go.'

'You'll die.'

'Trust me, when it comes to stealing, I'm the right voyant for the job.' I paused. 'Wait. Cyril, did you say there were weapons in there?'

'Paige?'

Liss had opened her eyes. I went back to her at once, taking the frail hand she held up.

'Liss,' I said softly. 'How are you feeling?'

'I've felt better. Being voyant is what put me in this place, but … I'm just now realising how much I would miss the æther.' Liss swallowed. 'Jules, Cyril, could you leave us alone for just a moment?'

They did as she asked. I waited, braced for her to tell me she hated me.

'Jules said you went to London,' Liss said in a faint voice. 'But you're here now. You didn't try to escape, then?'

'They put a tracker in me. But even if I had escaped, I would have come back.'

'Then you're not the White Binder.' She wet her cracked lips. 'I won't ask you why you worked for him, Paige. I'm sure you had your reasons … but I don't think you're like him. If he was the King of Wands in your reading, I might be afraid you admired him, but the card was inverted. I think you see him for what he is.'

My eyes filled again, my jaw clenching. I had cried more in the last few days than I had in over a year.

'I had a question.' Liss whispered it. 'Where is home to you, Paige?'

London had both held and hurt me. I had been cut away from Ireland.

'I don't know,' I said.

'I feel the same,' Liss said. 'A few years after the Rephs came, my ancestors sailed from the free world to Edinburgh. I've often wondered how long it took them to stop being homesick, if they ever did. For years, this place has been the only home I know, but my dreamscape … is still a bonny clearing in the Highlands.'

'We'll find a new home.' I stroked her dark hair. 'Liss, I'm going to get you a deck of cards. And then I'm going to get you out of here.'

'How?'

'The Rephs really did help with the first rebellion. I think I know which one of them started it,' I said. 'I think we could try again.'

'You make me feel brave, Paige.' A tiny smile lifted her cheeks. 'Be careful, won't you?'

'I promise.'

She nodded and slipped back into her deep sleep. Julian soon returned, folding his arms. He still had plenty of muscle from training.

'Are you serious about going to the House?'

'Not just for the cards,' I said. 'When I was in London, I saw a single voyant fend off three Rephs. They're not unbeatable, Jules. I want to at least get a glimpse of the supplies that might be in there.'

'For a rebellion?'

'Maybe.' I arched an eyebrow at him. 'Say that was the general idea. Are you in?'

'Of course I'm in.' The flame on the stove played in his dark eyes. 'If you risk going to the House, I'll start the work here. I can rally the troops.'

'Don't do it.' Cyril spoke from behind the shelves. 'You'll die, like the ones who came before. The Buzzers came in and—'

'They're not going to rebuild the Rookery, Cyril,' I cut in. 'After the Bicentenary, that's it. You're back out in the cold with nothing.'

Cyril fell silent.

'That settles it, then.' Julian grasped my elbow. 'Paige, we have to do this. A prison break. We leave them with no voyants again.'

'Jules.' I gripped him back. 'I agree, but we can't rush this. There are over three hundred people in this city, and we don't have any way out. I looked for one during my second test. There really are landmines in Gallows Wood.'

'But you do want to fight.' He gave me a serious look. 'You're from the syndicate, aren't you?'

After a moment, I nodded. 'Did Liss say?'

'Yes. I can also just … tell.'

'Not sure if that's a compliment, but thanks.'

'Liss mentioned you hold a high rank in the underworld. If that's true, you might be able to give the performers the sort of hope they've not had in a decade,' Julian said. 'You could promise them that there will be something more after this. That they'll have a home in London.'

I needed to explain that I didn't have the power to make that kind of promise. Only Jaxon could give them a place in the syndicate, and he never would. To him, none of these prisoners were diamonds among stone.

Before I could articulate this, Julian continued: 'I know what you mean, about biding our time. But I need something to hold on to, Paige. All of us do. Let's start to plan this – you and me. Let's show them that even after two hundred years, they still have something to fear.'

His conviction was invigorating.

'Okay,' I said. 'I have my own irons in the fire, but you can plant seeds, too. Start with people who have good reason to hate the Rephs – but Jules, be careful who you trust. Ask them questions. Nothing more.'

In unison, we both looked at Cyril.

'No.' Behind his ruined glasses, his eyes were feverish. 'You two muttonheads do what you like, but I'm not getting involved in this. The Rephs are immortal. How are we supposed to fight them off, exactly?'

'They're not all the same,' I said quietly. Julian frowned. 'I can't say anything yet, Jules. You talk to the performers; I'll break into the House.'

'What, right now?'

'No. I'll take a couple of days to plan my approach.' I stiffened, sensing a dreamscape I knew well. 'The Overseer is coming. I'd better go.'

'Okay.' He ushered me out. 'Come back and see us soon, if you can.'

'I'll try.'

Liss was about to lose her clairvoyance. I had to stop it. Not only that, but Julian had galvanised me into acting. What Cyril had mentioned was a temptation. I needed to see what they had in the House.

The Bicentenary would take place on the first of September. If Scion could take Dublin in a day, I could make a plan for payback in two months.

Warden continued to give me space, allowing me to scheme. In the library, I found a floor plan of the House, tucked among other documents pertaining to Oxford.

On Midsummer Eve, I donned my backpack and pulled up the hood of my coat. The paramedics had been right – with the help of the best medicine in Scion, I had made a full recovery in twelve days. I still took a dose of scimorphine before I slipped out of the Founders Tower.

I only had a few tools with me – my set of crude lockpicks, a torch, and the vial of mysterious pollen from Warden. It would have to be enough.

After some deliberation, I had decided that it would be too risky to enter the House by day. I needed the cover of darkness. As night fell, I left the residence by vaulting over the wall again, unnoticed by Gail.

The House was among the largest of the Rephs' buildings. Fronted by a daunting tower, it had several vast courtyards, including Tom Quad. To infiltrate and search it, I would have to bring to bear every skill I had ever learned from Eliza. She was the one who had taught me thieving and burglary, as part of my education in the art of being a criminal. Meanwhile, Nick had taught me to climb.

The House had no permanent residents. Thuban Sargas seemed to go there frequently; otherwise, few keepers visited. I still expected guards if there was treasure to be found, but my gift would allow me to sense them.

Magdalen Walk would lead me directly to the House, but I didn't want to be seen tonight. Instead, I cut down Rose Lane and followed a narrow path that took me along the back wall of the Residence of Merton.

No humans were permitted in the House. That made it all the more tempting. As I scaled a wall into its grounds, I compiled a mental list of things I might need to escort people through Gallows Wood.

Crossing the minefield had to be a last resort. Weapons would be crucial, given what lurked in the trees, but medical supplies would be an extra asset. Adrenalin was valuable – not only could we use it to sharpen our performance and dull pain, but it could also revive me if I had to leave my body.

For tonight, the cards were my priority. I could always come back to the House.

I had pondered over the floor plan for a long time, trying to work out which of its many rooms might contain numa. Suspecting Gail might have chipped in with its maintenance, I had asked her a few questions, feigning curiosity. From her, I had learned that only one building was generally used for storage.

The Meadow Building had large windows and plenty of footholds. Thick ivy grew in swathes across its façade, which faced Cherwell Meadow and Gallows Wood. I used the ivy to climb to a balcony.

At once, I sensed two Rephs and stopped, concentrating. They were in the House, but not close.

The storage rooms would be locked. I needed to pick the right one. Moving between the balconies, I tried to see through the windows, risking my torch. When its beam caught on metal, I stared. In this room, there were racks of weapons: swords, hunting knives, a crossbow. This must be where they stored arms to distribute to the red-jackets.

Julian was right. I wanted to make Scion afraid. To start, I was getting some of these weapons.

Now I just needed to enter the building. On the floor above the balcony, a sash window had been left open, just a crack. I used a drainpipe to reach a ledge, then shimmied across to the window, pulling myself through it.

I descended back to the middle floor. Finding the right door, I started to work on the lock with my picks. Hopefully the Rephs were unfamiliar with the telltale signs that a lock had been meddled with.

This whole city was old enough that its locks were no real obstacle. I slipped into the room and shut the door behind me. When I looked up, I found myself facing a large, yellowed map.

THE PENAL COLONY OF SHEOL I
OFFICIAL TERRITORY OF THE SUZERAIN

All the familiar landmarks were there: Magdalen, Amaurotic House, the Residence of the Suzerain, the Townsend, Port Meadow. I shone my torch across it, looking for any details I had missed.

Something caught my eye on Port Meadow. The printed letters next to it were faded, but I made them out.

OXFORD TRAIN STATION

It hadn't even crossed my mind.

We had all been brought here by train. Why couldn't we leave on it, too? It would take us under Gallows Wood. The average Scion train could hold nearly four hundred people, more if they were standing. I could get every single prisoner out of this city and still have room for more.

Even as the plan formed in my mind, I forced myself to take a steadying breath. The entrance to the station could be locked or booby-trapped. Even if we got past it, the Rephs would make sure Scion was ready at the other end.

We definitely needed weapons.

I searched the room. There were multiple net guns and air rifles, with boxes of acid and flux darts, as well as old horse pistols, which had to be more for comfort than anything. The air rifles would be handy, but I imagined they were counted with care, and I had no way to carry one. Still, I could probably filch a few small items. I took a sheathed knife and an air pistol, along with a case of acid darts.

In a metal case, I found boxes of ammo. Nick had tried to shoot Warden and Tertius, to no avail, but firearms would get rid of loyal red-jackets.

The sound of footsteps drifted to my ears. Without pausing, I shut myself into one of the gun cabinets, just as the creak of hinges came.

Two Rephs walked into the room. I could have kicked myself for not paying closer attention to the æther. Now my exit was blocked. The cabinet also had no room for a human. I had to suck in my stomach to fit.

Thuban Sargas was first in the room, drawling in Gloss. I pressed back, eyes closed.

That was when the cabinet doors opened.

Terebell Sheratan stared at me. I stared back, paralysed.

Neither of us moved. I waited for her to alert Thuban. My fingers strayed towards the pollen around my neck, but I thought better of it. Even if this vial did somehow hurt Terebell, Thuban would disembowel me.

But Terebell surprised me. Giving me a scathing look, she shut me back into the cabinet.

'Amaurotic weaponry is unsettling,' she said in English. 'Small wonder they destroy one another so often, with minds that can devise such things.'

'Are we speaking the fell tongue now?'

'Gomeisa told us to maintain our fluency in English and French. I see no harm in practice.'

'If you insist upon fouling our mouths.' Thuban walked across the room, making the floorboards strain. 'Count the weapons.'

My throat closed.

The pair stayed for a while, taking stock. Terebell either missed that I had taken the knife and the pistol, or simply chose not to remark upon it.

'I wonder that you would stoop to this work,' Terebell said. 'I have not heard of humans stealing from the House in a very long time. What is your fear?'

'The dreamwalker has sown the first seeds of unrest in our city. It is clear she is a criminal by nature. Suhail foolishly allowed her to overpower him. Next, she burned the Rookery,' Thuban said, disdain in his tone. 'You should know better than most that a lack of order is the root of dissent, Terebell. The scars on your back should remind you of that.'

My heart was pounding.

Terebell was one of them.

'It must be very hard for you to come here,' Thuban said, softer. 'Does the bell in Tom Tower ring in your memories?'

Nashira had the perpetrators tortured in the House.

'I hear you took the palmist there earlier.' Terebell was good at concealing her emotions, if she had any. 'You take her there often, Thuban.'

'What of it?'

'If she displeases you, there is room for her in Oriel.'

'No,' Thuban said. 'She was part of the syndicate. I will make her speak.'

'You are not tormenting her simply for information.'

'That is true. The creature has no pride, no hope. I confess, I enjoy seeing humans that way; I enjoy being the architect of their despair. Do you never wish to punish them?'

'I was a warrior. I take no pleasure in the suffering of beings weaker than myself.'

'So you admit they are weaker.'

'In body. Only a fool would not see it – but they created these weapons,' Terebell said. 'They may be frail, but their minds are sharp, inured and primed to violence. One day, they may turn that violence against us. You have seen their methods of torturing each other.'

'Indeed. I have used them on the palmist.'

'Yet you underestimate them, as you always have, Thuban.'

'I disagree,' Thuban said. 'Their minds did not save them on that fateful Novembertide.'

I listened, absorbing it all.

Ivy was part of the syndicate. Thuban must be trying to wring her for information about Jaxon. My limbs were beginning to ache, and a rifle was pressing into my back. I froze when something fell off it.

'Did you hear that?'

'I hear nothing,' Terebell said. 'The stocks are all in order, Thuban.'

Thuban left. Terebell rose next, walking towards the door. When Thuban was at the end of the corridor, I peeked out of the cabinet.

'You,' Terebell said, her voice low. 'Did Arcturus send you?'

'No. I need a deck of tarot cards,' I whispered. 'Where are the numa?'

'Tom Tower.'

She shut the cabinet on me and left.

That had been the closest shave of my life. Not waiting to question my good fortune, I waited for their dreamscapes to retreat, then slipped out. Terebell had left the door ajar.

I made my escape from the Meadow Building, blood thumping through my veins. Every shadow looked like Thuban. As I ran through a cloister, heading for Tom Quad, I tried to pluck some rational thoughts from my mind.

Terebell had concealed me. She was a scarred one. I needed to find out more about their history, to wrap my head around what was happening – but first I had to break into Tom Tower, grab the goods, and get back to Liss.

Tom Tower, where the scarred ones had been tortured, where Thuban had been hurting Ivy. Going there seemed like a bad idea, but I would do it for Liss.

The House was linked together by a series of closed and open-air passages. They were mostly unlit, which worked in my favour. Feeling like a rat in a maze, I rushed through, securing the straps of the backpack more tightly. I stopped at the edge of Tom Quad, took a deep breath, and broke into a dead run across the grass. As far as I could tell, no one was coming.

Tom Tower loomed above the main entrance to the House. I spotted the narrow archway at once. The door was locked. Taking out my picks, I tried to steady my hands and my breathing. As soon as I was inside, I shot up the steps, hoping no Rephs would appear.

At the top, I found a large chamber. A stained table stood in the middle, with a chair on either side. On this table lay a set of thumbscrews.

Sweat broke out on my forehead. Pushed against one wall, there was another kind of chair, its back and seat and arms lined with spikes, crusted with dried blood. Other instruments hung from the walls.

Warden had been scarred here. Thuban clearly still used it to torment humans, away from prying eyes. Ivy had been with him for months.

The numa filled a chest in the corner. Since they were in a torture chamber, they must be used for cruelty. I thought of the poor cartomancer whose cards had been passed around to be damaged. I caught sight of a shew stone, various sortes – and a single pack of cards, clearly old.

Hardly breathing, I flipped through it, assessing the illustrations. A different design to the one Liss had before, but they could still be used for cartomancy. I fastened the deck into the front pocket of my backpack.

There was another door, probably to the belfry, but I didn't go through it. This was enough for one night. Looping the straps back over my shoulders, I turned back towards the steps, only to lock gazes with a Reph.

Kraz Sargas blocked the doorway. His orange eyes seemed to smoulder.

'It has been twenty years,' he said, 'since there were traitors in the tower.'

I backed straight into a wall. His dreamscape was so faint, so hard to detect. The Rephs must have some way to cloak themselves in the æther.

'I'm sorry,' I said at once. 'I was looking for medicine.'

'Indeed, in a building reserved for your betters – though I wonder if you think yourself above us, dreamwalker. Suhail and Aludra certainly believe so.' He gave me a mock bow. 'Did Arcturus send you?'

'No.'

'So he lets his tenant go wandering off by itself. Nashira will not be pleased.' He moved towards me. 'Do sit, 40. I have been craving a word with you.'

'Which chair?'

'For now, the one without the spikes.'

With little choice, I did what I was told. Kraz took the opposite seat.

'Nashira believes that you are the Pale Dreamer,' he said. 'Have you worked alongside the White Binder?'

'I live in his section,' I said. 'But I just work as a waitron. Check my record.'

'This act does not fool me. You chose to hinder the assignment in Trafalgar Square. Thanks to your interference, the Seven Seals escaped. We may never find them again,' Kraz said. 'Either you are incompetent, or you helped them leave.' He leaned towards me. 'Allow me to explain your situation. Since your keeper clearly has no idea you are here, I can do whatever I wish to you, without his interference.'

There were no spirits in here; nothing I could use to repel him. Kraz tapped the thumbscrews.

'My cousin does not want us to put your life at risk,' he said. 'There are limits to what I can do. But even she would agree that you and your gift will survive a maimed hand.'

'Arcturus might disagree,' I said.

'I do not answer to Arcturus.'

My fear was climbing by the moment. Kraz held out a hand for mine.

I moved without thinking, sprinting for the door.

Kraz caught me at the top of the steps. He picked me up by my coat and smashed me into the wall. My side and ribs screamed in protest; I crumpled to the floor in a heap. Chuckling in that nightmarish way, Kraz grabbed my hair and used it to drag me upright.

'What do you think resistance will achieve here, dreamwalker?'

'Don't touch me,' I snarled.

'Arcturus cannot protect you now.'

My right arm was pinned, but my left was free. I stabbed Kraz straight in the eye with my finger. An irritated grunt escaped him, but he didn't let go.

He shoved me across the room, towards the iron chair. If he forced me into it, all those spikes would cut into my back, my arms, my thighs. It would be agony. In panic, I mustered my gift and went for his dreamscape.

Kraz let go. I blinked away stars and crawled, but Kraz rallied, pinning me to the floor. He was enjoying this too much to remember his orders. His hand closed around my splinted wrist. A cry escaped me as he tightened his grip, making him laugh again. Desperate, I groped for the vial in my gilet. I twisted to face him and smashed it against his cheekbone.

Now it was his turn to scream. He let go of me, his eyes turning white. Gloss ground from his throat, incomprehensible to me, as he rose and made a wild swing. I ducked it.

My palms and face were slick. Even after what I had done to the Underguard on the train, the very crime that had landed me here, I had no idea if I could do this – but I had to try. Kraz would report me to Nashira. If that happened, I would be killed immediately, never mind the Bicentenary. I had got away with making Suhail look a fool, but now I had defied the heir, the sacred blood.

When Kraz pulled his hands away from his face, I knew he was beyond saving. I took out the air pistol and managed to load an acid dart.

I sent it straight into his brow.

Kraz collapsed against the wall, staring into nothing. Within moments, his face became mottled and grey, as if he was decaying before my eyes. As I stared at him, a huge figure appeared in the doorway, and I flinched to face it, eyes wide, instinctively pointing the gun.

'Warden,' I said, my voice hoarse. 'What the fuck are you doing here?'

'I could ask the same of you, Paige.'

Warden came to me, only to see Kraz. I watched my keeper consider his choices, his eyes burning with an old grudge. I watched him come to a decision.

He took my hand and led me down the steps of Tom Tower, abandoning the ruin of Kraz Sargas.

24

THE GOLDEN CORD

23 June 2059
Midsummer Eve

The journey back to Magdalen was a blur. Warden escorted me through the city, using the same unlit paths. At first, I was afraid he was taking me to Nashira. Instead, he almost carried me from Rose Lane into the Porters' Lodge.

Gail looked up in alarm when he entered. Seeing us, she opened her mouth, shut it, shook her head, and went back to her crossword.

'Good evening, Warden.'

'Gail,' Warden said grimly.

Without another word, he led me up to the Founders Tower. I sat on the daybed and folded my arms tight. My side was killing me, even after the dacrodiorin and scimorphine. Nick had struck with surgical precision, and being flung about by Kraz had brought the pain back with a vengeance.

Warden bolted the door, then went to stand beside a window. For some time, he kept watch through a gap in the curtain, a sliver of torchlight dividing his face.

Now I was out of immediate danger, I could take him in. Aside from the usual black trousers, he wore his quilted jerkin over an ivory shirt. Outside the residence, he usually wore a doublet, at least. He had left in a rush.

'I would be obliged,' he said, 'if you would tell me why you were in the House.'

'I was looking for a new deck of tarot cards for Liss,' I said.

'You could have asked me to retrieve them for you.'

'I didn't need or want your help.' I held my aching side. 'Fuck. Is there any more scimorphine?'

Warden brought it to me in the form of a white pill. I tucked it under my tongue.

'Be honest,' I said, swallowing. 'Have I just killed Kraz?'

'Acid darts cannot destroy us. Only slow us,' Warden said. 'You must have used the pollen I gave you.'

'Yes.'

He looked me over, while I gazed at the grey dust on my hands.

'I must speak to Michael and Gail,' he said. 'In the meantime, you should wash. Leave your clothes outside the bathroom for laundering.'

I nodded. There was pollen on my shirt, in my hair.

As he opened the door, I said, 'Warden, wait.' I took the cards from my backpack. 'I need you to get these to Julian – 26. He should be in the Old Library. Tell him it could take a few days for Liss to bond with them.'

'I will deliver them by morning.' Warden slotted the deck into his jerkin. 'Divest yourself of the evidence now. Do not tarry, Paige.'

He left.

In the bathroom, I avoided my reflection. Even my face was dusted with pollen. While the bath filled, I stripped off my clothes and placed them outside the door with my splint. My wrist was sore and red.

Kraz had thrown me with ease. It shook me that I had trained for three years to run and fight, and it all meant nothing to the Rephs. They must be able to move through the world without any fear of harm.

Except, apparently, from a bit of pollen. That had been one extreme bout of hay fever. I clapped a hand over my lips to stop a laugh.

Keep it together, Paige.

I sat in the hot water, up to my collarbone. A fresh cake of honey soap had been left. As fast as I could, I scrubbed away the pollen, using a brush to clean it from under my nails. I washed my hair twice, just to be sure. Only once the water had drained and I had rinsed the bath did I start to calm down.

The evidence was gone. Wrapped in my nightshirt and robe, I sat down on the daybed, waiting.

Warden returned at midnight. By that point, I was as tense as a piano wire.

'You were gone for hours,' I said.

'I was keeping watch for any sign of a disturbance in the city,' he said. 'I also wanted to ensure I was seen on the Broad, and in the Residence of Queens, so no one would suspect that I had visited the House.'

'Is there any disturbance?'

'Not so far. Kraz will likely not be discovered for a day or two. Even when he is, Nashira will not want any word of this to spread. Our immortality must not be questioned.' He sat opposite me, looked me in the eye. 'Paige, did anyone see you?'

'Terebell,' I said. 'Thuban suspected an intruder, but he didn't catch me.'

'Terebell will keep your secret. She is one of us. If she was the only one, we have nothing to fear.' Pause. 'Your wrist is swollen.'

'Kraz was going to torture me for information about Jaxon.'

Warden clenched his jaw. There was something in his eyes that struck me: a brewing darkness, a resolve.

'Michael will bring another splint,' he said. 'He and Gail will swear that you were here all night, if they are questioned. Since I am the sole oneiromancer in this city, only I would be able to contradict their testimonies.'

'You definitely trust both of them.'

'Yes.'

'And you're happy to conceal the fact I just killed your heir to the empire.'

'I do not recognise the legitimacy of tyrants.'

His face held all the shadows in the room.

'There's something deeper here,' I said. 'It goes beyond how this city is managed, doesn't it?'

'Yes.'

'Well, I've been a criminal long enough to know that it doesn't pay to get involved in other voyants' grudges, so you can keep that to yourself,' I said. 'I would like to know more about the pollen, though.'

'It is the pollen of the poppy anemone, also known as the windflower,' Warden said. 'Why it harms us, I cannot tell you, but I do know a human tale about its origins. Have you heard of Adonis?'

That rang a bell. The year before, Eliza had found a book of Greek myths on the black market and used some of her earnings to buy it for us. I had been about halfway through it when I was detained.

'I think so,' I said. 'Was he a god?'

It had been years since anyone had last told me a story. My grandfather, whispering of mighty Aoife, who had transformed her stepchildren into swans. Warden had a tough act to follow.

'Adonis was a mortal hunter, beloved of Aphrodite,' he said. 'The goddess of beauty was so taken with him, she preferred his company even to that of the other gods. As the myth goes, her paramour, the war god Ares, grew so jealous of the pair that he slaughtered Adonis.'

He was a fine storyteller. His voice was slow and deep, calming.

'Aphrodite wept over her beloved. Her tears mingled with his blood, and from that mingling sprang the windflower, as red as the drops on the earth. Adonis died in her arms, and was sent, like all spirits, to languish in the underworld.'

I could almost see it.

'Zeus, the ruler of the gods, heard Aphrodite lamenting her lover,' Warden said. 'Out of pity for her, he agreed to let Adonis spend half the year in life, and half in death.'

Kraz had looked as if he was half in death, at least.

'To my knowledge, it is the only plant that harms my kind,' Warden said. 'It is illegal to either grow or possess it across the Republic of Scion.'

'If it's illegal, how do you have it?'

'I grow the flowers in a glasshouse in the Fields of Mercy.'
Warden reached for the wine. 'I wanted you to have the pollen
for your own protection. I did not expect you to have to use it so
quickly.'

'Do you have more?'

'A modest supply. The flowers will not bloom again until April,
and even that is no guarantee, given the unseasonal cold in this city.'

At least we had a weapon that worked against Rephs.

'The cartomancer must be a good friend to you,' Warden said.
'You took a great risk for her tonight, Paige.'

'She deserves to live.' I breathed out. 'Warden, I ... didn't mean
to drag you all into another mess. I'm sorry. Thank you for helping
me get back.'

'I owed you that much.'

Warden drank from his goblet. I watched his face, narrowing my
eyes a little.

'I didn't tell you where I was going,' I said. 'How did you know
I was there?'

'That is a grave matter I wanted to discuss with you.'

'Graver than the fact that I'm after killing a Reph?'

'Yes. May I stay?'

'It's your tower.'

'And it is still for your private use until July.'

'Then I give you my gracious permission to stay.'

'Thank you.' Warden sought my gaze. 'There has been a complication, Paige.'

'You say that like every single thing that's happened to me since
March hasn't been a massive and horrific *complication*. You personally, by yourself, have permanently complicated my life.'

'I fear I may be about to do it again.'

'Fire away. I doubt anything can surprise me at this point.'

Warden stood again, taking his goblet with him. He rested an
arm on the mantelpiece, staring into the flames.

'I do not know how it happened,' he said, 'but in the aftermath
of London, the æther has bound our spirits. I felt it for the first
time while you had your fever, and saw it in my dreamscape. It is
... a golden cord.'

368

'Right.' I paused, waiting. 'Has it got anything to do with the silver cord?'

'The silver cord binds the spirit to the dreamscape. This one appears to bind us to each other.'

'I don't understand.'

'I cannot say that I do, either.' Warden looked at me. 'I did hear of the golden cord in the Netherworld. It was a myth, a mystery – a powerful bond atwixt two spirits. From what I can tell, it gives us a seventh sense, keeping us aware of each other. Even when I left you just now, I could feel you from the Broad. I even shared your lingering fear.'

It took a while for his words to fully sink in.

'No,' I said in a whisper. 'That isn't possible.'

'How many impossibilities have you seen in this city?'

'I don't believe you. Why would something like that have happened?'

'I do not know.' Warden set his goblet on the mantelpiece. 'Can you feel this?'

A moment later, I did.

If you had offered me the world, I would not have been able to fully describe it – just as I could never explain how I breathed while I was sound asleep, or how my heart kept beating. I just knew he was calling me.

'Great,' I said. 'First you steal my memories, and now you've put a spiritual leash on me. Just what I've always wanted.'

'I do not intend to misuse it, Paige.'

'So get rid of it. Sever it,' I said hotly. 'You're the immortal. If you knew how to call me with it, you must be able to work out how to break it.'

'A silver cord is broken only by death. I cannot imagine the golden cord is any different. As for how I knew how to call you, I am following my instincts.'

'Why do I feel like you did this on purpose, to keep tabs on me?'

'You are under no obligation to believe otherwise.'

I took a deep breath. As angry and unnerved as I was, I was too exhausted to argue with him. Kraz had left me shaken, and I wanted to be still.

'So even if I left this place,' I said, 'you would be able to find me?'

'I believe so. I knew you had gone to the House,' Warden said. 'Your fear was palpable. That must have been when you saw Thuban. I left at once. I knew exactly where you were in Tom Tower.'

'Fuck.' I pressed both hands to my face. 'Why can't I feel it that strongly?'

'You are mortal. It may reveal itself to you more slowly than it did to me.'

'Because you have the æther in your blood.'

'Yes. It is called ectoplasm,' he said. 'Humans are fully corporeal; we are not. We exist within the æther, but also carry it in us. If your dreamscape is a glass float in the sea, mine is flooded with water.' He paused. 'I would release you from this binding if I could. I will seek counsel. For now, however, the cord exists.'

'Better not tell Nashira. I'm sure she wouldn't like you to be tethered to someone else.'

'She and I have no affection for each other.'

'You don't say.' I lifted my face. 'Warden, why are you with her?'

Warden sat back in his wing chair. I thought he wouldn't answer me.

'Do you remember what Thuban called me,' he finally said, 'when I first took you to Port Meadow?'

I nodded. 'I don't know what it means.'

'It is a cumbersome translation of a Gloss word, but Thuban was attempting to humiliate me – to sneer at my low standing, and my lack of choice in the matter of my union with Nashira.'

'She forced you to be her consort.'

Warden gave a stiff nod.

'I would tell you how it happened,' he said, 'but I would not burden you with my past.'

'You're burdened with mine, whether I like it or not.'

'The cord should not give me any further access to your memories. I will not attempt to see them without your consent.' Warden looked at me. 'Paige, this is an intimate connection, and I have no way to break it. I would prefer not to share it with someone who despises me. Tell me what I can do to earn your trust back.'

'Who says you had it in the first place?'

'You were close.'

Now he had told me about the cord, I was becoming conscious of it – a wisp of awareness, like a draught, telling me how and where he was. Without a scrap of concrete evidence, I was sure he was being honest.

'Show me the heart of your dreamscape,' I said. 'So I can see you.' He seemed to mull it over. 'You know I'll never get that far unless you let me in. You used your gift to judge my character. This is how I judge yours.' I paused. 'I want to trust you, Warden.'

'So be it. If you are to train with me again, we should take the first step,' Warden said. 'Will the scimorphine affect your gift?'

'No idea.' I shifted on to my side. 'I might hurt you.'

'I will cope.'

'In case you'd forgotten, I have actually killed people by dreamwalking.'

'I accept the risk.'

'Fine.' I cleared my throat. 'It would help if I was a little closer to you. Could you … lie on the floor next to me, or something?'

Warden did as I asked without protest, positioning himself by the fire on his back. His gloved fingers clasped on his chest.

Once, I would have relished this opportunity to break him. Now I was only intrigued. Before I had taken hold of the butterfly, I had savoured the freedom of walking in its dreamscape. It would be fascinating to see one that had existed for centuries.

'I won't stay long.' I passed him a cushion. 'I can't, without oxygen.'

'Very well.' He tucked the cushion under his head. 'I am ready when you are.'

There was something absurd about seeing him this way – this giant of a man, lying free and easy on the floor. I looked away to hide my smile.

'Brace yourself, then,' I said.

He nodded. I lay on my side across the daybed, letting my eyes close.

The poppy field was a blurred painting. Everything was melting, softened by the scimorphine, but I could still move. I cut through my flowers, heading for the æther. When I reached the final boundary, I pushed my hands through it, watching the illusion of my body fade away.

In my dreamscape, I had a dream-form, which appeared as I perceived myself. Once I left, I took on my spirit form, amorphous and faceless.

As I approached his dreamscape, a ripple crossed its surface as he lowered his defences. I slid past the dense walls, into the darkness of the hadal zone, where I took shape again. A golden thread stretched before me, making me think of the story of the Minotaur, another one in that book from Eliza.

Like Theseus, I followed it. I had reached this point during our training sessions, but only in bursts. Now I could take my time. I walked through the dwindling gloom, heading for the middle of his mind.

Unlike the tiny mind of the butterfly, his was cavernous, like a cathedral. Each circle took a while to cross. It seemed that dreamscapes widened by the year, the way a tree grew new rings over time.

Though this place dwarfed me, I felt no fear. I passed a spectre, a dark manifestation of memory. It watched me, but did nothing.

Warden waited in his sunlit zone, covered in scars, his face gaunt. This was how he saw himself – bleak and weary, drained of all hope. I approached him. Now I was in his dreamscape, I was playing by his rules. My hands looked almost the same as my real ones, except with a soft glow. A new dream-form, shaped by his personal impressions of me.

There were no mirrors in a dreamscape. I would never be able to see his Paige – just as he could never see his melancholy picture of himself.

I stopped at the edge of the twilight zone. His dream-form inclined his head.

'Welcome. Forgive the lack of décor,' he said. 'I do not often have guests.'

'It really is minimalist,' I agreed.

My dreamscape was alive with flowers. Warden had grown nothing here. His dreamscape was barren, like an abandoned house, down to the dust on the ground.

'Our dreamscapes are where we feel safest,' he said. 'Perhaps I feel safest like this.'

'In a great emptiness.' I paced the edge. 'I think I prefer my poppies.'

'Strange that the poppies are your place of safety. You were in terrible pain there.'

'It's where I met Nick.'

The golden thread reached from my spirit to his. It was as clear as the silver one that trailed behind me, pointing the way back to my own body.

'This is surreal,' I said. 'How are we even speaking?'

'In Gloss. Your spirit is intrinsically fluent, but once you return to your body, you will lose all command and knowledge of it. It is not a language for the living.'

'Aren't you living?'

'I am neither living nor dead.' He raised a hand to his chest, where the light ended. 'Behold the golden cord. Have you seen enough, Paige?'

'Just about,' I said. 'Thanks for having me.'

He inclined his head. I let my silver cord lift me away.

Back in my own body, I sat up and heaved, eyes prickling. When I looked at my fingers, I saw their very tips were grey. I really did miss Danica.

Warden raised himself on to his elbows. The golden light in his eyes guttered, then settled and calmed, before he got up and returned to his chair. Once my heart had slowed, I shifted a little closer to the fire.

That was probably the most intimate experience I had ever had with another person. Seeing the cord had made it real, sharpening my awareness of it.

'Tell me,' Warden said, 'how do you find my dreamscape, Paige?'

'I'm glad I saw it.'

'I am also glad.'

'Are you?'

'Yes. I was not in pain,' he said. 'I found it was pleasant to have company.'

'That's nice to know,' I said quietly. 'When I worked for Jaxon, I never thought I'd be able to use my gift without hurting someone. Before I knew what I was, all I could really do with it was cause pain.'

'You did not know what you were doing.'

'Oh, I did. I didn't know how, but I knew who was making people bleed. I knew who was giving them headaches. Whenever they sneered at me – whenever they brought up the Molly Riots – they would start hurting. Even when I was ten, I liked it. It was my small act of vengeance.'

'Nick was the one who told you what you were.'

'As you're well aware.'

My tone was clipped. I could forgive him, but I wasn't about to forget.

'When a memory does not leave a great impression on a person, I see it out of focus, dark and faint,' Warden said. 'Your memories of him are extraordinarily sharp – full of colour, every sound clear as a bell. Every moment at his side was precious to you. You miss him.'

'Keep telling me how I feel, and my patience with this golden cord is going to wear very thin, very quickly. Can you sense my growing irritation?'

'Yes.'

I raised an eyebrow.

'Some of your memories were locked fast,' Warden said. 'There is one in particular, quite recent. A knot in your flowers' roots. It troubles you.'

'Do you want to see it?'

The offer must have surprised him. He tilted his head, eyes narrowing.

'You showed me your dreamscape by choice,' I said. 'I don't mind, Warden.'

'I desire to know you,' he said, 'but I would not see what you do not wish to share.'

'You saw Dublin. That was the event that changed my life – when I came so close to death I could smell it, taste it. Anything else is small in comparison,' I said. 'Anyway, I wouldn't be so cruel as to deny you one last glimpse. Nothing's worse than a story without an end.'

'Is this memory the end of your story, then?'

'It's the last chapter of my life before I came to you.' I smiled joylessly. 'And to think, I really thought it would be the worst night of my life in London.'

I thought I knew what this memory was. The only way to be sure was to dream.

Warden took his pillbox from his doublet. I accepted a green tablet.

'This is the last one I will ever give you,' he said. 'Are you sure, Paige?'

'Yes.'

'Then sleep,' he said. 'I will do the rest.'

25

DANCE UPON NOTHING

14 December 2058

We gathered in a circle, like we might in a séance – five of the mighty Seven Seals. Jaxon Hall had dreamed us to this place, and here we stood.

From our name, an outsider might think that each of us came from one of his seven orders, but Jaxon still had no great love for soothsayers or augurs, whatever his publisher had forced him to say. He just happened to like the number, given the name of our district.

Seven voyants from five orders, blown from six countries to blossom in London.

Nadine Arnett was about to either weep or kill someone. Her arms were wrapped around her brother, whose wrists were tied with velvet sashes to the chair she stood behind. His face was drenched in sweat, hair stuck to his brow.

Jaxon was perplexed by Zeke, and Jaxon did not like to be perplexed. A short challenge, yes, to be unpicked with cleverness – but more than a year of mystery had chipped away at his patience. So he sat in his chair, smoking a cigar, waiting for one of us to break Zeke.

We had been put to work at dusk. Now the sky was dark. No matter how much Zeke pleaded for us to stop trying, Jaxon would not relent. If unreadability could be mastered, it would be a tremendous asset to the gang – the ability to resist all external influence from the æther. It would make us invincible in spirit combat. All we had to do was learn how to mimic it without losing our gifts.

Zeke already had. Once, he been a whisperer – like Nadine, and like their mother, Ayuko. When Zeke played his piano in Oaxaca de Juárez, every nearby spirit had flocked to him. Since his dreamscape had collapsed and regrown, he had lost that gift, changing his aura. Now he could sense the dead, but could no longer make them dance.

I had no idea why he had become unreadable. Only Jaxon knew that.

While Jaxon obsessed over Zeke, the rest of us had been forgotten, me included. Jaxon tended to pick a flavour of the year, and I was off the menu. I had shown no progress in months, and he was giving me the cold shoulder for it.

At last, my shine was rubbing off.

Zeke sobbed in agony. After so much pondering, even Jaxon had failed to predict that he would be in this much pain. We had flung spool after spool at him, to no avail. His mind sent them ricocheting all over the room, like water off a marble slab, hard as his syndicate name – Black Diamond.

'Come on, come on, you wretched rabble,' Jaxon shouted. His fist pounded the desk. 'I want to hear him scream three times as loudly as that!'

All day, he had been drinking wine and listening to 'Danse Macabre' – never a good sign. Eliza gave him an exasperated look.

'Jaxon,' she said. 'I need you to take several deep breaths, then some laudanum. Did you wake up on the wrong side of the chaise longue today?'

'Again.'

She looked away, grasping her own arms. This was the first time I had ever seen her confront Jaxon.

'Again,' Jaxon said.

'He's in pain,' Nadine said hotly. 'Jax, look at him. He can't take this!'

'I am in pain, Nadine. Agonised by your lack of ambition,' came the soft reply. 'Don't make me get up. Do it again, and do not stop until he breaks.'

'Jaxon, I can't watch this,' Nick said. 'I'm an oracle, but I'm also a medic, and—'

'If you so enjoy your sterile life, kindly return to it for good,' Jaxon said icily. 'Perhaps I am tired of your moonlighting, Dr Nygård. Scion takes the bulk of your time, while I receive scraps of it.'

'Stop it. You can snap at the others, but you don't scare me, Jax. I've known you too long.'

'Far too long,' Jaxon said pettily.

Nadine held on to Zeke, her hair tumbling over her brow. It was dark brown now, and shorter. It attracted less interest without the dye, but she hated the change, like she hated the citadel. Most of all, she hated us.

When Jaxon looked expectant, Eliza called one of her spirit aides: John Donne, a famous muse, won at auction for the same cost as one of her forgeries. Since he was a writer, not an artist, he was usually good enough not to possess her at random.

'Let me try John,' she said reluctantly. 'If an Elizabethan spirit doesn't work, I don't think anything will.'

'The obvious answer would be a poltergeist,' Jaxon said, perfectly serious.

'Jaxon,' I whispered.

'We are not,' Nadine gritted out, 'using a fucking poltergeist on my brother.'

'I will make that decision, Nadine.'

'You'll have to come through me.'

'I am quivering with terror.' Jaxon carried on smoking. 'Have it your way first, Eliza.'

Zeke couldn't take the suspense. His fevered eyes were on the spirit.

'He needs rest,' Nadine said to Eliza. 'You set that muse on him and I'll—'

'You'll what, play me an angry tune?' Jaxon said, smoke curling from his mouth. 'Please, be my guest. I do enjoy music from the soul.'

Her chin puckered, but she knew the punishment for disobeying Jaxon. She had nowhere else to go, nowhere else to take her brother. Zeke shivered against her, as if he were the younger sibling, not the older.

Eliza glanced at Nadine, then at Jaxon. On her silent command, John whipped forward. I didn't see the impact, but I felt it – and from his cry of distress, so did Zeke. His head slammed back against Nadine, his neck cording. Nadine tightened her arms around his shoulders.

'I'm sorry.' She dropped her chin on his head, eyes shut. 'I'm so sorry, Zeke.'

Old and determined, John was naturally obstinate. He thought Zeke was going to hurt Eliza, and fully intended to stop that from happening. Zeke's face shone with sweat and tears. He was almost choking.

'Please,' he said. 'No more—'

'Jaxon, stop it,' I snapped. 'Don't you think he's had enough?'

His eyebrows leapt for his hairline. 'Are you questioning me, darling?'

My courage faded. 'No.'

'Oh, the mouse squeaks at last,' Nadine said bitterly. 'You're pathetic, Paige. Always the last to object when he acts like a fucking—'

'Paige is your mollisher,' Jaxon reminded her sharply. 'As such, she is an extension of me. Not only that, but she is a dreamwalker. What are you?'

'I don't care about your fake categories!'

'You should, since I am your only protector,' Jaxon barked. 'The man who keeps you from starving like the wretched buskers.' He chucked a wad of money into the air, sending notes fluttering across the carpet. 'Ezekiel has only had *enough* when I say so – when I care to release him for the day. Do you think Hector or the Wicked Lady would ever show the generosity I have to a common whisperer, of all things?'

'We don't work for them,' Eliza said firmly. 'Come back, John. I'm safe.'

John slunk away, placated. Zeke shuddered.

379

'I'm okay,' he managed. 'I'm fine. I just need a minute.'

'You are *not* okay.' Nadine rounded on Jaxon. 'You preyed on us. We told you about what happened to Zeke and you promised you would make it better. You said you would fix him, not make him worse!'

'I said I would try.' Jaxon was unmoved. 'Am I not trying now?'

'We left our lives for this. For the chance you were offering,' Nadine exploded. 'I was an idiot to believe you. You're a liar. You're a con man.'

'Nadine,' Eliza warned.

'If I am so villainous, by all means, leave my home,' Jaxon said. 'The door is always there, Nadine.' His voice dropped a few notes. 'The door to the cold, dark streets of London. No one else in the syndicate would shelter you.' He blew a grey plume in her direction. 'I wonder how long it would take for the Vigiles to … smoke you out?'

Nadine shook with anger, a tiny flicker of dread on her face. 'I'm going to Chat's,' she said, snatching her jacket. 'No one is welcome to join me.'

She grabbed her headphones and purse before she stormed out, slamming the door behind her.

'Dee,' Zeke called, but she didn't return. I heard her kick something on her way down the stairs. Pieter came shooting through the wall, furious at being disturbed, and went to sulk in the corner with John.

'Jaxon, that really is enough,' Eliza said, shaken. 'We can try again next week.'

'Wait.' Jaxon pointed a long finger at me. 'We haven't tried our secret weapon yet.' When I frowned, he gave me a winning smile. 'Oh, come now, Paige – don't play the fool. Break into his dream-scape for me.'

The temptation to do as he asked was immediate. It had been weeks since Jaxon had smiled at me like that, as if I were his pride and joy.

'We've discussed this,' I said, standing my ground. 'I don't do break-ins.'

'You don't *do* them. I see. I didn't realise you had a job description. Oh!' Jaxon snapped his fingers. 'Now I remember – I didn't give you one.'

'Jaxon—'

'We are clairvoyants, unnaturals, lords of misrule. Did you think we were going to be like Daddy, sitting in our little offices from nine to five, sipping *tea* from our little Scion-made cups?' All of a sudden he looked disgusted, as if he couldn't abide how amaurotic people could be. 'Some of us defy Scion, Paige. Some of us want silver and satin and sordid streets and *spirits*.'

All I could do was stare at him. He took a huge gulp of wine, his eyes fixed on the window.

'This is getting ridiculous.' Eliza stood akimbo. 'Maybe we should just—'

'Who pays you?'

She sighed. 'You do, Jaxon.'

'Correct. I pay, you obey. Now, run upstairs and get Danica for me. I want her to see the marvels unfold.'

With her lips pursed tight, Eliza went upstairs. Zeke shot me a look of exhausted desperation. Over the past year, we had become good friends. I liked him. For his sake, I forced myself to speak up again.

'Jax,' I said, 'I'm really not up to it right now. I was tailing the Threadbare Company for—'

'You have two hours off tomorrow, honeybee. You can use it to catch up on sleep.'

'You know I can't break into dreamscapes.'

'I am painfully aware.' Jaxon poured himself some more wine. 'Go on. Try to impress me, as you once did.' My cheeks warmed. 'I've been waiting for this for years, Paige – a dreamwalker pitted against an unreadable, the ultimate ethereal confrontation. Never could I conceive of a more consequential or chaotic encounter.'

'Are you still speaking English?'

'No,' Nick said quietly. Every head turned towards him. 'He's speaking like a madman.'

After a short silence, Jaxon raised his glass. 'An excellent diagnosis, Doctor. Cheers.'

Nick ground his jaw.

In the strained aftermath of that moment, Eliza returned with a syringe of adrenalin. With her was Danica Panić – the final member of our septet. She had grown up in the Scion Citadel of Belgrade, but transferred to London to work as an engineer. Nick had been the one to headhunt her, having spied her aura at a welcome event for new recruits from elsewhere in Scion. Fortunate that Nick had noticed her before a Vigile.

'Come and see, my Chained Fury,' Jaxon purred. 'It will be quite extraordinary.'

Danica stood next to the spirits and folded her broad arms, which were pitted with scars and burns. She was solid as a brick, with crimped reddish hair, worn in a low bun. Her only soft spot was for waistcoats. When Pieter gave her a tentative nudge, she batted him away.

'Okay,' she said. 'What am I looking at?'

'My weapon.'

Her eyebrow went up. She had only been with us for a few months, but she already knew what Jaxon was like.

'Looks like you're having a séance,' she observed.

'Not today.' Jaxon waved a hand. 'Begin.'

I had to bite my tongue to stop myself telling him where to stick it. He always buttered up the newcomers. Danica had a spiky aura that he hadn't been able to identify – but as usual, he was convinced she would be something valuable. No doubt she would be his next target.

Taking a deep breath, I sat down. Nick stood ready with the adrenalin.

'Do it,' Jaxon said softly. 'Read the unreadable.'

'I don't know what you want me to do, Jax.'

'Whatever you can.'

Zeke braced himself. I couldn't invade his dreamscape, but its armour was so sensitive, even a nudge could hurt. I would have to be careful.

I shifted my spirit. As I tuned in to the æther, I registered all five of their dreamscapes, tinkling and shivering like wind chimes.

Zeke's rang on a darker note, a minor chord. I prepared myself to exert the lightest pressure I could.

I jolted back to myself when a hand grasped my shoulder.

'No.' Nick was behind me. 'She's not doing this, Jaxon. Unlike the others, I don't need your money. I'll take mine elsewhere if you don't ease up on Zeke.'

Jaxon watched us, his eyes shooting darts of annoyance. I hovered. Nick grabbed both of our coats, put his on, and shoved the window open.

'Come on, Paige,' he said. 'You're taking a break. I'll check on you later, Zeke.'

'Okay,' Zeke rasped.

I was tired to my bones, but I would never refuse Nick. Zeke sighed in relief and slumped in his chair as I donned my coat and left.

Jaxon would be fine by tomorrow, once he had slept off the hangover. I climbed out of the window and on to the drainpipe, my vision blurred.

Nick was already on the roof. As soon as I reached it, he started to run, fast and hard. I followed him.

At least once a week, Nick and I would take a *dérive* (as Jaxon dubbed it) in the citadel. I had once hated London in winter – it was grey and stern, ruthlessly cold – but after two years of training with Nick, learning how to navigate the rooftops, the heart of Scion had become my haven. I could race like blood along its streets. I could leap over traffic, fly above the unsuspecting Vigiles. On nights like these, I was full to the brim, bursting with life.

Up here, if nowhere else, I was free.

Nick eventually dropped to the pavement. We walked along the busy road until we reached the corner of Cranbourn Street, where he assessed a grand building – a popular spot for voyants, the Old Hippodrome.

'Nick,' I said, 'what are you doing?'

'I need to clear my head.'

'In a gambling house?'

'On top of it.' He rubbed chalk between his hands, then tossed the pouch to me. 'Come on, sötnos. You look like you're about to fall asleep.'

'Yes, well, I didn't know I was giving my spirit *and* my muscles a thrashing today.' I let him boost me to the first ledge, earning a puzzled look from a soothsayer with a cigarette. 'Why here?'

'I found something.'

We reached the top without incident. Nick had been climbing buildings since he was young; he found footholds where none seemed to exist. Soon my boots fell on artificial grass. On my left was a small fountain – no water – and on my right, a bed of shrivelled flowers, killed by the cold.

'What is this place?'

'Just a roof garden,' Nick said. 'I thought we could make it our new bolthole. Perfect view of Leicester Square.' He sat on the parapet. 'Sorry to snatch you like that. It was getting … claustrophobic in there.'

'Just a little.'

I sat beside him. We looked down at the square, its blue streetlamps.

'I don't know why he's like this.' Nick shook his head. 'Jaxon is the most charming person I've ever met. He is the sun, and all of us lean towards him, like flowers hungering for his light … but there is a darkness and cruelty in him that I have never understood. He did have a tough childhood, but it's no excuse. You suffered worse in Dublin.'

'You didn't have it easy, either.' The wind ruffled my hair. 'Nadine is braver than we are, to tell him what he is. She was right to call me a mouse.'

'No.'

'Yes. I should have spoken up for Zeke.'

'Paige, you're the mollisher. You're not supposed to contradict Jax in public, or even in private,' Nick reminded me. 'Nadine knows that.' He breathed out a puff of fog. 'She needs to be careful. Jax will lose his patience one day. He hired Nadine because without her, he wouldn't have got Zeke. She's far more vulnerable than the rest of us.'

'Nadine works so hard for him. She makes plenty of coin.'

'I've been his friend for years, and I can't tell you how his mind works.' Nick shook his head. 'He has them in a bind, and he knows it. They can't go home. They probably can't even go elsewhere in the citadel.'

'He trapped them here.'

'Yes.' He rubbed his forehead. 'At least we all still have each other.'

With a nod, I leaned against him, my head on his shoulder. Nick wrapped one arm around me with a quiet sigh.

'Paige,' he said, after a while. 'Can I tell you a secret?'

'Of course.'

Nick drew a deep breath, his chest rising.

'I think I'm in love.'

I drew away from him, so I could see his face. 'You're … in love?'

'Yes.' He was gazing out at the citadel. 'I've known for a while, but I've been too afraid to say. Jax doesn't let us fall in love for longer than one night.' He rubbed his brow. 'I've never felt this way before. I've been … consumed by a person, back in Sweden. But this is different.'

Hearing this, I felt strange and detached, as if my spirit had finally come loose from my body. Nobody in the gang fell in love. Eliza had her flirtations and flings, but otherwise, none of us had the time.

'Okay,' I said. 'Is it someone from work?'

'No.' Nick glanced at me. 'Someone closer to home.'

I looked back at him, chilled.

Someone in the gang. If Jaxon resented the idea of one of us being with a stranger or acquaintance for more than one night, he would fume at the realisation that a romance had blossomed under his roof.

'I don't know whether to risk telling them,' Nick continued, 'because I know how much unhappiness and tension it will cause, even if it's reciprocated. But I also don't feel like I can hold it in much longer. Is it selfish to want to say how I feel, even knowing it will hurt?'

I reached for the right words, steering him towards telling me, trying to ignore the shattering din in my head.

'You should be honest.' I heard my own voice as if from a distance. 'Otherwise you're living a lie. Jaxon doesn't see everything, does he?'

'The risk isn't really to me.' Nick sank deeper into his tweed coat. 'Jaxon would never cut me off. He respects me too much. That aside, I have my own apartment, my own income. But we both know that not everyone is in the same position.'

My skin was cold, my eyes hot. I tried to breathe slowly, but in my head, a terrible reality was dawning. Nick was not talking about me.

And part of me wished he was.

Nick was gazing at the sky, his mouth tight at the corners. He still looked just the same as he had on the day he saved me from the poppy field.

'Don't leave me hanging,' I said, forcing a smile. 'Who is it?'

'Zeke.'

'Zeke,' I echoed.

'Yes. I've loved him for a few months now.' He looked at me. 'Jaxon would never allow it. And if he caught us, he might be angry enough to punish Zeke.'

'You never let on,' I said. 'Why didn't you tell me sooner?'

'Because I hoped I would stop feeling that way. It would be simpler.' He pinched the bridge of his nose. 'I wish it could be someone at work. It would be easier to hide. But it's been months, and I still think he's the most beautiful person in the world. I really care about him, Paige.'

I sat there in silence for a good while, still feeling as if a numbing agent was seeping into me.

'I think I could help him,' Nick said, real passion in his voice. 'There could be a way to bring his gift back – a gentler method than Jaxon is using. Zeke wants to play again. He misses hearing the spirits' voices.'

I wished I could hear them, so I wouldn't have to listen to this. My throat was drawn like the knot on a noose.

Nick loved someone. I had never said a word to him about how I felt; until now, I had barely known it myself, except as a vague feeling of warmth and joy when I was with him. I ought to be happy for him. I didn't understand why I wasn't – why I felt afraid and shaken.

'I thought I could send Zeke a vision to explain,' Nick said, a faint smile on his lips. 'Or I could just talk to him, like a normal person. A chilling prospect.'

'The normality, or the talking?'

Nick chuckled. 'The latter. This is the one time in my life where being normal – not a criminal with an imperious boss – would be helpful.'

It warmed me to hear him laugh that way. It had been a long while.

'You should tell him in person.' I smiled. 'How else will you know if he feels the same way?'

'Like I said, it doesn't matter, because we all know the rules. No commitment,' he said. 'Jaxon would burst every blood vessel in his body if he knew.'

'Let him fume for a while. It will pass,' I said. 'It's not fair for you to carry this.'

'I've managed for nearly a year, sötnos. I can manage longer.'

Now the truth was staring me in the face, I was finding it harder and harder to hold myself together. The facts were cold and stark: Nick was not mine, the way I had once thought he was. I had never meant the same to him as he had always meant to me.

The stars were out, clear and bright. Looking at them, I felt small enough to disappear.

'You really could have told me sooner,' I said. 'I won't tell Jax.'

'I never thought you would, but you've had problems of your own. It wasn't fair of me to burden you with mine,' he said. 'Sometimes I think I should never have brought you into this, Paige.' I looked sharply at him. 'I see the way he treats you sometimes, too. Part of me wishes I had just left you alone.'

I shook my head.

'Nick,' I said, 'you gave me a life.'

'You had a life with Colin. You can still go back to it, if this is too hard.'

'That wasn't a life. My father and I both died in Ireland,' I said, my voice thickening, 'but you brought me back. Seven Dials is my world now. I love being in the gang. I love the chaos and the danger, all of it; I thrive on it. It is so hard, but every day is worth it. I can finally be myself, and I can be with you. I've never felt happier than I am now.'

I said it with as much conviction as I could, as I had many times before. It was still true on most days, even if Jaxon had darkened others. Even if I sometimes feared he would sever me from the under-world – from my lifeline – if I didn't agree to become his weapon.

Even if it was a lie in this moment.

'You saved me,' I told Nick. 'Sooner or later, I would have suffo-cated – lost my mind, lost control. I had to know. You made me part of something that matters. I'll never be able to repay you for that.'

Gradual shock registered on his face. 'Paige, are you crying?'

'No.' I turned away. 'I'm sorry, but I have to go. I'm meeting someone.'

I wasn't.

'Paige, wait.' He grasped my wrist. 'I've upset you. What is it?'

'I'm fine.' I drew my coat close. 'If you want my advice, you should go back right now and tell Zeke how you feel, while Jaxon is sleeping it off. If Zeke has any sense, he'll say yes. I know I would, if it were me.'

His brow tightened, then released, his lips parting. And I saw him understand.

'Paige,' he started.

'I'm late.' I lowered myself over the edge. 'I'll see you on Saturday, okay?'

'Paige, wait. Let's just—'

'Please, Nick. I need to go.'

He didn't try to follow me, but his eyes were still wide, utterly stunned. I picked my way back down the building, leaving him alone beneath the crescent moon. When I reached the bottom, the rest of the tears came. I closed my eyes and breathed the night air.

I couldn't go back to the den like this. This was not the Pale Dreamer.

Something would have to be done.

I took the Underground to Islington, despite the risk of travelling that way at night. My father worked long hours, and he wasn't expecting me. I would be able to slip in and out unnoticed.

I reached the Barbican without running into any trouble. For a long while, I stood in the empty apartment. For the first time since I was a child, I wished for a mother or sister, or even a friend outside the syndicate. As it happened, I had none of those things.

Not that I would have known how to explain what I was feeling – or not feeling – if I had. I had just let Nick down in his moment of need, and I had no idea why.

I thought back to my time at school, when I had been the only voyant among amaurotics. Suzette Fortin – my one friend – had broken up with her Parisian boyfriend in our final year. I tried to remember how she had coped with it. My instinct was to spend a week in bed, but Jaxon would never let that stand, and he expected me tomorrow. I couldn't work until I had purged myself of this feeling.

For all I tried, I couldn't remember what Suzette had done to get over Gérard.

I did know how Eliza brushed her cares away.

In silence, I untucked my jersey and blouse from my trousers. I showered, then straightened my hair. I dabbed on a flick of lampblack. Finally, I slipped into a dress and matching heels, bought for a leavers' dance I had never attended. The Schoolmistress had warned me not to come.

I needed to feel nothing like myself tonight. Shivering a little, I covered the dress with my woollen coat and walked on to the icy streets.

At some point, I found a cab. There was a club in the East End that Nadine frequented, with cheap mecks (and illegal alcohol), called Dance Upon Nothing. It was in a rough part of II-6, a section ruled by the Wicked Lady. That meant there would be no night Vigiles.

A huge bouncer guarded the door. He nodded me through without checking my card.

It was dark and hot inside, the music almost deafening. The space was packed with sweating bodies. According to Nadine, it was a converted bell foundry. A bar ran the length of one wall, serving oxygen and mecks from different ends; to its right was a dance floor, where lights flashed through dry ice. I sensed a seer, a physical medium.

For whatever absurd reason, Nick being in love was hurting like a punch to the gut. I would make it a clean break, and not allow myself to stop and feel.

I forged into the crowd. When I reached the bar, I sat on a stool, glimpsing my dim and distorted reflection in a mirror. This bar was a mixed bag of voyants and amaurotics. Even now, I had no idea what I was doing among them.

The waitron – a seer – raised his bushy eyebrows. I had a bad feeling I had seen him before. If this establishment paid tax to the Wicked Lady, it was best I didn't stay for long, and vital that I didn't associate with any voyants here. They would have me hurled off her turf.

'Evening,' he said. 'Can I get you something?'

'Blood mecks,' I said.

'Coming up.'

I risked a look around, already out of my depth. Eliza could drift into any club in the citadel and waltz out with a ride for the night. I had no idea how she did it, except that she drew admirers, the way her dreamscape attracted spirits. I clearly lacked her magnetism.

Nobody was looking my way. It was hard to catch a single eye in this darkness, let alone signal to a stranger.

There was a group of amaurotics at the other end of the bar. I was just about to give up and leave when one of them approached me. Nineteen or twenty, he was clean-shaven and a little sunburned. A mess of dark hair flopped on to his brow.

'Hey,' he called over the music. 'Are you here by yourself?'

I nodded.

'Reuben Evans,' he said. 'Can I get you a drink?'

'I've ordered, thanks.'

'Mind if I sit?'

I shook my head. He took the stool next to mine.

'I haven't seen you before, and I come here a lot,' he said. 'Are you from around here?'

'No,' I said, calling up my English accent out of habit. 'I live in Piccadilly. I take it you're local.'

'I'm from Cardiff, but I'm at the University.' Now I could hear the mellow accent. 'My digs are over in Shadwell. What brings you here?'

The Welsh had felt the sting of the Molly Riots. Scion had outlawed Cymraeg, along with the other Celtic languages, enforcing the blanket use of English. Reuben must come from significant privilege, to not bother to hide the way he spoke. Scion parents, perhaps.

'A friend recommended this place,' I said.

'It's good.'

It had been years since I had socialised outside the syndicate. I was coming to the swift realisation that I had forgotten how to make small talk.

The waitron handed me a glass of blood mecks, edged with honey. In winter, it was the most popular of the alcohol substitutes, made with cherries, black grapes and plums. Reuben gestured for the same.

'So,' I said, clearing my throat, 'what are you studying?'

'History of Scion Art. I'm in my second year,' he said. 'I want to be a curator at the Imperial Gallery.'

'That's interesting.'

'I assure you, I am a very interesting person,' Reuben said, with a dashing grin. 'Sadly, all my friends are studying Inquisitorial Law, the most tedious subject. Rosie there wants to be a Vigile, of all things.'

'That's tough work.'

'It's honest work, but not for me. Good thing I spotted you,' he added. 'You look far more interesting.' He accepted his drink. 'What do you do?'

'I work in an oxygen bar.'

'Ah. I've always been curious,' he said. 'What do waitrons do in those places?'

'Clean the equipment, chat to the customers, run social events, that sort of thing. But the bottom line is just ... watching people breathe.'

'Better or worse than watching paint dry?'

'Marginally worse. Your friends over there probably *are* more interesting.'

'Absolutely not.'

'That'll be nine bob and a penny,' the waitron said curtly. Reuben and I both handed our coin over. 'Can I see your identity card, young lady?'

I flashed my fake one from Leon. With a curt nod, he went back to cleaning out the glasses, but he kept an eye on me as I sipped my drink.

This man could not shake his suspicion that I was the Pale Dreamer. I rarely visited II Cohort, but about a month ago, Jaxon had sent me to broker a deal with a local gang called the Hempen Widows. Quite a few people had been at that meeting.

'Hey,' I said to Reuben, 'do you want to dance?'

'Sure.'

He threw back his drink and followed me into the gloom.

Fortunately, I knew how to dance. Eliza had taken me out with her enough times. Reuben was decent, too. For a while, I forgot what had happened with Nick and listened to the soulless music, approved by the Ministry of Arts. It vibrated in my very bones, filing away the æther.

After a while, Reuben drew me in, cradling my hips. I linked my arms around his neck, feeling his breath on my face, scented with apples. His stubble brushed my jaw. He drew back a little, looking at me.

'Do you want to go somewhere?'

It was now or never. Somehow, I had worked the same charm as Eliza. I nodded.

Reuben linked his fingers through mine and led me through the crowd, towards the toilets. He opened the door to a cloakroom. Before I could so much as breathe, he had taken me against the wall and kissed me. I smelled cigarettes and sweat, cheap aftershave.

I had never been kissed before. I wasn't sure if I liked it. He tasted of honey and mecks. A freckled hand came to cup my breast. Little by little, I grew used to the feeling, reaching up to grasp his shoulders.

When he started to unbuckle his belt, I almost stopped him. This was too much, too fast – but this was exactly what Eliza did, and she usually looked happier for it.

It was just sex. Just fun, just sweet abandon. No strings and no promises. I needed to be seen, desired. For a minute, I needed this stranger to think only of me. For a minute, I would become his world.

Reuben wanted me. I felt that. Yet as his other hand glided up the inside of my leg, as he nibbled along my jaw, every instinct told me to stop. I didn't know why I doing this. How had I ended up here, with a stranger?

Now he was on his knees before me, hiking my dress up to my waist. He pressed another kiss to my bare stomach, warm against my skin.

'You didn't tell me your name.' He traced the edge of my underwear. 'Who are you, girl from Piccadilly?'

'Eva,' I whispered.

He slid my underwear down to my knees. I shivered, closing my eyes. I didn't know him. I didn't want him. I didn't know what I was doing here.

'Do you want me, Eva?'

'Yes.'

Reuben reached up to touch me, taste me. Before he could, I pulled him up and crushed my lips back to his. He made a low sound in his throat.

I was covered in goosebumps now. Surely I was ready. While Reuben fumbled with his trousers, I pushed his shirt, allowing me to check his bare arm for the mark of a contraceptive injection. It was faded – he needed a booster soon – but still there. It would have to do.

Reuben bent to kiss the tops of my breasts. I had no idea what to expect when he drew me against him, both hands on my hips. He was trembling. I drank in the glazed desire in his eyes. He stared at me in a daze.

Then pain – stunning pain, like a swift uppercut into my stomach.

Reuben was oblivious. As he pushed into me, or tried, I could only hold still and wait, willing the deep ache to pass. He noticed my tension.

'Eva?'

'I'm fine,' I managed.

He blinked. 'Is this your first time?'

'No.' I wrapped my arms back around his neck, trying to distract myself. 'Go on.'

He kissed me again. When he moved, it came again – a vicious, racking pain. This time, I couldn't hold in a gasp of shock. Reuben drew back.

'It is,' he said. 'Eva, it's okay. We don't have to do this.'

'It doesn't matter,' I stammered out. 'Just try again. I want—'

'Eva, you're beautiful. But you don't look as if you're enjoying this.' His throat worked. 'Look, I just don't think we should. Can I call you?'

'Fuck you.' I pushed him away, so hard he fell into a rack. 'Just leave me the fuck alone, then. I don't want you. I don't need anyone. Got it?'

He stared at me, shaken.

I was already halfway out of the door, pulling my dress back down my legs, forgetting my coat. By the time Reuben came after me, I had already locked myself into the toilet. I sensed him returning to his friends, then leaving.

My lower stomach was cramping, the pain heavy in my pelvis. I held my head in my hands and shook with silent tears.

When I emerged, the old waitron blocked the passageway, arms folded. Seeing my tearstained face, he frowned a little. I tried to compose myself.

'I know a fake card when I see one, Pale Dreamer,' he said. 'I was going to tell the Wicked Lady.' Pause. 'But just this once, I'll let you off.'

I watched him. 'Why?'

'Because you've clearly already had a rough night.' He took me by the shoulder and steered me out. 'I'll call you a cab. Get back to where you belong.'

He shoved me on to the street. I stood alone in the slush of the citadel, tears chilling my cheeks, wondering where I would tell the driver to take me – the girl with no home, dancing upon nothing.

26

HALLS OF MAGDALEN

The intensity of that memory sent me into a long sleep. I had relived every detail of that night, down to the taste of my tears, and the pain. I woke to shadow and firelight. 'It's a Sin to Tell a Lie' strained from the gramophone.

Warden had covered me again. I stared into the fire, not wanting to face the music.

He had just seen the hardest night of my time as the Pale Dreamer. The night I had realised how terrible Jaxon could be, and the Seven Seals had strained at the seams. The night I feared I had lost Nick.

It could have been so many other memories. I had lived through the first two years of the Molly Riots, the separation from my grandparents, years of cruelty at school – yet it was that night, when I had needed something indefinable, that had been knotting up my poppies.

Jaxon did not believe in hearts. He believed in dreamscapes and spirits. Those were what mattered – but my heart had laid me low that day. For the first time in my life, I had been forced to acknowledge its fragility.

A tongue of fire still tantalised the embers in the hearth. It cast light on the figure by the window.

'Welcome back,' Warden said.

I sat up, braced for an echo of the pain. There was nothing.

'I hope that was entertaining for you,' I said.

'I did not expect that memory to be so intimate,' Warden said, very softly. 'You were under no obligation to share it with me, Paige.'

'I'm not ashamed of it.'

'You have no reason to be ashamed.'

'Thanks.' I sat up. 'Go on, then, sleep dealer. Interpret my past, like other voyants do the future. What does that memory tell you about me?'

Warden came to sit on his wing chair.

'I believe I understand why it affects you so deeply.' His gaze came to rest on mine. 'You are quite sure you wish me to speculate.'

'Yes.'

'You have a profound fear there is nothing to you beyond your gift. That is the part of you see as truly valuable – your livelihood, your unique asset. You rely on Jaxon Hall, who treats you as his commodity. To him, you are nothing more than quick flesh grafted to a ghost; a priceless gift in human wrapping. But Nick Nygård showed you more than that.'

'I didn't love Nick,' I said. 'I thought I did.'

'But it hurt you when he fell in love with Zeke,' Warden said. 'You saw that you were not the axis of his world, the way he was yours.'

'Nick saved me twice. He was my home, but I wasn't his.'

'And you felt lost.'

'Yes,' I said. 'I didn't have anyone else. I still don't. My family was scattered or killed in Ireland, and my father is chained to Scion. Reuben was just a tourniquet. I never saw him again. It was stupid.'

'No. The White Binder was losing his interest in you – or feigning a loss of interest, at least, in order to manipulate you. Without him, you had no safe place.' He spoke without judgement. 'You feared you might never find a home, or mean the world to anyone.

396

That night, you found the first person who knew nothing of the Pale Dreamer, to prove to yourself they could want you. You found Reuben.'

'Something like that.' I glanced at him. 'Don't even think about pitying me.'

'Never, but I can empathise. I know how it feels to be wanted for one specific aspect of yourself.'

For a moment, I looked away. I hated that I had let him work me out.

But it was also a relief, to have got it off my chest. I could breathe a little easier. That night had been only six months ago. Even if I had thought I was over it, it had formed a stumbling block in my dreamscape.

'You were in pain.'

'Yeah,' I said. 'I never found out why.'

'He was amaurotic,' Warden said. 'He could not see all of you that night, and you knew it. You could not be yourself with him. You might not wish to be seen only as a dreamwalker, but it is integral to you. You are the sum of all your facets.'

I digested this. 'You're saying I couldn't relax around him.'

'In short. In those circumstances, your dreamscapes were like oil and water; yours was richer in all ways. Your spirit did not call to his, nor his to yours.'

He made a fair point. If Reuben had realised what I was, he would have sent me to the gallows without a second thought.

'If voyant minds are like oil' – I weighed my words – 'what are yours like, Warden?'

The flames crackled.

'Fire,' Warden said.

Against my will, I thought of what oil and fire did together. I looked away.

'Paige, there was another memory. I saw it unintentionally before you fell asleep,' he said. 'It surged up from the depths of your dreamscape.'

'What memory?'

'Blood. A great deal of it.'

'That was probably the Dublin Incursion.'

397

'I have seen that memory. This blood was all around you, choking you.'

'I really have no idea.'

Warden regarded me for a while.

'Now you've seen everything – my life, my memories,' I said. 'Do you trust me, Warden?'

'I do.'

'Then what are we going to do next?'

He lapsed back into silence, his gloved hands clasped against his chin.

'I saw a map in the House,' I said. 'I know there's a train station under Port Meadow.'

'Yes.'

'I want to know where, exactly. I want to be gone before the Bicentenary.'

'And you assume I will let you go.'

'Yes, or you can safely assume that your snuffbox will find its way to Nashira,' I said coolly. 'I trust you only for as long as you help me. If I get any sense that you've crossed me, I'll run – not walk – to the Residence of the Suzerain. At that point, you'll have made it personal.'

His fingers drummed on the chair. He didn't try to bargain; he just looked at me.

'You cannot take the train,' he said.

'Watch me.'

'You misunderstand me. The train is programmed to come and go on particular dates, at particular times. Those times cannot be changed from this side,' he said. 'That lies with the Westminster Archon.'

'When is it next coming?'

'The Bicentenary.'

'Of course.' I shook my head. 'Everything comes down to that night, doesn't it?'

'Yes.' Warden held my gaze. 'For three years, you have lived in the shadow of the White Binder. Here, that shadow cannot touch you. When you arrived in this city, I did not meet the Pale Dreamer. I met Paige Mahoney – and I think that she is a force to be reckoned with.'

He spoke with such obvious sincerity that a lump came to my throat.

'You have craved belonging with others, but you have a choice to be the pillar of your own world. To embrace your independence,' Warden said. 'Do this, and you may inspire others to do the same. I need this from you, Paige.'

'Why?'

'I think you know by now.'

His tone was even, but he spoke from the depths of his throat, chilling me.

'You must be very tired.' He made as if to rise. 'I will give you privacy.'

'Stay,' I said.

He stopped, waiting. I pushed off the heavy mantle and went to the writing table, opening the middle drawer, where I had stowed his key.

'I'm still fuming with you. But you chose me over Kraz.' I offered it to him. 'I'd say you've earned your own bed.'

Warden took it, a new and soft light in his eyes. I pressed his wrist once before I let go.

On Midsummer Day, Warden entrusted me with the key to Water Walk. By day, it was a scenic retreat – a footpath that circled a water meadow by the River Cherwell. I spent the morning out there, savouring the sun on the mist, the crispness of the air.

That day, I understood how little I could miss Jaxon. In London, I rarely had a moment to myself. Since I had refused to practise dream-walking, Jaxon had worked me harder and harder. It had been almost a year since I had last spent a morning as slowly as this.

I sat down on the riverbank. As I soaked up the weak sunlight, I glimpsed a rabbit, the blue flash of a kingfisher, a squirrel darting up an oak. So much life still endured in this place.

After a while, another movement caught my eye. Nuala was gazing at me from the other side of the Cherwell. I smiled a little.

Warden was still talking around the question. I thought I knew what it was now, though I still wasn't sure how to answer. I was a mollisher, not a mime-queen. I hadn't thought I would lead for decades. I had been content to serve Jaxon, a moon that could only reflect others' light.

But I did have the skills to help Warden win. I knew how an underworld was organised; I knew how to move unseen by the anchor.

At this point, I had nothing left to lose.

Two days later, a rattled Michael returned from a feast. I was treating the cut on my arm while Warden pored over paperwork. They had a conversation before Michael left, shutting the door behind him.

'That looked intense,' I said. 'What did he say?'

'Nashira has called her entire family to the Residence of the Suzerain.' Warden looked out of the window. 'Kraz must have been found.'

'Better steel ourselves for questioning, then.'

'So far, no suspicion has fallen on either of us.'

Rephs clearly had no concept of forensics. I went back to studying a plan of the Guildhall, where the Bicentenary would take place.

Later that day, at sunset, I was making a list of voyants' names when someone used the iron knocker. The sky outside was rosy, bloodshot.

I recognised the dreamscape outside.

Warden stood by the fire. His gaze slashed towards the door, then to me.

'It's her,' I said under my breath.

'Hide, quickly.'

With no way to get to the attic, I squeezed into the bottom of the linen closet. Warden closed it before he let Nashira in.

The Suzerain stepped into the parlour. I watched through the crack between the doors. Warden knelt before her, as he always did.

'Arcturus.' Her eyes were a bright yellow, with no trace of green. 'Where is our dreamwalker?'

'She sleeps. It is not yet night.'

'I smell her.' Pause. 'Do you share your own parlour with her, Arcturus?'

I tensed. She must have a sniffer in her entourage, giving her the ability to smell auras and spirits.

'No,' Warden said. 'She came to beg for a meal.'

'I see.'

She looked out of the window. Three of her fallen angels drifted near her.

'Kraz is gone. A broken vial of the pollen was found with him,' she said. 'Do you happen to know anything about this?'

'No. I am grieved to hear it,' Warden said. 'When did it happen?'

'Three days ago. There was a disturbance in the House.' Pause. 'He was discovered in Tom Tower. Is that not a curious thing, consort?'

'I trust it absolves me. That is the one place in this city I will not go.'

'You are wise. The chains still hang.'

The silence was painful.

'Kraz was beyond saving. No word must be allowed to escape into the Rookery,' Nashira said. 'I have trusted you to watch over 40, yet she continues to find ways to indulge her criminality. Did she have anything to do with this, Arcturus?'

'Not to my knowledge.'

'She is brazen enough. You have been too lenient a keeper.' Pause. 'If you think to repeat your treachery, know that I will not spare a single life. Not even yours. Is that understood, Arcturus?'

'I am well aware of my position, Nashira.'

Out of nowhere, she struck him across the face. I felt the hot sting of it across the golden cord, as clearly as if she had done it to me.

'That was for your lack of respect,' she told him. 'Do not forget yourself.'

'Forgive me.' He looked up at her. 'I have had twenty years to reflect on my folly. 40 has proven to me that you are right about humans — but she has not left the Founders Tower. I would not wish you to misidentify the perpetrator, whose actions must be punished.'

There was another brief silence.

'Very well,' Nashira said.

Her voice was softer. She took hold of his chin, looking him in the eyes.

'Her possession of 12 in the citadel was a pleasant and reassuring surprise,' she said. 'You have nurtured her gift well, Arcturus.'

'Only for you.'

'We will see at the Bicentenary. Should the event go smoothly, all suspicion of you will be lifted. You will be welcomed back into the fold, and all those who question your integrity will be castigated for it.'

'It will be done. Will you claim her in the shadows, or before the emissaries?'

I frowned.

'The latter,' Nashira said. 'Let them all see her bridled at last.' She let go of him and placed a small vial on the mantelpiece. 'This will be your last dose of amaranth until the Bicentenary. I believe you need time to reflect on your scars. To remember why you should look to the glory of the future, not the failures of the past.'

'I will endure whatever you ask of me.'

'You will not have to endure it for long. Soon I will have the power we need to fortify our rule, and the season of conquest will truly begin.' She turned towards the door. 'See to it that no harm comes to her, Arcturus.'

The door closed.

Warden stood. For a moment, I had no idea what he would do. Before I could ask him if he was all right, he swung open the parlour door and left. I went to sit beside the fire and listened to the silence.

Sunset turned slowly to night. By one in the morning, rain was thundering from black clouds – a summer tempest, thickening the air. I cracked open a window before I lay in the dark, my eyes wide open.

Warden had ensconced himself in the Old Chapel, where no human was permitted to go. It was his sanctuary. But he and I had both thrown any concept of privacy to the wind.

I got off the daybed and tied the sash of my nightshirt. Barefoot, I left the tower.

A chill wind howled through the cloisters. Even in the summer, the cold never left. I probably should have put on a coat, but I wanted to feel the night on my skin.

As I walked, I heard a muffled sound, soaring above the rain. I followed it to a vast pair of doors, which stood ajar. The entrance of the Old Chapel.

Gail was in the Porters' Lodge. Michael and Fazal were in their rooms. Nobody was around to see me. I slipped into the forbidden wing.

Candlelight staved off the darkness. The sound had been organ music. It filled and awakened my entire body, resonating in my bones.

A small door stood open. I went through it, up the steps beyond, to the organ loft. Warden sat at the bench with his back to me.

His music roared through the ranks of pipes, up to the vaulted ceiling – a sound that pervaded each alcove and corner, straining against the ancient roof, as if it were fighting to escape into the sky. A sound that surged with terrible melancholy.

Nobody could play this without some degree of feeling. I listened for a long time.

When I finally approached him, the music stopped. I sat on the bench at his side. We faced each other in the gloom, with only the light from his eyes and a candle.

'Paige.'

'Hi.' I touched my fingertips to the keys. 'I didn't know you could play.'

'We have mastered the art of mimicry over the years.'

'That wasn't mimicry. That was you.'

There was a long silence.

'I'm sorry she hit you,' I said. 'You shouldn't have to put up with that, Warden.'

He glanced at me.

'I should not have taken your memories,' he said, 'but they allowed me to escape from Oxford. I walked with you through a meadow of poppies. I flew with you on the rooftops of London.'

I listened.

'Magdalen is my home, but also my purgatory. I am both its master and its captive,' he said. 'Living within these walls for so long has afflicted me with a terrible wanderlust – yet here I am, two hundred years after I arrived. Still a prisoner, though I masquerade as a king.'

All the while, both of us had been captives. I wished I had known sooner.

'Tell me about Novembertide,' I said.

'That night, I planned to launch a rebellion,' he said. 'I hoped that, with new prisoners among them, the humans would have the hope and pride to fight back. No sooner had I sown word of my plan than one human chose to betray us all. In exchange for his own freedom, he sacrificed the others. The cruelty of it shook me.'

His brow was dark. I wondered how many years of work had come crashing down around him.

'We're mortal.' I gave him a bleak smile. 'Our instinct is to survive at any cost.'

'So I learned. For many years, I did not understand why a man would bite the hand that fed him,' Warden said. 'In the end, I did see. It was because he knew his right to feed himself, as well he should.'

'You're getting it,' I said. 'What made you want to try again now?'

'You.'

I blinked.

'Nashira did not fear a second uprising. I dared not risk one,' he said. 'But when you arrived, I saw potential. All of us did. Those who remain.'

'I don't understand why she let you stay here. Why were you allowed to train me?'

'I convinced her that I was the only one who could. Because of what she did to me,' Warden said. 'I told her there were many times when I longed to abandon my body; that I had taught myself to cast my thoughts from it. That was true. She believed I could use the experience to help you dreamwalk.'

I thought on those words, putting the shreds of knowledge together.

'The scars,' I said quietly. 'They still hurt?'

'Yes.'

'You take amaranth for them.'

'She used a poltergeist.'

A fresh chill bloomed in my palm. My scar no longer hurt, but that had been a glancing blow. I couldn't begin to imagine the pain he must have endured in that tower.

I thought about reaching for his hand, inches from mine on the keys.

In the end, I decided not to take the risk.

'I had to be cautious,' Warden said. 'I have tested you, Paige. Your compassion and patience. I was not reticent with you because I disliked you, but because I feared you. Yet for the first time in twenty years, we all took an interest. Even before you arrived.'

'You saw the footage?'

'Yes. You eluded capture far longer than the others. The more I learned, the more I hoped. A survivor of the Imbolc Massacre, trained to fight, with a rare gift, a strong will, and a hatred of Scion. There are no coincidences. Every thread in the æther has its purpose.'

'Tell me what you want from me,' I said. 'No more riddles, Warden.'

'The prisoners would never trust a Rephaite to organise or lead them. They would think it was a trick. It must be a human,' Warden said. 'I need you to help me tip the scales of justice – to bring this place down, as I could not without you. Will you, Paige?'

Even now, I had a seed of doubt. Too many people had abused my trust.

But the only way his actions had ever made sense was if he was telling me the truth.

'I think I could,' I said. 'I think ... I want to.'

'Even though you must stay here for another two months,' Warden said. 'Even though you and I must cohabit and train in that time.'

'Even then.' I tilted an eyebrow. 'It's not like there's any other way out, is there?'

'You could still risk crossing Gallows Wood.'

'No, thank you. I want to survive,' I said. 'We take over the train.'

'Yes. On the evening of the Bicentenary, it will bring a number of Scion emissaries to this city, to witness the glory of the Bone Seasons – among them Benoît Ménard, the Grand Inquisitor of France. The train will also take them back to London.'

'Do you know what time?'

'Not yet, but Michael is a keen eavesdropper. He will discover the schedule. What matters is that all of you can leave,' Warden said. 'Your escape will show that the reign of the Sargas will not be eternal.'

He spoke as if this was really possible. I thought of Liss, at the end of her tether, hope dying in her eyes. I thought of Julian, his conviction.

Let's show them that even after two hundred years, they still have something to fear.

'Maybe we can do better than just a jailbreak,' I said, very softly. 'I'm a criminal. Let's apply a little more chaos.'

'I rather hoped you would say that.'

'Really?'

'Nashira knows you are the Pale Dreamer. You have the potential to wield the might and misrule of the syndicate against her. You saw her determination to avert the union between Dublin and London.'

'You're romanticising it a little. It's full of petty criminals and backstabbers.'

'That is dependent on its leaders. It has the potential to become something much greater,' Warden said. 'The syndicate would not exist without Scion. It was an unexpected complication, a hitch in her plan to conquer this world. More than your reputation, she also fears your gift, even as she prepares to claim it. You have already used it against Suhail and Aludra.'

'Which means I could also use it against her,' I said, catching his drift.

'Scion believes we are too powerful to destroy. That we have no weaknesses. You could prove them wrong,' he said. 'Nashira will try to kill you at the Bicentenary. There is one simple way to humiliate her.' He placed the very tips of his fingers under my chin, lifting it. 'Stop her.'

I searched his face. His eyes were dim, soft.

'I just have to survive,' I said. 'I don't have to defeat her. Just survive.'

'Yes.'

Something in me was turning to steel.

'Scion left me alive thirteen years ago, to bear witness. To spread fear,' I said quietly. 'I want to remind them that if you leave one spark aglow, it can still burn everything down.' My face hardened. 'Let's give them a day to remember, like they did for us in Ireland. I'll help you get your vengeance. You help me get mine.'

Warden held out a hand. I shook it, then watched as he clasped my fingers to his chest.

'Our equivalent of a handshake,' he said, by way of explanation. 'In some circles.'

'Suitably dramatic.'

'You consider me dramatic.'

'You own a gramophone, play the organ, and wear a cloak.'

'Touché.'

He did have a heart. It beat against my palm, strong and steady, unchanging. Even through his doublet, I could feel his warmth.

'We have plans to make,' Warden said. 'Will you join me?'

After a moment, I nodded. 'I will.'

Magdalen had many rooms. One of them was the Old Kitchen, which Warden had walled up at some point in his many decades in Magdalen. Now it could be entered only through a bookshelf on hinges. He opened it for me and let me go ahead of him, into the room beyond.

Michael was already there. He warmed me a mug of creamy saloop, a popular winter drink in London.

'Oh, I've missed this.' I blew on it. 'Thank you, Michael.'

Michael signed to Warden, looking pleased.

'Yes,' Warden said. 'I am glad Paige is joining us, too.'

He sat on the other side of the oak table, as did Michael.

'Okay,' I said. 'We have two months to plan this. Are Faz and Gail in on it?'

'They know a little.' Warden clasped his hands on the table. 'I made several mistakes during the last rebellion. You must not repeat them, Paige.'

'Before we get into that, I need you to understand that I am not a strategist. I'm a career criminal. We don't have battles in the syndicate – we have ambushes and occasional brawls. It's not honourable.'

'Honour did not help us last time. That is why I am engaging the services of a thief.' Warden nodded to a map of Oxford. 'We have several advantages that I did not have before, including the train. The celebration will also help disguise our movements.'

Michael cleared his throat and chimed in, with Warden observing him.

'We will need to establish a route through the city, to Port Meadow,' Warden said, for my sake. 'Only a trusted few performers and amaurotics should know where we are going.'

'I agree,' I said. 'Warden, I assume you spread word to all the humans last time.'

'Yes. Naïvely, I believed they would keep the secret, since my intention was to help them.'

'We can't do that again. Among the performers, I trust Liss and Julian,' I said. 'You could lead the amaurotics, Michael.' He shook his head at once, cutting a hand across his throat. 'Who, then – Faz?'

Warden was studying me. 'You trust none of the other performers, Paige?'

'Not enough to give them specifics yet. Maybe Guy, at a push. Jos, too, but he's young. I don't think it's fair to put that on him.'

'He may be useful as a courier.'

Michael signalled his agreement – probably vouching for a fellow polyglot.

'I don't think we should trust any of the red-jackets. Most of them are too indoctrinated. They've benefited from this system, unlike the performers,' I said. 'Was the traitor one of them, last time?'

408

'Yes.'

'So let's not repeat that cock-up.'

'How do you propose they are handled, then?'

'There are guns in the House, but they look antique, and Thuban clearly has them counted. We don't want to raise the alarm too early.'

'Hm. Terebell may be able to conceal any unavoidable theft.'

'Good to know, but we could avoid fighting them at all. I thought we could either drug or poison them. That way, Nashira will see they weren't involved in the rebellion. Even if we leave them behind, I don't want to condemn them to death,' I said. 'Liss should be able to find herbs that will make them sick, or we could use white or purple aster. Duckett grows it in the physic garden.'

'An admirably devious idea, Paige.' Warden seemed to consider it. 'The weapons in the House would not be effective against us.'

'Oh, really?'

I put my air pistol and acid darts on the table.

'Fluoroantimonic acid injures the Emim, but it only slows us,' Warden said. 'Since it is an earthly substance, our bodies purge it quickly.'

'You're telling me that if I hit you with one of these, *nothing* would happen?'

'It would hurt considerably, but I would be able to remain standing.'

'What about fire?'

'As above.'

'Fucking hell.' I took a deep breath. 'Okay, next scheme. What if we made projectiles that contain the pollen?'

'A sound idea, but our resources are limited.'

'If you have the right ones, I do know how to improvise crude guns and bullets. Even if we can only make a few, it could be worth it. If not, we could use our existing resources – replace the acid or flux in these with our own mixture. Does the pollen still work if it's diluted?'

'Yes.'

'Then we can just switch the contents. With care, obviously.' I patted the pistol. 'How many Rephs would be willing to fight the Sargas?'

'Not all of them who share our sentiments can – one, in particular, has a trusted position we do not want to risk,' Warden said. 'I will be able to muster six of them to your defence. Other than Terebell, I will not share their names.'

'That's a lot better than none. Something else did occur to me,' I said. 'First, I assume there's no phone reception here.'

'No.'

'Good. The emissaries won't be able to call for help unless they have a satellite phone. But Nashira must have a way to contact London.'

'Balliol has electricity and a single computer with access to the Scionet. It is heavily guarded.'

'We need to cut the power. If not, Nashira will be able to alert London *and* Winterbrook to the rebellion. Even if we got away from the Vigiles, Scion would either stop the train, or we'd be killed at the other end,' I said. 'Do you have any allies at Balliol?'

'No,' Warden said, only for Michael to nod vigorously. 'Very good, Michael.'

'Yes, great. The amaurotics' network will be crucial,' I said. 'Michael, help me out again. Since Warden here drinks like a fish, I assume you have plenty of wine in the residence.' Michael nodded. 'The emissaries will probably have bodyguards, and we'll have to fight our way past them. We can make fire bottles.'

They glanced at each other, Michael looking torn between concern and pride.

'Look, I know some … enthusiastic pyromancers. Magdalen is safe,' I said, impatient. 'Now, would you two kindly get some imagination?'

Warden said, 'I fear we could not match your personal brand of chaos, Paige.'

I pursed my lips. Just then, the bookshelf swung open, and in came Gail.

'Warden,' she said, a little flushed. Warden stood. 'I'm sorry to disturb you, but there's a performer outside. He's asking to be allowed to see Paige.'

I rose at once, brushing past her and breaking into a run to the Porters' Lodge. None of them would have risked coming here without good reason.

When I pulled open the heavy door, I ushered Julian straight in and shut it. His eyes were bloodshot.

'Jules,' I said. 'Did anyone follow you?'

'No.' He was hoarse. 'Paige, it's Liss. We got the new cards and gave them to her, but she's rejecting them. Her aura is still there, but she won't eat or drink, and—' A tear seeped down his cheek. 'She's dying.'

Warden entered the Porters' Lodge. Julian backed away, grasping my arm.

'Bring Liss here,' Warden said, eyes burning in the gloom. 'Do not be seen.'

I gave Julian a nod. He left the way he had come, and I leaned against the wall, holding myself.

Dawn broke while Julian was gone. I paced the cloister. When he returned, Jos was close behind. Fazal had woken by then, ready to relieve Gail. They both watched Julian carry Liss Rymore into Magdalen.

In the Old Kitchen, Julian laid Liss on the table, with a cushion to support her head. Liss had turned pale to her lips. In a few days, she had lost so much weight. A few numa were twisted into her hair.

'I don't know what to do.' Julian swallowed. 'Her spirit wants to go.'

Warden surveyed the scene. Jos gave him a tentative smile. Mustering a breath, I took Warden by the sleeve and led him back into the cloister.

'You still owe me a favour,' I said. 'I know we've helped each other a few times, but—' My voice shook. 'If you can save her life, that's what I want.'

'She has been in spirit shock for several weeks. Even if I can save her, she will need amaranth to recover.'

'I know.'

'You are aware that Nashira stopped my supply.'

'Yes.' I had to force the next words out: 'But you do have the last dose.'

Warden glanced towards the Old Kitchen. We both knew what I was asking.

'Without the entire vial, I may be weaker than my wont at the Bicentenary. There is also no guarantee that a reconnection will work,' he said, 'but if this is what you desire, I will try to grant you the favour I promised you, Paige.'

'It is what I desire.' I kept hold of his sleeve. 'Please, save her, Warden. Do this for me, and I'll lead your rebellion.'

Warden looked at my hand on his sleeve, then my face. After a moment, he nodded.

In the Old Kitchen, seven of us gathered around the table – five voyants, an amaurotic, and a Reph. Jos came to stand just in front of me.

Warden assessed Liss. She looked fragile, her dark hair fanned across the table. He took the vial of amaranth from his doublet and removed its stopper.

'I will need the deck of tarot cards,' he said. 'And a sharp blade or tool.'

Fazal handed over the penny knife on his belt, while Julian gave up the cards. Lips pressed together, he glanced at me. I gave him a tiny nod.

'Paige.' Jos looked up at me tearfully. 'Is Liss going to die?'

I couldn't bring myself to answer. All I could do was grasp his shoulder, hoping to comfort him.

Warden tipped the vial against his thumb. I felt a twinge of guilt. Taking Liss by the chin, he dabbed a drop on each of her temples, and a third under her nose. Julian kept a firm grip on her limp and unresponsive hand. Warden offered him the knife, holding it by the blade.

'Prick her fingers.'

Julian hesitated. 'What?'

'I require a little of her blood. If you care for her, you should do this.'

Steeling himself, Julian did as he was told, nicking each of her fingertips, drawing tiny beads of blood. Warden nodded his approval.

'Spread the cards.'

Michael and I were the ones to do it, laying the deck in rows across the table. Warden took Liss carefully by the hand and wiped her fingers across the Major Arcana, smearing the pictures with blood.

Liss made no sound. The only sign that she was alive was the slightest rise of her chest. Warden kept going, now marking each of the suit cards.

Now the cards knew Liss, but Liss still did not know the cards.

Warden wiped the blade clean and returned it to Fazal. Next, he unlaced the cuff of his doublet and drew it up, showing the corded muscle of his forearm. He sliced his inner elbow, and his blood seeped from the cut, the same greenish yellow as his eyes, sharpening my perception. It cast all our faces in a strange light.

'Wow,' Jos breathed.

Michael smiled.

Nearby, spirits were gathering – drawn to a numen, to Liss, to Warden. It reminded me of a séance. The ectoplasm dripped on to the cards.

Warden gathered the deck back together and placed them on her breastbone, then folded her hands over them. He spoke in soft Gloss, and the æther quaked around us all, the light of his blood flickering.

Liss opened her eyes.

We all waited, on tenterhooks. Liss sat bolt upright, breathing hard. The deck fell into her lap. While she stared at it, we stared at her.

'I'm still voyant,' she said, stunned.

Before she could say another word, Julian and I had both embraced her, crushing her between us. She laughed weakly and clutched us back, tears on her cheeks. Suddenly mine were damp as well.

'Liss.' Julian kissed her brow. 'We thought we'd lost you.'

'You'd be so lucky.' Liss grasped my hand. 'Paige, how did you do this?'

Wordlessly, I looked up at Warden. Liss followed my line of sight and immediately recoiled against Julian, who curled an arm around her.

413

'Warden,' she said in a faint voice.

He inclined his head.

'You will soon be missed in the Rookery, Liss,' he said, 'but you may stay in the halls of Magdalen until dusk falls anew, to recover your strength. You will need it for the weeks ahead.'

Without another word, he left the Old Kitchen, and the darkness swallowed him back into Magdalen. Part of me wanted to go after him, but all I could do was hold on to the shaking Liss.

'He's on our side,' she said. I nodded. 'Then we have a chance, Paige.'

'Yes.' I looked at Julian. 'I need a favour, Jules. I want you to go back to the Rookery and tell everyone who will listen that I am the Pale Dreamer, heir of the White Binder. Tell them I survived the Dublin Incursion. Tell them that even the Rephs fear me – and that if we ever get out of here, you're certain I would find a place for them in London.'

Julian took all of this in his stride. 'Are you sure you want to do this, Paige?'

'I'm sure.'

The three Magdalen residents stood by as Jos scrambled on to the table and joined the hug. I released my first easy breath in weeks. Liss was right. Maybe we did have a chance.

On the first day of July, I got up at sunset. I left the yellow tunic in the cabinet and put on my undershirt and combat trousers. I laced up my boots, as I had too many times before. I trimmed my hair back into its bob.

Arcturus Mesarthim waited underneath the stars. I met him on the grass of the Great Quad.

'I'm ready,' I said.

He nodded. I nodded back.

PART THREE

AUTUMN

27

THE BICENTENARY

1 September 2059

In the lost city, summer died like a weak fledgling. Late in August, autumn killed it.

Almost overnight, the leaves turned red as my aura, gold as the eyes of our merciless gods. A week later, they were falling in heaps. The Cherwell iced over. I woke to frost on the windows of Magdalen.

Before I knew it, it was the day of the Bicentenary.

Two centuries since Britain was placed on a silver platter and handed to Nashira Sargas. Two centuries since the inquisition into clairvoyance began. Two centuries since the first Bone Season.

Tonight was the celebration of all of it.

A woman watched me from a gilded mirror. Her cheeks were hollow, her jaw set. It still took me by surprise that this hard, cold face was mine. Though Warden had fed me as much as he could, food supplies had dwindled in the days leading up to the Bicentenary.

Nashira had not invited me to another feast.

I smoothed down the front of my dress, which had cap sleeves and a tight waist. The pleated skirt fell almost to my knees, worn over sheer black tights. A pair of small gold hoops hung from my ears.

After Warden appealed my demotion, Nashira had reversed it, supposedly as a mark of goodwill. More likely, the red dress was meant to conceal the blood she was going to spill for my gift. Scion emissaries would be used to violence, but too much of it could unsettle them – perhaps even put them off their negotiations for new places to imprison us. Then again, those might now be in question.

A month ago, Warden had told me the nature of the Great Territorial Act, which had been due to be signed at the Bicentenary. It was an agreement to establish another penal colony near Paris.

Fortunately, Michael – an intrepid spy, able to eavesdrop on both Rephs and humans – had discovered a hitch in these plans. Benoît Ménard, the Grand Inquisitor of France, could no longer attend the Bicentenary due to illness. He had been the guest of honour.

It was too much to hope that his absence would stop Sheol II. Ménard might have sent a representative. If not, it was only a matter of time. Regardless of what happened tonight, the Rephs would keep establishing these prisons. If they had the most powerful voyants locked up, there would be no way for the rest of human-kind to fight. Scion, the Bone Seasons – they were built to shackle and silence the people most able to resist the Rephs' rule.

Whether or not anyone was there to sign the Great Territorial Act, the Bicentenary was still on. The emissaries had arrived on the train at noon, along with squadrons of armed Vigiles. All day, the Overseer had been entertaining the visitors at the Residence of Queens.

Now I sensed them moving towards the Guildhall. Warden would be escorting me there soon. I needed to stop killing time.

Then again, I might not have much time left at all.

I sat to adjust my shoes yet again. They were uncomfortable, with a buckle and a narrow heel, red brocade to match the dress – clearly meant to hobble me, in case I had a mind to run.

My hair shone, curling to my shoulders. The Overseer had insisted on me wearing makeup: powder, blush, eyeliner. I was to look well and presentable for the emissaries. Most of all, I was to look happy.

Nashira had never formally told me I was going to die. No doubt she meant to take me unawares.

In the gloom, I wound the gramophone and moved the needle. Soft, echoing voices filled the parlour. I checked the name of the record. 'I'll Be Home' – a song I had never heard before now. It was calming.

If everything went to plan, I *would* be home by morning. No matter what happened tonight, I would never return to the Founders Tower.

The thought opened an unexpected hollow in my chest. Over two months, Warden and I had spent almost every night and day in this parlour. Even after Gail repaired the roof, I had rarely chosen to sleep in the attic. Every day had worn down my old fear of him.

We had weathered a few losses. In early August, a sickness had burned through the Rookery, killing Tilda and Guy, among others. I had caught it myself. Michael had ended it by stealing the medicine from the House.

I was still not convinced it had been a coincidence. At first we thought rats had caused it, but it could also have been contaminated water. The performers collected rain in kegs, which anyone could access.

For those long two months, a silent war had unfolded between the Residence of Magdalen and the Suzerain. Nashira must suspect dissidence – enough to want to cull our numbers – but she had no proof.

Paper hissed on the floorboards. I knelt by the door and picked up the note.

Julian had organised a small network of couriers, like the one Jaxon had in the citadel, to keep our trusted contacts informed of new developments. They included Felix Coombs – a tenant of Aludra – and Jos Biwott. I unfolded the note.

Delighted to report that the feast was delicious.

– Birdy

A smile crossed my lips. I had encouraged all my allies in the city to use aliases, as we did in the syndicate.

Michael had managed to spike the red-jackets' food at their autumn feast, which had been held at dusk in Merton. He had bribed his way into the kitchen, giving him access to the pots of chestnut soup.

In July, Warden had overseen our raid on the glasshouse, keeping watch from Magdalen Tower. Led by Liss, we had cut our way through the physic garden and stolen all the aster Duckett had been growing.

Liss had learned a few things from the courtiers. When purple aster was cut with valerian, it would take effect slowly, over several hours. By a stroke of luck, valerian grew on the edge of Gallows Wood.

Duckett had been handled with ease. The performers had ransacked his shop and forced him to confess where his supplies were stashed. After the Novembertide rebellion, he had stripped the city of anything valuable and buried it all in Gallows Wood.

We had dug up his trove, making it look as if one of the Buzzers had uncovered it. Warden, our expert in matters of memory, had measured out the white aster we needed to give Duckett, to make sure he had no memory of who had raided him, or why. I had, quite literally, shoved it in his pipe and forced him to smoke it.

He would not be joining us on the train.

I took a steadying breath. There was no point in prolonging the inevitable. I was supposed to meet Warden at nine, but I needed some air.

Before I left, I wound the gramophone, just once more. It comforted me, somehow, that music would be playing when I left – that whatever happened, a song would still be rising in this chamber for a while.

I closed the door of the tower behind me.

It was only the first of September, but a deep frost had already set in. In this city, autumn was as cold as winter. Nashira had failed to provide me with a coat, naturally. I walked briskly through the cloister.

The Great Quad was empty. I didn't know if I was strong enough to hurt Nashira, but I thought I might have a fighting chance now.

Fazal was just rounding off his shift. I caught him in the Porters' Lodge.

'Warden is in the Rose Garden,' he told me. 'Are you leaving now?'

'Soon.'

He and Gail both knew something big would happen tonight, but not exactly what. Both would remain here and wait for instructions.

'Thank you for being so good to me, Faz,' I said. 'Can you thank Gail, too?'

'Of course. Best of luck tonight, Paige.'

Fazal knew his grounds. I soon found Warden in the Rose Garden, or what remained of it. Wearing his livery collar and a black doublet, its front and shoulders rich with goldwork, he was as beautiful and terrible as he had been on the very first night I saw him.

Well, perhaps not so terrible. Even if we had disagreed on certain aspects of the rebellion, we had always been able to talk it out. Over eight weeks of training and plotting, I had come to respect him, if nothing else.

As I approached, his eyes darkened a little. I picked my way towards him.

'I know,' I said. 'I look like a doll.'

'Hm.' He glanced down at the goldwork. 'I empathise, to some degree.'

'You do look quite shiny.'

'I am a concubine. I must be suitably adorned.'

'What a pair we make.' I reached his side. 'Why are you out here?'

He nodded to a single frosted rose, clearly on the verge of death.

'Fazal tells me this is the last rose of summer,' he said. 'After we spoke of flowers last night, I had a mind to give it to you.' He gazed at it. 'And then I decided that it was better to let it choose its own time.'

The night before, I had told him which flower I wanted him to plant on my grave if we failed. He could still be cold and distant with me, but I knew he would do it. Wild oat grew on the grounds of Magdalen.

Nearly half a year of living at close quarters, and I suddenly had no idea what to say. Soon I would be waking in the den at Seven Dials, and it would be as if I had imagined him. The giant in the tower.

'Warden,' I murmured, 'as I've said, meeting you was … an experience.'

'Yes.'

'But I want you to know that it wasn't always a bad one.' I searched for the right words. 'I don't know if we'll have any time to … say goodbye, on Port Meadow. I just wanted to say that I'm glad we did meet. And I don't want to kill you now.'

'You honour me, Paige.'

There were shadows under his eyes. The lack of amaranth was getting to him, but I couldn't regret asking for it. Liss had come alive since the reconnection.

'Last chance to back out,' I said. 'Are you sure you're able for this?'

'Yes. It is time,' Warden said. 'Thank you. For reminding me what it was to hope.'

'Glad I could pass on some of my criminal skills.'

The bell rang. We both looked towards Magdalen Tower.

'We are summoned,' he said quietly.

He offered me his arm. Just for tonight, we had been instructed to put on a display of unity for the emissaries. And I was the special guest.

I tucked my hand into the crook of his elbow. For the last time, we left the Residence of Magdalen.

The Guildhall was at the end of Magdalen Walk. Almost everyone would be at the Bicentenary: jackets, performers, amaurotics. Most would be allowed to eat and dance. In return, they had to pretend they were grateful for their *rehabilitation*. Tonight, Warden and I were part of that performance.

He kept a gloved hand over mine as we walked. On any other night, the Rephs would never have allowed this, but clearly they wanted to give the impression that they were compassionate masters.

Nashira would clearly prefer me to be a willing sacrifice. I would not give her that satisfaction, but I knew I would be silenced before I went on stage.

'The train will leave this city at midnight,' Warden said. 'You will be called at a quarter to eleven – the last scene of the play, the grand finale.'

That was bad. If every prisoner was to reach the train, they would have to move quickly.

'So the execution won't take long,' I said. 'If she overpowers me.'

'She will not.'

'You don't know that.'

'I was attempting to be optimistic.'

He led me to the doors of the old building, which had been scrubbed to the last stone and step. Half the red-jackets were on duty tonight, armed with batons and flux guns, while the others were allowed to mingle and enjoy themselves.

David had drawn the short straw. He gave me a nod as I passed with Warden. I looked away.

In August, David had seen Michael entering the House. He had offered to help with whatever we were plotting – an offer I had summarily refused. At least he seemed to have kept his suspicions to himself.

As we waited for two Rephs to enter, the æther prickled, and I shot a glance over my shoulder. Two women came rushing from Cornmarket, carrying rolls of fabric. They slipped out of sight, into Carfax Tower.

They were stowing more tinder.

Julian had been the one to propose burning more than just Balliol, to distract both the Rephs and Vigiles from our escape. He had taken well and quickly to strategy. He and some of the performers would set the fires, clearing the way for others to head north. To avoid detection, they would try to use the unlit paths.

In Magdalen, Michael had helped me craft fire bottles, converting the wine cellar into an armoury. Those bottles were stashed around the city, along with matches and paraffin and other supplies.

I had got that idea from dead drops, used in the syndicate to hide items or messages.

As for guns, I had been able to improvise two from old plumbing scraps. Terebell had skimmed another three from the House. One was for Julian, and the other for Crina Nistor, leader of the amaurotics. The third was for me, waiting in a drop on Bear Lane.

Warden had brought me all the pollen he had stored in his glasshouse. Terebell had sent two boxes of darts. Over the course of a few days, Gail and I had carefully dismantled them, poured out the corrosive acid, and filled each chamber with a mix of water and pollen. We had stored everything in the Old Kitchen.

Magdalen might not escape the imminent devastation, but I had requested that Julian try to spare the Founders Tower. I wanted it to remain, as proof that all of this had happened. A monument to a memory.

Oxford would burn after all, in the end.

Thousands of candles lit the main chamber of the Guildhall. The façade was from the eighteenth century, but the interior was Victorian, with a gallery and a domed ceiling of intricate white plasterwork. A polished floor reflected the warm light of the chandeliers.

The emissaries were easy to clock – mostly in black suits and red ties, with gold cufflinks. The amaurotics were serving them drinks and bites to eat.

A steward rang a bell and called out:

'Lord Arcturus, Warden of the Mesarthim, consort to the Suzerain!'

Hundreds of curious glances came in our direction. From what I understood, only the Grand Inquisitor and a select few trusted officials had seen the Rephs until tonight. Now Frank Weaver had sent most of his staff from the Westminster Archon, as well as representatives from equivalent headquarters elsewhere in Scion.

Warden released my hand. Behind us, Pleione and Alsafi were announced.

'I must show my face to Nashira. I imagine there are people you would like to see,' he said. 'There is a trap room under the stage.

I will be there at half past ten. If you can slip away, I would speak to you.'

I nodded.

High overhead, Liss was on the silks with her understudy, Nell. The chandeliers lit them both, casting their shadows on the ceiling. The emissaries gazed up in wonder as Liss struck an elegant pose.

She was hanging up there with no safety net, relying solely on her strength and talent.

Julian was too new to performing to be allowed into the Guildhall. He was content with that. It left him free to pave the way.

Warden strode off, leaving me on my own. Fortunately, Michael appeared with a platter, offering me a glass of hot mecks.

'Well done,' I said under my breath. 'They should start feeling it by eleven.'

Michael smiled. We stood close together, surrounded by the din of conversation.

'Are unnaturals allowed in the gallery?' I asked. He shook his head. 'Shame. I was hoping for a decent look at all these syco-phants.' I glanced at him. 'You're going back for Faz and Gail, aren't you?'

He nodded.

'Okay,' I said. 'Just get to us before midnight. It sounds like we can't hold the train.'

Holding the platter in one hand, Michael reached into his sleeve with the other, passing me a note. I subtly opened it and read.

I got your backpack from Trinity. It's waiting with your boots — those shoes are too small. I hope you don't die. It was nice to meet you.

I closed the note, touched.

'And you, Michael,' I said quietly. 'Go on. Let's not raise suspicions.'

Michael went bravely to offer a drink to a Vigile. I accepted a finger sandwich from Crina, who gave me a nod.

It was only twenty past nine. Over an hour to kill, and small talk would be torture at this hellish party. I was already feeling the pinch of the shoes.

The hall flickered with candlelight and Chopin. As I wandered its edge, obscured by the gloom, I kept my focus off the æther. Too many people, crushed too close together. Instead, I observed the Rephs.

Several of them were newcomers to the city. Like Warden, they all scrubbed up very well. Some were on my side, but I had no way of telling which. I couldn't blame them for hiding. If this rebellion failed, they wouldn't just be scarred.

Liss executed a difficult climb, applauded by the guests. As I drank, I felt a tingle on my nape. Suhail watched me from a corner, his eyes ablaze.

I melted back into the crowd.

Warden now stood with Nashira, who was surrounded by an adoring flock of humans. I had to hand it to the Suzerain – she really was dressed to kill. Her hair was a golden cascade, matching the clasps of her cloak. From a distance, they were the perfect couple.

I gave them a wide berth. After seeing Nashira hit Warden, I had found it even harder to stomach the sight of their false courtesy.

My wandering took me into the arches under the gallery, where I leaned against a wall, safe in the shadows. Everyone in the hall but me was dressed for winter. My bare arms prickled with goosebumps.

The Rephs mingled like old friends with the emissaries, who were clearly both unnerved and mesmerised by these beautiful giants. It didn't surprise me that they could launch a charm offensive when it suited them. They must have charmed the wits out of Lord Palmerston.

Terebell was talking to a French aide. I watched in silent fascination, shot with disgust, as Thuban laughed with Priscilla Lane, the Minister for Culture – the woman who oversaw all censorship. Of the two of them, I wasn't sure who had the worse laugh.

Fortunately, Priscilla hadn't brought her team of professional dryshites tonight – someone was presiding over the piano with a measure of talent. A magnificent organ dominated the back of the stage, but Warden would not be playing. I doubted Nashira even knew he could.

Ivy was nowhere to be seen. Over the weeks, I had done my best to track her down – of all the people in the city, she needed to be at Magdalen – but Thuban must have locked her in the Residence of Corpus. Two performers, both with grudges against Thuban, had attempted to break her out. Neither of them had returned.

Corpus was the only residence where we had no firm allies, but Ivy would be freed. Michael had found an amaurotic who knew where its spare keys were kept. With the rebellion in full swing, getting Ivy away would be easier.

I took a small bite of the sandwich. My nerves had kept me from eating all day.

'You know there's cake.'

David had sauntered to my side. A flux gun was holstered at his hip.

'Savoy cake,' he added, as if I cared. 'After all, it is an anniversary.'

'I'm not hungry.'

'I can't imagine why.' He folded his arms. 'I'll give you some food for thought. Do you think Scion likes taking orders from the Rephs?'

'Looking at all this, I'd say so.'

'Some of them are buying into it,' he conceded. 'But the Rephs are clearly unnatural, and they're in charge of Scion. That must be confusing the anchorites. All this is chafing against their overriding instinct – to fear what they don't understand.' He glanced at me. 'Do you not think one person in history would have thought about resisting that hypocrisy from the inside?'

'If they did, they clearly failed. Are you steering for a point, David?'

'Just answer the question.'

'They wouldn't dare,' I said. 'They're too afraid of the Buzzers.'

'But you're not.' David lowered his voice. 'I've been keeping an eye on your friend. Don't worry. I won't tell anyone about the purple aster.'

He was out of sight before I could answer. In a flash, my whole body turned cold.

David knew. He had a way of seeing things that others blinked and missed. If he went to Nashira now, the rebellion would die before it

427

could begin. I thought of killing him, but stopped myself. If there was one thing more suspicious than poisoned soup, it was a corpse.

The clamminess was getting worse. The dress seemed to constrict around my ribs. When I tried to step outside, two Vigiles closed ranks in front of me.

'I just need some air,' I said. 'You don't want me to faint. I'm the main event.'

'Get back in there, unnatural.'

Defeated, I cast my eye around the hall again, looking for Frank Weaver.

The Grand Inquisitor of England was nowhere in sight. Scarlett Burnish was another notable absence. They must both have been given leave to stay in London, since they were so vital to Scion. Still, I could see a few other recognisable officials, including the Chief of Vigilance, Bernard Hock. He was a huge bald man with a muscular neck, who also happened to be a sniffer. Even now, his nostrils were flared.

I made a note to murk him if I could. He had detained many of his own.

The sight of another man stopped me dead.

It couldn't be him. Then again, he must have fled to London. If he had dared stay in his own country, he would have been assassinated.

Cathal Bell.

Cathal the Sasanach, the betrayer. The facilitator of the Dublin Incursion.

In his early fifties, he had been a charismatic and passionate man, with a crooked grin that endeared him to voters. Now his sweep of hair was grey.

I had never met Bell, but he knew my father. He had arranged our flight to London. It must have made him feel better, to bring other defectors across the Irish Sea. How my father had felt, I might never know.

Bell blotted his face with a pocket square. Every now and then, he straightened his tie and fussed with his collar. He seemed to be making stilted conversation with a Serbian official, Radmilo Arežina. Bulgaria had taken most of the blame for resistance to the

Balkan Incursion, but Arežina must have annoyed someone – both were getting as wide a berth as if they had lung fever.

At first, all I could do was drink in the sight of him, a worm squirming on the end of a hook. Bell must have thought he was buying himself a life of privilege, the day he betrayed Ireland. Now he understood that all Scion saw was another brogue – the king of kerns.

I almost walked towards him, to confront him, but I stopped myself. It was good that he was here. Let the dog see its masters fall.

Seeing him had set me to shaking. When Michael passed again, I took another glass of mecks. Bell had noticed my look, and was frowning, as if trying to place me. I started to turn away.

And then my willpower just snapped.

Bell and Arežina both clocked me coming at once. Seeing my red dress – the mark of an unnatural, in this context – Arežina backed away and made a beeline for the Greeks, leaving Bell stranded.

'Mr Bell,' I said. 'You look a bit different to how I remember you.'

I thickened my lilt as much as I could, getting his back straight up. 'Do I know you?'

'I was about to ask if you did.'

'I've never seen you in my life.' He spoke defensively. 'I don't make a habit of associating with unnaturals.'

He had tried very hard to shed his accent, but I could still hear it, plain as the nose on his face.

'You might remember Cóilín Ó Mathúna – Colin Mahoney, these days,' I said. 'Eleven years ago, you booked two tickets from Shannon to London. One was for him. One for his daughter.'

'Paige Mahoney.' He had turned white. 'I've no business with you now.'

'Oh, but I have business with you, Mr Bell. After all, you're part of the reason I'm even in this country.' I stepped closer, making him back into a pillar. 'First, I want to know something. Did a Trinity student named Finn Mac Cárthaigh survive the Dublin Incursion?'

'If he did, he's dead now,' Bell said, his face hardening. 'Other than a certain few who escaped, the survivors were executed at Carrickfergus.'

429

I had known, but hearing it still stoppered my throat.

Carraig Fhearghais, up in Ulster. Its castle was a former English military outpost.

'You will not shame me, unnatural.' His eye twitched as he said it. 'Scion is necessary. Ireland needed the anchor as much as the rest.'

The golden cord gave a sharp tug. Across the hall, Warden was now engaged in conversation with a handsome Greek woman. He shot me a warning look over her. I forced myself to smile at Bell. I couldn't risk the rebellion. He needed to think I was powerless.

'I may be trapped here now,' I whispered to him, 'but your ghosts are coming for you, Mr Bell. Trust me – they've told me themselves.'

Bell watched me with constricted pupils. I walked away.

The Overseer had been preparing this night for months. Surely the performance had to begin soon. Liss and Nell were just the opening act. I needed a distraction to stop me going back to gut Bell.

'40.'

Apparently, I had one.

'Come here,' Nashira said. 'I would like you to meet these emissaries.'

Somehow I had almost walked straight into her. The emissaries in question all jostled for a look at me, equally intrigued and repulsed.

'This is Aloïs Mynatt, the Grand Raconteur of France. He is here to represent its Grand Inquisitor, Benoît Ménard,' Nashira said to me. 'And this is Birgitta Tjäder, Chief of Vigilance in the Scion Citadel of Stockholm. I imagine you are familiar with their faces.'

'Very,' I said coolly.

Mynatt was a small man, stiff in posture, with no distinguishing features. Tjäder returned my contemptuous look. She was in her fifties, with thick blonde hair and eyes like olive oil.

Nick called this woman the Magpie. To her, every voyant life was a glinting prize she meant to take.

This was his archenemy, his reason for joining Scion. Tjäder had enforced such a cruel regime in Stockholm that even minor infractions had been punished with death. Her soldiers had killed his sister and several others for sharing a bottle of wine on the sly.

Tjäder looked tense. Her pale lips were pulled tight over her teeth, as if she was about to bite. I wasn't exactly relishing her presence, either.

'I don't want her near me,' Tjäder said. 'I work hard to clean my surroundings of filth.'

'That is precisely why 40 is here,' Nashira said. 'We contain their unnaturalness in our colony, Commander Tjäder. Once Tuonela III is established, you will start the gradual process of cleansing your citadels.'

Tuonela III. That had to be a third colony – possibly with the Magpie as its procurer, and a different name for a new region of Scion. Stockholm was officially Scion North; the other two were Scion West.

Nick was going to lose his mind when he found out about this.

'Inquisitor Lindberg will consider this proposal,' Tjäder said. 'The day there are no unnaturals in Stockholm will be a happy one, Suzerain.'

The performer at the piano stopped playing, prompting a round of applause. Nashira glanced up towards a large clock.

'The hour draws near.'

'Excuse me,' Tjäder said. 'I should rejoin my party.'

She turned and marched towards a group of Swedish emissaries.

The pianist started a new piece, accompanied by a fellow whisperer. Together, they sang a duet I recognised, even if I had forgotten its name. This song was thought to have been written by a voyant, to banish a spirit – the ghost of her lover – in the days before the threnody.

Nashira observed the performance. For the first time, I noticed an object on the piano. It was the bell jar from the Residence of the Suzerain. With Nashira distracted, I took the opportunity to return to the shadows under the gallery, where I watched the two whisperers sing a few songs.

At some point, Terebell Sheratan came to my side. I gave her a wary look.

'Most spirits in this city are confined to Port Meadow,' she said, 'but the victims of the Novembertide rebellion will be with you tonight.' Her voice too low for anyone but me to hear. 'They serve us, not Nashira.'

She left before I could utter a word.

The music drifted to a close, and applause rang out, an overpowering din. I put my glass down to join in. Above, Liss had made a hammock from her silks and sat in it. Nell swung to one of the chandeliers.

Nashira now stepped up to the stage, to continued applause from her audience. A Reph with a livery collar stood on her left, and Alsafi on her right.

'Honoured guests,' she said, 'I bid you welcome to Sheol I, formerly known as the University of Oxford. Thank you for joining us for this celebration – the bicentennial anniversary of our arrival in England, and the forging of our friendship with the late Lord Palmerston.'

I glanced around. The emissaries must have been informed of what they were going to see before their arrival. Most were nodding along.

'I well recall those early days, when Queen Victoria agreed to oversee the end of her monarchy, and dear Henry invited us to be the custodians of Earth. He entrusted us with this realm and its empire, but we knew we must begin afresh. We wished to build a new empire upon new foundations. An empire that united all humankind.'

More applause.

'For many years, we have been the hidden guardians of this world,' Nashira said. 'Tonight, we wished to reveal ourselves to the many of you who have carried out our bidding, making our dream possible. You have spread the message of the anchor far and wide. Now we rule over nine countries. In the years to come, we will knit more into our fold.'

As she spoke, I remembered the rattle of gunfire, the blood on the streets.

'Like the former university,' Nashira said, 'our city is a place of learning, curiosity, and respectful exchange of ideas.' (I almost choked on my drink.) 'The Bone Seasons allow well-meaning clairvoyants to receive the best possible quality of life. It saves them from delinquency and pain, and protects them from their worst instincts, allowing them to contribute to Scion. Their unnaturalness is an affliction, preying even on the innocent. Many are beyond our help – but some can be saved, and this is their house of correction.'

I walked out from beneath the gallery, so I stood under Liss and Nell.

'Let us celebrate two centuries of progress, and look forward to far more,' Nashira said. 'We are honoured to be friends to humankind. You are inventive, enterprising and benevolent. Forced to flee our world, we found kindness in this one.'

She really was trying to puff these people. From their gracious smiles, it was working.

'In return for your hospitality, we bring the wisdom and temperance of immortality. We have not only provided a compassionate means of culling the unnatural population of your countries, but prevented thousands of attacks by our enemies, the Emim. They are drawn to us – like moths to a flame, as the saying goes.'

I hated that she kept using our sayings. It was an unconvincing attempt to sound human.

Still, the emissaries were lapping it up. Tjäder remained wary, and Bell had retreated to the back of the hall, but otherwise, they were transfixed by the Suzerain. Her eyes were their own beacons in the gloom.

'We must not be complacent,' she said. 'The Emim took our home, and they now covet our new one. In the years to come, one city will no longer be enough to protect everyone. There have been sightings in France, the Balkans, and most recently, the forests of Sweden.'

I wondered if that was true.

'Within the next two years, we mean to establish Sheol II and Tuonela III,' Nashira said. 'Our system has been tried and tested. With your help – and your cities – we hope that our alliance will hold stronger than ever.'

The more I listened, the more I realised the vulnerability of the Rephs. Even if they controlled Scion, they had no home of their own. This appeal to the emissaries' consciences was rooted in genuine need.

'At the strike of ten, we will present a masque to celebrate our shared history, written by our talented and loyal servant, Beltrame,' Nashira said. 'But first, I wish to introduce my fellow blood-sovereign, Gomeisa Sargas.'

The Reph on her left took a step forward. He was as tall and pale as Nashira, with the golden hair of their family, worn long, some of it drawn away from his face. His thin lips tilted down at the corners.

He seemed older than the other Rephs – something about his bearing, his dreamscape. Then again, Warden had said they were ageless.

Perhaps it was power I was feeling. Gomeisa cast a very long shadow in the æther. No wonder Liss feared him. I tried to catch a glimpse of her, but she was hidden by her silks.

'Good evening,' Gomeisa said. 'To the humans of this city, I apologise for my long absence. I spend much of my time at my residence in London, where I am chief advisor to the Grand Inquisitor.'

His voice was soft, but it carried. It seemed to ring both in the hall and my head.

Gomeisa could have been the stranger in London. He probably lived near Westminster, but he must walk in the citadel sometimes.

'As the Suzerain has said, a new age is dawning – an age of greater collaboration between human and Rephaite. One day, all humans will know of us, and celebrate those who were first to embrace us, including all of you,' he said. 'Tonight, we renew our promise to protect and guide you, just as you gave us succour after our tragedy. We celebrate the end of the old world, where ignorance and chaos reigned – but if we are to look to the future, we must first remember the past.'

The amaurotics had been snuffing the candles. Nell had taken care of both chandeliers. Now the only light that remained was on the stage.

Gomeisa looked towards the bell jar. I saw his eyes flare a little brighter, and the barest nod of satisfaction. He looked back out at all of us.

'Let the masque begin.'

28

AMARANTH

The three Rephs took their leave of the stage. In their place, the Overseer bounded out, wearing a red cloak that covered him from the neck down.

'Welcome, one and all,' he called. He must be wearing a microphone. 'Welcome to our crowning glory, the Guildhall. Beltrame is my name. I am the Overseer, humble writer of this masque. A particular welcome to those of you who have joined us from abroad.'

Above, Liss and Nell swung to opposite sides of the hall, into the gallery.

'As Overseer, I am honoured to help the humans of this city adjust to their new life, and to develop new and useful skills. The Bone Seasons enable us to mould young unnaturals into model denizens before they can do any harm, preventing the need for execution.'

I had seen hundreds of hangings in my time. Even after the introduction of nitrogen aspyxiation, Scion liked to send us warnings from the Lychgate.

'We truly regret that the Grand Inquisitor of France is unable to join us tonight, and trust he will recover soon,' the Overseer said.

'In the meantime, his Grand Raconteur, Aloïs Mynatt, has come in his stead. We are all delighted to announce that Sheol II is already under construction in the Scion Republic of France, with unnaturals to be harvested from Paris and Marseille. Glory to the anchor! Vive la France!'

Aloïs Mynatt raised a glass as the hall erupted with cheers. My stomach curdled.

I had assumed negotiations for a second colony had only just started. Even if I burned this place down, another one was already rising.

'As the blood-sovereigns have said, tonight is both a celebration of our future and a grave acknowledgement of our past,' the Overseer said. 'Our repentant unnaturals have worked very hard to entertain you this evening. Their performance will remind us of the dark days before the Rephaim arrived – the days of the Bloody King.'

I watched as the performers walked out in a line. More of them filled the gallery, standing among the emissaries.

Liss had told me about this. They were going to re-enact the life story of the Bloody King. She had been cast as one of his five victims, Elizabeth Stride. She walked out with a seer named Lotte, cast as Kate Eddowes.

Most of the actors were masked and wore authentic Victorian costumes. Standing among them, the Overseer threw off his cloak to reveal the regalia of a monarch, complete with furs and jewels. The crowd jeered. He would be playing the Prince of Wales, the future Bloody King.

'Now, we are proud to present our masque, *The Fall of the Bloody King*.'

What an original title.

Cathal Bell led the applause, naturally. The performers efficiently circled the stage, moving scenery and props. It was all so well oiled; I could only watch.

The first act seemed to take place in a bedchamber. Affecting a pompous English accent, Cyril introduced himself to us as Lord Frederick Ponsonby, Baron Sysonby, devoted secretary to Queen Victoria.

'Your Highness,' he said to the Overseer, 'shall we take a turn outside?'

'Do you have your short jacket, Ponsonby?'

'Only a tailcoat, Your Highness.'

'I thought everyone must know,' the Overseer declared, 'that a short jacket is always worn with a silk hat at a private view in the morning. And those trousers are quite the ugliest pair I have ever seen.'

Hissing ensued. I had no idea if any of this was real, or made any sense to the audience. Cyril turned to us, anguish in his eyes.

'It was after a long awakening of afflictions – for example, with my tailcoat, and my poor trousers,' he said (to sympathetic laughter), 'that the prince first grew dissatisfied with his privileged life. He drank and he whored, he feasted and gambled, but none of it sated his appetites. On that very afternoon, he asked me to accompany him on an excursion.'

The next setting was a park. A fairground organ piped out 'Daisy Bell' – a reference that won a few knowing chuckles. That song was said to have been inspired by Lady Frances Greville, Countess of Warwick. Edward the Caresser had been notorious for his many affairs.

Ponsonby was clearly our narrator for the evening. Cyril shot us desperate looks as the two of them took a slow turn around the stage.

'I say, I don't mind praying to the Eternal Father,' the Overseer boomed, lighting a cigar, 'but was ever any man in England cursed with an Eternal Mother, Ponsonby?'

'Oh, my friends, human suffering has never surpassed that of my queen, watching her son tread the path towards evil,' Cyril said, as an aside. 'She knew, as did the good Prince Albert. How did I ever miss the signs?'

I kept watching, morbidly fascinated by this web of truth and fiction.

'I knew that you were thoughtless and weak,' a contortionist (playing the aforementioned Prince Albert) despaired in one scene, 'but I could not think you depraved.'

'Your words have no meaning to one who now sees as clearly as I do,' the Overseer said, laughing. 'Come, test your courage against my depravity!'

A climactic duel followed, delighting the audience. This part had definitely never happened.

Prince Albert fell into bed and died. After a fraught silence, the widowed Queen Victoria appeared, played by one of the tightrope artists.

'That boy. Oh, that boy,' she said bitterly. 'I never can, or shall, look at him without a shudder. His listlessness and want of attention are great, and cause me much anxiety. In truth, he is unnatural to me.'

Alone in the candlelight, she was a bastion of goodness, the last unsullied monarch. As the emissaries applauded, I caught sight of the clock and looked for Michael, finding him close to the stage, entranced by the spectacle.

'Michael.' I touched his shoulder. 'Do you know how I can get into the trap room?'

He nodded and showed me the way. I disappeared beneath the stage.

The trap room was stacked high with storage crates, which must have been used to bring in the props. Some of the candlelight leaked from above. Otherwise, all was dark.

I stood in that gloom for a minute, catching my breath. The dress felt even tighter. Despite the cold, I had broken into a sweat again.

For once, I wanted to see Warden. I wanted his calm and familiar presence. I followed the golden cord.

Over the last two months, I had got better at using it. Sometimes I would feel a flicker of emotion I couldn't explain, that didn't feel like mine. Now I was racked by fear and uncertainty, and both of those belonged to me.

Warden waited in a corner of the trap, behind two layers of crimson drapes – grand theatre curtains hung all around, perhaps to be dusted. The masque continued above us, but the sound was muffled.

'I assume we're alone here,' I said.

'The performers may descend to collect their props, but there is no reason for them to come this far,' he said. 'Besides, I believe we are quite hidden.'

'Why did you ask me here?'

'To make you an offer.' He met my gaze. 'If you wish to leave now, I will escort you directly to Port Meadow. You need not face Nashira.'

'Warden, I told you I wanted to do it. You've trained me for months.'

'Not just for this. For you, so you might understand your own power.'

The light from his eyes made the shadows deeper. I faltered, unsure.

'That power,' he said, 'is yours to wield as you wish. You are not obliged to use it. We can proceed to the train station and wait for the others. Say the word, and I will lead you past the Vigiles.'

It was tempting. If I confronted Nashira, I knew I was likely to die. I would not defeat her in single combat. I had thrown myself into training, but for all the work I had done with Warden, I had never managed to possess him.

And yet.

'No,' I said. 'I want to do it.'

'Are you certain?'

'Yes. Are you certain you want to turn your back on your own kind?'

'I do not see it that way. I am fighting on their behalf,' Warden said, his face set. 'We were not always tyrants, Paige. The Sargas have made us so, to consolidate their rule on Earth. I know we are better than cruelty and violence. We can share this world peacefully with humans.'

'I hope you're right.' I lifted my chin. 'Cathal Bell is out there.'

'Yes.'

'Then you understand why I need to stay. I will not leave while I can remind them of Dublin.'

'If you die, so does the memory.'

'No. Antoinette Carter is still alive. And you saw it,' I said, my voice strained. 'You saw the Dublin Incursion through me, so it can never be forgotten.' As I spoke, warmth lined my eyes, but I held it back. 'I have to do this, Warden. Whether or not I die is irrelevant.'

439

'Not to me.'

Warden spoke quietly, as he always did, but those words reached a part of me I had never known was there. I grew very still, watching him.

'I respect your decision,' he said. 'Whatever happens when you attack her, I will be there to help you, Paige.'

'I should think so.'

Warden inclined his head. I thought his gaze darted to my lips, but it was so quick, it might not have even happened. No, I had to be losing my wits.

He looked trapped by his clothes tonight, bound up almost to his chin in that rigid doublet. Where the last fastening gave way to the small parting of his collar, I knew I would be able to see just a little of his throat, if not for the darkness. I knew because I had glimpsed it before.

'I can't stand this makeup.' I glanced away. 'I hate that they've tried to … polish me, like the rest of this hell. I want them to remember my face.'

'Then show them.'

I looked back at him, curious. He tore off part of a drape with ease – a casual display of strength – and offered it to me. As I reached for the red velvet, I faltered.

'I don't think I can. I've no mirror,' I said. 'Would you mind?'

'As you wish.'

Warden closed most of the space between us. His left hand came to my jaw, tipping my face into the faint candlelight. Our auras tangled.

The golden cord was taut. I was more aware of it now than I had ever been, sensitive to its every vibration.

He brushed the cloth over my cheek, to help erase the blush. Without any water, there was only so much he could do to get the greasepaint off, but he could try, at least. I wanted them to see how tired and pinched I was.

As he tucked a curl behind my ear, lingering on the shell, I had the strangest desire to touch his face in return. It was the only part of him he had ever been supposed to show me.

Even if his reason for saying it had been absurd, Duckett had been right to call Warden striking. For the first time in six months, I saw it.

I closed my eyes at once. I could be dead in half an hour, drifting around Nashira. That fear was overwhelming me, forcing me to look for distractions. Of course I would find one in the nearest person. As my breath caught, I concentrated on the soft brush of the cloth on my chin, my lips.

Now my heart was hammering on my breastbone, as if it wanted to get out.

Warden stopped, assessing my face.

'I fear that is all I can do.'

'Thank you,' I said.

'Your hair must be tied.' He offered me a small box. 'Forgive me.'

'Will you do that, too?'

I had asked before I could think better of it. He nodded, and I turned around.

I told myself it was because I was about to die, and my fingers were shaking too much to do it. It was because I was so cold in the red dress, which left my arms and neckline bare. Those were the only reasons I could want to move closer to him. To want him to touch me again.

Warden placed the box on the corner of a crate and opened it. Inside were hairpins and gold ribbon.

It was some time before he started. In that prelude, I tried to understand what I was feeling. My skin quickened with goosebumps. I was aware of the sound of my breath, the depth of it, the rising cadence.

And I wondered if this was how it should have felt. That night with Reuben.

The thought shook me. I had to snap out of it, now. Warden had no interest in me, and I should have no interest in him. He was a Reph.

Warden seemed to finally decide on his approach. His first touch drew my back straighter, tightening my stomach. He felt the change and stopped.

'Paige?'

441

He had never said my name like that. A low thrum in the depths of his throat.

'I'm fine,' I said.

After a moment, he set to work. He gathered a thick bunch of curls at my nape, securing it there with satin. Then he began to wind and tuck.

Never in my life had I been so aware of someone else. He worked on my hair as if we had all night, careful with every strand. Even the gentlest tug went right the way through me.

I had thought he would stick to a bun – plain and simple, serving its purpose – but this was something more intricate. Now and then, he would slide a pin into my hair, sending a chill across my scalp and down my sides. I lost track of time, rooted by the fragile intimacy of it.

It took me far too long to notice.

He had taken his gloves off.

Now I was twice as conscious of him. Even if he had been ordered to make sure my hair was done up, the way he was touching me now – it had to be forbidden.

I had no idea why he would risk it. Still, I willed him not to stop.

By the time he was done, it was all I could do to take a steady breath. I reached up to feel my hair. He had worked it into an elaborate chignon, leaving a few loose curls at the front, framing my face.

'Warden,' I said, 'where did you learn to do this?'

'An old duty I no longer have cause to perform.'

I looked over my shoulder at him. His eyes were burning.

'I have another small gift for you.' He reached into his doublet. 'Nashira has a violent breacher in her entourage – a poltergeist. If she wields it against you, this pendant will deter it.' Pause. 'By your leave.'

I could only nod in answer, almost too aware of his soft voice to hear the words.

He fastened a thin silver chain around my neck. The pendant in question was like filigree, woven into the shape of wings.

'If she kills me, you have to lead the others,' I said. 'Get them to the train.'

'I will not need to lead them.'

'Warden, please.' When he gave me a small nod, I said, 'If she does turn me into a fallen angel, I need you to promise you'll set me free. It would be worse than torture, to watch her using my gift.'

'I vow it, but it will not be necessary. You survived the Dublin Incursion, Paige Mahoney,' he said. 'I believe you can survive the Bicentenary.'

'You're not wearing gloves,' I said, very softly. 'Why not?'

My senses heightened, taking him in.

'I do not fear humans' touch,' he said. 'I am weary of pretending otherwise.'

'Why do the others fear it?'

Warden just looked at me, his eyes bright enough to limn his cheekbones.

Before I could think better of the idea, I took him by the hand, threading my fingers between his knuckles, holding tight. His palm was callused against mine.

'There,' I said. 'The world didn't end.'

His gaze moved from our hands to my face. 'I never thought it would.'

Perhaps it was a kind of madness – the madness I had seen in people as they faced the noose, a wild desperation for escape. Perhaps I had just lost my fear of consequences, or I wanted to defy Scion.

Either way, I guided his warm hand back to my cheek, clasping it there. He let me do it, watched me do it. The lure of his touch was excruciating, and I was too cold to deny myself.

I wanted this, before the end. I didn't know exactly what I felt for him, but I needed to be touched, to be seen – here in this dark room, this red silence. And here he stood, willing. He was here, like the amaurotic had been there, in the flash house. This time, it had to be enough.

Except this wasn't like Reuben. I already knew that Warden could see me.

When he let go of my hand, I thought he would refuse me. Then he brought his palm up to lie flat between my shoulders, drawing me towards him.

Now I was cradled to his chest. My fingertips came to the front of his doublet, circling one of the fastenings. His other hand came to the back of my head.

And I wanted to touch him where I had before, when he was injured. I wanted the comfort of being held. I wanted to search for his scars from the first time.

I could not ask for any of this from a Reph.

Except the golden cord was echoing my need. Even if I didn't understand the link I shared with him, our spirits were connected now.

Warden moved to meet me, still supporting my head, sparing my neck. I gripped his arms, partly to keep myself from falling backwards.

'Paige.'

When he touched me under the chin, I looked him in the eyes, forcing myself to think only of this moment. To clear my mind and see.

'I know this can't mean anything,' I whispered.

Now he was cupping my face with both hands. Slowly, I understood that he was giving me time to think, to change my mind. He had seen me running blindly to the flash house in that memory.

I nodded, not breaking his gaze. He nodded back.

Rephs might not even do what I wanted from him. He might not have a clue what he was doing. A moment later, he taught me otherwise.

Who moved first, I'm still not sure.

I had always known there was no heaven. Jaxon had told me so. There was only the outer darkness, then light – a final rest, an ending. Beyond that, who knew.

Warden leaned in close. In that first moment our lips touched, I wondered if Jaxon was wrong.

And then I cast all thoughts of Jaxon Hall out of my head, and there was only Arcturus.

He wrapped an arm beneath mine, tipping me back a little. I was being held up by the æther itself, touching it with my bare hands. As I grasped him, drawing him closer, my mind fractured with realisations.

He was kissing me.

Arcturus Mesarthim, consort of Nashira Sargas, kissing an Irish thief in the dark.

Straight away, I knew that it was nothing like the night with Reuben. My body, my spirit, my dreamscape – every part of me knew Warden. The cord trembled with sensation, matching his touches, the chills his kiss raised. His lips were firm and warm on mine.

Don't stop.

It was all I could think, all I could breathe. I needed this embrace to last.

Kissing a giant was no easy task. Warden took me by the waist and hitched me up, sitting me on a crate. He was still taller than me, but not by such a long shot. At once, I framed his face and brought it close.

Warden let me look at him. I searched his eyes for the glazed look I had seen before. His gaze was sharp and clear. As his nose touched mine, he brushed the stray curls behind my ear, pressing our foreheads together. My dreamscape scorched. He set fire to the poppies.

For a sweet moment, it was slower, softer. I took the opportunity to dislodge my shoes, which fell to the floor with the ribbon and pins. My hand found his jaw, then slid into his tousled hair. With the other, I took hold of his nape, and he kissed me again, lips nudging mine apart.

Not like us, yet so like us.

He must have felt how cold I was. Now he pressed me close, so my bare arms were tucked between his chest and mine, sheltering them from the chill. I used the opportunity to start unfastening his doublet, working the stiff buttons. I had never felt anything like this in my life – this rising in my chest, this need to touch.

Stop, the voice of reason said.

Someone was going to find us and realise. This was reckless. I was gambling with far more than coin. I broke the kiss, and a word escaped me – maybe *no*, maybe *yes*. Maybe his name. He stopped at once. We looked at each other, both dishevelled, curls sprung loose from my chignon.

Only a moment passed. I looked at him, and he looked at me. A moment. A choice. My choice. His choice. I kissed him again, deeper. His arms came back around me, tighter. And I wanted it, all of it – too much, so much. I couldn't help myself. His lips brushed my eyelids and cheeks. He slipped a sleeve off one shoulder, placing a soft kiss there as well, then did the same to the other.

My hands went straight back to his doublet. I got some of the buttons loose and parted the black linen – only to find a shirt underneath. Without a word, he unlaced it. He swept up a thick handful of my hair, loosening a few more curls, and lowered his lips to my neck.

I had been sure his skin would feel ethereally cold. Instead, it was a silken warmth I wanted against mine. I smoothed my hands under the doublet and shirt, reaching over his broad shoulders. I slowed when I felt the scars under my fingers.

Not just the scars of a traitor, but scars left by a poltergeist. They held the same chill as the ones on my palm.

Our gazes met. I touched his face with my left hand, tracing around his cheekbone.

'I won't betray you,' I murmured against his lips. 'I'm not him.'

Warden nodded, resting his forehead on mine. I spread my hands on the tops of his scars.

The Novembertide rebellion was history, and it would not repeat itself.

Two hundred years was more than enough.

Warden suddenly tensed. He strengthened his embrace around me, drawing me straight to his chest. That was when I noticed the æther beyond him, and followed his line of sight.

Nashira Sargas was silhouetted against the dim candlelight from above, her eyes gold and ablaze. All I could do was stare back, my blood freezing.

The Suzerain took in the scene. The red drapes. The crate. My dress, its sleeves off my shoulders, the skirt gathered around my hips. Her consort, his doublet and shirt unfastened, my fingers still trespassing on his skin.

'So the two of you have been hiding in here,' she said. 'I expected a number of things when I noticed your absence … but not this degree of depravity.'

Warden lifted me straight down and swung me just behind him. 'I forced it on her,' he said, his voice thick and rough. 'She refused me.'

'I must say,' Nashira replied, 'that she did not look as if she was being forced.'

My cheeks burned with anger and mortification, knowing she had been watching us, and I had failed to sense it. I tasted fear, sour and metallic, as the terrible danger sank in. I had risked the rebellion for a kiss.

I might have just destroyed everything.

Somewhere in my panic-stricken haze, I found a grain of calm. Nashira still had no idea we were plotting anything. She was picturing a secret liaison. If she thought that was all there was to this, I could still protect everyone.

'Tell me,' Nashira said, 'when did you first touch the blood-consort, 40?'

'After the assignment to London,' I said quickly. 'He saved my life. He looked after me.'

'Paige,' Warden rasped.

I gave the golden cord a forceful pull, trying to shut him up. He had to let me bear the blame. Nashira was taking me to my death either way.

She also seemed to be listening. I stepped forward, in front of Warden.

'He refused my advances, but I kept pushing. I told him I wouldn't train if he didn't—' I was saying anything I could, laying my neck on the block of my acting, hoping she would stay her sword. 'He knew you wanted me to hone my gift, so he did it. Forgive me, Suzerain.'

'You are forgiven.'

That surprised me.

'You are human, 40. Of course your base needs overwhelmed you, living alongside my consort for so long,' she continued. 'He is, after all, the most … striking of us. Many have agreed as much.' She reached over me to take him by the chin, too hard. 'But if your story is true, he allowed a mortal to manipulate him. He had the option of coming to me. Such poor judgement, such weakness, is inexcusable.'

I had given it my best shot. Warden cupped my elbow, as if to console me.

'I divest you of your position as blood-consort, and the mantle of the Warden of the Mesarthim,' Nashira said. 'I have done all I can to bring you into the fold, to no avail. When you are sequestered, I may hang your sarx from the walls of this city, to serve as an eternal warning.'

'So be it. Others will still rise,' Warden said quietly. 'I am not alone.'

'Neither were you alone last time. You never knew when to let go of a cause.'

Thuban and Situla strode in. Situla shoved me aside, and the two of them laid into Warden, using their fists and the hilts of their blades. At once, I lashed out at them with my spirit, but Nashira was clearly at her limit. She struck me with her open hand, right across the head.

The corner of a crate glanced off my brow. I hit the floor and lay on my side, stunned. A sharp twinge came first, then a deep throbbing.

Warden took his punishment without falling. He would not kneel again. Dizzy and bleeding, I tried to rise, but Nashira pinned me, her boot heavy between my shoulders. All I could do was strain uselessly as Situla and Thuban took it in turns to beat Warden, hard enough to kill a human. I felt each shattering blow through the cord.

'Enough, for now,' Nashira said. 'Take him to the gallery and chain him. Let him watch his own concubine die before I deal his punishment.'

'With pleasure, cousin.' Thuban paused. 'And the flower?'

'It will be removed at the end of the masque. Draw no more attention to it.'

Situla and Thuban restrained Warden. His gaze caught mine, almost devoid of light. They had ripped off his livery collar, which now lay in separate gold links on the floor. Between them, they marched him away.

Nashira took her boot off me. I looked up at her, blood seeping down my face.

'Your time in this city has come to an end,' she said. 'Tonight, you and I will end the masque.'

'I know,' I said. 'I know about your fallen angels.'

'It is no great secret. I suppose Arcturus told you,' she said. 'Now I think of it, perhaps he meant to save your life.' She turned away. 'You ought to rejoice, 40. A dreamwalker must long for the æther; now you will enter it for good. Not only that, but you will find purpose in death. Together, you and I will not just possess one man, but the world.'

'And what about the syndicate?'

'A gathering of vagabonds is no threat to the Republic of Scion.'

'And yet,' I said, 'you're fixated on the White Binder. And you never did manage to catch Antoinette Carter.' I looked up at her with a smile. 'You were right, Nashira. I am the Pale Dreamer – and I meant what I said, when you murdered Seb. Even if I can't destroy you all myself, the Unnatural Assembly will.'

'Oh, Pale Dreamer,' Nashira said. 'You are as naïve as all mortals. And as blind to your own nature.' She brushed a drape aside. 'Take her, Alsafi.'

Alsafi picked me up, grasping me under the arms. My tears mingled with the blood on my cheeks as he lowered a black bag over my head.

He walked me up a flight of hollow steps. I had left the red shoes behind in the trap room. Beneath the bag, my lips were tender, my cheeks feverish. The rest of me was turning cold again.

The bad people do when they hate other people for no good reason. Finn appeared out of the dark. Alsafi kept a firm grip on my arms. *They put bags over their heads and ropes around their necks, to kill them. Even little girls, like you.*

Finn had been amaurotic, like all my father's relatives. He had still foreseen my fate.

Warden was gone. My only Reph ally, and I had let him get caught, just when I needed him most. The only way to save him now was to get one over on Nashira.

The bag came off my head. I was stage left, out of sight of the audience, watching the end of the masque. Ponsonby had just discovered the hoard of evidence in Buckingham Palace – the séance table, the knives, the portal to the pit of unnaturalness, or however the amaurotics understood the æther. Liss was already back on her silks, still in her bloody costume.

Terebell came to my other side. Grasping my shoulder, she lowered her head.

'Where is Arcturus?'

'They took him to the gallery,' I said. 'They ... think he was trying to help me escape.'

'Terebell and Pleione will assist him,' Alsafi said. I stared up at him. 'Distract her, 40.'

One, in particular, has a trusted position we do not want to risk.

'Alsafi,' I whispered. 'You're a scarred one?'

'I was not captured the first time,' Alsafi said. 'I walk among our enemies unscathed, but always loyal.' He nodded across the stage. 'Behold the sign, dreamwalker. The amaranth now blooms on Earth. After all these centuries, the scales tip in our favour.'

I looked towards the piano, which the whisperer still played. The bell jar was slightly aglow. Blood dripped into my eye from my cut, keeping me from seeing clearly.

The Overseer fled the stage. His screams echoed around the Guildhall. The emissaries cheered and laughed as a group of performers chased him into the crowd, all wearing the anachronistic uniforms of Vigiles.

In their wake, Nashira took to the stage again. Terebell handed me the red shoes. I placed them on the floor and stepped back into them.

'My thanks to you all,' the Overseer called. 'I trust that you enjoyed our masque, *The Fall of the Bloody King*. Now, I give you ... the Suzerain!'

Nashira stood in the candlelight to be applauded, surrounded by stage blood.

'My congratulations to the Overseer. His skills as a writer and thespian have shone tonight,' she said. 'Alas, the end of the masque also heralds the end of our celebration. At midnight, our train will return you to London – but before you are escorted to the station, I wish to show you the future, as our performers have shown you the past.'

'Your mouth was to be sealed,' Alsafi said to me. 'I will leave you free to speak.'

He left my side, and then so did Terebell. Warden was in the gallery – I sensed him. The memory of the kiss burned through me again. I grasped the pendant.

'The Overseer and his performers have proven that rehabilitation is possible, with the Bone Seasons. Their talents beautify our city,' Nashira said. 'Sadly, not all clairvoyants' abilities can be moulded for good.'

The hall fell deathly silent.

'This year, a woman was sent to this city from London. As a child, she was accustomed to sedition, for she hails from the Irish province of Munster, known for its wanton violence during the Molly Riots.'

Cathal Bell must be sweating again. A few of the emissaries muttered.

'After receiving a home in London, as well as a private education, this woman chose to repay Scion by devoting her life to crime,' Nashira said. 'Early in March, she murdered two of her fellow clairvoyants – both serving Underguards, loyal to Scion. It was a cold-blooded and cruel affair. Neither of her victims died quickly. She was transported here at once, in the hope that she could be redeemed. I believed we could improve her, teach her to control herself.

'It pains me to admit that our endeavour to reform her has failed. She has answered our compassion with insolence and brutality. There is no option left for her but to face the judgement of the Grand Inquisitor.'

Thuban brought my death to the stage. I recognised the great sword he carried. A blade of steel, coated with gold. A black hilt with a cross guard.

The Wrath of the Inquisitor. Scion almost never used it. The last time I remembered was about six years ago, when a voyant had been found to be working in the Westminster Archon. The streets had been full of people that day, drawn to the sight of a new kind of bloodshed.

I was the daughter of a defector. That was why. Scion had sent me to one of their best schools, and I had repaid them with defiance.

'Fortunately,' Nashira said, 'we have educated this woman just enough for her to understand the danger she poses. Tonight, she willingly passes her unnaturalness to me, so I might harness and destroy it. Dear friends, we are merciful, but not foolish. I wish to prove this to you now.'

So it was to be decapitation. The head was the part of the body we associated with the dreamscape. She was removing the house of my spirit.

This was it. With clammy hands, I reached up to my hair, tucking the stray curls back into the chignon, and took a shaking breath.

'Come forward, 40.'

I obeyed.

There was a hush as I emerged, my heels loud on the stage. I walked as if they were all beneath me, ignoring the anchorites' murmurs and hisses. All I had to do was live. By morning, I could be in London.

When I was close to Nashira, I stopped, folding my hands placidly in front of me. I made sure to keep my lips together, as if Alsafi had sealed them.

From here, I could see the bell jar, and what it now contained – a flower in bloom, as clear as if it had been spun from ice or glass, its petals touched by a curious, iridescent glow. It had a small presence in the æther.

The amaranth, a flower that grows only in the Netherworld. Its history extends to the time before we came here. Now it is a forbidden symbol of rebellion. A rejection of the legitimacy of the Sargas.

Nashira was clearly aware of it, but for now, she had eyes only for me, her most pressing concern. The amaranth looked as if it could shatter. It wept small drops from the ends of its petals.

'You face the Wrath of the Inquisitor,' she said. 'Kneel and be at rest, 40.'

I should do as she said, to keep her off her guard. But Warden had never knelt when they were beating him. I stared her down.

And then a voice came from the gallery. I couldn't see Jos, but I recognised the voice of a polyglot, sweet enough to call every spirit:

In fair Dublin City, where the girls are so pretty,
'Twas there I first met with sweet Molly Malone
She drove a wheelbarrow thro' streets broad and narrow,
crying 'cockles and mussels, alive, alive, oh'

The audience was stricken into panicked silence. Even the Vigiles seemed to have no idea what to do with this outburst of forbidden song. I glanced around the hall, but Jos was hiding, wisely. Crina launched into the next verse:

She was a fishmonger, and that was no wonder
Her father and mother were fishmongers, too
And they drove wheelbarrows thro' streets broad and narrow,
crying 'cockles and mussels, alive, alive, oh'

Crina was Romanian, from occupied Bucharest. Some of the other humans had joined in with her and Jos. Last to sing was Liss, defiant in her cradle of silks, dark fire in her eyes as she glared at Nashira.

She died of a fever, and nothing could save her
and that should have ended sweet Molly Malone –
but her ghost wheels a barrow thro' streets broad and narrow
crying 'cockles and mussels, alive, alive, oh'

And I knew this must be a Scottish take on that old anthem of Dublin, blown across the Irish Sea to Inverness.

Liss had thought my mouth would be sealed. She had reminded them for me.

Nashira looked with chilling emptiness at Liss, and then at me. The Vigiles tightened their grips on their rifles, but they couldn't shoot in here. Not without running the risk of hitting their own employers.

'Thirteen years ago,' I said, 'I was six years old. I was in Dublin on the first of February, when Scion murdered thousands of unarmed people – all to send a message. A warning to anyone who thought they could defy the anchor.'

'You will be silent,' Nashira said.

'I will not.'

One of the Vigiles aimed his rifle straight at my heart, the red light hovering on my chest. Nashira raised a hand to stop him.

'Cathal the Sasanach,' I called. 'Thirteen years ago, you left me alive – one child on Grafton Street. You let me live to bear witness to a day of reckoning, as you saw it. Now you will bear witness to this one. You will bear witness to the beginning of the end of Scion.' My voice was rising, my teeth bared. 'Go dtuitfeadh an tigh ort.'

Even from here, I could see him staring back at me, surrounded by hostile eyes.

He still knew his Gaeilge, all right.

Nashira flung one of her fallen angels at me – the poltergeist. I stiffened, but the pendant on my collarbone deflected it, with such force that it sent me lurching, almost off my heels.

One of the Rephs spoke in resonant Gloss, and spirits came surging back to the Guildhall. I took flight with them, abandoning my body.

They joined me at the edges of her dreamscape, helping me break down her armour. The fallen angels were moving to defend her, but now twenty, now fifty – now over a hundred spirits – were descending on their killer, and those ancient walls were starting to give.

I tumbled into the first ring, the darkest circle of her dreamscape.

Like other Rephs, she had a mind as large as a cathedral. I paid no mind to anything but the light at its heart, far away. Launching into a dead sprint, I pictured myself with a massive dream-form, growing myself into a giant, taking longer and longer strides. Outside, the spirits were still distracting her. Otherwise she would have stopped me.

There she was, in that pool of light – another giant, regal and glowing, not looking at me. I braced myself just before I slammed into it.

When her eyes opened, I saw.

The Guildhall appeared, afire with colour. Auras flared and spirits danced, the latter appearing as hairlines and zigzags of light. For the first time, I was grateful I didn't have the sight – it was sickening in its intensity, making it impossible to focus. Her sixth sense threatened to sweep me away.

A moment later, I was struck blind. Nashira must be trying to shut her own body down. I forced her eyes to work again and looked down at her gloved hand, clenching it.

Pressure mounted in her skull. Her spirit was fighting back in her dreamscape, recovering from the shock of my entry. I had moments to act.

Paige Mahoney lay on the stage, the dress garish against her pallid skin. Jos clambered up to shake me, jolting my silver cord. I could see it, with these sighted eyes, stretching between that body and this one. The golden cord, however, was invisible to Nashira.

Hurry, Paige.

I had to find a way to prove how weak she was. Straining to move her arm, I reached for the Wrath of the Inquisitor.

Even with full control of my host, the sword would have been heavy. I lifted it from its stand. Rephs were resistant to amaurotic weaponry, but this performance was for the emissaries' sake, not hers. I turned the sword, planting its hilt on the floor.

I threw Nashira on the blade, just as she hurled me out of her dreamscape.

The Guildhall was in chaos. When I opened my own eyes, my ears were full of shouts, and my head was in such agony that tears welled, hot and stinging. I looked up, hair falling over my brow.

Nashira Sargas was impaled on the Wrath of the Inquisitor.

'Suzerain,' the Overseer cried, aghast. 'Red-jackets, to arms, to arms!'

The red-jackets did not reply. Across the hall, they were collapsing.

Nashira opened her eyes. I watched her come back to herself. The blade had gone into her middle and out of her back. She gripped it with both hands, uprooting it from her body. Drops of light scattered the boards and coated the blade; more of it spread in her doublet.

'A clever display,' she said to me. 'Arcturus trained you well, after all.'

I was frozen. Even knowing the Rephs were immortal, seeing her pull that sword out of herself, as if it were just an inconvenience, was paralysing.

The sword fell to the ground. Instead, she unsheathed a knife. It came flying towards me. With so much pain in my head, I barely moved in time. The blade caught my right cheek, leaving a shallow wound.

'You can do better than knives,' I said hoarsely. 'What are you – a common thief?'

My voice was slurred. Each time I returned to my body, it took a moment for each part of me to wake up. My fingertips were numb; my heart laboured. The poltergeist came back for a second go, only for the pendant to send it packing. In a fury, the poltergeist shot towards the golden sword, the sword coated in the blood of its binder.

The possession had disoriented Nashira. I could see it in the flicker of her eyes, her stiffened gait. Her fallen angel would finish the job.

The Wrath of the Inquisitor began to shake, its blade clattering on the boards. As with angels, I had seen poltergeists lift and hurl objects before, an ability we called *apport*.

The nearest candles went out in a rush. A Vigile found Crina, the second dissident to sing. He lifted his rifle and shot her clean in the head. I flinched as she died and fell to the ground, blood on her grey tunic.

The gunshot elicited screams from the audience. They broke like a wave on the doors of the Guildhall. I watched Birgitta Tjäder try another door. Someone had sealed the entrances.

Had that been part of the plan?

I had no time to think about it. The Vigile aimed his rifle at Jos, the first singer. My nose bled as I tried desperately to dream-walk. Jos backed away, his small hands raised.

Liss swept down from the ceiling and grabbed Jos with one arm. With incredible strength, she swung him into the gallery. He scrambled over the balustrade and ran, pursued by the same Vigile.

A film of cold sweat coated my skin. Turning back to the poltergeist, I watched the golden sword rise of its own accord, casting a long shadow on the wall. Heaving for breath, I dreamwalked yet again.

This time, I had lost the element of surprise. Nashira threw up all her centuries of armour, slamming me back into my own skin. This time, I woke to my own scream of agony. A tight helmet was crushing my skull, more excruciating than when I killed the Underguards.

That was it. I was done.

Nashira recovered faster than I did. As she rose, four of her angels ripped into my dreamscape, trying to destroy a threat to their binder. In the distance, I heard myself sob again; I felt myself thump my head on the boards, as if that could dislodge the invaders. They were tearing at my poppies like a plough, scattering petals.

Her outline came back into focus. As the angels withdrew, she grasped me by the hair.

'How tired you look,' she said. 'Give in, dreamwalker. The æther calls you.'

I was tempted, just to escape the pain. All I could smell or taste was blood.

Nashira held up a hand. The sword snapped into it, delivered by the poltergeist. 'A willing angel is better,' she said. 'But that would be too much to ask from someone as wilful as you.'

Suddenly she let go of my hair. Michael had thrown himself on to her back, forcing her to deal with him first. It gave me time to crawl away, but I was so weak, so racked with pain. My gift burned like a curse.

Nashira pitched Michael off the stage. He landed on a performer, sending them both crashing to the floor in a heap.

Her face appeared above mine again, her eyes turning as red as my dress. The draining was the final insult. I was cut and bruised, in more pain than I knew how to hold. I couldn't stop her forcing me to my knees, shoving my head down, baring my nape to the sword.

At least I had spoken.

At least I had reminded them of Dublin.

'You are too feeble to wield this gift. You should never have possessed it,' Nashira told me. 'No human can harness such power. I am pleased you did not die in Dublin, or it might have been lost for good.' She held up the Wrath of the Inquisitor. 'Rest easy, dreamwalker. All you need do is watch as I conquer.'

I managed, with my last scrap of strength, to look up, into her eyes.

The golden blade swung high, reflecting the candlelight.

Arcturus Mesarthim stopped it.

The blade sank deep into his shoulder. He wrenched free and attacked Nashira, whirling immense spools. Merope and Alsafi leapt into action, with Alsafi battling his own secret allies, keeping up his long pretence. Pleione and Terebell joined the fray, fighting on the same side as Warden. Their outlines ran together.

All the while, the amaranth shone.

I was surrounded by the Rephs. My survival instinct urged me to get out of their way. As I started to get up, my dreamscape sent mirages across my line of sight – candlelight and poppies, hall and field. My knees buckled again, the pain pounding at the front of my head.

Then Warden was there, one arm across my chest, turning me. He scooped me into his arms and bore me from the stage.

'The train will leave erelong,' he said. 'We must go.' I could hardly speak. 'Paige?'

The main doors to the Guildhall suddenly opened. A solitary figure emerged from outside, wearing a suit and tie and an ornate white mask.

'Good evening, one and all.'

His voice was slightly muffled, but he still managed to silence the room. All skirmishes came to a standstill. I stared towards the man in the doorway, convinced I was still hallucinating.

That could not be his voice.

He could not be here.

'I hear you've all been looking rather hard for me – to no avail,' the same deep voice said, with a familiar tinge of amusement. 'All those secrets and clever defences, and I still found you first.' He walked into our midst, undaunted by the guns, the giants. 'But for those of you who somehow don't know, I am the White Binder.' His charm gave way to a terrible chill. 'And I want my dreamwalker back.'

'Jaxon,' I breathed.

He was here. They had come.

Just as I passed out, the windows shattered.

29

HIS PARTING FROM HER

Another storm raged in my dreamscape, months after the last – memories pouring unchecked from their places, flowers torn apart by wind.

Outside my ravaged mind, glass now covered the floor of the Guildhall. I still didn't know how the windows had exploded – only that Warden was still holding me, carrying me away from the chaos. Even in this murky stupor, I knew his aura, the shape of his dreamscape.

For a short while, I could barely remember where I was. A callused hand cupped my cheek. I blinked, trying to make the lines stop blurring.

'Paige.'

My fingers went to his chest. I was so weary, I could hardly keep my eyes open.

'Warden,' I murmured.

'I have you.' He brushed a curl out of my eyes. 'You should not have attempted a second possession. The first display was more than enough.'

'You knew I was … an opportunist.'

'I did.'

His arms drew me closer, warming my skin. The poltergeist might not have been able to touch me, but the ethereal skirmish had left a chill.

Warden must be waiting for someone. Given our lack of time, it had to be for a good reason. With no choice but to trust his intentions, I leaned on his chest and checked out for a moment, succumbing to exhaustion – only to jolt awake at the deafening blast of a shotgun.

There had been no shotguns in the House. They were also not standard issue for Vigiles. The one place I had seen one was the black market.

Danica had bought it.

Warden had carried me to the gallery, above the turmoil. Bursts of gunfire lit the ceiling, the sound cutting right through my head. Two hammers drove hot nails into my temples. A drill was boring straight into the bone above one eye, setting off a deep throb. Every faint sound was too much to bear. Even his eyes were a little too bright.

As if he could tell, they dimmed. He hitched me up, so I could lean forward, and helped me stem my fresh nosebleed. From the taste, it was heavy.

'Help is coming,' he said, his voice calming me. 'This pain will not last.'

'Nashira.' I forced her name out. 'Where is she?'

'For now, she has retreated. She may be trying to save the Residence of the Suzerain.'

I reached out to the æther, to pinpoint her, but my eyes watered in protest.

'Balliol,' I said thickly, grasping Warden. 'Did they—' He leaned closer to my lips to hear me, and I tried again: 'Did someone cut the power?'

'Gail assured me she would. London will not hear of this until it is too late.' He glanced up. 'Julian and his allies seem to have done their part. The residences are burning. They have also set bonfires across the city, to further divide attention. Our rebellion has begun, Paige.'

461

'Good.' I kept hold of his sleeve. 'How long until the train leaves?'

'Fifty minutes.'

'Then why … are we still here?'

'The Vigiles have almost surrounded the Guildhall. Terebell is leading our allies through a secret corridor, but she cannot move too many at once, or our escape route will be spotted.' Warden ran a hand over my hair. 'They came for you, Paige. The Seven Seals came.'

Before I could fully absorb this, Liss landed catlike in the gallery, barefoot and dishevelled, cheeks flushed. She rushed straight to my side.

'Paige—'

She had taken off most of her costume, leaving her in skintight black, her face still flecked with stage blood.

'Liss,' I rasped. 'You need to go.'

'Not yet.' She looked at Warden. 'Are you getting help for her?'

'Yes. You should make for the meadow as soon as you can, Liss.'

Liss shook her head. 'Too many people are still trapped in here, and the Vigiles are taking shots while they get the emissaries out. I have to help.'

'Liss.' I reached for her. 'Thank you. For the song.'

'They deserved to be reminded.' Liss crouched to press my hand, her grip firm. 'Get well, Paige. We need you strong.'

She leapt back off the balustrade and caught her purple silks, which now hung almost to the floor. From what I could make out, she and Nell were using them to swing across the hall, distracting the Vigiles.

'I have to help them,' I said faintly. 'I need … my gun. The drop on Bear Lane.'

'You can retrieve it soon.'

'Crina is dead.'

'Michael is leading the amaurotics. We will follow,' Warden said, 'but your dreamscape is damaged. You cannot go back to London like this, Paige.'

'Michael was … meant to get Gail and Faz.'

'I sent one of my other allies for them.'

Port Meadow was over a mile from the Guildhall. We were going to have to run all the way. With this in mind, I tried to kick off the red shoes of anguish. Noticing my predicament, Warden unbuckled them for me.

Only a few candles lit the gallery. The pendant caught their light, a cool weight on my neckline. Warden watched my face, clasping my cold fingers to his chest. Their tips and nailbeds had turned a purplish grey.

Another pair of gunshots rang out from below. When I opened my eyes again, a vicious light scalded them. I tried to block it, my head in agony.

'Paige.' A hand in a tactical glove clasped my shoulder. 'Paige, it's me. It's Nick.'

Nick had a ski mask on, but I knew his voice, his aura. He wore a winter boiler suit, like an engineer.

'Nick,' I whispered. 'You found me.'

'I told you I would.'

'Vision, we have to go, right now,' Nadine said from the balustrade, holding a pistol. 'We can treat her when we get back to London.'

As she spoke, she made a precise shot. I distantly sensed a dreamscape wink out.

'It could be too late by then.' The light gleamed back into my eyes, and a hand took mine. 'Cyanosis, and no pupil response. She's not doing well.'

'You said cyanosis was normal for her.'

'She has it persistently in her lips. Now it's in her fingers, too.' Nick breathed in. 'She needs more oxygen. Fury has the mask.'

'I'll get it.'

Nadine swung a leg over the balustrade. I watched her drop out of sight.

Another blackout. When I stirred, there was something fastened over my nose and mouth. I recognised the smell of it. Someone was feeding me extra oxygen. Nick cradled me in the crook of his arm, keeping the mask cupped over my mouth. I breathed deep, heavy-eyed.

Warden was gone. I looked for him in the dark, my chest heaving. Instead, two covered faces hovered above me.

'It's not working.' Nick sounded grim. 'She's pushed herself too hard.'

'Our train will not wait, Vision.' The other voice had an edge. 'Drag her if you must. I will not be left here when it proceeds to London.'

'Jax, I think she's dying.'

'Save her, then. Aren't you a medic?'

Just then, Warden returned. He knelt beside me and looked at Nick.

'Paige was attacked by four spirits, controlled by a binder of exceptional strength. I suspect they have damaged the barrier of her dreamscape. Her overuse of her gift has not helped,' he said. 'I have a remedy.'

'Excuse me,' Jaxon said icily. 'Nobody – including you, whatever you are – will be feeding poison to my dreamwalker without my express permission.'

Warden ignored him, which I would have found mildly funny if I hadn't been an inch from death. Nick looked at me, then at Jaxon.

'This remedy,' he said. 'What is it?'

'Explaining it to you would take some time. It will mend the injury, but only if I act now.' Warden glanced up. 'If you do not wish to lose Paige, you will not stand in my way, Jaxon.'

'How do—' Jaxon collected himself, but his eyes remained wide and fixed, his nostrils flared. 'Very well. If you insist upon fritter-ing our time away, try whatever potion you like.' He checked his pocket watch. 'During this century, if you please. Our window of escape is closing.'

Nick patted my cheek. 'Paige,' he said in a soft voice, 'this man says he can help you. We don't have much time to decide. Do you trust him?'

Trust. A small flower on the edge of my perception, beckoning me into a different world – a different, safer life, before the poppy field.

'Yes,' I said.

Pleione was standing behind Warden. He took a vial from her – another gilded vial of amaranth. The scarred ones must have been stockpiling it.

He placed one drop under my nose, and two more on my temples, just as he had with Liss. Tipping up my chin, he helped me take a sip. It tasted sweet, and warmed my throat on its way down. Distantly, I thought of that book of myths, which spoke of a nectar drunk by the gods. A nectar that healed wounds and sickness.

And I wondered if all our stories – tales of deathless gods and giants – might have roots in the Netherworld.

Little by little, the agony subsided, tears of relief washing my cheeks. The tension in my neck unwound. I could sense the amaranth working like drops of water on my poppies, quenching and soothing.

'Paige.' Warden sought my gaze. 'Hearken to me. Come back.'

I blinked several times.

'I haven't a clue what *hearken* means,' I informed him. 'But I'm back.'

His eyes glowed.

'Paige.' Nick bundled me straight into his arms. He was shaking. 'You're okay.'

'I don't understand.' I clutched his back. 'Nick, you can't be here. Your job—'

'Dani got us on to the train. I'll explain in London.' He got me to my feet, to the stairs. The Rephs followed. 'Hurry. We don't have long.'

The Guildhall was in disarray. Radmilo Arežina had been shot in the chest, and now bled on the floor. One of the Greek officials was already dead, her eyes open and dull, observed by her own spirit.

We had agreed that none of the emissaries should be harmed, allowing them to return to London with doubts about the Rephs. Either someone had gone rogue, or the Vigiles had been hitting their own. I couldn't blame anyone for losing it. These people were the architects of voyants' misery, sending us to our deaths by the thousand.

Most of the Rephs had vanished. The Vigiles were helping the surviving emissaries out of the main doors, taking potshots at the rest of us. I could already see their plan. Once their employers were safely out, they would lock us in and burn this building to the ground.

Scion could not allow us to escape. If we did, we would be loose cannons, armed with the knowledge of the truth behind the anchor. We would all be witnesses – but not the kind they wanted to be left alive.

On the lower floor, Danica and Nadine were returning fire, using the pillars for cover, both in the same woollen masks and boiler suits as Nick. We had precious few weapons in the gang, but everything we did have, they must have brought with them.

Seeing us, Nadine detached a small grenade from her belt. It was a modern one, which meant it had been expensive. She pulled the pin, switching on its red warning light, and hurled it towards the doors.

The Vigiles fell back, shouting to one another. The explosion blew the doors off their hinges, giving us enough cover to sprint across the hall. One amaurotic used the opportunity to flee, only to be gunned down on Magdalen Walk.

'Paige.' Nadine wrenched me behind a pillar. 'Are you all right now?'

'I can reach the train.' I gripped her shoulder. 'Thanks for coming.'

'You are not welcome. We expected a jailbreak, not … whatever this is.' She reloaded her pistol. 'What the hell is going on here, Paige?'

'Long story. Warden, where do we go?'

Nadine did a double take when she saw Warden, her eyes widening.

'The way out is through the trap room,' Warden said. 'Paige, you should avoid using your gift. The amaranth will take some time to heal you.'

I nodded, stoking the lingering ache in my temples. My best weapon against Rephs, and I would have to keep it holstered. Just my luck.

'Quite an entrance you made there,' I said to Nadine, who huffed a laugh.

'You know Jaxon loves theatre. And he didn't take kindly to Scion using you as a soldier.' She leaned out to shoot a Vigile. 'Ready to go?'

'Absolutely.'

Nadine lobbed a second grenade before she came after me, followed by some of the performers from the masque. Zeke joined us, grasping my arm in a wordless greeting. Liss landed on the chandelier.

'Liss,' I shouted up to her. 'Liss, come on, let's go!'

'I still need to get Lotte,' Liss called back. 'I'll be right behind you.'

Before I could answer, a Vigile fired at us from the entrance. Zeke slammed me to the floor just in time. As we took cover behind a mecks fountain, bullets chipped at the floor and walls, and shattered a few glasses.

Liss saw. Using her silks like a trapeze, she soared down and kicked the Vigile in the chest, hard enough that he fell back in surprise, even with his armour. Seizing her chance, Nell abandoned her own silks and dashed after us, clearly exhausted. I pushed her after the others.

At the entrance to the trap room, Warden held the heavy drape so we could all pass. Jaxon shoved a dazed Cyril aside to go down the steps first. I ushered Cyril in front of me before I went myself, with Warden and Pleione bringing up the rear.

We filed after Danica, who had a headlamp on. I caught up with her.

'Dani,' I said. 'I hear I owe you for this rescue.'

'Yes,' she said. 'You know, none of this would have happened if you had not insisted on taking a weekend off.' She checked her watch. 'The train will leave at midnight. There is no way to delay it. Can you make it?'

'I can try.'

As we crossed the trap room, Terebell arrived, back from guiding another group. She showed us to a gap in a wall, one I would never have seen in the dark. Nadine went first, turning sideways to edge through.

Jaxon went next. Just as I was following, Lotte caught up with us. She tripped on her bootlaces, still in her bloody skirts from the masque.

'Lotte, over here.' I flashed a torch. 'Where's Liss?'

467

'She covered me.' Lotte reached us, breathless. 'She's coming, Paige.'

'She'll be fine. She always is,' Nell said. 'Just show us where to go.'

But now I was concentrating on the æther, and my blood was turning cold. Every remaining dreamscape in the main hall had just disappeared.

All except for Liss, and she was very still.

I ran back to the steps. Jaxon called after me: 'And you are going *where*, darling?'

'Just get to the train, Jaxon,' I snapped.

At the top of the stairs, I stopped, chills racing up my arms. The Vigiles had retreated, leaving the doors wide open, letting in an icy wind from outside. More of the candles had blown out. By the light of the very few that remained, I saw the shape on the floor.

'No.'

The word escaped me before I accepted what I was sensing. I rushed towards the heap of fabric, using her dreamscape as my guide, and sank to my knees beside it.

This could not be Liss.

Liss never fell.

Yet these were her silks, recognisable by their rich soothsayer purple. The only pride they had ever allowed her. With shaking hands, I searched the silks until I uncovered her face.

Liss lay quiet. As I lifted her lolling head into the crook of my arm, my fingers sank into her wet and tangled hair.

'Liss.' My voice sounded nothing like mine, thin and unsteady. 'Liss?'

She cracked her eyes open, just a little. Her lips formed a tiny smile when she saw me.

'Funny,' she said. 'I never fall.'

'You didn't fall. You just … needed a little rest. Now you need to get up.'

'No.' Liss drew a laboured breath, lashes fluttering. 'The æther warned me. In August, I drew two cards for myself. One was the Tower. The other was … Fortitude. I'm glad I still chose Fortitude.'

The Tower, the card of change and destruction. It showed two people falling to their deaths from a great height. Sometimes the æther sent complex riddles.

Sometimes it could be plain as a picture.

'That's the problem with … seeing the future. I told you and Jules that knowledge is dangerous.'

'No,' I said, my jaw trembling. 'Liss, I told you I'm getting you out of here. We're going to London, and then I'm going to take you back to Inverness. We'll find that beautiful clearing, the one in your dreamscape. You'll be safe in the Highlands.'

Even as I spoke, tears were dropping down my cheeks. My fingers had found the back of her skull, the place the blood was flowing thick.

'Nick,' I screamed over my shoulder. 'Nick!'

Liss gazed at the ceiling. I could sense her silver cord, frail as a cobweb, thinning. This could not happen – not to her, after everything.

Nick rushed to my side, holding a torch. When he shone it across the scene, I saw the spreading pool of blood. He did his gentle checks before he shook his head at me. I swallowed against the knot in my throat.

Perhaps he could have saved her life, if there had been a hospital – but if Nick couldn't help Liss now, no one could.

'You already brought me back once, Paige,' Liss said. 'You have to live. For the last card.' A tear ran down her cheek. 'It's all right. You can leave me.'

'No,' I whispered. 'You never left me.'

Liss moved her hand, and I took it. She drew one more rattling breath before her fingers loosened. Her spirit rose, a kite cut from its line, drifting into the æther. I clasped her body close, numb to my core.

'You should say the threnody,' Nick murmured. 'I don't know her name, sötnos.'

He was right. Liss wouldn't want to stay here, in her prison.

'Liss Rymore, be gone into the æther. All is settled. All debts are paid.' My voice was shaking. 'You need not dwell among the living now.'

Her spirit disappeared.

I lowered her with care. This was no longer Liss – just the shell of her, an empty house that would grow cold. Liss was on her way to the outer darkness, where no one would ever be able to imprison her again.

'Paige.' Nick placed a hand on my back. 'I didn't know Liss, but I'm sure she wouldn't have wanted you to give up. We have to go now.'

'I think not.'

I knew that voice. Now the candles had gone out, I couldn't see Gomeisa Sargas, but his words resonated. Even the walls seemed to magnify them.

'Gomeisa,' I said. 'Did you do this?'

The silence was damning.

I looked up. Liss had not fallen. Both of her silks had been physically ripped, right below their rig – a straight cut, almost impossibly so.

A low voice came from behind me: 'You should not hide in the shadows, Gomeisa.'

I looked back over my shoulder, my cheeks damp. Warden had returned to the hall, and his gaze was fixed on the gallery.

'Unless you fear Paige,' he continued. 'None of us could blame you for it. Beyond these walls, your city burns. Your façade of power is already dissolving – you who stole that power unjustly, long ago.'

'We have not forgotten,' Pleione said.

'I do not fear the amaranth, nor these emissaries of Scion. They handed their world to us on a platter,' Gomeisa said. 'One night of fire will not break our reign.'

'I'd tell you to go to hell.' I rose. 'But I'd say we're already there.'

'Indeed. Hell is for the dead, and we are death incarnate, 40. Where blood flows through your body, the æther itself is coursing in mine. Tell me, what fire can scald the sun? Who can drown the ocean?'

Gomeisa was walking along the gallery, his footsteps loud. Behind Warden, one of the newly arrived Rephs had appeared, along with Terebell.

'I would like you all to reflect on our situation. Especially you, Arcturus,' Gomeisa said. I could see him now, a silhouette in the gallery. 'Given what you have to lose.'

Warden came to stand beside me. When he saw Liss, his eyes darkened.

'He killed her,' I whispered.

'I want you to picture a butterfly,' Gomeisa said. 'Behold its ornate wings. See how it helps flowers to grow – graceful and beloved.' He ran his gloved hand along the balustrade. 'Now I want you to imagine a moth. It takes the same shape, but humans spurn it for its dullness; how it feeds on dust and rot.'

'Maybe you're the moths,' I said. 'You're the ones who come out at night.'

'A flawed comparison, to be sure. But your ancestors knew the difference,' Gomeisa said. 'They saw in us a greater rendering of themselves – divine beings, stronger and wiser. They gave us your world out of respect for the natural order. Moths, after all, cannot rule themselves. They see a fire and fly to it, unable to separate it from the sun. That is how we see your world, Paige Mahoney. A box of moths, just waiting to be burned.'

His dreamscape was in range. I readied my spirit, not caring how much damage it would do.

'The Sargas family is your sun,' Gomeisa said. 'Let us be your guiding light.'

Before I could jump, Warden grasped my shoulder. His glove was back in place. 'We can distract him,' he said quietly. 'Get to the meadow.'

'He has to pay for this.' My nose bled again, pressure building. 'He can't just—'

'This is not one of your street brawls, dreamwalker. You cannot avenge your friend this night, but there will be others.' Pleione never took her eyes off the enemy. 'Go to the meadow. Ours is an old battle.'

Gomeisa was on our level now. When I saw his eyes – a rich purple, more red than blue – my stomach turned, my anger flaring. He must have fed on Liss as she was lying there.

'If you survive this night, you will come to realise it was not so terrible here, 40,' he said. 'We offered you our sanctuary and wisdom. You were not unnatural here – lower, yes, but acknowledged. Here, you have learned to master your gift.' He held out

471

a hand. 'The Sargas family is merciful. Even your allies know this. Arcturus betrayed us once, yet Nashira still allowed him to remain as blood-consort, respected.'

Nick was retreating towards the trap room. I glanced at the clock on the wall.

It was now or never.

'I urge you not to risk Gallows Wood,' Gomeisa said as I backed away. 'It is an orchard of death, sown with mines. If they do not kill you, the Emim will – and we cannot allow you to waste your gift, a gift we had thought lost. Come back to the fold. This is your last chance.'

He knew his twisted logic well. The Rephs had relied on it for two centuries, using it to tempt the weak.

Pleione ran towards Gomeisa. Terebell and Warden went after her, both gathering spools. Nick seized the opportunity to tug me towards the trap room, but I hardly felt it. All I could feel was the æther.

The Rephs met in a great clash, like bells slamming together, making the planes of being ring. They fought not with guns or swords, but with the dead as their weapons. Each flex of muscle, each turn and step, sent a shockwave across the æther. They were dancing on the edge of life – a dance of giants, the danse macabre.

The spirits of the Bone Season still lingered in the hall. Terebell sent a spool weaving around the pillars – thirty spirits, all spinning and rising together, converging on Gomeisa. I waited for the blow to fall. By now, Nick was transfixed as well.

With a sweep of his hand, Gomeisa shattered the spool. Like glass shards from a mirror, spirits burst across the hall. As I watched, Terebell went flying into a wall, Pleione into a pillar. When the Reph I didn't recognise charged, Gomeisa simply cut his hand upward. The motion flung his attacker on to the stage. The boards splintered under his weight, sending him into the trap room.

Gomeisa could use apport. For all intents and purposes, that made him a living poltergeist, able to move objects – and people – from a distance. My heart thundered as his gaze turned on me.

Warden stepped between us. He faced his enemy, unarmed and unarmoured.

'Always a slave to the past, Arcturus,' Gomeisa said. 'Always last to give up.'

'Go, Paige,' Warden said. 'Do not linger.'

I only hesitated for a moment. If Gomeisa threw me, I would not get back up, unlike Terebell and Pleione. A human was no match for that power.

Warden gave me a nod. For as long as I could feel the golden cord, he would be able to find me. At last, I let Nick pull me away, towards the stage.

Halfway there, a hand wrapped around my ankle, almost tripping me. I looked down to see a young Scion emissary, bleeding from a deep gash in his neck, which he was trying to stem with a handkerchief.

'You,' he rasped. 'You're the dreamwalker.' His eyes were bloodshot. 'Listen … to me.'

'Paige, come on,' Nick said, but the man refused to let go. I didn't recognise him. Someone of low rank. A clerk or administrator in the Archon, not the sort of person to appear on ScionEye.

'Bone Seasons,' the emissary rattled. 'This goes deeper than you know. Some of you … eat your own.' His cough spattered the floor with blood. 'Find … Rackham. He is the one … who hunts. Find him.'

With those words, he slumped to the floor. I exchanged a shaken look with Nick.

Zeke had come back to cover us. I shoved the words and the name from my head. As we made a break for our exit, Zeke threw a flashing canister behind us. Thick white smoke billowed from inside, and the four Rephs vanished into it. So did all that remained of Liss Rymore.

Through the darkness of the trap, where the fifth Reph was recovering from his fall. Into the hidden opening. Along a corridor, then into a small room. Nick guided us with his torch until we burst into the night, taking a few steps down to Fish Street.

In the morning, I would grieve for Liss. For now, I had to save the others. She would have wanted that. All of us had been her family.

The city reeked of smoke. The sky was dirty red, the streets hazy. The residences might be made of stone, but their contents were flammable, and Julian and the others must have set plenty of bonfires.

Every bell was ringing, the old siren droning out from the Broad. I had never heard so much sound in this city. The bells were the amaurotics' signal that all the buildings had been opened. Every prisoner could flee.

Warden had been right to warn me. As I tried to extend my perception to locate Julian or Michael, I could feel that my dream-scape was too fragile to withstand the pressure. I was going to have to rely on just five of my senses.

Nick looked at the unfamiliar city, exchanging a silent look with Zeke. 'Jax led us,' he told me. 'What's the fastest way to Port Meadow?'

'I need my gun first.'

We had emerged at the back of the Guildhall. I led them a short way to Bear Lane, where I retrieved my air pistol, loaded a windflower dart, and laced on my boots. Finally, I grabbed my backpack, which Michael had filled with provisions, including a flare gun. Nick wrapped his coat over my dress before I put the backpack on.

'Eliza,' I said to them, hitching up its straps a little. 'Where is she?'

'She stayed in London.'

We ran on to Fish Street. I had memorised every possible route to Port Meadow. Now the Guildhall was fully evacuated, the Scion emissaries were fleeing, trailing Vigiles. My instincts told me to take the safest way, but speed was of the essence. Nick and Zeke followed me without question, on to the cobbles of Cornmarket.

The Rephs had their hands full with the fires. This was the only home they had, and it was burning. As we emerged at the end of the Broad, a scream reached my ears, and I saw Nell, restrained by two familiar Rephs.

'Your first pitiful rebellion failed, and so will this,' Merope said, pulling her towards the nearest building. 'Do you think you threaten us, 9?'

'Get your hands off me!' Nell was kicking and twisting for all she was worth. 'You are never feeding on me again. I'd rather die than—'

Her screams were cut short when Merope clapped a hand over her mouth. I wavered, then broke away from Nick and Zeke and sprinted towards Nell.

'Paige,' Nick bellowed.

I steadied my aim and shot Merope. The dart struck her arm, and I knew the needle would be piercing its cap, driving the mixture into her body.

Merope had not been expecting a human to deal any real damage. She plucked the dart out, but the windflower was in her blood. When she felt it, her tawny eyes flickered. Like Kraz, she let out a discordant sound and fell as if her bones had melted.

I grinned in triumph. While I loaded another dart, Nell hurled a spool at a surprised Aludra, who grabbed her by the wrist.

Cursing in Swedish, Nick covered Nell with a few rounds from his old rifle, hitting Aludra until she let go. Nell lunged away from her, almost falling.

'Paige,' she called, 'did Liss make it?'

'Just go, Nell!'

Aludra glanced at the bullet holes in her jerkin with irritation, as if Nick had used a toy gun. Nell snatched her supplies and sprinted north.

'There you are,' Aludra said to me. 'I still owe you for your display in the chapel.'

I took aim at her. 'Sure you want me to dent the family pride again, Aludra?'

Without a word, she drew a blade. In unison, Zeke and Nick opened fire on her. It slowed her approach, but she kept coming. She must have stewing in hatred for months, waiting for a shot at me. Rephs had plenty of time to nurture their grudges.

Nick ran out of bullets. Taking a deep breath, he closed his eyes and extended a hand towards her. The æther hummed as he sent a vision.

'An oracle,' Aludra observed. 'It has been some time since I fed on your kind.'

Her eyes changed.

Nick dropped his gun in shock, blood seeping into his tear ducts, the cords in his neck straining out.

'Nick,' Zeke said, grasping his shoulder. Nick gripped his knees, trying to hold himself upright. 'Paige, what is she doing to him?'

'I destroyed your heir, Aludra. I've just done the same to Merope,' I warned. 'Don't think I won't do the same to you. Back off, and I won't shoot.'

'We can recover from the pollen,' Aludra said. 'Did the concubine give it to you?'

'Warden did.'

'So he betrays his own kind yet again. The blood-sovereign should never have pardoned him,' she said. 'The Sargas may forgive, but do not think you can insult the Chertan and escape with your life, 40.'

She ran at me. With my hands raw with cold and my senses unbalanced, I missed, sending the precious dart into the night. Nick reloaded and fired just in time, and Aludra buckled, riddled with bullets. I reached into my backpack for another dart, but Zeke pulled me away.

'We have to move, Paige,' he said, his voice muffled. 'What are these things?'

'Rephs,' I said. 'All you need to know is that they're strong as rocks, feed on aura, and don't take kindly to humans. Best practice is just to run.'

'What did you shoot at them?'

'Pollen,' I said, earning a bewildered look. 'How long do we have left?'

'I'd stop asking,' Nick said. We broke into a run. 'You won't like the answer.'

Once we were past the Broad, we saw no more Rephs. They must be trying to round up the arsonists. I hoped Julian was heading for the meadow.

We passed Amaurotic House, which was unlocked, and took a left into the ghost town. At the end of the street, a figure came racing towards us. I caught him by his red tunic and slammed him into the wall.

'Going somewhere, Carl?'

'Get off me!' Carl was drenched in sweat. 'You've killed us all. We have to hide. The Rephs will let them into the city any moment now.'

'Who?'

'The Buzzers,' Carl shouted, his breath fluttering white. 'You've broken their trust in us. They'll do what they did last time we rebelled!'

'We accounted for that, you fool. The Rephs won't kill the emissaries.'

'You poisoned the others. I can't fight by myself.' He shoved at me, almost in tears. 'I knew there was something wrong with the soup. This place is all I've got in the world. You are not taking it, Paige—'

'Come on,' Zeke urged.

'Carl, there's a world beyond Scion. I know,' I said tightly. 'I came from it.'

'Even outside Scion, people will never accept us when they understand what we are. We're freaks,' Carl said, his cheeks flushed. 'That's why we need the Rephs. Because they're like us, and they get it. This is the only place that's safe for voyants. I'm never going out there again, so you can keep your precious world. You're welcome to it!'

He shoved me off and bolted. Nick watched him go, lowering his gun.

'You've got a long story to tell when we get home.'

I nodded. 'Let's keep going.'

'Yes,' Zeke said, running again. 'Come on. We can make it.'

I expected a fight before this was over. Our enemies must be hot on our heels, and clearly not every red-jacket had taken our concoction. When I heard an explosion in the distance, I glanced back.

Warden had told me that Rephs were vulnerable to blast injuries. An explosion at close range wouldn't kill them, but it would hurt.

Port Meadow was close now. When we reached the short bridge on Ironwork Street, Nick slung his rifle across his back and swung his legs over the wall. Zeke dropped first, into the overgrowth under the bridge.

'Nick,' I said, 'where the hell are you going?'

'To meet the others. Come on.'

He jumped down before I could ask, landing in a crouch. Just as I was about to follow, the golden cord gave a tug. I turned to see Warden.

'There you are.' I released my breath. 'Did you beat Gomeisa?'

'For now. Paige, time is very short,' Warden told me. 'The Sargas and their loyalists will be following any stragglers. We should not tarry here.'

'I know, Nick was just—' I blew out, my breath clouding. 'I don't know what they're playing at, but I need to get them. Will I meet you there?'

'No. I will wait,' Warden said. 'The entrance is not far into the meadow.'

He still needed me to front this. Steeling myself, I cleared the brick wall and jumped from the low bridge, heading for the pool of torchlight.

Danica was squatting beside an open hatch. It must have been hidden deep in the weeds, or I would have noticed it. Over my first couple of months in this city, I had searched long and hard for an escape.

'Quickly, darling.' Jaxon pointed his cane at the hatch. 'Down you go.'

'What?'

'This is a maintenance shaft. It will take us straight to the tracks,' Danica said. 'We can use it to slip back on to the train and seal ourselves in the rear compartment. The Scion guests will have no idea we are there.'

'I agreed to meet the other prisoners on Port Meadow. There's an entrance there, too.'

'Yes, I know,' Danica said impatiently. 'That leads to the station the emissaries will be using.'

'They aren't getting back on the train,' I said. 'We're taking the whole thing.'

'What?'

'I'm not leaving anyone behind.'

There was a strained hush before Jaxon marched towards me. He pulled off his mask and hood, rumpling his hair. His appearance shocked me into silence – dark circles under his eyes, a sheen to his white skin, pupils down to pinpricks. Jaxon Hall was never stressed enough to break a sweat.

'You have been away for some time, Dreamer,' he said, low and cold, 'so I will forgive this sudden display of idiocy. But enough is enough.'

'Jaxon—'

'I have spent a great deal of time and coin on this little extraction. Danica and Nick have both risked the careers that help sustain our enterprise. We are the dominant gang of I-4, not a charity for the poor and needy.'

'What are you saying?'

'I came here for my dreamwalker, not to adopt the great unwashed.'

Even knowing Jaxon as I did, his tone hit me like a punch to the chest. I looked at him as if for the first time. A man on the edge, all his focus on himself and his own. He expected me to abandon the others.

'Jaxon,' I said hotly, 'they're voyants—'

'A rabble of the lowest sort, along with some amaurotics, of all things. What do you expect they'll do to earn their keep in London, Paige?'

Liss on the floor, bleeding from her cracked skull. *The first card in the tarot, and somehow I still wound up at the bottom of the pile.*

'I appreciate the rescue,' I whispered, 'but I already had an exit plan in place.' I forced myself to sound calm and reasonable, even as my voice shook. 'You stick to yours, Jaxon. I'll meet you on the train.'

Jaxon grasped my nape, hard enough to hurt.

'Paige,' he said, 'are you disobeying me?'

Suddenly I was almost eighteen, and his temper had fallen on me for the first time. I went limp, like a rabbit faced with a fox – playing dead, curling small.

'If we take the entire train,' Jaxon said, 'and you fill it with however many scores of imbeciles you want to drag back to London, Scion will notice us.'

'We killed the power. London doesn't know.'

'More idiocy.' His grip on my neck tightened. 'Has captivity made you stupid, Paige?'

Warden had moved as soon as Jaxon laid a hand on me. Now he strode towards us from the bridge. I willed him to stop, and he did, eyes ablaze.

'Let me use small words for you.' Jaxon spoke to me slowly, as my teachers often had at school. 'Six stowaways is one thing. We can slip out of the train, just as we slipped in. But do you really think that you can drag a horde back to a guarded station and pass unseen in Westminster?'

'Let go of her, Jax,' Nick said.

'Okay, I'm leaving.' Danica entered the shaft. 'Nick, take my gun, if you want.'

Jaxon was ignoring them all. Our gazes locked fast. My cheeks burned, the humiliation worse for knowing that Warden was hearing all this.

'If you do anything more to compromise this endeavour – the endeavour to rescue *you*, I might add,' Jaxon said, 'there will be consequences. You may have claimed a little independence here, but it is time to remember your place. If not, you will find yourself quite alone.'

The same threat he had made to Nadine. This was the Jaxon Hall I feared, the man who all but owned my life. My only chance at belonging.

What he was saying made sense – six of us were more likely to escape on the other side. I could go down this hatch and be done with it. The emissaries would eventually get back on the train, taking us with them.

Not so long ago, I would have done it, because there had been no one in my life outside the syndicate. Now there were people counting on me. Warden was still waiting. I saw myself as if from a distance, caught by the scruff of my neck like a kitten. Once, a clear threat to banish me from the underworld would have had me whimpering for mercy.

I would not beg for anything now.

'I'll take my chances,' I said. 'I quit.'

Jaxon tilted his head, dangerously. Zeke looked as if he might pass out on my behalf.

'What,' Jaxon said, 'did you just say, Paige?'

The words had come out of my head, then. I was turning numb, down to my fingertips.

'You heard me,' I said, trying to make my voice stronger. 'If you won't let me go to Port Meadow and still work for you, I quit. See you down there, Jax.'

With that, I started towards Warden.

'No one walks away from me, Pale Dreamer,' Jaxon said, stopping me. 'If I can't have you, no one does. I will ensure you never work in the syndicate again. You will be discarded goods, exiled from the underworld. Who else but me would dare succour an Irish fugitive?'

'Oh, get fucked, you stretched weasel.' I spun to face him again, unleashing all my bottled anger. 'I'm meant to be your mollisher, your second. If you won't let me speak my mind, I may as well stay here. I joined you so I could be myself, Jaxon. I refuse to be less, even for you.'

This time, his silence was even more frightening. When I turned my back on him again, he said nothing. None of the others followed me.

Warden gave me a boost on to the bridge, making a step with his clasped hands, then joined me. I drew my gun as we pressed on to Port Meadow.

'Paige,' Warden said.

'Don't.' I loaded another dart, my breath shaking. 'I just threw my life away. Now I have no power to help the others in London. I've sold them a lie.'

'Wait, Paige!'

I turned. Nick and Zeke had just hoisted themselves on to the bridge. A few moments later, Nadine clambered after them. No sign of Jaxon.

'He can't fire all four of us,' Nick said firmly, once they caught up. 'Come on. We'll cover you.'

I looked between them, afraid to believe it. 'You're sure?'

'Apparently,' Nadine said, 'but we have less than twenty minutes to get there. And the stretched weasel might still come after us with his cane.'

'No,' Nick said. 'Jax will save his own skin. The shaft is the safest way.'

'And we've picked the dangerous one. I love this job.' Nadine snapped a new magazine into her pistol. 'Where are we going, Dreamer?'

Port Meadow was dark, except for the sally port, flanked by lanterns. Oliver and Emil – the brothers who had attacked me in June – were out cold beside it.

Michael waited beside them, along with a large group of amaurotics, some performers, and one thin palmist in a white tunic. She was gaunt and shivering, her dark hair freshly shaved against her skull.

'Ivy.' I approached her first. 'Are you okay?'

She nodded. 'One of the amaurotics let me out of Corpus.'

'I'm glad you made it.' I looked at the drawn faces around me. 'Has anyone seen Julian?'

No one answered. Nick regarded Ivy with concern.

'If Julian has been killed or captured, his allies may not know where to go,' Warden said. 'I believe there was a flare gun hidden on Bear Lane.'

'Paige,' one of the performers said, 'why is he here?'

'He's on our side.' I looked back at Warden. 'A flare will attract the Vigiles.'

'They will be coming here either way, to take the train to London,' Warden said. 'The emissaries will not want to be stranded in a burning city.'

He had a point.

Julian Amesbury had been my unwavering ally from the first night to the last. The thought of leaving without him was more than I could stomach. He knew where to go, but if he was dead or detained, he would want me to help the people who had been relying on him to lead them.

I took the flare gun from my backpack and loaded it, then found a point above the meadow, cocked the hammer, and fired. The military flare shot into the clear sky, where it erupted into red brilliance.

'Okay,' I said. 'Let's move.'

Warden went first, opening the sally port. I stepped right over Oliver.

Nick and Zeke lit our path. As we followed Warden, I tried to ignore the roil in my gut. I had just thrown away my job, my security. Not only that, but I had insulted Jaxon.

If I stuck to my guns, he would ensure that no other mime-queen or mime-lord would hire me. And if I did survive the night, Scion would hunt me for the rest of my life. I needed protection. I needed my gang.

Who else but me would dare succour an Irish fugitive?

I couldn't think about it now. Instead, I sent up another flare, replacing the one that had just sputtered out. The red glow illuminated the whole meadow. Behind us, a few more humans had reached the sally port. With the help of the amaranth, I forced my perception a little farther.

At once, I sensed far older dreamscapes.

'Rephs,' I barked. 'Move it!'

Without question, everyone sped up, Michael pulling Ivy along with him. Our boots pounded on the hard earth, but the Rephs were hot on our heels, faster than us. Nadine drew a knife, and we both turned, me pointing the flare gun. It might set fire to their clothes, at least.

'Warden, keep going,' I urged him. 'Get them to the station!' I looked at Nadine. 'A knife won't do much. Use your gun and don't hold back.'

She switched to her pistol. When the Rephs came near enough to see, I recognised Terebell and Pleione, the former carrying a coughing Jos, and grabbed Nadine by the wrist. Felix was just behind them, as was a tall male Reph, one of the visitors to the city.

'Jos,' I said, relieved. Terebell lowered him to the grass. 'Go on, follow Warden.' I steered him north. 'Felix, do you know where Julian is?'

'No. We got separated near Balliol.' Felix reeked of smoke, and his black hair was now grey with ashes. 'He's not going to make it, Paige.'

'Just go with Jos.' I ushered him that way. 'Terebell, was one of you meant to get Faz and Gail?'

'I was,' the newcomer confirmed. 'They chose to remain at Magdalen.'

'They can't,' I said, shaken. 'Nashira will think they helped us plot this.'

'We will do all we can to save any humans who do not reach the train before it leaves,' Terebell said. 'I give you my word, 40.'

I would have to trust her. There was no time for me to go back and convince Gail and Fazal, or to search for Julian. If I stayed here, the performers and amaurotics would have nowhere to turn in London.

'Warden said you wanted to fight for the city,' I said. 'Why are you here?'

'We are not bound for London,' Pleione said. 'We came only to bring your friends. Now we intend to launch our attack on the Residence of the Suzerain. Nashira has locked herself inside.'

'Please,' I said, 'if you can, find Julian. He's the reason we got here.'

'We shall try.'

Just as quickly as they had come, the Rephs were gone, heading for the sally port. I exchanged a nod with Nadine, and we sprinted after Warden.

Julian wasn't going to reach the train. It killed me to keep going.

Ahead, Warden had stopped, as had the others. Halfway to his location, I glimpsed a pair of performers from the masque, locked in an argument.

'You two,' I called as I passed. 'Come on. What the hell are you doing?'

'You're working with the Rephs,' the man snapped, his voice embittered. 'This could be a trap.'

'You want to risk the minefield instead?'

'Paige, come on,' Nadine burst out. 'If we miss this train, I *will* kill you.'

Leaving the performers to decide, I kept running, hoping they came to their senses.

We passed the frozen pool, the watchtower, the training grounds where Merope had drilled me. Warden waited near a corner of the ethereal fence, beside an iron hatch, much larger than the one Danica had opened. The survivors were huddled around it.

'The entrance to the station is here,' Warden said. 'But we face an unexpected obstacle.'

'That isn't what I wanted to hear.' I caught my breath. 'Where are the guards?'

'There were none.' Warden nodded to the hatch. 'But there is this.'

When I looked closer, I saw it. A large silver padlock held the hatch shut. A bar of white light glowed down the middle.

'This is an ethereal padlock, which uses the same hybrid technology as the fences,' Warden said. 'Nashira is the only binder in the city. The poltergeist inside the padlock must be hers. No doubt she intended to escort the emissaries here personally.'

'You're strong.' I looked at him. 'You can't break the hatch open?'

'No. The iron has been fortified with adamant, a rare material from the Netherworld,' Warden said. 'It resists all physical force.' He demonstrated, giving it a pull. 'The binding is very weak, made to be swiftly broken. The threnody may be powerful enough to override it.'

'We'd have to know its name,' I said. 'The name it held closest when it was alive.'

'Yes.'

The marks on my hand smarted. When I tried to sense the poltergeist, my nose bled again.

'Fuck this,' I said. 'We'll backtrack and use the same hatch as Jaxon. We can still—'

'They're coming,' came a frantic cry. I looked over my shoulder to see a performer. 'The Vigiles, the Overseer, the Rephs, the whole lot of them. They're at the sally port.'

I pinched my nose. That scotched my plan to retrace our steps.

'Julian,' I said to her. 'Where is Julian?'

'I don't know. Where's Liss?'

'She's—' I could hardly get it out: 'Liss is dead. Gomeisa killed her.'

'No,' Nell whispered. 'Not her.' Several of the other performers stared at me, including Jos, whose eyes filled with tears. 'Paige, are you sure?'

I nodded stiffly.

'Enough. I'm not dying here, and I'm not going back.' The voice came from a sallow augur in his forties. 'Get away from that hatch, Reph.'

'I would not advise touching it,' Warden said.

'I'm done taking orders from parasites,' the augur sneered. 'You'll have to deal with a voyant doing what he pleases with his own life. Got it?'

Warden set his jaw. The augur had a heavy length of pipe in his hands, one of our many improvised weapons. Before anyone could stop him, he swung it overhead and brought it down hard on the padlock.

A shockwave cut through the æther. My hair crackled as the augur was blasted away from us, screaming.

I glimpsed scores of electric torches in the distance, replacing the vanishing light from the flare. For now, the darkness was still hiding us.

'Everyone stay calm,' Nick said. 'Falling apart now will get us killed.'

'Who *are* you people?' Cyril demanded. 'How do you have proper weapons?'

'Later, Cyril.' I tried to keep a level head. 'Fine. The lock is unbreakable, but—' I swallowed. 'Could I persuade the poltergeist in spirit form?'

'That may be our last hope. If you leave your body, you could speak to it in Gloss,' Warden said. 'I have already tried, but it will not respond to my voice.' Against the darkness, his eyes burned. 'I did not want it to come to this. You have already done too much, Paige.'

'I can do it,' I said, with more conviction than I felt. Only a fool would try to reason with a poltergeist. 'Do you have any more amaranth?'

Warden gave me the vial from Pleione. Our fingers brushed as I took it and removed the stopper. He had been quick to put the gloves back on.

'Drink every drop,' Warden said. 'It is the only way to fortify yourself.'

'You're sure?'

'Yes.'

I nodded and drained the whole vial in one go. It mopped up the last of my headache, reinforcing my dreamscape.

The Vigiles were armed with ballistic shields and guns, defending the emissaries. Birgitta Tjäder was among them, as was Cathal Bell. When Tjäder spotted us, she gave a shout of rage. Nick raised his rifle, aiming for her head. No point using spools on amaurotics.

I faced the huddle of prisoners. For the first time since their arrival here, they needed to be encouraged. They needed to hear a voice telling them that they were capable, that they were worth something, that everything was going to be all right, even if it was a lie.

That voice would have to be mine.

'Scion left me alive in Dublin,' I said, raising it enough that they could all hear. 'That is not a mistake they're going to make again. Right now, those Vigiles and their employers – even the Rephs – are terrified of us. They don't want us to tell our stories. If they trap us here, they will leave no witnesses. No survivors. Each of us carries a secret Scion must deny. Each of us carries the key to its downfall.'

They all watched me, including Warden. My throat was already sore, and words had never been my forte, but I pressed on:

'Listen to me, all of you. You fought your way to this meadow. You're here,' I said. 'So are the people who died here twenty years ago, on Novembertide. Their spirits are with us now, ready to help.'

As I spoke, those spirits moved closer. 'If you can hold the Vigiles off, I will open this hatch – and I promise you, when dawn breaks, you will be in London. And there will be no day bell to send us to our cells.'

There were murmurs of assent, of anger.

'I know you're all exhausted,' I said, 'but I need you to dig as deep as you can, and fight once more. I need you to defend me while I dreamwalk. Do this one last thing, and we can leave this hell for ever. You've fought so long, and so hard, and we are so close to freedom.'

Cyril swallowed. 'Are you really the Pale Dreamer?'

'I am,' I said quietly.

'Then you'll help us find somewhere, once we get to London?'

'I will.'

It was a lie. Without my position as a mollisher, I was nothing. I had no sway to get them work; I had nowhere to give them refuge. But I needed them to believe me, so they would fight to save themselves.

The prisoners shared weary looks. There were no battle cries, no shouts – nobody had breath or strength to spare – but in unison, they picked up their weapons and surged towards the incoming Vigiles. Nadine and Zeke flanked them, both firing at the enemy. The Novembertide spirits rallied, flying alongside my allies with a vengeance.

'I need my oxygen mask,' I said to Nick.

Nick reached into his boiler suit.

'It's running low,' he warned, handing it over. 'Make it count, Paige.' As I lay on the grass, he looked hard at Warden. 'You'd better keep her alive. If this goes wrong, I will hold you personally responsible.'

'Gallows Wood is the only other way out of the city. Even if you survive the minefield, there is a wall,' Warden said. 'Unless you can think of an alternative, Dr Nygård, the train is your only means of escape. And Paige is your only means of accessing it.'

Nick pumped the shotgun and went after the others. I strapped the mask over my mouth and nose. It sealed and illuminated, confirming a steady flow of oxygen. Warden joined me on the ground.

'Warden,' I said, 'if I don't deactivate the padlock on time, don't wake me. I can't—' My voice wavered. 'I can't watch them all die around me.'

'I will not abandon you to the æther,' Warden said. 'You are stronger than you believe. If you can hold your own against Nashira Sargas and Jaxon Hall, a poltergeist will not defeat you, Paige Mahoney.'

He brushed my cheek. I wanted to be held again, in that moment – selfishly, like a fool. I was so tired, so threadbare from dreamwalking. My own gift, my greatest strength, was eating me alive.

Just one more fight, and I could go. Trusting Warden to guard my body, I leaned on him and dislocated, letting my spirit drift.

I sensed abrasion in the æther, just as I did when I stood near the fences. The hybrid technology was affecting it in a way that felt artificial and strange.

Unlike a ghost, a breacher was not meant to stay in one place for long. Forced into a haunt, this one had chiselled a space in the æther, like a tiny aching hole in a tooth, reflecting the confines of the padlock. I fit my own spirit into that space with it.

This cavity was not a dreamscape, but I found myself taking a shadowy form. In a rushing darkness, I could make out a faint outline.

Who are you?

The language was not one I had ever learned, but I could speak it.

No, please, don't. I don't want to die, the figure whispered. *I don't want to die.*

I hear you. I mean you no harm. I saw without eyes, spoke with no voice. *You haven't been this way for long. Tell me how you died. Do you remember?*

My neck snapped, as if I was hanged with a noose. I sat and waited to be saved. I was in pain. I could not move, it said. *I am still bound in place, but I am glad. It was not my time to go, and I will not. It wasn't fair, not fair, not fair.*

So this was what Warden had called a willing poltergeist – determined to stay, chained by its bitterness. I pushed myself towards it, fighting the tide of its fury. In this form, I could exert almost no pressure of my own.

I don't want to go. She told me not to go, the poltergeist said. *I must not go, I cannot go.*

You have to go now. It's time. I was close enough to touch the other spirit, but I kept a careful distance. *She is holding you here, but you are stronger. You can be at peace. If you just will it, you can go. Leave and be free, spirit.*

This close, I could see its neck, bent at a ghastly angle.

I cannot go, it repeated.

I had the vague sense that I needed to hurry. In the near distance, I was aware of Warden holding me, the golden cord providing a second harness.

You, the poltergeist said. *I know your spirit. You did not save me, walker.*

Now I knew this spirit, too. I knew the name it had given me in March.

Let me save you now, I said. *I can send you a long way away, to the outer darkness, so nobody can ever hurt you again. All I have to do is speak your name. When you hear it, you can break your binding and leave. Let me set you free.*

The figure blurred. *There is an old secret*, it said. *It pertains to you, walker.*

What secret?

Some are for the dead alone. You dance among us, but you live. I see the cords that join you to both flesh and sarx. I see as I never saw with my eyes. The poltergeist touched my outstretched hand, or whatever passed for a hand in this place. *Save them, and you will pass unscathed. Speak my name, and I will go.*

Our fingers connected. The shock of it jolted me back into my own body. I sat up with a heaving gasp, staring at my hand, the scarred one.

'Paige,' Warden started.

'Sebastian Pearce. Did you see—' My throat was refusing to work, but I managed to ask the question, misting the oxygen mask: 'Did you see his database entry?'

'Yes.'

'Did he have a middle name?'

'Albert.'

No sooner had he spoken than I was reaching for the ethereal padlock, clamping my scarred hand tight around it. The cold went all the way through me, but I held on, holding that pocket of æther in my palm.

'Sebastian Albert Pearce,' I forced out, 'be gone into the æther.' The mask delivered a fresh hiss of oxygen. 'All is settled. All debts are paid. You need not dwell among the living now.' I closed my eyes. 'Goodbye.'

Seb heard me. The artificial haunt collapsed as he tore free of the flimsy binding and vanished. When I removed my icy hand from the padlock, the white light went out, and the shackle clicked up.

Warden wasted no time. We must have almost run out. Gathering me to his chest, he cast off the padlock and lifted the hatch. I heard distant shouts, saw the flash of torchlight, as our allies spilled down the concrete steps. Michael rushed past us with Ivy.

As if in slow motion, I saw Birgitta Tjäder grab a gun. Her bullet hit Cyril in the neck just as he reached the hatch, killing him. Nick roared at her and emptied his rifle. She raised a ballistic shield just in time.

Warden waited for everyone to descend. His warm, solid frame was my only comfort as my awareness returned in excruciating jolts, soaking me in cold sweat.

'Julian,' I said thickly. 'Warden, can you see him?'

He scanned the meadow.

'No,' he said. 'I am sorry, Paige.'

Liss and Julian, my two closest friends in this city. After everything we had survived, I was going to have to leave without them.

Warden pulled the hatch back down and bolted it shut. The shouts from above blurred into a senseless cacophony, like the barking of dogs. I clenched my fingers, holding on to Warden as he followed the others down the steps. The feeling came back to my skin.

Only stolen torches lit the darkness underground, where the survivors had gathered on a short platform, which smelled of disinfectant. A stack of stretchers stood at the far end, just visible in the torchlight.

The train was the sort you saw on a light rail, sleek and modern. The words SCION AUTOMATED TRANSPORTATION SYSTEM were emblazoned across the back. The carriages were white, the anchor printed on each door. As Warden approached, the nearest ones slid open, and the lights turned on inside.

'*Welcome aboard the Pentad Line,*' Scarlett Burnish said. '*This train will depart in three minutes. Destination: Whitehall, Scion Citadel of London.*'

With gasps of relief, most of the survivors poured into the carriages, leaving their makeshift weapons on the platform. Some of them stayed where they were, clearly unable to believe this was happening, braced for a trick.

Warden set me down. I looked up at him, wishing I had the words.

'Thank you,' I finally said. 'You never had to help us, Warden.'

'You owe me no thanks for your freedom. It was already yours by right.'

'You have a right to freedom, too.'

'Yes. It has taken me twenty years to find the strength to reclaim it.' Warden took my hands. 'I have you, and you alone, to thank for that.'

My reply caught in my throat. A few more people boarded the train, Nell and a cryomancer named Charles among them. Zeke leaned out.

'Paige, get on,' he shouted.

'I'm coming, Zeke. Give me a minute.'

'You have two,' Nadine called down the platform. 'See you on the other side.'

She hit a button inside their carriage, and the doors closed. An amaurotic and a soothsayer lurched into the next one, supporting each other. I needed to join them, but I could only hold on to Warden.

'How strange and unexpected,' he said, 'that this should be so difficult.'

An empty ache filled my chest. I glanced down at his gloved hands, cupping my pale ones, with their grey nail beds and blue rivers of vein.

The realisation came slowly, like dusk encroaching on the sun. The realisation that I might never see him again, as long as I lived. These could be the last moments I ever spent with him.

'Come with us,' I said. 'Come with me, to London.' I let my hands drift to his shoulders. 'Oxford is already burning. Save yourself, Arcturus.'

Warden held my gaze. I saw him with clear eyes, grounded in myself.

I didn't love him, even if I had kissed him. Our fragile bond could never have survived in this place, in our circumstances – but I wanted to understand what I did feel. To let it unfold, let it breathe, let it steep, far away. I didn't want him to die here, lost to the lost city.

But anything between us was impossible. In the end, he was immortal. And from the look in his eyes, wanting might not be enough.

'One minute to departure,' Burnish said. *'Please make yourselves comfortable.'*

'I cannot forsake my allies,' Warden said. 'But you must go without me. You have survived to fight another day. That is what I wanted for you.'

'It's not all I want.'

'Hm. And what else do you want?'

'So much. More than I can say,' I said quietly. 'I just know I want you with me.'

Warden drew me close, silent. Perhaps our worlds were too different to unite – the dreamwalker, the sleep dealer. The thief and the giant.

But I could sow a seed of secret hope, somewhere in my poppy field. I could plant it and tend it and wait for a flower to blossom, red as blood.

'My allies and I will attempt to seize the city,' Warden told me. 'We will save any humans we can. If we destroy Nashira, her loyalists may scatter. Our chances are very small, but we can only try.' He lifted my chin. 'Paige, hear me. If you never see me again, it will mean all is well. But if we fail tonight, and Nashira still holds power by dawn, I will come to warn you.'

'Find me either way.' I tightened my hold on him. 'I don't know where I'll be. Not in Seven Dials. I'm … not sure I have a home now.'

'Wherever you are, I will know where to seek you.' He pressed my hand to his chest with one hand, framing the curve of my cheek with the other. 'The night we met, you told me I had brought the wrong voyant to this place. It seems you were exactly the right one, Paige Mahoney.'

I managed a smile.

'Don't forget me,' I said softly. 'In the end.'

'An oneiromancer cannot forget.'

My smile widened.

The seconds were counting down. I could hear the train preparing to move. Warden lowered his forehead to mine for a long and tender moment.

'Tell me,' he said. 'Do you trust me now?'

'Should I?'

'I cannot tell you that. That is the cruelty of trust.' He looked at my face as if he was trying to learn it by heart, down to the smallest feature. 'For trust to live, you cannot know for sure if you should let it.'

'Then I trust you.'

'*This train is ready to depart,*' Scarlett Burnish said. '*Mind the closing doors.*'

Along the platform, they snapped together and locked. Our time was up. Warden released my hands and took a step away from me, eyes hot.

'Run,' he said. 'Run, little dreamer.'

Nick slammed on to the shelter at the back of the train, his ski mask abandoned, face pinched with dread. The train was starting to move.

'Paige,' he roared.

My heart leapt, and all my senses hit me like an iron wall.

I sprinted along the platform. The train picked up speed at once, almost leaving me in its wake, but I was fast. I had always been fast.

Nick flung out a hand. I made a grab for it. My fingers almost slipped from his before he leaned out and grabbed me around the waist, lifted me right over the rail – and I was on board, I was there, I was safe. Sparks flew across the track, and metal shook beneath my boots. Nick steadied me as I looked back, my hair ruffling around my face.

Warden had already disappeared into the dark, a candle blown out by the wind. In all likelihood, I would never see him again.

But as I watched the tunnel race before my eyes, I was certain of one thing: I did trust him.

Now I had only to trust in myself.

Glossary

Æther [noun]: The spirit realm, which exists alongside the physical or corporeal world, Earth. Among humans, only *clairvoyants* can sense the æther.

Adamant: [noun] A metal from the Netherworld.

Amaranth: [noun] An iridescent flower that grows in the Netherworld. Its nectar can heal or calm any wound inflicted by a spirit; it can also fortify the *dreamscape*.

Amaurotic [noun *or* adjective]: A human who is not clairvoyant. This state is known as amaurosis, from an Ancient Greek word referring to a dimming or dulling, especially of the senses. Among voyants, they are known colloquially as *rotties*.

Anchorite: [noun *or* adjective] A disparaging term for people who work directly for Scion, or are especially committed to its message. It can also be used as a descriptor, e.g. *anchorite propaganda*.

Angel [noun]: A category of *drifter*. There are several known sub-types of angels:
 — A *guardian angel* is the spirit of a person who died to protect someone else, and now remains with the living person they saved
 — An *archangel* protects a single bloodline for several generations

— A *fallen angel* is a spirit compelled to remain with their murderer.

All sub-types of angels can be *breachers*.

Apport [noun]: The movement of physical objects by *ethereal* means, derived from Latin apportō ('I bring, I carry'). Among spirits, this ability is unique to *breachers*. Rarely, clairvoyants or Rephaim may be able to use apport.

Aster: [noun] A genus of flower. Certain kinds of aster have *ethereal* properties:
— **Blue** strengthens the link between the spirit and the dreamscape. It can sharpen recent memories and produce a feeling of wellbeing
— **Pink** strengthens the link between the spirit and the body; consequently, it is often used by voyants as an aphrodisiac
— **Purple**, highly addictive, is a deliriant that distorts the dreamscape
— **White** causes amnesia

Aura: [noun] A manifestation of the link between a clairvoyant and the æther, visible only with the *sight*. Since the Netherworld began to deteriorate, *Rephaim* have required human auras to sustain their own connections to the æther.

Biblioclasm: [noun] A book burning.

Binder: [noun] A type of clairvoyant who can compel and tether spirits. A spirit that serves a binder is called a *boundling*.

Bob: [noun] Slang term for a pound. The Scion Inquisitorial Pound is the official currency of the Republic of Scion, used across all nine countries.

Bob cab: [noun] An unlicensed cab, generally used by clairvoyants.

Bone: [adjective] Good or prosperous, from thieves' cant; originally from French *bonne*.

Bone-grubber: [noun] A derogatory term for a *red-jacket*. The term refers to individuals who collect and sell unwanted items, such as rags and bones.

Boundling: [noun] A spirit controlled by a *binder*.

Breacher: [noun] A category of spirit that can affect the corporeal world, e.g. by injuring the living or moving objects. The ability to breach is usually related to the manner of a spirit's death – a violent death is more likely to produce a breacher. The most common types of breacher are *angels* and *poltergeists*. When breachers touch either a human or a Rephaite, they can leave cold scars and a profound chill.

Broadsider: [noun] An archaic term for a *cartomancer*.

Brogue: [noun] A hibernophobic slur in the Republic of Scion, referring to an Irish accent.

Busking: [noun] Plying a skill for money in public. For clairvoyants, this is a type of mime-crime.

Buzzers [noun]: See *Emim*.

Cartomancer: [noun] A clairvoyant who uses cards to connect with the æther.

Clairvoyant: [noun] A human who can sense and interact with the spirit world, the æther. They are identifiable by their *aura*.

Cohort: [noun] An administrative division in the Scion Citadel of London. The citadel is divided into six large cohorts, each of which is internally divided into six sections. I Cohort is the centre; the other six cohorts extend in concentric circles around it, with VI Cohort forming the outermost edge of the citadel.

Cold spot: [noun] A portal between Earth and the Netherworld, which manifests as a perfect circle of ice. Humans cannot pass through a cold spot, but *Rephaim* and *Emim* can.

Courtier: [noun] A habitual user of purple *aster*. The name comes from Mayfield Lane in Soho, formerly known as St Anne's Court, where the aster trade began.

Dacrodiorin: [noun] An expensive medicine, created by the Republic of Scion, which significantly accelerates healing.

Data pad: [noun] A tablet computer, widely used in the Republic of Scion.

Denizen: [noun] A resident of the Republic of Scion.

Dethroned: [adjective] A slang term among *courtiers*, referring to complete recovery from the influence of purple aster. The opposite is to be *reigning*.

Dreamscape: [noun] The house or seat of the *spirit*, where memory is stored. The term is often used interchangeably with *mind* by clairvoyants.

The dreamscape is thought to be how the brain manifests in the *æther*, and often resembles a place where an individual feels safe. Clairvoyants can access their dreamscapes at will, while amaurotics may catch glimpses in their sleep. The dreamscape is split into five zones or rings:

—**Sunlit zone**, the centre of the dreamscape, where the spirit is supposed to dwell. The *silver cord* fastens it in place
—**Twilight zone**, a darker ring that surrounds the sunlit zone. The spirit may stray here in times of mental distress. Only *dreamwalkers* can go beyond this zone without injuring themselves

—**Midnight** and **abyssal**, the next two zones

—**Hadal zone**, the outermost and darkest ring of the dreams-cape. Beyond this point is the *æther*. There may be *spectres* – manifestations of memory – in this zone

Dreamwalker: A contraction of *dreamscape walker*, referring to an exceptionally rare and complex form of *clairvoyance*. Comparable to the concept of astral projection, dreamwalking involves the dislocation and projection of the *spirit* from the *dreamscape*. Dreamwalkers have an unusually flexible *silver cord*, allowing them to not only walk anywhere in their own dreamscape, but possess other people.

Drifters: [noun] Spirits that have not gone to the *outer darkness* or the *last light*, instead remaining within reach of the living. They are broadly divided into two categories: *breachers* and *common drifters*. Within these categories are numerous sub-types of spirit, including *angels* and *ghosts*.

Ectoplasm: [noun] The Rephaite equivalent of blood. It is luminous and slightly gelatinous, and considered to be molten *æther*. As such, it heightens *clairvoyant* abilities.

Emim: [noun] Large and violent creatures that have infested the *Netherworld* and are now venturing to Earth. They are known colloquially as *Buzzers*, due to a distinctive sound that voyants hear when they appear. They feed on human flesh to sustain their earthly forms, and are also believed to devour spirits.

Ethereal: [adjective] Pertaining to the æther.

Finewiring: [verb] A slang term for skilful pickpocketing.

Fell tongue: [noun] A collective term for all human languages, used by the *Rephaim* to distinguish them from *Glossolalia*, the *ethereal* tongue.

Flam: [noun] A slang term for a lie, used exclusively in the under-world of London.

Flash house: [noun] Formerly a term for a brothel, it now refers to any entertainment venue where clairvoyants gather to socialise, particularly nightclubs. They are often owned by clairvoyants and pay *syndicate tax*, but may be frequented by both voyants and amaurotics.

Floxy: [noun] A brand name for scented and enriched oxygen, inhaled through a cannula. Served in most entertainment venues across the Republic of Scion, including dedicated oxygen bars. It is considered a legal alternative to alcohol and recreational drugs, both of which are forbidden under Inquisitorial law.

Flux: [noun] A colloquial name for Fluxion 14, a deliriant that has a particularly intense effect on clairvoyants. One of the key ingre-dients is purple *aster*. The number refers to the version of the drug.

Ghost: [noun] A spirit that prefers to dwell in one place – often their place of birth or death. Moving a ghost from its *haunt* will upset it.

Gilet: [noun] A sleeveless jacket.

Glossolalia: [noun] The language of spirits and Rephaim, distin-guished from the *fell tongue*. Usually shortened to *Gloss*. It is impossible to acquire Gloss; one can only be born with it. Among humans, only *polyglots* are capable of speaking it.

Glow: [noun] A clairvoyants' slang term for *aura*.

Golden cord: [noun] A connection between two spirits. It creates a seventh sense, allowing the linked individuals to track one another and share their emotions.

Grand Inquisitor [noun]: Leader of a Scion country. Each has its own Grand Inquisitor, but they all submit to the authority of the Grand Inquisitor of England, currently Frank Weaver.

Grand Raconteur [noun]: The main propagandist of a Scion country, who makes public announcements and reads the news. News reporters are known as *little raconteurs*.

Greasepaint: [noun] A slang term for makeup.

Haunt: [noun] A place occupied by a spirit – typically a *ghost* – for a long time.

Harlie: A derogatory term for a *performer*, derived from *harlequin*.

Inquisitorial [adjective]: Referring to the authority of a Grand Inquisitor, e.g. Inquisitorial law.

Jarker: [noun] A forger of documents in the underworld, employed to provide fake travel papers and identity cards, and to send clandestine messages across Scion. Some jarkers also specialise in making counterfeit money. They may be clairvoyant or amaurotic.

Kern [noun]: A derogatory term for Irish defectors to the Republic of Scion, from Old Irish *ceithern*, referring to Irish or Scottish soldiers.

Last light: The end or heart of the *æther*, the place from which spirits can never return. What lies beyond it is unknown.

Ley lines: [noun] A term for the trade routes between the various underworlds of the Republic of Scion.

Macer: [noun] A slang term for a cheat.

Mecks: A non-alcoholic drink. Comes in white, rose and blood (red) to imitate wine.

Mime-crime: [noun] Any act involving contact with the spirit world, especially for financial gain.

Mime-lord or **mime-queen**: [noun] A high-ranking member of the clairvoyant syndicate of London. Generally heads a dominant gang of five to ten followers, but maintains overall command over clairvoyants within a section of the citadel. Together, the mime-queens and mime-lords of London form the Unnatural Assembly.

Mollisher: [noun] The heir and second-in-command of a mime-lord or mime-queen.

Netherworld: [noun] The home world of the *Rephaim*, which once functioned as an intermediary realm between the æther and Earth. At some point, the Netherworld was overrun by the *Emim* and began to fall into decay, forcing the Rephaim to relocate to Earth.

Nose: [noun] A spy or informant.

Numa: [noun] [singular: numen] Objects used by soothsayers and augurs to connect with the æther, e.g. mirrors, tarot cards and bones. The term originates from the seventeenth century and refers to a divine presence or will.

Off the cot: [adjective] A slang term for *mad*.

Oracle: [noun] One of the two categories of *jumper*. Oracles receive sporadic visions of the future from the æther, often experiencing intense migraines at the same time. They can also learn to make and project their own visions. Like dreamwalkers, they have red auras.

Ossista: [noun] A waitron in an oxygen bar.

Outer darkness: [noun] A distant part of the æther that lies beyond the reach of clairvoyants. Spirits sent to the outer darkness are rendered incommunicado, but may be able to return through sheer force of will. See also *threnody*.

Paddy wagon: [noun] A slang term for a vehicle used to transport prisoners.

Penny dreadful: [noun] Cheap, illegal fiction produced in Grub Street, the heart of the clairvoyant writing scene. They are often serialised horror stories.

Performer: A human who has either been evicted from the residences or received the *yellow streak*. Performers specialise in various arts to entertain the red-jackets, and are under the command of the Overseer. Also known as *harlies*.

Phantasmagoria: [noun] A colloquial name for the delirium induced by *flux*, referring to the vivid hallucinations it causes.

Pink-jacket: [noun] The second rank for humans in Oxford. Pink-jackets have passed their first test by verifying their gift.

Querent: [noun] A person who seeks knowledge of the æther. They may ask questions or offer part of themselves, e.g. their palm, for a reading.

Red-jacket: [noun] The highest rank for humans in Oxford. Red-jackets are primarily responsible for patrolling Gallows Wood to protect the city from the *Emim*. Also called *bone-grubbers*.

Reef: [verb] To hit; to strike.

Regal: [noun] Purple aster.

Reigning: [verb] Using purple aster.

Rephaim: [noun] [singular: Rephaite] Humanoid beings of the Netherworld. Among humans, they are known colloquially as *Rephs*. Since their proper Glossolalic name is untranslatable in the *fell tongue*, Lord Palmerston named the arrivals after the eponymous Biblical giants, referencing their imposing stature.[1] Since their world fell into decay, the Rephaim have been forced to use human *aura* to sustain themselves.

Rookery: [noun] A Victorian slang term for a slum. In Oxford, it refers to a shantytown on the Broad, where the *performers* live.

Rottie: See *amaurotic*.

Sarx: [noun] The skin of Netherworld beings. Rephaite sarx is slightly metallic and more durable than human skin, showing no signs of age. While Earth-made weapons may pierce it, it will heal quickly, while *breachers* and Netherworld metals cause significantly more damage.

Sasanach: [noun] An Irish word for an English person, literally meaning *Saxon*.

Scionet: [noun] The intranet of the Republic of Scion.

Scimorphine: [noun] The most effective painkiller in Scion.

Scrying: [noun] The art of seeing into and gaining insight from the æther, especially through *numa*.

Shade: [noun] A type of *drifter*, older than a *wisp*.

---

[1] The word may also refer to ancient demigods or kings, or the shades of the dead who dwell in Sheol. Several alternative names were proposed, including *Titans, Manes* and *Ettins*.

Sheol I: [noun] The code name given to Oxford under the rule of the Rephaim. It was agreed that each of their earthly abodes would be named after a human conceptualisation of the afterlife in honour of the Netherworld: Sheol (Biblical) for cities in Scion West, Tuonela (Finnish) for those in Scion North, Erebus (Greek) for those in Scion East, and Orcus (Roman) for those in the proposed Scion South.

Shew stone: [noun] A type of *numen* used by seers. Like a crystal ball, a shew stone can offer glimpses of the future.

Silver cord: [noun] The link between the body and the spirit. The silver cord wears down over the years and eventually snaps, resulting in death.

Skilly: [noun] A thin gruel, made of meat juices or oats.

Soothsayers: [noun] One of the seven orders of clairvoyance according to *On the Merits of Unnaturalness*. Broadly agreed to be the most populous order, soothsayers are reliant on *numa* to connect with the æther.

Spirit sight: [noun] Sometimes referred to as the *third eye* or simply as the *sight*. The ability to perceive the æther visually, indicated by one or both pupils being shaped like a keyhole. Most voyants are sighted, but some are not. Half-sighted voyants can choose when to see the æther, while full-sighted voyants must see it all the time.

Spool: [1] [noun] A group of spirits; [2] [verb] to draw spirits together. All *clairvoyants* are capable of spooling.

Strides: [noun] A slang term for *trousers*.

Syndicate tax: [noun] A monthly sum of money paid by London clairvoyants to their local mime-lord or mime-queen, to buy a place on their turf.

Syndies: [noun] Members of the clairvoyant syndicate of London.

Threnody: [noun] A series of words used to banish spirits to the *outer darkness*. There are many threnodies, developed by clairvoyant communities across the world.

Toke: [noun] A slang term of uncertain origin, referring to low-quality bread.

Underlord or Underqueen: [noun] The head of the Unnatural Assembly and mob boss of the clairvoyant syndicate of London. The incumbent Underlord is Haymarket Hector.

Unnatural: [adjective *or* noun] The formal name for clairvoyants under Inquisitorial law.

Veil: [noun] A word used to describe the boundaries between the three known planes of being – the corporeal world, the æther, and the Netherworld.

Vigile: [noun] A member of the police forces of Scion. Day Vigiles are amaurotic and work for the Sunlight Vigilance Division (SVD), while night Vigiles are clairvoyant and work for the Night Vigilance Division (NVD). Night Vigiles agree to be euthanised after thirty years of service.

Voyant: [noun] A common shorthand for *clairvoyant*.

Waitron: [noun] A gender-neutral term for anyone in the service industry of the Republic of Scion.

White-jacket: [noun] The preliminary rank for humans in Oxford. A white-jacket is expected to take a test to demonstrate their proficiency in clairvoyance and their loyalty to the system; upon passing it, they become a *pink-jacket*.

Windflower: [noun] A red flower, also known as the poppy anemone. In Greek myth, it grew from the blood of the hunter Adonis, a lover of Aphrodite. Though named for its short-lived fragility, its pollen can inflict serious damage on *Rephaim*.

Wisp: [noun] The weakest type of *drifter*. Wisps are often used in *spools* to bolster their strength.

Yellow-jacket: [noun] A rank given to humans in Oxford if they show defiance or cowardice. Earning a yellow tunic three times is called the *yellow streak* and usually results in permanent eviction to the *Rookery*.

People of Interest

CLAIRVOYANTS

Humans with the ability to commune with the æther. They are identifiable by an aura, the colour of which is related to their specific means of connecting with the spirit world.

Paige Mahoney

Order: Jumper
Type: Dreamwalker
Alias: The Pale Dreamer

Believed to be the only living dreamwalker, Paige was raised by her paternal grandparents on their dairy farm in Munster. In 2048, she was forced to move to England when her father relocated there to work for the Republic of Scion. Paige attended the Ancroft School in Bloomsbury before accepting a job offer from Jaxon Hall, a mime-lord in the clairvoyant syndicate of London. She is now mollisher of his gang, the Seven Seals.

Amelia Denslow

Order: Soothsayer
Type: Astragalomancer

A clairvoyant detained for the nineteenth Bone Season, stationed at the Residence of Queens. She is a seasoned red-jacket who often leads external assignments to London.

Antoinette Carter

Order: Fury
Type: Unknown

One of the celebrity speakers at the protest that preceded the Imbolc Massacre of 2046. Carter hosted a popular TV show, which involved her predicting the future. After narrowly surviving the slaughter on St Stephen's Green, Carter went into hiding, but continued to speak out against Scion through a pamphlet, *Stingy Jack*. She is currently a fugitive with a significant bounty on her head.

Beltrame

Order: Medium
Type: Physical

A clairvoyant detained for the nineteenth Bone Season. He currently holds the position of Overseer, making him responsible for the performers' welfare and training. He lives at Kettell Hall.

Bernard Hock

Order: Sensor
Type: Sniffer

The Chief of Vigilance, who heads the Night Vigilance Division. Despite his clairvoyance, he is a trusted agent of Scion, using his keen abilities as a sniffer to detect and detain his fellow clairvoyants.

Bill Bunbury

An member of the clairvoyant syndicate of London. Bill owns an oxygen bar in I-4, which he uses to facilitate illegal activities.

Carl Dempsey-Brown

Order: Soothsayer
Type: Seer

A clairvoyant detained for the twentieth Bone Season, stationed at the Residence of Oriel.

Charles Lanvin

Order: Augur
Type: Cryomancer

A clairvoyant detained for the nineteenth Bone Season, stationed at the Residence of Queens.

Cyril Foxworth

Order: Augur
Type: Botanomancer

A clairvoyant detained for the nineteenth Bone Season. Cyril is a performer, specialising in drama and dance.

Danica Panić

Order: Fury
Type: Unknown
Alias: The Chained Fury

A member of the Seven Seals. In her early twenties, Danica moved from the Scion Citadel of Belgrade to London, where Nick Nygård prevented her from being detained at an event. Like Nick, she now leads a double life, dividing her time between the syndicate and working as an engineer for Scion. She created a life-support machine for Paige, allowing her to sense the æther at a distance without fear of dying.

David Fitton

A clairvoyant detained for the twentieth Bone Season, stationed at the Residence of Merton.

Divya 'Ivy' Jacob

Order: Augur
Type: Chiromancer

A clairvoyant detained for the twentieth Bone Season, stationed at the Residence of Corpus.

Duckett

Order: Soothsayer
Type: Catoptromancer

A clairvoyant detained for the sixteenth Bone Season. A retired performer, he keeps a stockpile of vital supplies in the Rookery, offering them to those who agree to run dangerous errands for his amusement. Duckett was one of the three human survivors of the Novembertide Rebellion of 2039.

Ella Giddings[1]

A clairvoyant detained for the twentieth Bone Season, stationed at the Residence of Trinity. Aludra Chertan is her keeper.

Eleanor 'Nell' Nahid

Order: Guardian
Type: Summoner

A clairvoyant detained for the nineteenth Bone Season. Nell is a performer, specialising in trapeze and aerial silks.

Eliza Renton

Order: Medium
Type: Trance
Alias: The Martyred Muse

---

[1] Ella's surname was originally Parsons – specified in *The Mime Order* – but on reflection, this surname is unlikely to have survived in Scion.

A member of the Seven Seals. Eliza was raised by aster dealers in Cheapside and worked for an underground theatre before applying for a job with Jaxon Hall. She is a trance medium who specialises in ethereal forgery – painting copies of famous pieces of art while possessed by the spirits of their creators.

Emil Viklund

Order: Medium
Type: Physical

A clairvoyant detained for the nineteenth Bone Season, stationed at the Residence of Exeter. He is a red-jacket.

Ezekiel 'Zeke' Sáenz

Order: Fury
Type: Unreadable
Alias: The Black Diamond

A member of the Seven Seals. Born in Mexico, Zeke later moved to Boston to live with his younger half-sister, Nadine Arnett, while she was at college. Formerly a whisperer, he is now unreadable.

Felix Coombs

Order: Augur
Type: Hydromancer
Alias: Lucky

A clairvoyant detained for the twentieth Bone Season, stationed at the Residence of Trinity. Aludra Chertan is his keeper.

Gail Fisher

Order: Soothsayer
Type: Seer

An amaurotic detained for the nineteenth Bone Season, stationed at the Residence of Magdalen. Gail formerly lived at Queens with her keeper, Alsafi Sualocin. Upon realising Gail had a condition that required frequent medication, Alsafi allowed her to move to Magdalen, which needed a night porter. Gail takes the bulk of the responsibility for maintaining the buildings.

Guy Morrow

Order: Soothsayer
Type: Dactylomancer

A clairvoyant detained for the nineteenth Bone Season. Formerly a successful tailor in Leeds, he is now a performer, specialising in dexterity skills.

Hector Grinslathe

Order: Soothsayer
Type: Macharomancer
Alias: Haymarket Hector

Underlord of the Scion Citadel of London and head of the Unnatural Assembly.

Jaxon Hall

Order: Guardian
Type: Binder
Alias: The White Binder

Mime-lord of I-4 and head of the Seven Seals. He lives in Seven Dials, a district in Covent Garden. Although he is Paige's employer, she knows very little of his past. Jaxon is a powerful binder, able to exert sole command over multiple spirits.

Joseph Biwott

Order: Sensor
Type: Polyglot

A clairvoyant detained for the twentieth Bone Season, stationed at the Residence of Merton.

Julian Amesbury

A clairvoyant detained for the twentieth Bone Season, stationed at the Residence of Trinity. Julian grew up in London and has spent most of his life trying to blend in with the amaurotic population.

Kathy Lorimer

Order: Augur
Type: Rhabdomancer

A clairvoyant detained for the nineteenth Bone Season, stationed at the Residence of Exeter. She is a red-jacket.

Layla Stern

A clairvoyant detained for the twentieth Bone Season, stationed at the Residence of Trinity.

Liss Rymore

Order: Soothsayer
Type: Cartomancer

A clairvoyant detained for the nineteenth Bone Season. As a child, Liss moved from Inverness to London with her parents, Arthur Lin and Imogen Rymore, who had fallen on hard times. Since Imogen was amaurotic, the syndicate turned the couple away. They later died of lung fever. Left to fend for herself, Liss fell prey to a sting, resulting in her imprisonment in the Tower of London. After three years, she was transported to Oxford. She is now a performer, specialising in aerial silks.

Lotte Gordon

Order: Medium
Type: Physical

A clairvoyant detained for the nineteenth Bone Season. She is a performer, specialising in acrobatics and contortion.

Michael Wren

Order: Fury
Type: Unreadable
Alias: Birdy

A clairvoyant detained for the nineteenth Bone Season, stationed at the Residence of Magdalen. He takes responsibility for housekeeping.

Nadine Arnett

Order: Sensor
Type: Whisperer
Alias: The Silent Bell

A member of the Seven Seals. Born and raised in Québec, she moved to Boston in early 2056 to share an apartment with her half-brother, Zeke. In 2057, the siblings joined a student trip to the Grand Conference in London, where Jaxon Hall convinced them to join the underworld.

Nicklas 'Nick' Nygård

Order: Jumper
Type: Oracle

Paige's best friend, who saved her from a poltergeist when she was a child and later brought her into the Seven Seals. Nick grew up in the Scion Republic of Sweden, where he discovered a natural affinity for the sciences. Following the murder of his younger sister, Karolina, Nick resolved to bring Scion down. Now living in London, he leads a double life as both a committed member of the Seven Seals and a Scion employee.

Ognena Maria

Order: Augur
Type: Pyromancer

Mime-queen of I-5.

Oliver Viklund

Order: Medium
Type: Physical

A clairvoyant detained for the nineteenth Bone Season, stationed at the Residence of Exeter. He is a red-jacket.

Tilda Lee

Order: Sensor
Type: Whisperer

A clairvoyant detained for the twentieth Bone Season, stationed at the Residence of Oriel. Tilda was born in Liverpool and came to London to find work. She takes purple aster as a means of coping with her clairvoyance, which causes her to hear spirits' voices in Gloss, a language she does not understand.

The Wicked Lady

Order: Augur
Type: Pyromancer
Mime-queen of II-6.

William Linwood

Order: Soothsayer
Type: Seer

A clairvoyant who Paige meets on a train leaving Inquisitors Cross.

REPHAIM

Immortal humanoids of the Netherworld, a
decayed and uninhabitable dimension that once
served as an intermediary realm between the æther
and the corporeal world. Rephaim exhibit similar
abilities to clairvoyant humans.[2]

Arcturus Mesarthim
Warden of the Mesarthim and blood-consort of the Rephaim through his union with Nashira Sargas. Arcturus is the only Rephaite stationed at the Residence of Magdalen. He is known to the humans of Oxford as Warden.

Alsafi Sualocin
A Rephaite stationed at the Residence of Queens. He is a trusted confidant of Nashira Sargas and frequently serves as an intermediary between London and Oxford, occasionally travelling as far as Paris.

Aludra Chertan
A Rephaite stationed at the Residence of Trinity. She is responsible for confiscating and scrutinising prisoners' belongings.

Castor Sargas
A Rephaite formerly stationed at the Residence of Balliol, where he made a sport of targeting the amaurotics. He has since left Oxford to work alongside Vindemiatrix Sargas, one of the two blood-heirs.

Kraz Sargas
One of the two blood-heirs of the Rephaim. His female counterpart is Vindemiatrix Sargas, who does not live in Oxford.

---

[2] The names listed in this section are pseudonyms. Since the true Glossolalic names of the Rephaim are impossible for most humans to articulate, on Earth they use the names of stars – often associated with divinity and fate, and set high above humans.

Gomeisa Sargas
Warden of the Sargas and one of the two blood-sovereigns of the Rephaim, sharing his power with Nashira. He lives in London, where he acts as an advisor to the Grand Inquisitor of England, Frank Weaver.

Merope Sualocin
A Rephaite stationed at the Residence of Balliol. She oversees physical drills, which she leads on Port Meadow.

Nashira Sargas
Suzerain of the Republic of Scion and one of the two blood-sovereigns of the Rephaim. She is stationed at the Residence of the Suzerain – formerly All Souls College – and shares her power with Gomeisa Sargas.

Nembus Sheratan
A Rephaite stationed at the Residence of Exeter.

Pleione Sualocin
A Rephaite stationed at the Residence of Merton. She usually takes responsibility for 'welcoming' newcomers to Oxford.

Situla Mesarthim
A Rephaite stationed at the Residence of Corpus.

Suhail Chertan
A Rephaite stationed at the Residence of Balliol. He holds authority over the Rookery.

Tertius Chertan
A Rephaite stationed at the Residence of Queens.

Terebellum Sheratan
A Rephaite stationed at the Residence of Oriel, more often known as Terebell.

Thuban Sargas
A Rephaite stationed at the Residence of Corpus. He is feared throughout the city for his sadistic tendencies.

AMAUROTICS

Humans who are not clairvoyant, sometimes
known as rotties. They have no connection to the
spirit world and are unable to sense it.[3]

Abberline Mayfield †
The former Grand Inquisitor of the Republic of Scion England, who oversaw the invasion of Ireland. Upon his sudden death in 2054, he was superseded by his Minister for Finance, Frank Weaver.

Alice Heron
A Scion key worker who lives in the apartment next door to Colin Mahoney.

Aloïs Mynatt
Grand Raconteur of the Scion Republic of France.

Birgitta Tjäder
Chief of Vigilance in the Scion Citadel of Stockholm and commander of the Second Inquisitorial Division. Tjäder is notorious for her ruthless adherence to Inquisitorial law. She is the archenemy of Nick Nygård, whose sister was murdered by soldiers under her command.

Cathal Bell
The former Minister for Foreign Affairs in Ireland. Though he was popular with the general public, Bell was secretly plotting against his own country, culminating in the Imbolc Massacre (also known

---

[3]   It is rare, but possible, for a clairvoyant to become amaurotic through the process of *spirit shock* (see glossary).

as the Dublin Incursion) of 2046. Despite his loyalty to Scion, he was passed over as Grand Inquisitor of Ireland. He lives in London.

Clara Barnes
A former student at the Ancroft School in Bloomsbury. Clara and her friends would often make fun of Paige.

Colin Mahoney
Paige's father. Formerly known as Cóilín Ó Mathúna, he was a forensic pathologist and spent most of his life in Dublin, away from his family. During the Molly Riots, he was identified as a person of potential value to the Republic of Scion. Under intense pressure from Cathal Bell, Cóilín agreed to move to London. Expecting Ireland to fall to the anchor, he took Paige with him and anglicised their names. He lives on the secure Barbican Estate among other Scion key workers.

Crina Nistor
An amaurotic detained for the nineteenth Bone Season.

Evelyn Ancroft
Schoolmistress of the Ancroft School in Bloomsbury, which was founded by her grandmother. She is a known *anchorite* (see glossary) who frequently targeted Paige.

Fazal Osman
An amaurotic detained for the nineteenth Bone Season. Fazal was initially assigned to the Residence of Balliol, where Castor Sargas targeted him for standing up for his fellow amaurotics. He was quietly transferred to Magdalen, where he lives on a permanent basis as the day porter and gardener.

Finn Mac Cárthaigh[4]
Paige's older cousin through her paternal aunt. Finn was a history student at Trinity College in Dublin. He took Paige to the protest that preceded the Imbolc Massacre and is presumed to have been killed in the ensuing bloodbath, along with his fiancée – Kayleigh Ni Dhornáin – and their closest friends: Anjali Roy, Oscar Keeley, and Temiloluwa Adisa. The only confirmed survivor of the tight-knit group was Laoise Ní Cheallaigh, who had not been able to reach the protest.

Frank Weaver
The incumbent Grand Inquisitor of the Republic of Scion England. He succeeded Abberline Mayfield.

Kayleigh Ní Dhornáin †
A student at Trinity College who was believed to have been one of the first people killed in the Imbolc Massacre of 2046. Kay was engaged to Paige's cousin, Finn.

Nita Patel †
An amaurotic detained for the nineteenth Bone Season. Nita was stationed at the Residence of Queens and did her best to provide for the performers, especially during the winter.

Radmilo Arežina
An official from the Scion Republic of Serbia.

Reuben Evans
A student at the University of Scion London, who Paige meets at a flash house, Dance upon Nothing.

---

[4] The modern Irish spelling of this name is Fionn, while Finn is the anglicised form. During my revision of *The Bone Season*, I considered amending it, since I imagine Paige's cousin being a staunch opponent of anglicisation. However, since Finn is also the Old Irish spelling – something I suspected he might appreciate – I eventually decided to keep his name as it was in the original.

Sandra McCarthy
Paige's paternal aunt. Born Alastríona Ní Mhathúna, she used Sandra as a nickname and often gave an anglicised form of her birth name after leaving Tipperary. At the time of the Dublin Incursion, she worked at a hospital in Dún Laoghaire and was living with her spouse and their son, Finn.

Scarlett Burnish
Grand Raconteur of the Republic of Scion England. A fashion icon who is well-liked among the amaurotics of Scion, she reads the approved news and distributes propaganda on the flagship broadcast network, ScionEye.

Sebastian Pearce
An amaurotic detained for the twentieth Bone Season. Seb drew unwanted and dangerous attention when he was subjected to a prank by students at his school, who planted an illegal shew stone in his satchel.

Suzette Fortin
A former student at the Ancroft School in Bloomsbury. Raised in the Scion Citadel of Paris, Suzette befriended Paige[5] in their second year at Ancroft. They lost touch after Paige joined the Seven Seals, whereupon Jaxon instructed her to sever or restrict contact with the amaurotics in her life.

---

[5] Unlike the majority of her classmates, Suzette had not absorbed the hibernophobic sentiment that spread across the Scion Republic of England in the wake of the Molly Riots. In France, this sentiment manifested as a suspicion of Bretons.

THE SEVEN ORDERS
OF CLAIRVOYANCE

The Seven Orders of Clairvoyance is a classification system created by Jaxon Hall in his notorious pamphlet, *On the Merits of Unnaturalness* (2031). Jaxon proposed that there were seven broad categories of clairvoyant, each linked to an aura colour. The Seven Orders system is currently used by the syndicates of London and Paris, but should not be taken as the only or correct means of thinking about clairvoyance.

The below types of voyant are those listed in the first edition of *On the Merits of Unnaturalness*. However, in order to keep you in Paige's perspective, I have classified them as they would be seen in the most recent edition, which she takes as the official version. Some types of clairvoyance are unverified – these are marked with an asterisk – and some are subject to fierce debate on the matter of how they should be categorised. Other types have since been identified or proposed, and more have yet to be discovered.

Note: You do not need to learn the Seven Orders of Clairvoyance by heart to understand *The Bone Season*. If a type of clairvoyance is especially relevant to the story, Paige will explain it.

I. SOOTHSAYERS

Soothsayers use numa – objects with ethereal properties – to connect with the æther and foretell the future. They are believed to be the most populous group of clairvoyants. Most have purple auras.

The seers are broadly divided into two sub-groups: seers, who use reflective objectives, and common soothsayers, who do not. Jaxon later revised his opinion on certain seers and moved them into the second order (see footnotes).

COMMON

- Acultomancer[1] – needles
- Astragalomancer – dice

---

[1] Any voyant who casts their numa as lots may also be called a *cleromancer*.

- Axinomancer – axes
- Bibliomancer – books
- Cartomancer (or broadsider) – cards
- Cyathomancer – cups
- Dactylomancer[2] – rings
- Macharomancer – knives

SEERS

- Catoptromancer – mirrors
- Crystallist – crystal balls or shew stones
- Cottabomancer – wine in a bowl[3]

II. AUGURS

Augurs use the raw materials of the natural world to connect with the æther. Like soothsayers' objects, these are known as numa. Most have blue auras.

On the Merits of Unnaturalness divided the augurs into two classes: vile augurs, who use the human body for divination, and common augurs, who use other forms of organic matter.

COMMON

- Anthomancer – flowers
- Daphnomancer – bay or laurel leaves[4]
- Dendromancer – oak and mistletoe
- Sycomancer – fig and sycamore leaves
- Cryomancer – ice[5]
- Capnomancer – smoke
- Halomancer* – salt[6]
- Hydromancer – water[7]
- Libanomancer – incense

---

[2] Originally classified as a vile augur until Jaxon discovered they used rings to scry, as opposed to fingers. Nonetheless, the name (from Ancient Greek *dáktulos*, 'finger') stuck.

[3] Despite some debate, Jaxon has stood by his decision that cottabomancers are seers, given their need for a vessel to hold the wine. However, many cottabomancers see themselves as augurs.

[4] Any augur who uses plant matter (other than flowers) may be known as a *botanomancer*. Specific terms like *daphnomancy* refer to the preferred sort of plant. This also applies to anthomancers, who may choose to define themselves more specifically, e.g. as a *rhodomancer* if they favour roses.

[5] Originally classified as a soothsayer, specifically a seer. Jaxon later conceded that the reflective qualities of ice (as well as water and pearls) were less important than its elemental nature.

[6] Though not yet proven to exist, Jaxon still believes in the possibility of halomancy – a type of *abacomancy*, a category which would also cover the use of dust and sand. Abacomancy is still a mostly theoretical art, with the exception of spodomancy, which uses ash.

[7] See footnote for *cryomancer*.

- Margaritomancer – pearls[8]
- Pyromancer – fire
- Halomancer* – salt
- Rhabdomancer – able to locate cold spots[9]
- Spodomancer – ash
- Tasseographer – tea leaves or dregs
- Theriomancer* – animal behaviour

VILE[10]

- Anthropomancer (or splanchomancer)* – human sacrifice
- Chiromancer (also known as palmist) – palms
- Drymimancer – tears
- Extipicist – entrails
- Haematomancer – blood
- Podomancer* – feet
- Oculomancer* – eyes
- Osteomancer – bones

———— III. MEDIUMS ————

Mediums have exceptionally permeable dreamscapes, which allows spirits to take over their bodies with relative ease. *Trance mediums* fall into a state of unawareness when they are possessed, while *restive mediums* remain conscious. Most have green auras.

- Automatiste (art medium) – favoured by artists' spirits
- Psychographer (writing medium) – favoured by writers' spirits
- Physical medium – capable of great feats of strength, flexibility and agility while possessed
- Speaking medium – used by spirits to communicate in a human language, as opposed to Glossolalia

---

[8] See footnote for *cryomancer.*

[9] As with certain types of seer, Jaxon debated whether to categorise the rhabdomancer as a soothsayer – since they sometimes cast lots – or an augur. He acknowledged this uncertainty in the first edition of *On the Merits of Unnaturalness.* Given their connection with ice, as well as their use of dowsing sticks, rhabdomancers are now almost universally seen as augurs.

[10] The vile augurs faced significant discrimination after the publication of *On the Merits of Unnaturalness,* which stigmatised their gifts. Many were imprisoned in a slum in Bermondsey, where they remain.

IV. SENSORS

- Gustant – capable of tasting ethereal activity
- Polyglot – capable of speaking and understanding Glossolalia, the language of spirits; may have uncontrollable outbursts
- Sniffer – capable of smelling ethereal activity
- Whisperer – capable of hearing spirits' voices, but not understanding them

V. GUARDIANS

Guardians exercise a higher degree of control over spirits than most other clairvoyants. Most have orange auras.

- Binder – capable of commanding multiple spirits
- Exorcist* – capable of banishing a spirit without knowing its name
- Necromancer* – capable of animating the dead
- Summoner – capable of calling spirits across great distances

VI. FURIES

Clairvoyants whose powerful abilities are believed to stem from internal transformation, i.e. a change to the dreamscape.

- Berserker – capable of entering a battle trance, fuelled by spirits
- Sibyl – capable of making prophecies in a trance
- Unreadable – capable of deflecting all spiritual interference[11]

VII. JUMPERS

Clairvoyants with the ability to enter or significantly impact the æther.

- Dreamwalker – capable of projecting the spirit and possessing other people
- Oracle – capable of receiving, invoking and sending visions

[11] The process of becoming unreadable is the only known way for a voyant being able to move from one order to another. An unreadable is not born, but created, usually by a traumatic event.

Acknowledgements

My warmest gratitude to the readers who have followed this series faithfully throughout the last decade. Thank you for your support and enthusiasm, and, most of all, for your immense patience while I work on each instalment.

To my wonderful agent, David Godwin, without whom none of this would be possible. To Ali Smith, who gave me early feedback on *The Bone Season* and encouraged me to send it out into the world. To the staff at David Godwin Associates – Heather Godwin, Philippa Sitters, Rachel Taylor and Sebastian Godwin – and the team at Peters Fraser & Dunlop, including: Antonia Kasoulidou, Mariam Quraishi, Rebecca Wearmouth and Rosie Gurtovoy.

To the editors who oversaw both the original and revised editions of this book: Allegra Le Fanu, Alexandra Pringle, Alexa von Hirschberg. Thank you for seeing potential in me, in Paige, and in this universe.

To the global Bloomsbury team for continuing to champion my work, including: Alexis Kirschbaum, Amanda Shipp, Amrita Paul, Ben Chisnall, Ben McCluskey, Beth Maher, Callie Garnett, Carmen R. Balit, David Smith, Donna Gauthier, Elisabeth Denison, Ellen Chen, Emilie Chambeyron, Emma Allden, Genevieve Nelsson, Grace McNamee, Joanna Vallance, Joe Roche, Hattie Castelberg, Ian Hudson, Inez Maria, Kathleen Farrar, Katy Follain, Laura Meyer, Laura Phillips, Lauren Dooley, Lauren Molyneux, Lauren Moseley, Lauren Ollerhead, Lauren Whybrow, Lucie Moody, Mariafrancesca Ierace, Marie Coolman, Nancy Miller, Nicola Hill,

Nigel Newton, Paul Baggaley, Philippa Cotton, Phoebe Dyer, Rachel Wilkie, Rayna Luo, Rosie Barr, Sarah McLean, Suzanne Keller, Trâm-Anh Doan, Valentina Rice and Valerie Esposito.

I'd also like to thank some of my original team for *The Bone Season*, who have since moved on: Cristina Gilbert, Eleanor Weil, Katie Bond, Jude Drake, Laura Keefe, Oliver Holden-Rea, Rachel Mannheimer, Sara Helen Binney, Sara Mercurio and Terry Lee.

To David Mann, Emily Faccini and Ivan Belikov for somehow making *The Bone Season* even more beautiful than it was in 2013. You're a dream trio to have working on my books.

To Sharona Selby and Lin Vasey for combing through this one after my revision.

To the translators who will work on the Anniversary Edition, and to those who worked on the original, sending Paige and Arcturus all over the world (I'm glad I can finally acknowledge you in this new edition), including: Amanda Mlakar, Anna Petrushina, Benjamin Kuntzer, Charlotte Lungstrass-Kapfer, Cláudia Mello Belhassof, Devora Busheri, Deyan Kyuchoukov, Eli Gilić, Emma Jonsson Sandström, Fátima Andrade, Gan Zhenlong, Janet van der Lee, Juhász Viktor, Kjersti Velsand, Lena Jonsson, Lenka Kapsová, Lucia Halová, Marta Pera Cucurell, Nhiệt Xích, Penelope Triada, Regina Kołek, Saša Stančin, Selim Yeniçeri and Teodora Văcariu.

To the Home Bursar of Magdalen College, Albert Ray, for allowing me access to the Founders Tower so I could make the revised version of *The Bone Season* as accurate as possible.

To Ashleigh (@afrolicthroughfiction) for starting a Discord for the series, giving its readers a place to come together to discuss it; to the Bone Season Advocates who have supported each launch; to the booksellers and librarians who have got it into readers' hands, and to any other person who's ever shouted about it. It means more than I can express.

To my friends and fellow authors, many of whom have supported me through writing this series – I'm indescribably lucky to have met you all over ten years in the industry. Special mentions to London Shah for her generous early quote on this edition; Katherine Webber Tsang, who I first met because of *The Bone Season* and I now don't think I could function without; Ilana Fernandes-Lassman, Richard Smith and Vickie Morrish, my fellow Stanners, who were there for me after I first sold *The Bone Season* in 2012; and Kate Dylan, Saara El-Arifi and Tasha Suri, for constant encouragement, friendship and laughter as I worked on this revision.

Finally, thank you to my family, whose love and support has never wavered.

Just as I said ten years ago, thank you – all of you – for taking a chance on a dreamer.

PS: Paige, thank you for walking into my head on that summer day in 2011. Sorry for everything I've inflicted on you.

A Note on the Author

Samantha Shannon is the New York Times and Sunday Times bestselling author of The Bone Season series. Her work has been translated into twenty-six languages. Her fourth novel, *The Priory of the Orange Tree*, was her first outside of The Bone Season series and was an international bestseller. She lives in London.

samanthashannon.co.uk / @say_shannon

A Note on the Type

The text of this book is set Adobe Garamond. It is one of several versions of Garamond based on the designs of Claude Garamond. It is thought that Garamond based his font on Bembo, cut in 1495 by Francesco Griffo in collaboration with the Italian printer Aldus Manutius. Garamond types were first used in books printed in Paris around 1532. Many of the present-day versions of this type are based on the *Typi Academiae* of Jean Jannon cut in Sedan in 1615.

Claude Garamond was born in Paris in 1480. He learned how to cut type from his father and by the age of fifteen he was able to fashion steel punches the size of a pica with great precision. At the age of sixty he was commissioned by King Francis I to design a Greek alphabet, and for this he was given the honourable title of royal type founder. He died in 1561.